SO-AHZ-750

N THE ROGUE

ight © 1991 by Conan Properties, Inc.

rt by Ken Kelly

ook
ed by Tom Doherty Associates, Inc.
h Avenue
rk, N.Y. 10010

a registered trademark of Tom Doherty Associates, Inc.

812-52141-2

ion: November 1991
s market printing: August 1992

the United States of America

7 6 5 4 3 2 1

TO THE DEATH!

Now a pair of men bore down upon the Cimmerian from either
side. From the left, a man darted in, swinging a sword. From the
right came a spearman. Conan whirled right, leaned aside as the
spear lanced toward him and grasped the spearman's arm. Hauling him across his front, Conan sent him colliding into the
swordsman. As they smashed together, Conan gripped his hilt in
both hands and slashed both men across the waist with a single,
terrific blow.

CONAN
THE ROGUE

BY
**JOHN
MADDOX
ROBERTS**

TOR ®
fantasy

A TOM DOHERTY ASSOCIATES
NEW YORK

For Edgar Boggs, Jerry Hall, Rodney Roberson, and their fair ladies.

In appreciation for all the intellectual stimulation and the heroic doings.

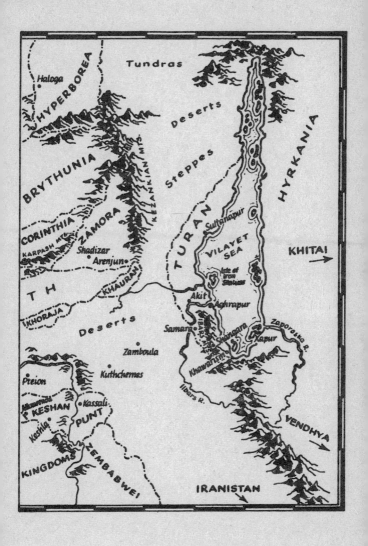

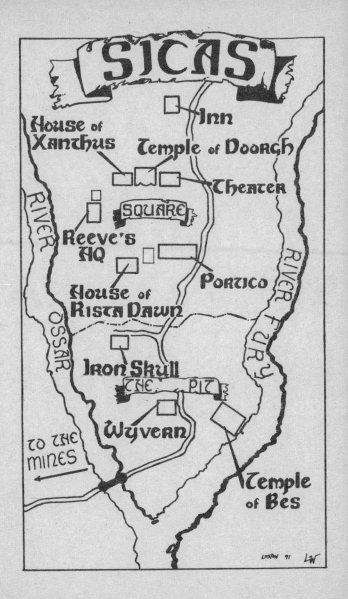

THE ROGUE

ONE
The Small Man

The cup of hardened leather slammed down upon a table stained with spilled wine and scarred with the nicks and gouges of a hundred barroom brawls. The hand that gripped the cup was equally scarred, the thick wrist banded with a broad bracelet of coral-studded bronze, as much a defense as an ornament. The hand snatched up the cup to reveal four dice, each showing a different face: the serpent, the dog, the skull, and the dagger.

"The beggar!" crowed a voice, naming the lowest score in dicing. "You lose, Cimmerian!"

"Set!" cursed the unfortunate gambler. He addressed the ivory cubes. "All the gods curse you and the beast from whose teeth you were carved!"

The winner, a sharp-faced man whose red hair was cropped close to his scalp, scooped up his winnings: a pile of silver coins, amid which the torchlight winked from a few thin golden coins of Nemedia. More luridly gleamed the many golden chains depending from his neck and the jewels that flashed upon his fingers, the trophies of a long winning streak.

"That cleans me out," the loser said, staring glumly into the interior of the dice cup. Its ridged surface ensured that the dice would tumble correctly. He saw no signs that it had been tampered with. And he knew that the dice were honest. They were as honest as dice could be, at any rate. The man who sat across from him was hard, but he knew better than to cheat Conan the Cimmerian, who had somehow lately been deserted by fortune.

The Cimmerian set the cup on the table and leaned back against the carved wooden pillar behind him. He brooded upon the many vicissitudes of fortune. He and his companions had hired on for a minor campaign when a border satrap rebelled against the king of Nemedia. They had been in the storming party when the border lord's citadel had been taken, and came through the fight with few losses and rich loot.

With purses bulging, they had come here, to Belverus, and settled down at The Sword and Scepter to drink, carouse and gamble for their takings. One by one, as they lost their loot, the others had left to seek employment for their swords. It had come down to Conan and the red-haired man, whose name was Ingolf. Now Ingolf was the final winner.

"You've still your sword," Ingolf pointed out. "Do you want to wager it on another roll of the dice?"

Conan touched the weapon that leaned in its leather sheath against the pillar. It was a long, straight-bladed brand, with hilt and pommel of plain steel, its handgrip of unornamented bone. It was severely plain, the way Conan liked all his weapons.

"Nay, for with this I will win yet more gold."

Ingolf shrugged. "As you will. Let me stand you to a final mug of ale before you go forth to seek your fortune." It was a traditional gambler's courtesy, and Conan nodded assent.

The serving wench who brought the ale had shown Conan much favor in the past few days, but now that he was clean of cash, she had not so much as a smile for him. Ingolf she treated as if he were her long-lost lover, suddenly returned from the wars.

Like the dice cup, the ale mug was made of leather, and it smelled faintly of the pitch with which its interior was waterproofed. Leaning against the pillar, the Cimmerian hooked a thumb into his broad, nail-studded belt as he raised the jack and drank. His sleeveless vest revealed strongly muscled arms and a neck corded like a great ship's anchor cable. His baggy knee-breeches and fur-topped boots showed long service and now, along with the sword, were his only possessions. Days before, he had gambled away horse and saddle, bow and arrows, lance, shield, even his dagger. It was nothing. He enjoyed the profligate life, and he would always find a means of livelihood with his warrior skills. As long as he had those, everything else was replaceable.

He set down the half-empty cup and studied his surroundings, as if seeking inspiration by which to restore his fortunes. The prospect was not promising. The hour was late and the cookfires had burned to embers. The few remaining patrons of The Sword and Scepter drank or gambled with little fervor. Most of the paid-off veterans of the recent campaign had been picked clean days before. At one table sat a lone man whose trousers, jacket and head scarf were made of silk and dyed a strange shade of violet. He seemed to be watching Conan intently, but the Cimmerian ignored him. He wanted nothing to do with any man who would wear clothes of such a color.

It was a typical soldiers' den, decorated with obsolete weapons and painted wooden busts of famous Nemedian generals from past centuries. Many of these busts showed signs of having served as targets for dagger-throwing contests. The serving women were at least as attractive as the wooden generals. Conan finished his ale and rose. He hooked the sword's hanger to the rings on his belt.

"Farewell, Ingolf. Perhaps we'll meet again and I will be as lucky in gaming as in war, for a change."

The red-haired man nodded. "Wars are many and good warriors few. We'll meet again." The two gripped wrists. Left unspoken was the likelihood that, next time, they might be on opposite sides. That meant nothing to professionals.

The Cimmerian made his way between the tables and went up

the steps to street level. As he always did when going from the illuminated indoors to the night-gloomed outdoors, he stepped to one side of the doorway and waited with his back against a wall while his eyes adjusted to the change. Most men needed minutes for their eyes to adjust, Conan only seconds. But he knew full well that a man could die in seconds and that often that sort of thing happened to men who walked forth blind. There was no sound on the street save the creaking of the pothouse sign overhead. In the distance, he could see a light. It was one of the city torches. These were planted at every corner and were supposed to be tended by the night watch. In practice, it was remarkable for one in four to be burning after midnight.

He tensed slightly as another patron emerged from the tavern. The man stood beneath the sign and stared down the street, first one way and then the other, as if he were looking for someone. He stepped into the street, stumbling slightly, then scanning in both directions once more. He vented a frustrated sigh and walked off toward the torch. Quietly, Conan fell in behind him. The man hurried, taking mincing steps on slippered feet. He stopped by the torch and peered down the side streets, then released another sigh. Conan's sword hissed from its sheath.

"Were you looking for me?"

The man whirled and his eyes bugged as he saw the blade leveled at his throat. As Conan had suspected, it was the fellow in the violet-silk garments.

"Peace, peace!" the man said hurriedly, his palms outward. "Indeed I came seeking you, but only to talk, not to rob!" His voice was quiet and breathy. Conan laughed at the thought of this effeminate little man, who stood no higher than his chest, trying to rob him.

"In that case, I have been spared a terrible fate." Then his voice lost its humor and he snapped: "Now, what do you want?"

"I could not help overhearing your conversation with that so fortunate mercenary back inside. Am I correct in understanding that you are a fighting man and that you are presently without either employment or funds?"

"Right on all counts," Conan said. "But I've never been destitute enough to come to the likes of you for assistance."

The long-lashed eyes lowered and the man seemed to flush. "You misapprehend. I wish to hire you for a mission. It is a mission for a warrior of strength, skill, and courage. Are you not such a man?"

"I am," Conan agreed. He sheathed his sword smoothly, without looking down at his sheath. "Why did you not come to me back there?" He jerked his black-haired head toward The Sword and Scepter.

"This is a matter requiring great discretion, great confidentiality. I could not speak where others might overhear." He came close and looked up at Conan. The Cimmerian immediately regretted that they were no longer separated by the sword's length; the man wore scent. Conan's revulsion was washed away by the man's next words: "I am willing to pay most handsomely for this service."

"Speak on," Conan growled. He had served stranger men than this one in his time. Gold was always the same, no matter whose hand bestowed it.

"Not here. Even here, there might be listeners. Besides," he hugged himself and shivered, "the night grows cold."

Conan, who was far more lightly dressed, ignored the chill breeze. "I am comfortable enough. Well, if you must, I have a room not far from here. Come along."

Without looking back, the Cimmerian strode from the circle of torchlight. Surprised by the abrupt departure, the little man stood for a second before scurrying after him. Then a cloaked form detached itself from the shadow of a doorway and followed the two of them on silent feet.

Conan turned down a short alley and his ears told him that the small man was still behind him. He stopped at a torch that burned in a sconce next to a door. Just beyond, wider doors identified the establishment as a stable. From within could be heard the quiet shufflings and snortings of horses.

From a box nailed just within the smaller doorway Conan took a candle and lit it from the torch. "Come on," he said, stepping inside. He ascended a flight of creaking steps and entered a tiny, cramped room. The candlelight revealed its sparse furnishings: a bed, a chair, and a small table.

The little man entered and wrinkled his nose in disgust. "This is a vile-smelling place." From a sleeve he took a kerchief and held it over his nose and mouth.

"Any stable smells better than that scent you've bathed in," Conan said. He unlatched the shutters of the room's sole window and threw them open. "There. All the fresh air you can breathe." He unhooked the sword's hanger from his belt and sat on the bed with the weapon across his knees. "Now, let's hear your story."

The other man sat on the spindly chair, first brushing the seat with his kerchief. "Very well. My name is Piris. I come from Shadizar, in Zamora. I am in search of a . . . a certain object that was stolen from me."

"What sort of object?" Conan asked.

"All in good time, my friend. I have looked long for this object, and there are others who would like to find it. The original thieves are dead, and it has been through more than one set of hands since they died."

"And you think it is here, in Belverus?"

"It was, but it is no longer. I have strong reason to suspect that it is now on its way to Sicas, in Aquilonia, if it is not there already."

"I've never heard of the place," Conan said.

"It is not a great city, but it is said to be a wicked one. It lies a few miles off the king's high road between Tarantia and Shamar, at the confluence of two rivers, the Ossar and the Fury. Its wealth comes mainly from its nearby silver mines, and this wealth has attracted persons of a rough sort. The royal officials there are, it is said, of an understanding and forgiving nature."

"Bribe-takers, eh?" Conan knew the breed.

"I would not wish to judge harshly on the strength of mere hearsay," Piris protested. "However, that does seem to be the impression. You can understand that I would not wish to search for my property in such a place, among rapacious and violent men, without the aid of one who is both strong and skilled in the combative arts.''

"That is reasonable," Conan agreed. "Now, just what is this thing you are looking for?"

Piris hesitated. "Ah, my friend—Conan, is it? Yes, Conan, this is something I am reluctant to—"

"Set take it, man, can you not speak plainly?" Conan all but barked.

"You see, I will wish you to go ahead of me to Sicas and learn something of the place. I will follow in a day or two. I have some inquiries to make here. In Sicas, I will tell you all you need to know.''

"I do not like this secrecy. I've a mind to toss you down the steps. No, perhaps out the window would be better.'' He gazed at the window as if measuring it for the throw.

"I am willing to pay one thousand golden dishas for this task, the sum payable in full upon the recovery of my property.''

Conan was mollified instantly. "I'll need something on account. I'll have to outfit myself for the journey.''

Piris smiled, revealing small, perfect, white teeth. "Of course.'' He took a fat purse from within his jacket and extended it. "You will take, say, one hundred dishas for your traveling expenses?''

Conan dumped the purse on the table. The coins that spilled out bore the likeness of the king of Koth, and each was worth ten dishas. He quickly separated twenty of them, scooping the rest back into the purse and tossing the bag to Piris, who caught it adroitly.

"I will take, say, two hundred dishas for my traveling expenses. How will you find me in Sicas?''

Piris hefted the bag, which was now far lighter than it had been. Sighing sadly, he returned it to his jacket. "Very well. Somehow, I do not think that you will be difficult to find, even in a city of scoundrels. Just take lodging in an inn near the main gate of the town. I will find you.''

"Then I think that concludes our business," Conan said.

"Until we meet again, in Sicas." Piris bowed, touching spread fingertips to his violet-sheathed breast. He left behind a dissipating cloud of flowery scent.

Conan shut the door and barred it. Fortune had turned again. Almost he was tempted to go back to The Sword and Scepter to reenter the game with a new stake, but he shook off the temptation. His gaming luck had deserted him in Belverus and it would not come back. He crossed to the window to draw in some unscented air. He did not see Piris in the alley, but for a moment he thought he saw a shadowy form moving amid deeper shadows. He stared, but his keen eyes descried no more movement. Deciding that fatigue and drink had made him see that which was not there, he closed and bolted the shutters. Blowing out the candle, he lay back on the narrow, hard bed and wondered why he had never heard of Sicas. He thought that he had heard of every city with a reputation for wickedness. Well, doubtless he would find out all about it when he got there. It sounded like his sort of city.

The next day Conan betook himself to the markets of Belverus to outfit himself for the journey. First he went to the armorers' quarter to furnish himself with suitable weaponry. In a cutler's stall he found a dagger to replace the one he had lost gaming. He chose a wooden-hafted weapon with a foot-long blade three fingers wide at the hilt, its thick spine and razor edge tapering to a slender point.

He wandered among the shops and stalls, admiring the long, slender lances and the powerful bows, but then, reluctantly, leaving them behind. He was headed for a city, not for a battlefield. Likewise he bypassed the shops of the shield-makers. Beneath a great awning erected in a small square, he found a bazaar selling soldiers' armor. This was a place where mercenaries between hires sold off their unneeded arms and to which they repaired when they needed to rearm at a reasonable price.

He tried on a knee-length hauberk of blackened mail, but rejected it as too heavy. The merchant tried to sell him the full-plate harness of an Aquilonian man-at-arms, but the panoply of a heavy cavalryman would be of no use to him in the dangerous alleyways of a city. On a table of light cuirasses he found just what he needed.

It was a brigandine that fit him perfectly. It was made of stout leather backed with thick canvas. Between leather and canvas were sandwiched hundreds of small, overlapping plates, fastened to the leather by rivets. The rivet heads showed on the outside and were gilded, making a brilliant show against the glossy black of the leather. It made an excellent defense, lighter than mail and almost as flexible. Had he been going to war, Conan might have worn it as a reinforcement over a hauberk. By itself, it was just what was called for when dealing with the daggers and swords common to dangerous cities. Best of all, it was a far more handsome garment than a shirt of mail. The brigandine was tailored to fit tightly at chest and waist, and its martial appearance announced that the wearer was not a man to be trifled with.

He examined a display of helmets, hoping to find suitable headgear. There were visored helms of Aquilonia and Poitain, spired casques from Turan, crested Nemedian helmets, even a horned helm from faraway Asgard. Conan chose a close-fitting steel cap lined with velvet. It was unpadded save for the cloth, and thus was smaller and lighter than the battle helms. It would turn a sword and save his crown from a wooden cudgel, although the lack of padding would mean a ringing headache the next day.

Satisfied that he was properly armed, he went to the clothiers' quarter for some new garments. The year was waning, the days were shortening, and the coming winter rode upon the north wind. Conan was inured to stern weather, but there was no point in suffering. He bought winter clothes and padded boots and fleece-lined gloves. He found a cloak of fine Shemitish wool that would serve as both garment and blanket on the journey. It was a broad, semicircular mantle, dyed red with madder.

Thus newly attired, he went to the horse market. Here he found every sort of horseflesh, from humble plodders suitable for the plow to fiery destriers so fierce that only experienced trainers could display them, working in pairs. There were hunters and race horses, and palfreys for noble ladies.

He mounted and tried out a dozen, settling on a bay gelding that was sound of wind and limb and capable of good speed when asked. It was well-trained and responsive, and Conan had to bargain for much of the morning to obtain a reasonable price. He took the beast to a blacksmith's to have it reshod and watched the process carefully to make sure that it was done properly. The best horse in the world could be ruined by a botched shoeing, and a lame horse was of less use than a dog when a swift flight was called for.

Satisfied that the horseshoes would stay on for a long journey, he led the animal to the saddlers' district and found there a Brythunian saddle that was satisfactory both to him and to the horse. The saddler threw in a set of worn saddlebags and a bridle when they had struck a bargain.

For the rest, Conan bought such items as were always useful on a journey: flint and steel for fire-making, ropes and picket pins, and a waterskin. He put these items in his saddlebags and went in search of a mapmaker.

The shop he sought was in a district catering to scholars and the practitioners of arcane arts. Sellers of books abounded, and a sound of steady scraping came from the shops of parchment makers. Many sorts of scribes plied their skills here, from the humble letter-writers, who sat at folding tables and indited missives for the illiterate, to copyists, who busily scribbled away copying manuscripts, to calligraphers, who grandly crafted official documents and certificates in the ornate styles of the powerful or the wealthy. There were illuminators who could spend days painting and decorating a single letter.

Conan was more accustomed to the quarters frequented by adventurers like himself, and he felt a certain interest in the place. He saw a shop selling the paraphernalia of the wizard's trade and stopped to gaze in its front window. What appeared to be a tiny demon capered among the wands, rune-engraved swords, celestially spangled robes, and crystal spheres. The creature had a body shaped like an egg set atop spindly bird's legs. The larger end of the egg had a fanged mouth above which were three red eyes on short stems. Its nether end was armed with a long barb. Conan noticed that as the thing jumped about, from time to time it would wink out of existence; at other times it became transparent. It was just a clever illusion.

By asking at various shops, he was directed to a small cul-de-sac at the end of which, wedged between an ink-maker's shop and a parchment seller's, he found the mapmaker he needed. The establishment's only sign was a pair of gilded dividers fastened to the wall above the low door. Ducking his head to clear the lintel, Conan went inside.

The interior was not as dim as he had anticipated. Light came in through a front window, and a good deal more was admitted by a skylight overhead. The place was scrupulously clean and it was full of maps, but there was no sense of clutter. The maps and charts were rolled neatly in leather tubes, all of them carefully racked, the racks bearing labels. At the rear of the shop was a low dais at which an elderly man sat, working meticulously at a tilted drawing table. He looked up as the Cimmerian entered.

"How may I serve you, sir?"

Conan walked back to the dais, glancing at the large display maps decorating the walls. "I need to find a certain place, a city named Sicas, in Aquilonia. I must fare thither and I wish to set out as soon as possible."

"Sicas," said the old man. "Let me see. I know the name, although it is scarcely a legendary metropolis." He rose from his chair and crossed to a rack from whence he selected a map tube. He extracted the rolled parchment and carried it to a flat table, where he spread it out and weighted its corners. While he did this, Conan examined some of the maps on the walls. These were of great antiquity, depicting nations that no longer existed. The mapmaker noticed him studying a particularly age-darkened specimen. The lettering was none Conan knew, and the outlines of the coasts were equally mysterious.

"Is this some land across the western sea?" he asked.

"No, but it might as well be, for its remoteness," the old man said. "In truth, the continent you see depicted there is the same as that upon which you now stand, but so long ago that the very oceans have changed their shape in the time since. I believe that to be one of the oldest maps in existence, and it is itself a copy of a far, far more ancient map. The written language is one no longer spoken, but I believe this to be a depiction of the western world as it was when the nations of Valusia and Commoria were supreme and the lands of the Picts were a string of islands in the western sea."

"Valusia and Commoria," Conan mused. "These are names from legend. The Picts I know, though. I learned to fight them from my earliest youth. Even the Vanir did not plague us as did the Picts."

"You are a man of Cimmeria, then?" queried the mapmaker. "I thought so, from your aspect. I have seen fewer than a half-score of your countrymen in my life."

"My countrymen like to stay close to home," Conan said, "but I was ever a wanderer."

"Come see this." Conan joined the shopkeeper at the table. With a spidery hand, the old man indicated the map before him. "This is a map of southeastern Aquilonia. Can you read the Nemedian letters?"

Conan nodded. "Fairly well, although the skill is new to me. These names are simple enough to make out." He pointed to a serpentine blue line at a spot where a tiny, stylized fort was drawn. "This is the Tybor River, and this is the crossing at Shamar."

"Exactly. And there," the mapmaker pointed to a tiny dot midway between Tarantia and Shamar, "is Sicas. From here, there are two easy routes to Sicas. The southern road will take you into northwestern Ophir; then it swings north and crosses the Tybor at Shamar. From there, you could take the royal high road toward Tarantia. About halfway to Tarantia, a road branches southwestward, and Sicas lies only a few miles beyond. However, there is civil war in Ophir just now and the border crossings are heavily guarded." His neatly manicured forefinger traced another route.

"You would be best advised to take the northerly route. The high road between Belverus and Tarantia is a good one, with many towns, villages, and wayside inns along the way. It intersects the Aquilonian high road just south of Tarantia, and from there you may proceed southward to Sicas."

"That is how I will go, then," Conan announced.

"Shall I make you a sketch-map? It will require only a few minutes. I will list the principal towns along the route, and the distances between them."

"Do so," Conan said. The old man opened a drawer and took from it a thin sheet. This was not the fine parchment he used for the detailed maps, parchment that, well cared for, could last for centuries. Rather, it was common paper, and upon it he began to sketch lines and letters with great skill, dipping his quill in ink made from lampblack.

"Know you aught of this place, Sicas?" Conan inquired.

"It is obscure, so there cannot be much to know," said the mapmaker, "but I will see what I can find." He rinsed his quill in a beaker of water and placed it in a rack, then took up a canister made of horn and silver from which he shook a fine powder over the new sketch-map to aid in drying the ink.

"Now, let us see what is to be found." He went to a tall case full of books and scrolls, some of them looking as ancient as the maps upon the walls. He selected a heavy tome and took it down. This book had a binding of brightly dyed Ophirian leather and appeared to be relatively new. The old man put it on the table and began to leaf through it.

"This is the most recent *Annal of the Kingdom of Aquilonia*," he announced. "Each king of that nation has one annal compiled in the early years of his reign. If he enjoys a long reign, he may have subsequent editions compiled. Although they are primarily used for purposes of taxation, they are invaluable to the cartographer as well. This one is but ten years old."

Conan was intrigued. "So this is how a king keeps track of who owes him what, eh?"

"That is the annal's purpose. It also records population, local products, and livestock and, especially, which feudal lord has the right to what piece of land. This is always a subject of bickering and dispute.''

"That I know full well.'' Conan had been involved in a great many such disputes.

"Here we are: Sicas. First its location is described. It lies at the confluence of two rivers, the Fury and the Ossar. From there the Ossar flows on to join the Khoratas a hundred leagues to the southwest.

"Sicas's population is about ten thousand. In the nearby countryside, the usual domestic livestock are raised: cattle, sheep, swine, and so on. Most of the land is cultivated, and there is river fishing. The major source of wealth, however, is from a great silver mine that lies near the city, just across the Ossar. When discovered three centuries ago, these silver deposits were vast, and for a while, Sicas was widely famed as the City of Silver. After a few decades, these early deposits played out, and ever since then, the ore has yielded a more modest but still quite respectable poundage of silver annually.

"This may be of some interest: As a source of precious metal, Sicas does not fall within any feudal fief, but rather is direct property of the Crown. As such, the local authority is a King's Reeve, who administers justice and is commander of the royal garrison. As commander, he is authorized to have one hundred men under his command.''

"No local lord, then?'' Conan asked.

"So it would seem. There is little more: Sicas has a small local production of woven and dyed wool. All the usual crafts are practiced. There are no ancient or famous public structures, although a few rather fine buildings were erected during the years of great prosperity when the silver was plentiful and fortunes were made. There are temples for the state cults, including a rather splendid Temple of Mitra.''

"It sounds a dull place,'' Conan said.

"Did you expect otherwise?'' the mapmaker asked.

Conan thanked the old man and paid him for the sketch-map.

Outside the shop, he unhitched his horse from a small statue and checked the angle of the sun. It was barely past noon. The day was young, and Conan decided that there was nothing to detain him longer in Belverus. He rode through the thronged streets to the west gate, an elaborate structure faced with purple marble, forty feet high and topped, like all the city gates, with a great, brazen alarm gong that gleamed like a second sun.

He rode out onto the high road, past the pens and campgrounds where late-arriving caravans spent the night when they found the gates barred. As the gleaming towers of Belverus disappeared behind him, the Cimmerian hoped that the bad luck that had plagued him there would likewise disappear.

TWO

A Lady in Distress

It felt good to be riding again on an open road with a good horse and a full purse, Conan thought. Then he corrected himself. His purse was no longer as heavy as when first he had filled it with the two hundred dishas he had extracted from Piris. Outfitting himself had taken nearly half the amount, and he had spent his nights on the road at decent inns. The map showed that towns and villages were many along this road, so there was no need to lay in a store of travel fare, nor to spend the nights beneath the sky. Conan had no taste for hoarding his money, so he spent freely as he went along. He was cautious enough to avoid the many games of chance that came his way at every halt. He had been given the gold on account against the completion of his task, after all. When he earned the other eight hundred dishas, he would be free to squander his money as he liked.

As he rode, women along the way cast many inviting smiles toward the big handsome Cimmerian. Nemedia was a land renowned for the beauty of its women. Conan smiled back, but rode on. The husbands of those women were equally renowned for the touchiness of their honor and their jealousy, and their readiness to fight anyone who should fall afoul of these qualities. It was not that Conan feared any Nemedian. It was just that he would never get to Sicas if he had to fight every one of them he met while journeying.

From time to time he passed patrols of Nemedian soldiers, and they eyed him suspiciously, this scarred barbarian with his black hair and blue eyes, in his gold-studded black brigandine and his steel cap. But they rode on and left him unmolested. His look and his well-used weapons were forbidding, and he was engaged in no outlawed activity.

Before he reached the Aquilonian border, a cold wind came whistling through the mountain passes to the north, and the sky grew leaden. In the borderland, the towns were father apart, and travelers tended to fare in groups for mutual protection. In this, as in every land, the farther one went from the centers of royal authority, the greater the abundance of outlaws.

Nemedia was noted for the strictness, even the cruelty, of its punishments, and in many areas the local lords grievously oppressed the peasantry. In result, many ruined men took to the hills and turned outlaw. Sometimes they formed powerful bands and descended on caravans or groups of travelers, leaving nothing behind save broken, mutilated bodies, stripped of valuables and even of bloodied clothes. A little questioning in the villages informed Conan that it had been many years since royal forces last swept these lands to clear out the bandits. He kept his attention on his surroundings and made sure that his sword was loose in its sheath.

One evening, still a half-day's journey from the border, darkness overtook the Cimmerian before he could reach the next village. He had resigned himself to a restless, wakeful night beneath the stars when he saw, not far away, the gleam of several camp fires. He approached them cautiously, ready to turn his horse and run at an instant's notice. More than once had he approached such friendly-seeming fires, only to find a trap set by outlaws to lure unwary travelers.

As he neared a fire, a man approached him, bearing a spear obliquely before him in both hands. "Who be you?" the man challenged.

"If I were any but a friend, you'd be nursing a split skull," Conan answered. "When you challenge a man, present your point to him, don't stand at high port like a recruit on inspection." He saw that the fellow was nervous, and probably with good reason. "I'm a soldier," Conan announced, "and it looks as if you could use one this night."

Another, older man came forward. "That is so. Come in, soldier, and share our fire."

Conan rode into the clearing, where a few small tents had been erected near the fires. A miscellaneous group of travelers sat on logs or cushions, huddled near the flames for warmth. Most of them had the look of petty merchants, but there were a few entertainers and some families with children, and here and there the sort of ragged pilgrims who were always traveling from one temple or sacred site to another, seeking enlightenment but more often finding a grave along the way.

Conan found a spot where the grass was deep and drove a picket pin into the ground. After tethering his horse, he unsaddled and curried it, then left it to graze. He carried his saddle and bags to the fire where sat the man who had invited him. The man passed him a broad leaf bearing a half-loaf of bread and some sausage.

"This is a nervous-looking lot," Conan said around a mouthful of food.

"Word is all over this area of a band of robbers just come across the border from Aquilonia. They were here last year, then went looking for richer pickings to the west, but they were pushed back into Nemedia a short while ago and now harry the district."

Conan took a skin of wine offered by a woman and drank, then passed it on to the older man. "How strong a band?" he asked.

"Reports vary from a mere five or six to twoscore. It may be a number of small bands who sometimes combine for larger raids.

Such men always infest borders, fleeing to the neighboring country when the king's men finally make it too hot for them.''

"This has an ill sound," Conan said. "Am I the only fighting man here?''

The man nodded to a small fire where two men in rusty mail vests, belted with short swords, sat passing a wineskin back and forth between them. "There are those two. They claim to be soldiers.''

Conan snorted. "Those are such as hire out to watch over warehouses at night. Should bandits strike, they can be counted on to take to their heels, if they are not snoring drunkenly.''

"Well, you have the look of a real fighter, anyway," the man said. "I am Reshta of Asgulun, a dealer in spices." He offered a hand and Conan took it.

"Conan of Cimmeria. My trade you already know. I journey to a place called Sicas, in Aquilonia. Have you ever heard of it?''

"I know only that it has gained an evil reputation these last few years. I have passed the road to that town many times but never was tempted to see the place. And you fare thither? I had not heard that there was war in Sicas.''

"There may be before long," Conan said bemusedly.

Soon all save those appointed as sentries sought their beds as the night grew colder. Conan went a little way from the fire and unbuckled his brigandine. It would take a greater threat than a few bandits to make him sleep in his armor. He lay down with his cloak wrapped about him and rested his head upon his saddle. Last of all, he slid his sheathed sword beneath the cloak. With his right hand resting on its bone grip, he slept.

"Bandits!''

The cry woke Conan instantly from a sound sleep. Without conscious thought, he was on his feet, the sword gleaming bare in his hand. There was no time to don his cuirass, but he snatched up his steel helmet and clapped it upon his tousled head. He saw forms struggling in the dimness, and someone had dumped dry brush on the fires so that, abruptly, they flared up, exposing both raiders and victims. He had an impression of eyes widened in

terror and of teeth flashing whitely as his ears were assaulted by
the sounds of weapons thudding against bodies and the screams
of women.

He thrust these things from his mind to concentrate on the
attackers. A man saw Conan and charged him, yelling. With both
hands gripping a spear, the bandit ran in, trying to impale the
Cimmerian with the full weight of his body behind the weapon.
Almost idly, Conan gripped the spear just beneath the head and
jerked it sideways. Then, with a flicking slash of his sword, he
severed both of the man's hands at the wrist. The outlaw ran
screaming into the outer darkness.

The Cimmerian ran toward one of the fires. He passed another
outlaw about to ax a man lying on the ground, and he skewered
the attacker through the kidneys in passing. At the high-flaring
fire, he turned so that the flames were at his back. This way, his
enemies would have to come toward him well illumined, unless
one was hardy enough to attack him through the flames.

"There he is!" shouted someone, and suddenly it seemed as
if the whole band of rogues were bearing down upon him. He
dodged a descending ax and halved the axeman's head. Before
the man had a chance to fall, Conan snatched a handful of his
coat and swung the corpse across his body like a ghastly shield,
using it to catch the slash of a two-handed sword. The long, heavy
blade bit sickeningly into the dead spine and Conan dropped the
corpse. As it dragged the blade down, the sword-wielder tried
vainly to free his weapon. Conan's blade split his shoulder, carving downward through lung and heart.

Now a pair of men bore down upon the Cimmerian from either
side. From the left, a man darted in swinging a sword. From the
right came a spearman. Conan whirled right, leaned aside as the
spear lanced toward him and grasped the spearman's arm. Hauling him across his front, Conan sent him colliding into the
swordsman. As they smashed together, Conan gripped his hilt in
both hands and slashed both men across the waist with a single
mighty blow.

"That's enough!" shouted someone outside the circle of firelight. "Back, and away from here!" A sound of trampling feet announced the precipitate retreat of the bandits. Conan's trained ears told him that there were no more than four of them left.

In the sudden quiet there was no sound save the crackling of the fires. Then the sobbing of women, the groaning of wounded men, and the crying of children rose into the night sky. Reshta came near and surveyed the Cimmerian with something akin to awe.

"By all the Baalim!" exclaimed the Shemite. "You spoke no falsehood when you proclaimed yourself to be a fighting man!"

"How many are dead?" Conan asked, bending to tear a strip of cloth from a slain bandit's tunic. "Not counting these vermin, I mean." With the cloth, he cleaned his blade while the merchant went to take a tally.

"Five of us were killed," Reshta reported when he returned.

"Where were those two louts in rusty iron?" Conan asked.

"As you predicted, they never woke from their drunken stupor. Both had their throats cut. The other three dead tried to fight in the dark."

"That is always a bad idea," Conan said. "Fighting in the dark leaves too much to chance. Many a fine warrior has died at the hand of a lesser man he could not even see."

"Doubtless these unfortunate men lacked your experience," said Reshta. After a moment of pondering, he spoke again. "I think that like everyone else here except for you, I was confused in the early moments of the attack. Still, it seemed to me that these villains came in search of you."

"I do not see how that could be," said the Cimmerian. "No man knows me in these parts. I have no wealth and no enemies. Doubtless they saw that I was the best fighting man here and that they would have to slay me first if they hoped to accomplish their aim."

"Aye," said Reshta, sounding doubtful. "Perhaps that is how it was." He walked away to oversee the disposal of the dead. Despite his own words, Conan remembered the voice from the outer dark. It had called: *"There he is!"*

* * *

The next morning he parted company with the traveling band. He had no intention of reining his fine horse to the plodding pace of these merchants and mountebanks. Before he rode away, the Shemitish spice merchant came to him.

"Farewell, Cimmerian, and thanks for your aid. Even if those rogues were looking for you, I feel sure they would have descended upon us last night whether you were with us or not. They were in the district and we made a tempting target. I feel that when you reach Sicas, that town will grow very lively."

He rode alone, and he knew that the bandits might be in wait for him somewhere ahead. But he was mounted and fully armed and armored, and in such a state, Conan feared no four or five bandits in the world, in broad daylight. The sun had not yet reached zenith when he learned that he had no worries at all from that quarter.

No more than a mile from the border, he came upon a grim, ghastly, but not at all unusual sight. A small detail of Nemedian troops sat beneath a large tree, sipping at steaming cups of an herbal infusion. Above their heads dangled four bodies, each hanging by the neck from the same limb. Conan reined his horse toward the little group. A man whose helm bore the green plumes of a sergeant stood and approached him.

"A fine sight, eh, outlander?" said the sergeant.

"Are these the bandits who have made a nuisance of themselves here lately?" Conan inquired.

"Aye." White teeth flashed in the dark face. "We ran into these four this morning, captured them and hung them all in the same hour. You see that villain in the velvet coat?" He pointed to the corpse of a middle-aged man with a gray-specked beard. "That is Fabirio, who was once a good soldier of the king. He was my captain when I was a recruit; that is how I knew him for certain." The sergeant spat upon the ground. "He turned bad after he killed a comrade over a gambling debt. These last eight years he has plagued both sides of the border with his band. No longer, though."

"Good work," Conan commended. "I was with a group of travelers last night when these rogues attacked. We slew five and the rest fled. The other travelers will be along later today and will confirm this." Conan knew better than to boast of his own feats when he had no evidence for proof.

"Excellent!" exclaimed the sergeant. "Perhaps that was the lot. Their numbers have been dwindling of late."

"Did you have a chance to question them?" Conan asked. "Did they say anything?"

"We did not bother," said the sergeant. "What could these scum say that might interest us? We ran them down, disarmed them and strung them up. Why do you ask?" A suspicious light came to the man's eye, a light with which Conan was all too familiar.

"No reason," he said. "Were there rewards on their heads?"

"Oh, assuredly," said the sergeant. "If you do not mind tarrying about here in Nemedia for months while all the office vermin go through their paces and if you can assemble enough witnesses and so forth. However, you have the look of a man with an itch to visit far lands, so I would not encourage you to cultivate any vain hopes in that direction."

"I shall not," Conan said. "Greater rewards beckon me elsewhere."

"Then ride forth with the blessings of the gods, outlander," said the sergeant.

Conan rode away from the tree and its unnatural fruit, reflecting that this was not the first time that officers charged with enforcement had expressed an interest in seeing him out of their territory. He was quite sure that it would not be the last.

Just past noon, he crossed the border into Aquilonia. Two small forts marked the boundary, since at this point there was no natural feature such as a river or a mountain range to mark it. There had been peace between the nations for some time, and the border officials did no more than note his name and give him a wax tablet stamped with the date and the place of the border crossing. He was supposed to surrender this tablet to royal officers upon demand and give it back when he should leave the country. Conan accepted this process with the resignation with which he tolerated all such nonsense.

The border territories of Aquilonia were similar to those of Nemedia, but they were far more efficiently policed. The villages were, for the most part, cleaner and better ordered than those on the other side of the border, not that Conan considered this to be a great attraction. His own tastes ran to the colorful and the uproarious. If he had wanted a life that was calm and harmonious, as philosophers had assured him was that most to be desired, he would have stayed at home in Cimmeria. Life there could be brutal and ferocious, but most of the time it was dull. That was why he had left.

The high road was paved with cut stone, but Conan saw that there were gaps where weeds sprouted between the slabs of granite, and in places, pieces of the road had been washed out by storms. Clearly, the king of this place was failing. Conan was not a man of the civilized lands, but in his wanderings he had learned to read such signs. In the forested Cimmerian lowlands, the broken stub of a branch holding in its clefts strands of bristling black hair meant a wild bull grown old, clumsy and decrepit. Likewise, a fine road in such a state of neglect meant a king who was losing his grip.

Even in its deteriorated condition, the fine road brought him within a few days to the juncture of the high road leading to Tarantia. He would have liked to ride north and see the capital city, but instead, he rode south, toward Shamar.

This highway linked the two major cities of Aquilonia, and during the height of the traveling season, it would be thronged. With winter closing in, the traffic had dwindled, and for much of the time Conan could see no other travelers in either direction. The lands nearby were cultivated and had the look of great estates, with broad fields worked by peasants, and in the distance he could descry the fine villas of the wealthy. Standing near each country house was a fortified tower to which the owners could repair in unsettled times.

At intervals along the road stood shrines to the local gods, some of them bearing the remains of offerings: flowers, cakes, and incense. As he passed one of these shrines, Conan heard sounds from a copse of trees behind the structure. There were the growling voices of men, then the sharp, high scream of a woman. Without pausing for thought, he spurred his horse off the road and pounded for the trees.

Just inside the wood, three men looked up from their activity at the Cimmerian's arrival, hard-bitten men in ragged clothing, belted with swords and long daggers. They crouched over a struggling woman who was resisting the removal of her garments. Conan saw a flash of white limbs and grinned at this unexpected liveliness in the midst of his otherwise dull morning.

"Begone, fool," snarled a man whose rat-trap mouth was framed by thin, drooping black mustaches. His greasy black hair was parted in the center by a jagged scar. "You've no call to interfere with our sport."

"Sport, is it?" Conan said. "You call three men attacking one woman sport?" He drew his sword and thumbed its edge. "What I call sport is a three-on-one fight with a man who knows his business. Will you play with me?"

Setting spurs to his horse, Conan charged down upon them. The men looked at one another for an instant, then took to their heels as one man. Three to one was poor odds when the one was mounted and armored. Laughing, Conan chased them as they scrambled amoung the trees. He was forced to maneuver carefully among the boles, ducking low to avoid limbs. The men reached the edge of the wood ahead of him, and there they scrambled onto their horses. Conan burst from the trees just in time to see three horses' tails presented to him, their riders galloping the mounts for all they were worth.

Hallooing like a hunter with a stag fleeing before him, Conan pounded toward them, his sword cutting great circles in the air around him. To his astonishment, the three horses put on a great burst of speed and the men began to draw away. His own horse was already running at top speed, and it was clear that he would not catch these three. He reined in and turned, then trotted his mount back to the copse behind the shrine.

He found the woman rearranging her clothing. Her face was a furious red, but her smile was dazzling when he rode up.

"Oh, sir, I cannot begin to thank you. Who knows what my fate might have been had you not arrived as you did?"

"I can guess," Conan said. "But you need not fear now. Those were the best-mounted cowards in Aquilonia. They were riding racehorses, else I'd have collected their heads."

"If they were thieves, why should they not steal the best?" the woman said. "I would think that men who spend their lives fleeing must prize fleet animals."

"That makes sense," Conan agreed. "How came it about that you fell afoul of them?"

"I was traveling on the highway and stopped at this shrine to rest and make a small offering. When I emerged, they were waiting for me. I think they must have camped in these woods to catch lone travelers. They relieved me of my belongings, then dragged me here to make use of what I had left. I am sure that after that, they would have cut my throat." She shuddered, then looked up with another smile. "But you appeared, like a champion out of legend. I shall be grateful to you forever."

Conan studied her as she spoke, and he liked what he saw. The woman was slender, with long, tapering legs and a willowy waist. Her breasts were high and full. Beneath a mane of somewhat disarrayed chestnut hair, her face was heart-shaped, with generous lips and wide blue eyes.

"Did they get away with your belongings?" Conan asked, forcing his mind back to practical matters.

"Let me see." She looked around a little clearing. "I think they tossed them somewhere when they set about to . . . to . . ."

"Rape you," Conan finished for her. It was a simple enough word, he thought. The woman shouldn't have to fumble for it.

"Yes. Exactly. Here they are! They didn't get away with them." She stooped and picked up a shawl wrapped around a small bundle. "Not that there is all that much to steal."

Conan noted that something within the bundle jingled. He was always alert for such sounds.

"Whither are you bound?" he asked.

"I fare to a town called Sicas," she said. "It is not far from here. The road to Sicas branches off this one a few miles to the south."

"Sicas! That is my destination as well."

"Say you so?" She lowered her eyes, blushing again. "Sir, you have already done so much for me, I scarcely feel that I could implore you for another favor, but could you, of your kindness, allow me to travel along with you until we reach the city? I think that now I would be terrified to walk this highway alone."

"Assuredly," said Conan, who had had something of the sort on his mind since his first good look at her. "This is no racehorse, but it is strong and will carry double with no undue strain."

"Oh, thank you, sir! If you will let me take your hand, I will use your stirrup to mount behind you."

"No need," Conan said. He leaned low, grasped her about her slender waist and set her before him on his saddle.

She gasped. "I have never known a man so strong! And you are not only brave, but generous. I do not know how to express my gratitude."

"Doubtless we shall think of something," he assured her.

At an easy walk, he rode back onto the highway and turned southward.

"You speak with a strange accent," she said. "What land do you hail from?"

"Cimmeria," he said. "I am Conan, a free warrior."

"Cimmeria! It is almost a name from legend. I was just a girl when your countrymen sacked Venarium, but I remember the near panic that spread at the news. Aquilonia had been victorious for so long that it seemed unnatural for mere barbarians . . ." She clapped a hand across her mouth. "Oh, forgive me! I did not mean to . . ."

"No matter," Conan said. "I've seen enough of civilized places to know that it is a fine thing to be a barbarian. Yes, I was at Venarium. It was my first real battle, and it was a good one. Those we win are always good ones." He smiled down at her. The top of her head barely reached his chin. "Now, how do you happen to be traveling alone, on foot, to a place like Sicas?"

She sighed deeply. "It is not a pretty story. My name is Brita, and my home is in Tarantia. My father was a Master of the Drapers' Guild. Both my parents died in the pestilence that swept the city five years ago. I was left with only my younger sister, Ylla.

"We were left with our house and a small stipend from the guild. I had many offers of marriage, but I had promised our mother on her deathbed that I would not marry until I saw my younger sister grown and wed. The times were hard for a while, yet we scraped by.

"But as she blossomed, Ylla grew wilder. Soon I could not manage her. She spent much time out in the city, in its less savory quarters, with a string of male companions, each one more disreputable than the last. Finally she came home with a villain named Asdras." She all but spat at the name. "He was a handsome enough fellow, but he was a gambler and a thief, although a well-spoken thief. He was the ruined son of a prominent family and seemed to fancy himself some sort of raffish aristocrat, as if he followed his low pursuits only for the amusement.

"He demanded—not asked for, but demanded—my sister's hand in marriage. I banished him from our house, of course. For days there were terrible scenes between my sister and myself. She raged that I was ruining her life, that I sought to drive away the man she loved." Brita brushed a pair of tears that made twin tracks down her pale cheeks. "As if a man like Asdras could ever love anyone except himself." She released yet another deep sigh.

"Well, it could not drag on forever. One day Ylla stormed out, claiming that she would run away with Asdras. I thought it was just another of her childish threats and I awaited her return. She did not come back that night, nor all the next day. I went seeking her, only to find that she had truly run away with the rogue. Some of his friends told me that Asdras had heard that the town of Sicas was a veritable paradise for men like himself, even more wicked than the lowest quarters of Tarantia. Naturally he had to see for himself, and he took Ylla with him.

"I thought that my heart would break, but I still love my sister, and I must honor my pledge to our mother, so I resolved to fare to this evil city and fetch my sister back. I sold what possessions I could to raise money, and I set out on foot, feeling that a horse would be an extravagance. I have no idea of how long I must search for my sister in Sicas, or of what bribes may be necessary."

"I think that you had better go back to Tarantia," Conan said. "A city like Sicas is no place for a gently bred lass such as you. Go home and wait. I have known many girls like your sister, and a great many men like this Asdras. Sooner or later she'll tire of being a ne'er-do-well's woman and she'll come home. Just give the girl time." He said this only to comfort the distressed woman. He knew full well that such girls almost always became harlots after they deserted their rogues, or the rogues tired of them. They almost never went home.

"Ah, but I cannot!" Brita raised her tearful face to his. "I love my sister, and I am certain that her faults are merely those of headstrong youth. If I can bring her back home, I am sure that in time she will settle down and will wed decently."

Conan had his doubts. It sounded as if the young slut had cut a swath through the dissipated youth of Tarantia and, as such, would make an unlikely match for some plodding guildsman. He forbore to express these thoughts.

Stifling her tears, Brita spoke again. "I scarcely know how to ask this, since you have been so kind. But when we reach Sicas, could you help me search for my sister?" At his frown, she added hastily: "Oh, I know it is presumptuous of me, but I am so desperate! I have a little money, and I can pay you for your trouble."

The last thing Conan wanted was to be a woman's protector while he was in the city, and neither did he want to take from her what was undoubtedly a pitiful sum of money. Nor did he wish to dash her hopes, so he equivocated as best he could.

"Well, I've a task to perform in Sicas, and I've already accepted the hire, so that must come first. But when we arrive, I'll see what may be done. I'll see you settled there and perhaps talk to a few officials."

She beamed. "Oh, thank you!" She cast her arms around his neck and kissed his slightly bristled cheek. He had not shaved in several days.

Now it was Conan who sighed. He had always thought it foolish to take in wounded birds. At least, he thought, this time he had taken in a pretty one.

A tiny wayside market stood at the junction of the high road with the side road to Sicas. Conan questioned a seller of clothes about their route while Brita went to a fruit-seller's booth. She had pointed out, practically, that the produce here would certainly be cheaper than in the town.

"Aye, that is the road to Sicas," said the clothier. "And if I were you, I'd ride straight on to Shamar. Sicas is a wicked place."

"I like wicked places," Conan told him.

"So do I, within reason. But Sicas is more than just wicked."

"What makes it so bad?" Conan asked.

"I could spend all day telling you, but since you're going there anyway, you'll find out all too soon. Good luck to you."

Conan remounted and soon Brita rejoined him, her shawl now bulging with fresh fruits. He lifted her to the saddle before him and began to ride down the side road toward Sicas. Brita's eyes sparkled and she seemed exhilarated.

"What has changed your mood?" he asked.

"I spoke to some vendors back there," she reported. "They said that two people went toward Sicas a few days ago, riding from the direction of Tarantia. They match exactly the description of Asdras and Ylla."

"Well, that's something, anyway," Conan grumbled. He had few hopes for the success of the woman's mission.

In the late afternoon they stopped on a hilltop overlooking Sicas. The view was serene for a town with such an odious reputation. Its shape was triangular, with the two rivers joining at the

apex. The base of the triangle was a wall built across the peninsula of land formed by the converging rivers. A moat had been
dug at the foot of the wall, linking the River Fury on the east
with the Ossar on the west. A stone bridge built on arches crossed
the Fury just north of the wall. In the distance, on the other side
of the Ossar, Conan could just make out a cluster of structures.
This must be the silver mine, he thought.

"No sense waiting," he said, heading the horse down the hill.

THREE

The City of Rogues

The stone bridge rang hollowly beneath the horse's steel-shod hooves as Conan rode across, Brita propped on the saddle before him. On the far side of the bridge the road turned right and ran a quarter-mile to the single gate in the town's wall. They stopped at the gate and were looked over by a singularly scruffy guard. The man wore a dingy cuirass and a dented helmet, and he leaned on a halberd that appeared to be at least a hundred years old.

"Who're you?" the man demanded.

"Conan of Cimmeria and Brita of Tarantia," Conan answered. "We come to Sicas on legitimate business."

"D'you think anybody cares? All sorts of fools ride into this town. Some of them leave by way of this gate, but most of them leave by way of the river, floating." Even from the height of his saddle, Conan could smell the sour wine on the man's breath.

"That being the case," the Cimmerian said, "you'll not mind standing aside to let us pass."

"The fee's two silver marks," the guard said sullenly.

"A mark for the town and a mark for you, eh?" Conan said.

"What's it to you? A man must make a living."

"I will pay him," Brita offered quietly. "We do not want trouble with the authorities."

"No, you'll not," Conan grumbled. He reached into his pouch and withdrew four marks of silver, which he tossed to the guard. "Now we've paid. Let us pass."

The man stood aside and bowed with exaggerated courtesy. "Welcome to our fair city, strangers. You'll pay gold to get out again."

They passed beneath the lintel and into the town. "This town is living up to its reputation already," Conan muttered.

"It is just the sort of place to attract Asdras," Brita assured him.

A single wide street led from the gate into the heart of the town. All of the side streets were narrow and twisted. They had not passed the length of two blocks when they came upon a violent commotion.

"Draw!" shouted a voice. Instinctively, Conan gripped the throat of his sheath and pressed his thumb against the hilt of his sword, loosening it from the slight grip of the scabbard. But the shout was not for him. Three young men dressed in red leather had a fourth backed against a wall. The man at bay was a black-bearded, scar-faced fellow with a cast in one eye. He snatched forth a straight backsword with a half-basket hilt. The three in leather drew Khorajan sabers. These weapons had long, curving blades and handles long enough to grip with both hands.

"Cowards!" shouted the black-bearded man. He slashed at one of the youths, who jumped back, laughing. Another stepped in and slashed the lone man's exposed side. The man gasped and clapped a hand to the wound, whirling to face this assailant. As he did, he exposed his back to the third, who slashed him obliquely from shoulder to hip.

Screaming, the wounded man arched backward, trying vainly to keep his sword between himself and his attackers. One red-clad assassin struck the sword from his hand even as another thrust his blade into the man's belly. The bearded one collapsed to the cobbles writhing, his arms wrapped about his midriff. The laughing men ran him through a few more times, then walked away, wiping their blades. At last the victim was still as a pool of blood widened around him.

Brita shuddered and buried her face against Conan's armored chest. "Mitra! What kind of place is this?"

"At a guess," Conan said, "it's a place so lawless that men commit murder in public places in broad daylight with no fear of punishment."

One of the men caught sight of the Cimmerian and halted, regarding him insolently. "What are you looking at, outlander?"

"I always like to see experts at their work," Conan said.

Another youth spoke. "I think this black-haired barbarian saw something that displeased him. Is that so, foreigner?"

"Three, by my count, but rest easy. I fight for pay, so I've no quarrel with you."

"See that you keep to that course, savage," said the first speaker. "No one lives long who earns our displeasure." The three sheathed their swords and swaggered away. The people who thronged the street stepped quickly out of their way. Nobody took note of the corpse, except to avoid the pool of blood. Conan nudged his horse onward, and it shied sideways as it passed the corpse, upset by the smell of fresh-spilled blood.

Two streets beyond the fight scene, he saw an inn sign at the intersection of a narrow street. He turned the horse into the by-way, which ran for no more than ten paces, then opened onto a broad courtyard. The courtyard was surrounded by three galleried stories of rooms. At street level there was a stable on one side and a tavern on the other. A hostler took the horse's reins as Conan lowered Brita to the pavement. Dismounting, the Cimmerian addressed the man.

"Hold the beast. I want a look at this place before I see to the animal's stabling." They went into the tavern, where a chubby, white-haired man came forward wearing a professional smile but eyeing skeptically Conan's dangerous looks and ready weaponry.

"Welcome, sir and lady. Do you seek lodging?"

"We do," Conan said. "We need two rooms."

"Have you two that adjoin?" Brita asked hastily.

"Aye. A silver mark per room each night. A quarter-mark each day for the horse's stabling and feed. The rooms you need are on the top floor."

"Let's have a look at them," Conan said. They followed the man outside and climbed the stairs to the third floor. The landlord opened two rooms that were connected by a low door; the quarters were reasonably spacious and comfortable looking. The Cimmerian went to a bed and abruptly threw back the covers.

"No bedbugs, sir," said the host.

"Well, I see none, at any rate. I've stayed at inns where I had to fight the bed vermin off with a sword." He looked up. There were skylights in the ceiling, admitting abundant light.

"We allow no braziers in the rooms," the landlord said. "If you wish, you may have extra blankets, and should you desire it, the cooks will heat a brick for you to set at your feet, but you may have no open fires save for candles."

"We'll take these," Conan said.

"Have you a bathhouse?" Brita asked.

"Aye, next to the kitchen."

"Very well," Conan said, handing him the money. "Tell the hostler to stable the horse and bring up my saddle, pad and bags."

"I shall. In the taproom, the first mug of ale is on the house. I trust that all will please you here. If not, I am at your service." The man bowed his way out.

Conan unbuckled his brigandine and tossed it onto his bed. "I think I'll go in search of that ale."

"And I will find that bathhouse," Brita said. "I will speak with you this evening." She glanced at the skylight. "I may have time enough to go out and make some inquiries before dark."

"Be careful, then," Conan cautioned. When his saddle and bags were brought up, he stowed them before going down the stairs and into the tavern. He was not merely thirsty; he knew that there was no better place than a barroom in which to pick up the gossip of a town.

In the taproom, men and women sat at long wooden tables eating or stood at the bar drinking. At one end of the room, spits turned at an open hearth, where fat dripped hissing onto the coals. The air was full of a thin, savory smoke. Conan crossed to the bar. Behind it, a bald man wearing an apron tended his taps, bottles and cups.

"A new guest?" he asked.

"Aye."

"Light ale or dark? Or would you prefer wine?"

"Dark ale," Conan said. The barkeep set a tall wooden tankard before him, crested with a thin foam. Conan raised it and drank deep. It was uncommonly good ale. He surveyed the room and its occupants, noting that all of the men were armed. He had observed the same thing out in the street. Even those who clearly were not fighting men were girded with steel, and many wore light armor. In the confines of the taproom, they were nervous as well, starting at every loud sound.

"This is a jumpy crowd," Conan commented.

"With good reason," the barkeep said. "You've just arrived in Sicas?"

"Aye. Never been here before." The door opened and everyone grew even more tense. Fingers tightened on hilts. The man who came in was fat and looked to be harmless. The patrons relaxed and conversation resumed. Conan turned back to face the barkeep.

"What does red leather mean to you?" he asked.

"It means trouble. Why do you ask?" The man devoted great attention to polishing a horn cup.

"Today, as I rode into town, I saw three overgrown boys dressed in red leather cut down a lone man. He never had a chance, and they laughed as they slew him. They let him draw his sword, but it was nonetheless plain murder."

"The man they killed, what did he look like?" asked the barkeep.

"A scar-faced man with a black beard and a cast in one eye."

"That was one of Lisip's men. I do not know his name, but I

have seen him with that mob. The red-clad boys follow Ingas. They are a pack of young Poitainian thugs who came in town about a year ago. Give them wide berth. They love to use those two-handed Khorajan slashers they all carry.''

''Who is this Lisip?'' Conan asked. He drained his mug and pushed it across the bar for more. The barkeep held it below a tap and refilled it.

''He used to boss all the town's scum, and he owns most of the bawdy-houses down in the Pit. Now he has a great deal of competition.''

''And Lisip has a feud with this Ingas?'' Conan asked.

''They were at peace yesterday. It sounds as if that has changed.''

''So now these two gangs contend for control of the town's low life?'' Conan asked.

''Two?'' The barkeep chuckled. ''Stranger, there are at least four major gangs, plus a good dozen smaller packs that ally themselves now with one, now with another. The big gangs sometimes form alliances and break them as lightly.''

This sounded intriguing. ''How do they operate?''

''Sometimes they rob directly, but mostly they just get a piece of everything. The harlots have to pay a portion of their earnings, the gamblers of their winnings. Every merchant in the town must pay every month or have his shop and goods destroyed. Sometimes they hire themselves out as bullyboys. Businessmen hire them to wipe out their competitors. And all of them kill for money.''

''Is there no law?'' Conan asked.

The man gave a snorting laugh. ''Law? There is the King's Reeve, Bombas. He is in the purse of every gang leader in this town, and he knows better than to trouble the wealthy men, those who hire the gangs for their dirty work.''

''This is a royal town. Has no one complained to the king?''

The barkeep glanced around to see if anyone was listening. ''No. But many have died just for speaking of it.''

Conan thanked the barkeep, turned and carried his mug to a

table. He took a corner at the end of a bench, where he could keep the entirety of the room within his view. A server set bread and cheese and a platter of sizzling waterfowl before him and Conan tore into the viands.

As he ate, he thought over the barkeep's strange tale. He had been in many wide-open and roaring towns, where the authorities were happy to look the other way for a monetary consideration. But ordinarily they required that the wilder elements keep their drinking and brawling, their thieving, gambling, whoring and killing, to a single district. That way everybody made money and the respectable element of the city stayed happy.

Usually such a district was controlled by a vice-lord. Sometimes another gang came in and then there would be a fight for control. Never, though, had Conan encountered anything so wildly anarchic as here in Sicas. In such a town, he thought, there was a great deal of money to be made.

He had finished his meal and was enjoying another mug of ale when the door opened again. This time the diners in the room remained tense, their facial expressions strained. Hands stayed on hilts and all conversation ceased. Three figures swaggered in through the door. Three figures, each dressed in red leather. They surveyed the room haughtily, as if they had just entered a barnyard and saw nothing before them except pecking fowl.

The landlord scurried over to them, bowing. "I did not expect you until the day after tomorrow," he said. "I have not yet—"

"Payment is due early this month," said the tallest of the three, not bothering to look at the landlord as he spoke. "And the amount has gone up. Fifteen gold royals instead of ten."

"Fifteen?" sputtered the landlord. "Instead of ten? And early? But I cannot pay that!"

A youthful thug with a stringy yellow chin-beard affected to ignore the man, reaching overhead to rap his knuckles on a heavy, soot-stained beam. "Fine old timber here," he remarked. "Make a splendid fire. Probably take the whole block with it. Wouldn't your neighbors appreciate that?"

The landlord groaned, defeated. "Very well, I will pay. But I cannot pay today. I had not yet even gathered together the usual ten.''

The third youth patted the old man on the shoulder. "Do not vex yourself, Grandfather. Moneylenders always have an open purse, even if they do ask for high interest. We shall come by tomorrow, early.''

"Bringing torches," added the one with the thin beard.

The tallest nudged the other two. They looked at him and he nodded toward the rear corner of the room where Conan sat. Hands resting on the long hilts of their Khorajan swords, the three walked toward the Cimmerian with an insolent, loose-jointed amble.

"This is the second time today we have encountered you, barbarian. You are new here. Who have you come to join?"

"I work for nobody here." He left his hands on the table, in plain view. He knew that they would think him less dangerous that way, the fools.

"But you said you fight for pay," countered the bearded one.

"And no one is paying me to fight just now," the Cimmerian answered.

"Then what is your business here?" demanded the bearded one.

"It is, as you say, my business," Conan said.

"We do not like people who refuse to answer to us," said the third. He was a bit older than the other two, with quick, nervous brown eyes. Conan read him as the most dangerous of the three. If it came to a fight, he would kill this one first.

"Many people do not like me," Conan said. "I try not to let it grieve me too much."

"We don't like your tone, either," said the tall one. "Why not come outside into the courtyard and discuss this with us?"

Conan knew why they wanted him outside. The cramped corner, the tables, and low beams would make it difficult for them to wield their long blades. He fumed at their insolence but reminded himself that he had eight hundred dishas yet to earn in this town and becoming ensnarled in gang politics would hinder him in that task.

"As I told you, I fight for pay. Come back and see me when somebody is willing to pay gold to see you dead." The two shorter ones closed their fists around their hilts, but the tall one made a calming gesture.

"This one is afraid to fight. Come, brothers. We'll talk to Ingas about this . . . this . . . what sort of barbarian are you?"

"Cimmerian."

"This Cimmerian. Then if our master wants his head, we'll come back and fetch it. Farewell, savage." The three whirled and stalked out. Conan noticed that most of the room's inhabitants had either tiptoed out during the confrontation or had drawn back to the periphery. Now that there was to be no fighting, they resumed their places.

One man had not moved. He was a tough-looking specimen, and now he rose and approached Conan. He stood a little below medium height but was strongly built. He wore a vest of mail, old but clean and well oiled. Graying hair hung to his shoulders beneath the rim of a battle-nicked steel cap. Broad wristbands of studded leather encircled both wrists, and he carried his hands well away from his short cutlass and dagger as he drew near. From boots to steel cap, this one was every inch a professional.

"You handled those three well, Cimmerian. Do you mind if I join you?"

Conan gestured to the seat across from him. "It is not taken."

The man sat. "Let me buy your next mug." He called to a server and in moments two tankards arrived. The two men clicked the tankards together and drank. The graying man wiped his mouth with the back of his hand.

"I am Nevus, from Tanasul. Your homeland I know. What is your name?"

"Conan."

"You told those precious redbirds that you serve no one here. Does that mean that you have no wish to?"

Conan shrugged. "Just now I wait to meet with a man who

has employment for me. The job should be finished in no great time. After that, who knows?''

''Well, should you find yourself at loose ends, you could do worse than joining Ermak's band. We're a small troop, but we're the best. Ermak takes on only professional fighting men, no scum like those three. I cannot read letters, but I can read the years of experience on you.''

''I thank you for the offer, and I will think upon it. I noticed that the leather boys did not bother you.''

''Ermak and Ingas are at peace for the moment. There is so much profit to be had in this town that we don't need to fight all the time.''

''So I hear. What sort of work do Ermak's men perform?''

''Weapon work, mainly. All the gangs know that we're the best fighters. When there's a dispute, the gang that is allied with us is the one that wins. Then it has to pay us a piece of everything it takes.''

''That sounds agreeable,'' Conan said. ''Where is Ermak headquartered?''

''Southwest of the Square there's a big warehouse built up against the Ossar River wall. It's two-storied, and we have the top floor. There are usually about twenty of us, although men come and leave frequently.''

''You say that Ermak is at peace with Ingas. Is he at war with anyone?''

''Lisip has been making noises of late. We should have a brawl with his men soon, but they are of no account, just scum and sweepings like Ingas's.'' The man drained his tankard and stood. ''Think upon my words, Conan. There is more profit to be had in joining with Ermak than with any of the others. Better amusement, and far better company as well.''

''I shall think on it,'' Conan said. ''Farewell.''

The Cimmerian finished his ale and climbed the outside steps to the third floor. In his room he lit a candle, for night had fallen. He knocked on the door linking the two rooms but heard no sound. Assuming that Brita was asleep, he pulled off his boots and stretched out on the bed. Before he knew that he was nodding, he was fast asleep.

He awoke to the sound of knocking at his door. A glance at the candle told him he had been asleep for two or three hours. Silently he rose and picked up his weapons-belt. He drew the dagger and went to the door. The pounding continued. Abruptly he threw the door open and hauled the person who stood without into the room, slamming the door shut.

"Conan!" screeched a woman's voice.

"Brita? What have you been doing? I thought you asleep in the other room."

"When I went to the bathhouse, I spoke with the women attendants there, to learn something of the town. Conan, this is a dreadful place!" She sat on the chair and clasped her hands in her lap.

"I find it interesting, but then, you are a woman. So what did these gossips tell you?" He sat on his bed, first stripping off his weapons-belt.

"They said that this town is ruled by packs of savage, vile men who—"

"I've learned all about that this evening," Conan interrupted. "How did you come to be outside in the middle of the night?"

"Well, the bath-women said that if I sought some *particular* rogue, the place to inquire about him would be the Square. That is a public market and government center in the middle of the town. I am so anxious to find my sister, and it was still light, so I went there."

"You should have told me," Conan grumbled. "What did you find out?"

"I talked to a few stall-keepers who had not yet closed for the evening, and they told me that I should ask of certain ladies who lounge about in the south colonnade. I went there and spoke to some of them." She lowered her gaze and seemed to be studying her clasped hands. "I think that these women are not truly respectable."

"I can promise you that they are not," Conan affirmed. "So what did these knowledgeable ladies of ill repute tell you?"

She looked up, her face alight. "One of them saw Asdras this very day! She said that he has established himself in a house called the Wyvern. It is in a district known as the Pit."

"The Pit? I heard the name spoken this evening. It does not sound good. Did she say where this might be?"

"It is the southernmost quarter of the town, where the two rivers join. It is a notorious place; all the lowest elements gather there."

"In this town, notoriety truly means something," Conan commented.

"I know. It sounded so terrible that I was reluctant to go there."

"Go there!" Conan exploded. "You mean to tell me that you contemplated going to the Pit *alone*? *After dark?*"

"Well, it was not quite dark yet when I left the Square. I am *so* concerned for my sister, Conan. I just had to go and see for myself. It is a small town, really, and the Pit is not far. But by the time I drew close to the Wyvern, it was pitch-black and I was terrified. I could not force myself to go on. I came back, sliding against walls and ducking into doorways at every sound of approaching footsteps."

"That was wise. In fact, coming back here was the only wise thing you've done since taking a bath. Well, go in and get some sleep. In the morning, we'll—"

"But I cannot wait until morning!" Brita said. "Now that I know where Asdras is, I must confront him tonight! Who knows what he might do if he learns that I am in town seeking Ylla? He might run, or he might hide her someplace."

"Brita, this matter will keep until tomorrow," Conan said. "A grown warrior walks abroad in this town after dark at grave risk. It is far worse for a woman, even if escorted. And if the Pit lives up to its name, it is that much worse."

She stood. "Well, if you will not go with me, I must go alone. I will find a torch or a lantern and I will go down into the Pit by myself."

"And what do you hope to accomplish beyond your own death?" Conan demanded.

"I only know that I must try," she said.

Conan began to haul on his boots. "I can see that it is useless to try to get a night's sleep." He stood and buckled on his brigandine.

"Oh, I knew you would help," she exclaimed.

"Then you know me better than I know myself. I never ere now took myself for a fool." He strapped on his weapons-belt and clapped his steel cap on his head. "I suppose I am as ready as I will ever be. Let's go."

They went down the stairs, and in the courtyard Conan appropriated a lantern from its hook. By its light, they walked into the street. The night was chill, but Conan had not donned his cloak. Tonight he might have to fight or run or both, and neither activity would be improved by the voluminous garment.

All was quiet on the main street of the town. The buildings to either side blocked most of the moon's light, and they walked in the middle of the road to avoid unpleasant surprises. If anyone lurking in the shadows felt tempted by the couple out for a midnight stroll, the lamplight glinted on enough metal adorning the big Cimmerian to discourage any predatory thoughts.

The street passed along the eastern side of the Square. The spacious public plaza was flooded with moonlight, casting enough glow to reveal the colonnades and fine buildings around the periphery, although their details remained cloaked in obscurity.

Beyond the Square, the street narrowed. It was no longer straight, but began to twist this way and that. This was the oldest part of the town, Conan guessed, and had probably stood here before the silver mine brought fleeting prosperity, at which time the Square and the finer areas to the north had been erected.

"The Wyvern is down here someplace," Brita said, peering from side to side. The light of the lamp was quickly swallowed in the deep shadows on every hand. "Yes, there!"

Conan raised the lantern in the direction she pointed. A pole protruded over a low doorway. The pole was decorated with the figure of a wyvern, cut from thin bronze. Its mouth smiled sardonically and its barbed tail, after making several loops, pointed toward the door.

"There is no sense in waiting out here in the cold," Conan said. "Let us go in."

The tavern was below street level and they descended three steps to the door. Thrusting the portal open, Conan ducked his head low and went inside, closely followed by Brita. The door opened onto a landing, from which further steps descended to the floor. Conan stood on the landing and surveyed the scene before proceeding onward. Perhaps a score of patrons huddled around tables, and the predominant sound as the two entered was the rattle of dice and the slamming of leather cups onto tabletops.

Upon the opening of the door, all faces turned toward the landing to study the newcomers. Nearly every countenance was decorated, with cropped ears, slit nostrils and various fanciful brands predominating. These were not the scars of combat but of punishments inflicted by public torturers. Half-naked women wandered between the tables, plying their ancient trade. They eyed the Cimmerian with interest until they saw Brita step from behind him.

"Hold this." Conan handed Brita the lantern. He leaned forward, both hands braced against the wooden rail of the landing.

"We are searching for a man named Asdras," he announced. "He is a newcomer to this town, and his companion is a young woman named Ylla. Has any here seen him or the woman?" After staring at the outlander for a moment, the gamblers returned their attention to their gaming. No one said a word. Brita stepped even closer to Conan and whispered: "Perhaps if I offer money . . ." He silenced her with a raised hand.

The Cimmerian descended the steps to the floor, and Brita followed him as he made his way among the tables. He stopped at one where three men sat. The fourth seat was vacant, but a pair of gloves and a half-empty cup lay upon the abandoned space. Conan pointed to them.

"Where did he go?" Conan demanded. A man looked up at

him with a sneer. This one had traveled far in his pursuit of villainy. A great character from the Khitan language had been tattooed across his face in scarlet.

"Wherefore should we tell you anything, dog?" He spat copiously upon the filthy floor next to Conan's boots. Smiling, the Cimmerian leaned across the table and bunched the front of the man's leather tunic in one great fist. Hauling the tattooed man over the tabletop, he slammed him against the wall, holding him with his feet well clear of the floor. Conan drew his dirk and laid its keen edge against the man's jugular.

"You will tell me," Conan said, "because you want to live."

"Peace, my friend!" cried the tattooed one. "I meant no discourtesy! Asdras was here, but he left more than an hour ago. He sat there all evening, but the cleaning boy brought him a note. He read it and said that he must go out back to see someone but would return soon. He did not come back, which seems passing strange since he was winning."

Conan dropped the man. "Where is the boy?" Wordlessly the man pointed to the bar, where a stunted youth listlessly plied a mop, moving the accumulated filth about without removing any of it. Conan walked over to the lad.

"Who gave you a note to deliver to Asdras, boy?"

The boy stared at him vacantly, his mouth half-open and tongue lolling. After a while he spoke, in the slow monotone of a half-wit.

"I went out back to dump the slops. Someone gave me a paper, said give it to Asdras."

"Who was it? A man or a woman?" Brita asked. The boy thought for a while, clearly a difficult process.

"Don't know. It was dark."

"This is useless," Conan said. "He's gone now."

"Let's go out back," Brita said. "They may still be there."

"If it will set your mind at ease," Conan said resignedly. "Show us, boy."

The two followed the half-wit through a curtain at the rear of the public room and passed through a storeroom full of barrels and smashed furniture. The boy pointed to a door in the wall and Conan opened it. The alley behind the building reeked of a hundred years' worth of garbage. Rats scurried away from their feet as they went outside. They could hear pigs rooting in the muck.

"No one here," Conan reported. "Let's go back to our inn."

"Wait," she said, raising the lantern higher and pointing. "What is that?" Holding her skirts well clear of the filth, she stepped daintily toward a rat-swarming heap a few paces from the door.

Conan stepped over to the mound and gave it a kick, causing it to shift slightly. The rats scurried away, squealing. Brita gasped, her hand flying to her mouth. There lay a dead man, his eyes staring, his mouth agape in surprise. The rats had only begun to nibble at him, so his features were still handsome despite his expression. His hair was yellow and spread around his head in a broad fan.

"Asdras!" Brita cried.

A dagger protruded from his chest. Asdras had been neatly skewered through the heart.

Four

The King's Reeve

Conan rose late and breakfasted mightily. Before leaving his room, he looked into the adjoining chamber. It was vacant. He told himself that the woman was probably safe while the sun shone, although her incredible penchant for putting herself in danger and her tendency to go off without informing him were annoying. Then he cursed himself for caring. What was the innocent, addle-headed woman to him, anyway? Still, having aided her thus far, he felt a certain responsibility. Annoyed with himself for suffering this unwonted sentimentality, he buckled on his accoutrements and descended the stairs.

The public room was deserted except for a serving woman, who at his order brought a great platter of meats, eggs and hot bread. Polishing off this spread put Conan in a far better temper, and he went forth to see what he could learn of the town. First he walked to the city gate. The man on guard there was not the one who had greeted them the day before, but he was just as unsoldierly looking: a fat, aged man who limped as he paced before the gate.

"Has a man came through today who is—" Conan thought for a moment of how to describe Piris "—well, womanish-looking, and fond of clothes that would look well on a courtesan?"

"Nay. I see some odd types, but none like that has passed this way today."

Conan tossed the man a coin, which was caught neatly. "If he should arrive on your watch, tell him that Conan of Cimmeria is staying at the first inn on the street."

The watchman looked at Conan as if wondering what business the foreigner could have with such a man, but knowing better than to ask. "Aye, sir, I shall tell him."

Conan thanked the guard and walked back down the street. It was his first good appraisal of the town in full daylight, and what he could see of it looked fair enough. The local architecture was of the sort favored in this district of Aquilonia. Most of the buildings' lower stories were of a rough-cut gray fieldstone, and the upper stories were half-timbered.

One street was lined on both sides by the headquarters of various guilds. These were imposing edifices, but one was a fire-gutted hulk, looking like a rotted tooth in an otherwise healthy jaw. Over its door were a pair of crossed picks, identifying the place as the Guildhall of the Miners' Guild.

From one large building Conan heard a familiar music: the clashing of swords. The rhythmic sound of the weapons told him that this was a lesson in progress, not a fight. He wandered in and saw a good hundred men being put through their paces by a master and his assistants. The students stood in pairs facing one another, alternately attacking and defending as the master called out the moves. All wore padded coats and stout helmets. The swords were blunt and had basket hilts to protect the hands.

The walls were hung with a great variety of practice weapons and small bucklers, but the favored implement seemed to be the one-handed sword. It was the best weapon for fighting in city streets. The men had a grimly determined look, but Conan quickly saw that few of them had much aptitude. The master, a wiry man in his forties, called a rest and then noticed the Cimmerian. He walked toward Conan, looking him over with quick calculation.

"You've the look of a man who needs no instruction from me," he said by way of greeting.

"I heard the sound of arms and came to have a look," Conan said. "I never saw an arms school with so many overaged burghers as students."

The master's smile was a white flash in his dark countenance. "I heard about this town a year ago and came hither. It seemed to me that a frightened town would be a good place in which to practice my profession, and I was right. Cutlers and armorers do well here, too. The citizens wear so much iron beneath their clothes that the streets draw lightning."

"Do you teach the scoundrels as well as the respectable citizenry?" Conan asked.

Again the swift smile. "Them I teach in the evenings."

"How do they rate?"

"Few are good fighters. All are killers."

"Is that true of Ermak's men?" Conan knew that it was seldom difficult to get a professional swordsman to talk shop.

"Professionals. They are mostly competent second-rate swordsmen. Battlefield soldiers are seldom truly expert at the art of single combat. Ermak's men are far better than any of the others, but their real skills are with pike and halberd."

"How about the followers of Ingas, the ones who wear red leather?"

"They never come here. They have small skill, but they are the most vicious. They favor those Khorajan slashers because with one, you can inflict a terrible wound with very little skill. But the Khorajan two-hander lacks defensive quality, so if you don't want to be killed in the midst of cutting down your man, you have to be very quick, well armored, or else do all of your fighting in packs. Ingas's men prefer the latter."

"I have noticed that about them."

"Do you seek employment with Ermak?" the swordmaster asked.

"I have no such plans at present."

"Then consider coming to work with me. As you can see, I have more students than I can comfortably handle with just three assistants. I teach three classes every day. One class is even made up of women!"

"I will think about it. But you know as well as I that the knowing of technique is of no use to a man who is not a real fighter."

The master shrugged. "It makes them feel safer and they pay well for the instruction."

Conan bade the master farewell and walked outside. Behind him, the clashing of metal resumed.

Another few minutes of walking brought him to the Square. It was a large public area for a city so small, surrounded by splendid buildings and decorated with a number of fine statues. Some of the buildings were temples, others were mansions. One had the royal lions of Aquilonia over its main gate. This, he decided, must be the headquarters of the King's Reeve.

He began to wander among the numerous stalls set up by vendors. Although he had taken no particular path through the town, he did not meander aimlessly. He was exploring, fixing the plan of the town in his mind so that he would not become lost should he have to flee. It would be disastrous to run into a blind alley were there a large group of armed and angry men at his heels.

A number of beggars lounged in the shade of the colonnade Brita had mentioned. Apparently it was too early yet for the ladies to parade their wares. He was passing the statue of an Aquilonian king dead for a hundred years when he heard a commotion nearby. People began to flee past him, looking back over their shoulders.

With the agility of a mountain goat, Conan sprang up onto the pedestal of the statue. From his vantage point he stood above the heads of the crowd, which now had drawn back to leave a broad, clear space at the western end of the Square. Within the cleared space two groups of men shouted at each other, separated by about a dozen paces. The sun flashed on drawn weapons. It seemed that a fine brawl was in the making.

"Hey up there!" It was a woman's voice. "You, the black-haired foreigner! Help me up. I want to see!"

Conan looked down to see a handsome, brown-haired woman whose expensive gown was styled to show her lush figure to best advantage. He stooped to grasp her hand and with a tigerish surge of muscle, he hauled her onto the pedestal beside him.

"My, you are a strong one!" She smiled at him boldly. "I thought I knew all the rogues in this town. Who are you?"

"Conan of Cimmeria. If you know them all, who are these men making all the fierce noises?"

She surveyed the scene before them. "The bigger band over there on the right are Lisip's men. The others are Ermak's."

Now he saw Nevus, his drinking companion of the night before. Nevus stood with about fifteen comrades, all of them hard men like himself. Most of these wore light armor and carried drawn short swords or cutlasses, although one had a light, straight two-hander and another a quarterstaff. They were heavily outnumbered but stood unafraid, smiling and hurling insults.

Facing them were at least thirty men dressed in a motley assortment of garments, most of them marked like the men he had seen the night before in the Wyvern. They carried an equally grotesque assortment of weapons. At a glance, Conan identified a double-bladed ax from Shem, a Bossonian archer's bill, eight different types of sword, and an iron flail. One man was armed with a pair of steel gauntlets with three-inch spikes over the knuckles.

"Which one is Lisip?" Conan asked.

"You won't see him here," the woman said. "He rarely leaves the Pit, and he's too old and fat to fight anyway."

He did not need to ask which was Ermak. A tall, sandy-haired man stood a little before and to one side of the mercenaries, dressed in half-armor of excellent quality. It was the best position for controlling a small unit, and the man had the bearing of an experienced under-officer. The sword he held casually in one hand bore a blade that measured about two inches wide at the hilt and had a perfectly straight taper to its needle point. It was a sword for a true blade artist, and its hilt was a complex steel basket of graceful shape.

"This will be enjoyable," the woman said, "but they'll take a while to get started. We might as well be comfortable." She sat on the pedestal, her legs dangling over one edge. Conan sat beside her and gave her an admiring examination. If she noticed, she was totally unembarrassed by it. She was a large woman, but so well proportioned that every line of her was graceful. Her facial features were of the same proportions, but too finely formed to be considered heavy.

"Who are you?" Conan asked, "and how do you come to know so much about these men?"

"I'm Maxio's woman. My name is Delia." She stuck two fingers against her lower lip and vented a shrill whistle. A vendor looked around and she waved him over to the pedestal. She tossed him a coin and he held up a broad leaf that had been cleverly folded to form a pouch. She took a few nuts from the pouch and popped them into her mouth, then held out the leaf to Conan. He took some of the nuts. They were still warm from the oven.

"And who might Maxio be?" he asked.

"You *are* new here. Maxio is the leader of his own little band. Freelance, mostly, but sometimes they side with one of the other gangs. They specialize in housebreaking."

"And Maxio is your husband?"

She laughed heartily. "Husband? What would I want with a husband? I said I was his woman, but that is a matter that could change." She gave him an appraisal as open as he had given her. "It could change very soon, if the right man should appear."

Lisip's men had drawn closer to Ermak's, who held their ground. They were still well out of weapons range. A crowd of guards now stood on the steps of the Reeve's headquarters, but they did not seem inclined to rush between the two bands and prevent violence.

"Will they do anything?" Conan asked, nodding toward the guardsmen. This time she laughed even louder.

"That bunch of spavined, knock-kneed ex-beggars? If they

were horses, you couldn't boil them down for decent glue! You
see that fat face peering out from behind them, as if they could
somehow preserve it from harm?''

"I see the man,'' Conan answered.

"That is Bombas, the King's Reeve, one of the two men who
claim to own this city. He belongs to anyone who pays him. He
lets the rogues have free run of the town, but he hates Maxio, so
my man has to keep out of sight most of the time.''

"The royal guards don't look formidable enough to cause a
man of spirit any fear,'' Conan said.

"Bombas has three who are hard men, and he keeps them
close, as his personal bodyguards. One is a local man named
Julus. He was once Lisip's second-in-command, but Lisip expelled him for skimming more than his share. The other two are
a pair of Zingarans whose names I do not know. They have orders
to kill Maxio on sight.'' She continued to much the roasted nuts
as if the prospect of her paramour's imminent demise was not
terribly upsetting. "I wish they would hurry up and fight. This
sun will bring out my freckles.''

Ermak's men had now formed a double line, with intervals
between men and lines sufficient to allow free use of weapons but
close enough that each would not have to face two enemies at
once, except for the flankers. Conan noted with approval that the
strongest-looking men stood on the flanks. Lisip's men stood in
a disorderly mob, doing most of the shouting.

"Why this enmity for Maxio?'' Conan asked.

"Bombas thinks that Maxio murdered his brother last month.
His brother was heard arguing with someone in an upper room
of the Wyvern. A little while later he was found with a dagger
buried in his guts. The dagger was one that Maxio had been
carrying for weeks; it had an ivory grip set with garnets.''

"The Wyvern?'' Conan said, wonderment in his voice. "What
was the Reeve's brother doing in that place?''

"Oh, Burdo—that was his name, Burdo—had a well-known
taste for the women of that establishment.'' She said this with the
contempt of a well-placed courtesan for her lesser sisters. "And

he suffered from several of the consequent ailments. He was supposed to be meeting someone about a magical cure, but someone killed him instead.''

''Was it Maxio?'' Conan asked.

She shrugged. ''I do not know. What is it to me if he did kill him? I know of no reason why he should, but he does not discuss everything with me.'' She gave Conan another admiring appraisal. ''Just as I do not tell him everything.''

At that moment, Lisip's mob, their courage sufficiently worked up, charged at the smaller band of mercenaries. Instantly the air was filled with the sound of clashing arms. Shouts of rage vied with screams of anguish, and men began to fall. The mercenaries held their line, while most of Lisip's men could only wave their arms ineffectually. Any time one of Lisip's men tried to force a way through the front line, one of the men in the staggered second line repelled him.

''With that many men,'' Conan commented, taking another handful of the nuts, ''they could easily turn a flank. They have numbers sufficient to make up for their lack of skill. It is cowardice that keeps them from doing it.''

''That is so,'' she agreed. ''Everyone in town fears Ermak's reputation. He has killed ten men in single combats alone since he came to town, and who knows how many in brawls.''

Now Ermak shouted for the first time: ''Advance!'' Smoothly, the second line stepped through the intervals in the first. These men were fresher and they plied their arms with fury, dealing wounds with nearly every blow, taking but few injuries in return.

''It won't be long now,'' Delia predicted. ''Lisip's scum have no staying power.''

Conan saw that a number of the rearmost of Lisip's men were already slowly backing away from the mob, not wanting to run like cowards but having lost their taste for the fight.

''Advance all!'' Ermak shouted. The former first line now stepped into the intervals, thus forming a single line. All of the mercenaries began to advance forcefully and steadily, dealing a blow with each short step. It was too much for Lisip's mob. After a brief, defensive flurry, they broke, starting with the rearmost and quickly degenerating into a thinning crowd of fleeing men.

Ermak's professionals pursued them to the edge of the Square, then stopped at their leader's command. Laughing, they turned and walked back across the plaza, wiping their bloodied weapons. Some in the crowd cheered and clapped. Seven men, dead or mortally wounded, lay upon the pave. Some others dragged themselves away, favoring wounded limbs. All were Lisip's. Some of Ermak's men had taken minor wounds, but none needed the help of comrades to walk.

"Not much of a fight," Delia complained. "After a good one, I've seen as many as twoscore dead on the Square or in the street."

Conan was satisfied. It had been amusing, and he had learned much about the respective merits of two of the town's gangs. "You said that Bombas is one of two who claim to own the town. Who is the other?"

She pointed to a great mansion that hulked at the northern side of the Square, behind high, spike-topped walls. "The man who lives in that house. His name is Xanthus and he owns the silver mine, or rather, he leases it from the Crown. He is far and away the richest man in Sicas, and like all of that breed, he can never be rich enough. It was his problems with the miners' guild that started all this warfare between the gangs."

At last, Conan thought, he was learning the reason behind this uproarious activity. "The miners? How so?"

"The miners had a long dispute with Xanthus, and a number of times they marched into the Square here and made a demonstration in front of his house, shouting and waving their picks and hammers. Finally, they refused to work."

"What did they complain about?" Conan asked.

She shrugged. "I don't know. Pay or conditions at the mine or some such. I'll have nothing to do with any man who works for a living. That way, you die old and poor."

"If the mine is Crown property, why did he not go to the king for aid?"

"I cannot say, but he did not. Instead, he went to Ophir, where that civil war has been dragging on for years, and he came back with Ermak and his men. Ermak had more than fourscore men with him then. They broke the miners and forced them back to work. That was when the miners' guildhall was burned.''

Conan could see where this was leading. ''But when the mercenaries had restored control, they were of no mind to leave, eh?''

''Not when they found how agreeable life could be for them here. I think that Ermak has decided to retire from the wars and set himself up as a wealthy lord someplace.

''Of course, Lisip did not like all this. He had controlled the underworld activity in this town since before I was born, but he always stayed in the Pit. Soon he was sending agents out to hire rogues and bring them back here to reinforce him. The word spread that Sicas is a town where anything can be had for a price and where you can do anything you want, as long as you decorate the right palms with silver and gold. Now not a day goes by without some new villain coming through the gate.'' Again she gave Conan her bold stare. ''Like you.''

''I thank you for sharing this information with me,'' Conan said.

''I'm sure you will put it to good use,'' she replied with obvious amusement.

Conan boosted himself from his seat atop the pedestal and landed lightly on bent knees. He reached up and caught Delia by the waist as she pushed off from her own seat. Her waist was remarkably slender for so large a woman. She landed with her hands braced on his shoulders. They stayed there longer than absolutely necessary.

''Farewell, Cimmerian,'' she said. ''I expect to be hearing from you soon. Should you wish to see me, I am always easy to find.''

''Before you go,'' he said.

''Yes?''

''What do you know of a man named Asdras?''

She looked disappointed. ''The man who was found dead this morning behind the Wyvern? Just that he was a gambler who came here a few days ago and established himself at a table there. As for his being found dead in the alley, it's a rare morning when a corpse isn't found there.''

"What about a woman who arrived here with him? Her name is Ylla, but she may be using another. She is very young.''

"I'd heard of no woman, but that is not unusual. Sporting men often keep their women hidden away someplace. Now that she's without a protector, she'll probably show up beneath the colonnade there.'' She pointed to the structure, where the beggars had resumed their begging. "The beggars have it in the mornings. The professional women show up as the sun lowers.'' She smiled at him. "You shouldn't have to go looking for a woman, though.''

"I'm not. Thank you again, and good day to you, Delia.''

Still smiling, she turned and swayed away, contriving to make even her retreat an invitation.

"Who is that woman?'' hissed a voice behind him. He whirled to see a small, feminine figure standing near him. Her head was scarved and her face veiled.

"Brita?''

"Of course it is I. Who else would it be? I came down here this morning while you snored away. I've been combing the town since sunrise, looking for my sister. I saw you come into the Square a while ago, but then I saw that a fight was about to start and I was frightened and fled. Just now I heard that the brawl was over and I came back. Who was that hussy?''

"Is it any business of yours?'' he demanded, annoyed with her proprietary attitude.

"Well,'' she stammered, the blush concealed behind her veil but plain in her voice, "I . . . I . . . would think that you would not consort with such persons when we have a serious mission to perform.''

"We have, have we?'' he said. "I do not recall taking service with you. I said I would help you out while I wait to contact my employer.''

She was silent for a moment, then said primly, "I am sorry. I presumed too much. I will not trouble you further." She turned and began to walk away.

"Wait," Conan said. She paused. "As a matter of fact, that woman was telling me of how matters stand in this town. And I did ask about Asdras and your sister."

"What did she say?" Brita asked, hope bright in her voice.

"Not much," Conan confessed. "She knew of Asdras, but she knew nothing of your sister."

"Oh. Well, I have heard from several people that she has been seen. There is a scent that she loves, and I asked among the perfumers until I found a shop where she purchased some of it a few days ago. And other vendors are sure that they saw her. There are not that many gently bred girls her age with a Tarantian accent in this town."

"She would stand out," Conan agreed. He was angered at himself for justifying his actions to the woman, as if she had some claim upon him. But there was something in her vulnerability, and in her hopeful courage in this cesspit of a city, that appealed to him. Then he glanced over her shoulder and saw three men walking toward him across the Square with measured, deliberate stride.

"Go back to the inn," he told Brita. "I will speak with you this evening."

"What is it?" She turned to follow his gaze.

"I am about to be questioned by the royal authorities," he said. "Best that you do not attract their notice."

"I see. I will speak with you later, then." She left a few seconds before the three were within speaking distance. One was a huge, brute-faced man with black hair sprouting through the laces of his shirt. The other two were smaller, wearing the dress and ornaments of Zingara. The big man had a stout wooden club thonged to his belt, its knotty head studded with iron. The other two wore sleeveless vests of fine mail and boasted curved swords. They had the aspect of men handy with their weapons.

"Come with us," said the big man. "The King's Reeve wishes to speak with you."

"Is there some reason why I should go with you?" Conan asked. "I have done nothing illegal in this town."

"If you do not come with us," said the largest of the three, "you are resisting the Reeve's summons, and that is an offense."

"Am I under arrest?" Conan asked, his hand near his hilt.

"He just wants to talk to you," said the man in a bored tone. "Do not make this difficult."

"Then lead on," Conan said. The hulking man turned and Conan followed him. The two Zingarans fell in behind the Cimmerian. They crossed the Square, where a cleaning crew loaded the bodies into wheelbarrows and men wielded mops to clean up the blood. Scavengers had already appropriated the fallen weapons.

Conan followed the big man up the steps of the Reeve's headquarters, at the top of which two guardsmen leaned upon their pikes as if they truly needed the support. One man had a crooked leg. The second was one-eyed, and he squinted with the remaining eye as if the orb were none too sound. Except for his escort, Conan noted, every king's man he had encountered in this town was fat, elderly, or physically infirm in some fashion. It seemed an odd standard of recruitment, but he had no doubt that it tied in with everything else that was wrong with this district. He remembered the decrepit state of the royal high road he had traveled in coming hither. This sorry excuse for a royal burgh was yet further proof that the King of Aquilonia was losing his grip.

He was ushered into an office of palatial proportions, and a man looked up at him from behind a desk of equally imposing size. The man himself was fat, with sagging flesh drooping in unhealthy folds, spilling over the tight collar of his embroidered tunic and hanging over his belt like a suspended waterfall. His flesh was grayish, and his small brown eyes peered from the folds as from behind ramparts.

"Here is the foreigner, Your Excellency," the big man reported.

"Very well, Julus. You, barbarian, come here." He gestured

with a gloved finger. Over the gloves Bombas wore rings upon every finger. Even his thumbs sported large seal rings.

Conan stepped forward. "Yes?"

"I saw you watching that fight a little while ago," the Reeve said.

"And I saw you watching it, too," said the Cimmerian.

The Reeve's face gained a little color. "What is it to me if the riffraff of this town murder each other? Good riddance is what I say to that. But I make it my business to know what new villains afflict my town. I knew you for a Cimmerian the moment I saw you. I was a junior officer in Gunderland years ago, and I know your breed. You are all troublemakers, and there are still some of us who haven't forgotten Venarium."

"I've made no trouble in your town," Conan maintained, "although I've seen very little but trouble since I rode through your gate."

"What is your business here?" the Reeve demanded.

Conan decided that he had better say nothing about Piris. "A way back on the road, I drove off some bandits about to victimize a woman. A respectable, Aquilonian lady. She was on her way hither to find her sister, who had run away with a gambler, and I agreed to help her."

There was no belief in the Reeve's expression. "Knight-errantry is for aristocrats, not for a common sellsword like you."

Conan shrugged, knowing better than to plead nobility of purpose. "She is paying me."

"Well, I will have my eye on you from now on. This is my city, and I like to regulate the comings and goings of the scoundrels who infest it. Get your business done and move on. I have no need for the likes of you in this city."

Conan wanted to laugh in the face of this pig-eyed lout who would pretend to control this town when he was too fearful to leave his own palace.

"And further," said Bombas, "there is one man whose company you should particularly avoid. His name is Maxio. He murdered my brother, and the moment I see him, he draws his last breath.'' Now the Reeve's tone grew conciliatory. ''Still, so long as you keep to lawful employment, and stay not too long, you will have no trouble from me. You have been warned. However,'' and now his voice became almost friendly, ''should you learn of where Maxio is hiding, that is information for which I will pay handsomely. Keep it in mind. And now, good day to you.''

Conan turned and went to the door, then turned back. ''Your Excellency?''

The Reeve looked up from his papers. ''Yes?''

''As King's Reeve, you are empowered to have a hundred men-at-arms, all mounted, are you not?''

''That is so.''

''Yet I have seen only about a score, and none of them on horseback. Why is that?''

The Reeve looked at him coldly. ''When I need to consult with a penniless barbarian on matters of military policy, rest assured that I shall send for you instantly. Now, begone.''

Smiling, Conan turned and left.

FIVE

The Fat Man

From the Reeve's palace, Conan continued his exploration of the city. South of the Square, the buildings were older and a great deal shabbier. By the time he reached the Pit, they were truly dilapidated. Here the streets were nearly deserted, and the few inhabitants bore the ragged look of poverty and drunkenness. This was a district of predators and scavengers, who slept by day and preyed by night.

Apparently the cleanup crews never strayed far south of the Square, for here the streets and alleys were slick with filth and the rats were as abundant in the day as at night. He found the Wyvern, its door bolted at this early hour.

He walked to the confluence of the rivers and arrived in time to see some bodies floating by, most likely those of the men who had been slain in the riot. All had been thoroughly stripped, and the river fish already nibbled at the ghastly mess of exposed organs floating next to one of the corpses.

Satisfied that he understood the basic layout of the town, Conan turned his steps back northward. This time he took a different route, and he noted that the more prosperous, newer section of the town had a system of sewers beneath the streets. He knew from experience that these could be handy for escape in time of need, and he made a mental note of every access hatch he passed.

Once, as he stood next to a clothes-seller's stall, a procession passed by. A score of men and women, most of them quite young, followed a man bearing the image of a large-breasted female deity that bore a Vendhyan look. The followers clashed tuneless instruments and chanted endlessly. Conan inquired of the vendor who these people might be, and the man made a sour face.

"Followers of Mother Doorgah. Their leader is a priest who came here a couple of years ago and moved into the old Temple of Mitra on the Square. They're a nuisance, but harmless enough."

"Is that allowed?" Conan asked. "I thought that only state deities were permitted to have temples in a royal burgh."

The man looked at him pityingly. "It seems that this goddess has money. That is all that is required in Sicas."

Moving on, Conan checked with the gate guard and found that Piris had not yet made an appearance. Where was the man? Already, Conan was impatient with the waiting. Sicas was a town where a man of courage, strength, and enterprise could grow very rich, and the Cimmerian had thought of several ways that he might hasten his own growth in that direction. The eight hundred dishas he had yet to earn from Piris, which had seemed a goodly fortune just a few days before, now seemed a paltry sum. He decided to give Piris one more day to contact him; failing that, he would commence operations on his own.

There were still two hours of daylight remaining, so the Cimmerian went to the inn and saddled his horse. Both he and the animal needed the exercise. He wanted the beast to be in top shape should his leave-taking of Sicas be precipitate and not lacking in company.

Outside the city, he put the horse through its paces, finishing with a hard gallop and then a leisurely, cooling walk on the return to the city gate. Back at the inn, he oversaw the animal's currying and gave the stableboy specific instructions as to the mount's care and feeding, tipping the lad handsomely to be sure that his orders were carried out conscientiously.

As he walked from the stable, his stomach reminded him that he had not eaten since breakfast. His relatively active day had left him ravenous. He was striding toward the public room when a man stood in his way.

"Your pardon, sir," said the man, who, Conan realized, was not much more than a boy, and one with a weakly pretty face. By way of compensation he wore a brigandine of brown velvet studded with brass, and his open cloak revealed that he wore not one, but two swords.

"Yes?" Conan grumbled. Hunger always put him in an ill temper.

"My master would speak with you."

"Boy," Conan said, "I do not know your master, and I do not know you, and you stand between me and my dinner. Stand aside, and if your master wishes to speak with me, he may come here and ask for me within."

"I am sorry, sir, but I must insist. My master desires most urgently to speak with you, and in fact, he invites you to share dinner with him."

"That is better, but still not good enough. Stand aside." He pushed past the youth and walked toward the common room.

"Sir!"

This time Conan whirled. "Curse you, boy. What do—" He stopped when he saw the small crossbow that the youth leveled at him. He must have had it hooked beneath his cloak, already drawn and with a bolt fitted to the string.

"Now, sir, will you come with me?"

"Are you as good as you think you are? That thing lacks the power to punch through this armor, and I have slain many men while badly wounded." His hand went to his hilt.

The youth smiled. "Perhaps so. But do you truly *want* to get a bolt through your leg, or your arm, or perhaps even through an eye? That is a great annoyance to endure just to turn down an offer of dinner.''

"Your master had better be a very, very generous man," Conan said. "Let's go."

The youth walked just behind Conan and directed his route. From the inn they walked but a short distance, then went around to the rear of a fine stone house. The boy indicated that he should climb an exterior stair to the house's half-timbered second story and Conan complied, halting at a landing facing a heavy door.

"This is the place," the boy said. "Now, knock."

Conan knocked. Then he whirled and snatched the crossbow from the youth's hands and tossed it to the ground below. Cursing, the lad reached for his swords, but his hands closed on Conan's, which already gripped the hilts.

Conan grinned at him. "Men who are not confident in their swordsmanship sometimes think that two swords make them twice as dangerous." Abruptly the Cimmerian yanked the two blades free of their scabbards. Before the youth could even think to move, Conan was behind him, and the blades crossed just beneath his chin. "But it is not true," Conan concluded.

At that moment the door began to open and Conan barged through, pushing the boy before him. A man sprang back as they entered. Conan braced a knee against the boy's back and shoved him forward just as the blades snapped away from the lad's neck.

"Your boy is too young to be allowed to play with dangerous toys," Conan said, casting the twin swords at the man's feet. The youth sprawled in a corner, holding a hand to his head, which had made violent contact with the wall.

The man Conan addressed was immense, not only tall, but enormously fat. If Bombas was a wreck of sagging, pallid flesh, this man was a majestic monument of billowing fat, appearing to be constructed of spheres stacked one atop another. His immensity, poised on incongruously tiny feet, seemed to float weightlessly as he moved. He was dressed in richly ornate garments and wore many jewels; his fat face was as pink and cherubic as a babe's. But his eyes were as hard and sharp as sword points. He walked over to the youth and looked down sadly.

"Gilmay, Gilmay," he sighed. "What am I to do with you? I give you simple instructions. I say: 'Gilmay, go and ask, respectfully, mind you, that this Cimmerian gentleman come to meet with me, that we may break bread and hold converse together.' But do you follow my instructions? No, indeed you do not. Instead, you must measure yourself against a tried warrior. Simple courtesy is not sufficient, for you must play with swords. Well, this gentleman has very properly chastised you, and you should be grateful that he did you no harm in the process. Now, Gilmay, I adjure you to apologize to this gentleman."

The boy looked up, furious, but he saw something in the fat man's face that cowed him thoroughly. He turned to Conan and bowed. "I beg your forgiveness, sir."

Conan stood thunderstruck throughout the strange performance. "You did all the suffering," he said.

"And that being the case," said the fat man, "let us all be friends and sit down and have dinner like civilized men."

"I am not a civilized man," Conan said.

"And yet," the other said, "you displayed the true, the inner . . . that is to say, the spiritual . . . quality of civilization and gentility. I cannot tell you, sir, how much I admire one who has not only the strength and spirit to conquer, but tempers these manly virtues with the qualities of compassion and the fine judgment, the delicate discrimination, to know when the proper amount of force has been applied and that no more need be exercised. I admire that, sir, indeed I do."

Conan endured the torrent of words with equanimity. "Get to the point."

"The point? But, sir, is dinner not the very point of existence? Would any day be complete without it? And if not complete, how can any day be of profit? So let us to dinner, sir, and then we shall speak of other matters."

"A bite of dinner would not come amiss," Conan allowed.

"Gilmay, inform our host that we are to be served immediately."

The fat man turned to Conan. "And now, sir, that the air has been cleared between us, now that all hostility has been dispersed and an air of tranquility prevails over all, I pray you be seated and allow me to pour you a cup of this excellent wine of Poitain, laid down many years before either of us afflicted the ears of our fond parents with babyish squalls. This is a fine, full-spirited Altuga Red, its grapes grown on the southward-facing slopes of a vineyard of that province, brought to fullest maturity, picked by stout yeomen and trampled by the shapely bare feet of the most beauteous peasant lasses of that fortunate land. Those feet, where they are not crumbled to dust, are now gnarled and cankered with age, but their former beauty remains enshrined in this most excellent vintage." He poured two cups full and handed one to Conan. The Cimmerian watched the other man drain his glass before doing likewise. It was splendid wine, he thought, even without all the buildup. He held out his glass and the fat man refilled both.

"And now, sir," the man said, "I know that you are a Cimmerian and that your name is Conan."

"You're better informed than I in that matter," Conan said.

"Then let us correct that at the outset. Your humble servant whom you see standing before you, and eager to offer hospitality, is Casperus, a scholar and minor, I say *very* minor, wizard of Numalia, in Nemedia. Do you know the city?"

"I've been there," Conan nodded.

"A wonderful city. A place of scholars and artists, where even such an inept fellow as I could study and gain a humble reputation as a mage. The arts of magic, of course, are terrible and mysterious and require, alas, that one who would be a true master begin his studies in earliest youth, enduring all the sufferings and privations of the ascetic. Alas, I did not have the opportunity to do this, but instead came to study the mysteries only after reaching full maturity and, as you have no doubt observed," he gestured self-deprecatingly at his rotund form, "I lack the qualities of true self-denial. No, I was trained and spent much of my life as a dealer in art objects, rarities of which most persons cannot even guess the value."

The Cimmerian nodded, evincing polite interest, giving half an ear to the man's incredibly voluble words but far more attention to matters of gesture and expression. Once, as a naive barbarian youth adrift in the bewildering world of the great cities and city-states and empires, Conan had been gulled by appearances, taken in by words. That was no longer true. He had long ago learned to look beyond outward demeanor and make a far shrewder judgment of his fellow men, although by his own admission, he was a good deal less canny where women were concerned.

The man wanted to give the appearance of a fat, eccentric, rather foolish dabbler in magical arts. That he was indeed fat was unassailable fact. The rest was not. Behind the aspect of softness and the flood of words, Conan perceived a ruthless, brilliant mind at work, and a will as strong as any he had encountered in his life. He said nothing of this, and that, too, was a lesson he had learned early and at great cost.

"Despite my late and, if the truth be told, quite superficial studies," Casperus continued, "I acquired enough mastery of the arts thaumaturgic to be able to find a man of many rare qualities, just such qualities as I require, residing within a close radius of my own location. Allow me to show you, sir."

He walked to a low table, gesturing for Conan to follow. The Cimmerian did so. He disliked sorcery, but he scented something far more than sorcery here, something far sweeter and far more to his taste. Conan scented money, in large amounts.

On the table rested a wooden object resembling an open book. The hinged cover lay back, revealing strange characters carved into its inner surface. Set into the other half was a round mirror made of what appeared to be black glass.

"Know you what this is, sir?" asked Casperus with amazing brevity.

"A scrying glass," Conan said. It was a common device, used by sorcerers to discern distant or hidden matters.

"Exactly, sir, exactly. An elementary thing, but truly indispensable. I had but to concentrate my thoughts upon my requirements, speak a simple spell or two, and behold! There did my scrying glass reveal, in this very city, sir, just such a man as met my requirements. To wit: a warrior of Cimmeria, a bold and hardy son of that most notably bold and hardy race."

Before Conan could seek more explanation, the servers appeared, coming from belowstairs. They wore livery and performed their task with the swiftness and efficiency of well-trained domestics, setting up a trestle table, covering it with a snowy cloth and loading it with serving platters. When the last platter had been laid and the candles lighted, the table looked ready to collapse with the weight of opulence. There was a profusion of delicacies, but the centerpiece was an entire roast pig, its eyes replaced by cherries and in its mouth an apple studded with cloves.

"Where are the others?" Conan inquired.

"What others, sir?" asked Casperus, seating himself.

"The other diners, of course." Conan seated himself likewise. "Surely all this is not for just the two of us?"

"And wherefore not, sir?" the mage demanded.

Conan accounted himself a trencherman of no mean capacity, but he was certain that he could not have made his way through this spread in a week.

"As I have said, sir, I am at best a third-rate wizard, and before that, a most humble and obscure purveyor of works of art. I am upon no account an accomplished warrior, and to my chagrin, I must confess that in the arts amatory, my deeds must be accounted laughable. However, in the feats of the table, I yield second place to no man, sir, to no man! You and I, sir, each in his own way, possess qualities that border upon the heroic, so why should we feel ourselves bound by the cautions and the appearances of lesser men? Would you practice at arms with an untried youth who is no match for your strength and skill? Well, sir, neither will I face such a meal as would satisfy the paltry appetite of a common burgher or laborer. And you, I can see, are a man of abounding appetite for all the things that make life worth living, so let us set to, sir, let us set to!''

Forthwith, the fat man seized a bone-handled carving knife and removed from the roast pig a slab of flesh sufficient to feed a small family. Conan could bear the delectable smells no longer and began to heap his own plate. In silence the two men attacked the banquet, occasionally refilling their cups from the numerous flagons that dotted the table.

The Cimmerian made a substantial dent in the spread, but when at last he leaned back replete, the fat man still tore into the viands as if he had not seen food in weeks. He emptied plates, stripped bones and sopped up gravies, ingested mounds of pastries and devoured slabs of bread spread thick with herbed butter. Since his own hunger was now sated, Conan found the sight repulsive. He studied the chamber surrounding him to avoid the sight of the gorging Casperus.

It was an extremely long room, with windows in every wall. Apparently the merchant-mage had let the entire upper floor of the house. The furnishings were few, but rich: a huge bed, some chairs, the trestle table. Bundles of what looked like traveling gear were neatly stacked in a corner. Most oddly, considering what the man claimed to be, the only piece of wizardly paraphernalia in sight was the scrying glass. Usually the quarters of wizards were replete with astrolabes, ancient books, vials of strange liquids and powders, and bubbling retorts. This one was traveling, he reflected, and was by his own admission not much of a wizard.

At last Casperus sat back and released a mighty belch. The table was devoid of all but scraps of food. Daintily he wiped his lips with a silken napkin and dipped his fingers into a bowl of scented water in which floated rose petals.

''Monstrous fine, sir, monstrous fine,'' the fat man proclaimed. ''It is a repast such as this that gives true meaning to life. That, and the search for the ancient, the hidden and the truly valuable. It is of such a matter that we must speak, sir. If you will join me now, we shall discuss our business.''

Casperus rose from the table, moving as lightly as a Poitainian dancer despite the vast meal now lodged in his belly. He took his former chair and sat. He clapped his hands loudly and the servants entered to clear away the ruins of the feast.

Conan took the chair opposite, and the two men sipped at their wine in silence as the servants went about their work.

"Now," Conan said when the servants were gone, "what is this all about?"

"It is a long story, sir, but bear with me. It is worth hearing, for there is much profit in it." He leaned forward and spoke in a voice that was a virtual whisper. "Now, sir, what do you know of Selkhet?"

Conan shook his head. "I never heard the word."

"Few have, outside of Stygia. It is not a word, sir, but a name. The name of a goddess of the Stygian pantheon."

Conan shifted uncomfortably. He disliked Stygia. He loathed its priest-kings, its wizards, and its infernal collection of gods.

"For many centuries," Casperus went on, "Selkhet has been a minor deity, a mere protector of the grave, her image carved upon the grave-markers of the poor, or set as a statue atop the tombs of the wealthier. Like all Stygian deities, she has a tutelary animal. Selkhet's is the scorpion. Know you much of magic or godcraft, sir?"

"As little as I can safely manage," Conan assured him. "Crom is my god. One god is enough for any man."

"Ah, yes, Crom of the northlands, the rival of Ymir. An interesting deity, but one with whom little of magic is associated. Well, sir, doubtless you have learned in your travels that most peoples are not of your religious frame of mind. Most prefer a plethora, a veritable multitude of deities, and none of all the earth are as god-besotted as the people of Stygia." He sat back and smiled. "Now, sir, I have told you that I am a magician in my humble way, but that does not mean that I am superstitious. Matters of sorcery and divinity work according to certain immutable laws. These are laws studied and understood only by the highest of mages and priesthoods. Gods are not at all what most people fondly think them to be. To the typical worshiper, a god is just a sort of extremely puissant human being who must be placated, but gods are nothing of the sort, I assure you.

"Take this matter of the tutelary animals. Gods have their origins not upon this earth, but in the vast and awful gulfs of space, so why should they be represented by, or even take the form of, earthly animals? I will tell you why: because men want to give these unfathomable creatures a form that is familiar to them. Selkhet, for instance. Grave-robbers perform their unclean labors at night. In prying into tombs, one will encounter two sorts of noxious creatures: serpents and scorpions. Serpents are torpid at night and rarely bite then. Scorpions are at their most lively in the hours of darkness. Any tomb-robber will be stung by scorpions, and some of the scorpions of Stygia can slay with a single sting. Therefore, to the vulgar mind, the scorpion is sacred to Selkhet, the guardian of tombs. Do you follow me, sir?"

"Thus far," Conan said.

"Excellent, sir, excellent. Selkhet is an unthinkably powerful creature from who knows what distant star, but in Stygia she is portrayed in one of three ways: as a beautiful woman wearing a headdress crowned with the image of a scorpion, as a scorpion with the head of a woman, or simply as a scorpion. Now, what know you of Python?" He laced his fingers upon his capacious belly, and the candlelight winked luridly from the rings decorating the pudgy digits.

"A city of ancient legend, the capital of long-perished Acheron."

"Very good. Now, the people of Acheron were close relatives of the Stygians of today. Both were descended from the people of yet more ancient Lemuria. Acheron was their northern kingdom, Stygia the southern. Ah, sir, if you could only have seen purple-towered Python! I have, in mystic visions, and I can assure you that the most gorgeous cities of today are but poor and shabby places compared to Python. Its extent was ten times that of Luxur, the greatest city of Stygia; its obelisks were high enough to pierce the moon! Its wealth was beyond imagining, and its mages and priests the most powerful the world has ever seen.'' His voice took on a tone of sadness, but it was the tone of a professional storyteller.

"As the millennia turned in their immemorial rotation, Acheron grew decadent, and most of its magical lore was forgotten. The barbarian Hybori overwhelmed the degenerate heirs of a once-great empire and scattered them like chaff before the storm. Many of the Acheronians fled south, to take refuge with their cousins, the Stygians. Stygia, unlike Acheron, was at the height of its power and stopped the Hybori at the Styx, which they were never to cross in all the centuries since that time. Now we come to the meat of the matter.''

"And about time,'' Conan grumbled. The merchant went on as if he had not heard the rude comment.

"Much of the early part of this tale is related in the *Book of Skelos*, but you must understand that much of that most powerful of tomes was writ down in a raving delirium, leaving considerable doubt as to sequence and meaning, although every bit of it is reliable, and is understandable to a great mage, which I have already told you I am not.''

Conan suppressed a groan. This was just the *early* part of the tale?

"Among the Pythonian refugees were the priests of Selkhet. This once rich and powerful priesthood was sadly reduced, its temples and treasuries seized by the savage Hybori, able to bear away only such books as they could carry in their arms. These were sad times for them, but they found a protector in the god-king of that day, Khopshef the One Hundred Seventy-third. He gave them the town now known as Khet, the City of Scorpions, with broad lands extending from the river far into the desert. Of course their goddess had to accept a subordinate role. The cult of Set, the Old Serpent, was already predominant in Stygia and would brook no rival.

"In gratitude for this munificence, the priests of Selkhet crafted an image of their goddess as a gift to the god-king. It was to be no ordinary image. First, they set out to find the greatest sculptor of the age. This was a man named Ekba, who was a servant of the king of Budhra, a kingdom of that time of which nothing now is known save its name. He was quite mad and therefore suitable for the project. The priests ordered him to create an image of the goddess as a scorpion with a woman's head, and they subjected him to many spells and rituals to provide him with the correct inspiration. He was to have whatever materials he desired, however rare or valuable.

"These materials proved to be most remarkable; two years were required just to assemble them all. Many heroes of the day, men whom I fancy must have been much like yourself, sir, occupied themselves with the quest for these items, and many of them died in the attempt. Ekba demanded the bones of a living princess, the organs of a certain dragon, a pearl of a sort found only in Khitai, and so on. All of these substances were reduced to powders and mixed with the metal of the idol. For ten more years Ekba labored over the image, spending much time in prayer and ritual, seeking the true vision. He made many attempts to cast the figure, but was unsuccessful. The priests had to guard him at all times, for he frequently attempted suicide.

"At last, Ekba in his despair demanded that he be given a terrible decoction of the black lotus. It is a potion employed only by the greatest mages when attempting the most powerful of spells. With reluctance, the priests agreed and prepared the potion. Ekba drank it and fell into a swoon that lasted ten days and nights, dead to any but the practiced eye of a mage.

"When he awoke, he was a man possessed. He ordered that all of his materials be taken from his studio to the very sanctuary of the goddess. There he shut and barred the doors and began his final labor. For twenty days he worked without food or drink, and many were the uncanny sounds that emerged from the temple, heard only by the ears of the priests who surrounded the building. On the final midnight, as the moon reached its zenith over the temple, a terrible scream was heard from inside.

"The priests battered open the doors and rushed within. There they found, on a pedestal, the superb image of their goddess.

Below the pedestal lay the body of Ekba, an expression of unspeakable horror upon its countenance. It had been injected so full of venom that within minutes of the discovery, it exploded from the internal pressure of its bloating.'' The fat man seemed to take a certain satisfaction in this grisly revelation.

"Needless to say, the god-king found the image a wholly fitting gift, and he built a shrine in his palace to house it. Now, the image was not valuable for its material, for it was made of base metal, mostly bronze. Many valuable substances had been incorporated into it, but they had been reduced to powders of no intrinsic worth. No, good sir, what made this image so precious was the tremendous magical power that infused it. For centuries, the god-kings of Stygia employed the scorpion image in their most esoteric rites, and for a time, the priests of Selkhet enjoyed special favor and patronage.

"However, even in that haunted kingdom, time goes on and nothing is immutable. The power of Set grew and that of other gods waned. Less and less often was the image of Selkhet utilized, and her priests fell from power. The Years of Dissolution came: three centuries when Stygia broke up into warring provinces, the leader of each claiming the mantle of god-king, and great battles were fought both on the ground and on the magical plane.

"The few priests who tended the palace shrine did not want the image to be captured by one of the warring factions, so they moved it to the royal crypt to replace the guardian figure of the goddess that previously resided there. Then, to disguise it, they covered it with a thick, black lacquer so that it would resemble a common figure of black stone. There they left it.

"In the course of the disruptions, the palace changed hands many times, and it is to be assumed that the priests were killed early in this period, because the true nature of the image was forgotten. In time, the palace was abandoned and the desert sands covered it.''

The fat man sat back and peered into his cup, which had grown empty. He remedied this situation, then performed the same service for Conan, who was fascinated with the tale despite his abhorrence of sorcery.

"At some time," Casperus went on, "robbers must have tunneled into the palace to rob its crypts. There are whole villages in Stygia with no livelihood other than the robbing of tombs. They have a great mastery of the counterspells necessary to protect them from the defensive curses laid upon all such sites. It is certain that about five hundred years ago, the black scorpion was in the possession of the wizard Ashtake of Keshan. He had no concept of its full power, but he knew that it was a talisman of importance. It passed to one of his apprentices upon his death and then it disappeared for more than a century. It resurfaced in the *Annals of the Family Ashbaal*. For many years it appears among the inventories of that family of merchant-princes of Shem. They had no knowledge of its history or of its magical nature, but even with its unsightly coating of lacquer, it is an exquisite work of art. It resided in their treasury for generations, for as valuable as it plainly was, there was that about it which made the most devoted collecters of art wary.

"The *Annals* report that the scorpion was stolen, along with much other treasure, when the Argosseans invaded Shem three hundred years ago. It is next mentioned in the memoirs of Elsin Ataro, a high councilor of King Gitaro the Third of Zingara. This man Ataro was, like me, a dabbler in both art and magic. He knew that the scorpion was more than a fine work of art, wonderful as it was in that capacity. By consulting many rare and ancient tomes, he divined something of its true nature. He conjectured that it was the Selkhet image of the ancient god-kings, although of its origins and creation he knew little. When Ataro died, the scorpion was not among the inventory of his effects.

"Eighty years ago the scorpion reappeared in the possession of the famous wizard Shamtha of Shadizar. How the scorpion fared to Zamora is unknown. The mage became obsessed with the thing and spent many years seeking to unlock its secrets. He attempted numerous magical experiments with it, and he left behind a most unique manuscript detailing his efforts, which came into my possession some years ago. One evening, upon the rising of the gibbous moon, Shamtha attempted a last experiment, the nature of which is unknown since he did not survive to record the process. What is known is that his tower, which stood upon a rise of ground near his house and in which he conducted his wizardly labors, exploded like a mighty volcano, raining stones all over Shadizar. No trace of either wizard or scorpion was found amid the rubble.

"Fortunately, Shamtha kept his record book in his house, which was only slightly damaged. His heirs decided to have the unique document copied and to sell these copies to any student or practitioner of magic who could pay the rather steep price. It has been widely read in the years since, but only as a curiosity, for it was believed that the image of Selkhet was destroyed in the mighty upheaval that shattered the tower of Shamtha."

"But it was not?" Conan asked.

"Decidedly not. Almost forty years ago the image came into the hands of Melcharus of Numalia, a dealer in antiquities and works of art." Hands on knees, Casperus leaned forward and spoke with great emphasis. "That man was my father, and as a boy, I actually saw the fabulous image in the strongroom of his shop! Even as a lad, I was fascinated by something about the image. It drew my thoughts and desires as if by some inner power of its own." The fat man's eyes glazed and spittle gathered upon his infantile lips. He was a man speaking of his deepest, most secret lust. "I would seize every chance to visit the strongroom. As often as I could, I volunteered to dust and polish every object therein. My father thought I was merely being dutiful, but I just wanted an excuse to touch it, to stroke its glossy flanks and gaze upon, even stroke lovingly, the beautiful face of the goddess." His eyes cleared and he shook himself slightly, like a man emerging from a waking dream.

"One evening," he went on, "thieves broke into the strongroom. There were many treasures in that room, but the only thing taken was the scorpion. My father was relieved and thought that they must have been alarmed and fled without taking anything truly valuable, but I knew that they had found exactly what they had come for. I grieved for its loss, but I resolved to learn everything I could about the scorpion.

"To that end, I studied the arts of magic, although, as I have told you, with no ambition to become a great magician. No, I wished to recover the image of Selkhet. I tracked down every possible reference to this single end, and I became the world's greatest scholar of this one, obscure facet of magical lore. I set many spies and passed many bribes to divine the image's whereabouts. It has been through many hands since the thieves took it from my father's strongroom. It is restless because it has one sterling quality: It causes the death of any incompetent wizard who seeks to use it."

"Then why," Conan demanded, "since it has been the death of great wizards, and you say you are none such yourself, do you wish to own the thing?"

Casperus, hands still on his knees, sat back and laughed until his fat rolled about in the chair as if independent of the man himself.

"Because, sir, when I describe the feelings I had for the object, I describe the feelings of a boy! I was then under its spell, and I thought its beauty and mystery the most desirable things in the world. But I learned better, sir! When I grew to manhood, I discovered that I would never be a great wizard, but I also learned that there is something even better than power, whether it be earthly or sorcerous. Even better than these is great wealth! As a dealer in art objects, I have trafficked with many of the wealthiest people in the world, and I know that they are above worldly laws. They are courted by kings and are the patrons of magicians, who are but their servants. And—" he leaned forward again and resumed his emphatic whisper "—I have determined that the ancient scorpion image of Selkhet is the single most valuable object upon this earth!"

Conan started to speak, but the mage overrode him.

"Think of it, sir. The black scorpion is three things." He held up a fat hand with one finger extended. "It is an unthinkably ancient artifact of a long-dead kingdom, and perfect in every way." A second, beringed finger joined the first. "It is a work of art as great as any the world has ever known." The third finger went up. "It is, perhaps, the most powerful magical talisman in existence. I qualify this last only because it is believed by some that the legendary jewel called the Heart of Ahriman is as puissant, but I do not believe it to be so. In any case, the whereabouts of the Heart have been unknown for three thousand years. Now, when this scorpion is in my hands, I propose to hold a unique auction, an auction for sorcerers and art collectors and those rarified few who combine both activities. I shall send out missives identifying the work in question, and I shall offer far more than the scorpion itself, sir. There is also the formidable library I have compiled over the years concerning the image. Without this, even a great mage could waste a lifetime seeking to divine the object's secrets. Among these documents is included the *original* manuscript of experiments compiled by Shamtha, not the imperfect copies hawked by his heirs.

"I will send invitations to all of the greatest sorcerers of this decadent age, to the Order of the White Peacock in Khitai, to Thoth-Amon, and to all the others. I expect to realize the best offer from the current priest-king of Stygia. He is not the equal of his predecessors, the god-kings, but he is still the richest man in the world, and has a notable stake in things sorcerous."

"Then why not sell to the priest-king," Conan asked, "and forget about the others?"

"Because, sir, sorcerers may often have the power to summon and offer things of unique value. It is not unthinkable that a man like Thoth-Amon, who is no king but is yet a much greater sorcerer than the priest-king of Stygia, might be able to offer far more than that king, especially since earthly wealth is of little account to him, whereas sorcerous power is everything." Once again he slapped fat hands to fat knees. "In short, sir, I intend to transform the black scorpion into wealth incalculable, sir, wealth incalculable!"

"And what," Conan demanded impatiently, "has all this to do with me?"

"I was just about to come to that, sir."

"And none too soon," the Cimmerian grumbled.

"In recent years I have traced the scorpion through a long and tedious list of thieves and buyers. An art dealer such as your humble servant establishes many contacts helpful in such a quest. Upon several occasions I have been within days of laying my hands upon it, only to find that it was stolen or sold just before I got within reach of it. Last month, in Belverus, I tracked it to the home of a wealthy dilettante in the sorcerous arts. He would not let me see it and scorned my generous offer. Mind you, the man had no idea of its true worth, and any attempt on his part to employ it sorcerously would inevitably have brought about his own most painful and colorful demise, therefore rendering my acquisition of the image a veritable act of charity. Failing this, I employed an, ah, an agent, as it were, to obtain it for me."

"And was your thief successful?" Conan asked.

"Sir!" Casperus protested. "You use an ugly word."

The outlander shrugged. "I have been a thief in my time. I do not find the word distasteful."

"Well, in answer to your question, my agent was all too successful, not only obtaining the scorpion, but fleeing with it. I have reason to believe that it is now, or soon will be, in this very city!"

"And you want me to find the thing for you?" Conan asked.

"Exactly, sir!"

"Then why didn't you say so in the first place?"

For a moment the fat man was nonplussed. "Why, sir, how could one broach such a subject without the fullest preparation? Even to discuss so wonderful a treasure without first conveying a sense of the full majesty of its origin and powers seems to me little less than sacrilege, sir, sacrilege!"

Conan knew better than to talk sense to a man obsessed. "Who is this thief, and how should I find him?"

Casperus waved a dismissive hand. "That is irrelevant. The

idol has changed hands at least twice in the interim. My agent had partners and these, it seems, fell out. However, in this town there is only one possible buyer for the image. He is a man who calls himself Andolla and claims to be a sorcerer. In truth, I suspect him to be a mere charlatan, albeit a rich one. I must keep myself concealed here, or whoever has the image now will flee before even approaching Andolla. I need a man who is clever, who is a mighty man of arms, and who has a sensible wariness of magical things. In short, sir, I would like to employ you.''

"Now we come to the truly important part of all this," Conan said. "How much?"

"I am prepared to offer fifty thousand golden marks of Aquilonia upon delivery of the image into my hands."

It was a princely sum, but Conan affected to be unimpressed. "That is paltry if the thing is worth what you say."

"Only to me, sir, only to me. Were you to seek to sell it to the likes of Thoth-Amon, he would have it from you by force or by sorcery, whereas I know the proper safeguards. The idol has been the death of many men over the millennia. No, sir, I will not be paying you for the image, for it is already mine, and mine alone. I will be paying you for the performance of a few days' work, and fifty thousand golden marks should be more than adequate recompense for such a task. A man of your accomplishments should find it a simple matter. You will not be dealing with great sorcerers, after all, but with mere thieves. I have no doubt that they will have swordsmen in their employ, and it is because of this that I require a champion such as yourself. My bodyguard, Gilmay, is competent to defend me from the common footpads who would prey upon a man of my obvious prosperity, but as you have already discovered, this about exhausts his realm of expertise.''

"Very well," Conan said. "I accept your commission. I will need five thousand now. In this town the authorities alone have set a high standard for bribe-taking."

Casperus nodded. "Done. And may I say, sir, that you fulfill my highest expectations as a man of decisive action." The fat man rose and crossed to the pile of effects on the floor. He uncovered a strongbox and opened it with a key that hung from his neck on a golden chain. From the box he extracted five clinking bags of soft leather. Relocking the box, he returned to his chair.

"Each of these bags contains ten golden imperials of Aquilonia, each coin worth a hundred marks."

Conan took the weighty bags and placed them in his belt pouch. "Now describe the thing to me. I know that it is a woman-headed scorpion, but how large is it? Will I need help to move it? Is it heavy enough to require an ox cart?"

Casperus chuckled. "By no means, sir. The value of the object is in its beauty and the sorcerous art of its making. It is only about thus long," he held his hands nearly a foot apart, "and perhaps half as high."

"So small?" Conan said, astonished.

"That is what makes it so easy to hide and transport. Had it been the size of a great sphinx of Stygia, it would never have been stolen. Its color, as I have said, is black, and the lacquer itself is beautiful in its own way. You would think it made of obsidian until you should lift it. It is quite weighty for its size. This is not the weight of the base metal alone, but also the burden of its sorcerous power and its many curses."

Conan felt an involuntary shiver. "Do not speak so much of sorcerous things."

"Then just consider it a valuable object, sir, and fetch it for me."

Conan rose. "I will return when I have the thing in my hands. Good evening to you."

Casperus rose and bowed. "And the best of fortune to you, sir, the very best of fortune!"

The Cimmerian left the upper chamber and descended the stair to the street below. He was cheerful as he wended his steps toward the inn, the bags making a comfortable weight at his waist. Surely, his fortune had turned since he departed Belverus.

Within his room at the inn, Conan noticed something subtly wrong. He held his candle high and surveyed his surroundings. The scanty furniture was as he remembered it. Then he saw that one of his saddlebags lay on the floor a bit to one side of a crack in the wall. He distinctly remembered placing it directly against the crack on the previous night, to block a draft. He was sure he had not touched it since. He crossed to the bag and examined it. Nothing had been taken. There had been nothing in it of any value. The Cimmerian knew better than to leave valuables in a hired room. He shrugged. Doubtless, he thought, some thieving inn servant had rifled his goods in search of loot. He turned at a scratching from the adjoining door. He kept his hand on his sword-hilt until he was certain that it was Brita.

"Ah, there you are!" she said. "I grew worried, with you away for so long. Where did you go?"

"First, tell me what you've been doing," Conan said.

She sat on the bed, her look despondent. "Since the perfumer's, I have had no luck. It is as if Ylla has vanished into the air."

"Well, do not lose heart. This is not a large city, but it has more than enough room for one girl to hide herself for some time. As for me, I had an invitation to dinner and I accepted it." He began to unbuckle his brigandine, turning slightly to slip it off his shoulders. "It was from a strange man, an unbelievably fat fellow named Casperus." He turned back to see that her face had gone deathly pale. "What is it, lass?"

She shook herself and the look vanished. "Oh, nothing. I but had a fleeting memory of a fat man I detested when I was a girl." The strange look had disappeared so quickly that Conan thought it might have been a trick of the flickering candlelight. She smiled at him brightly. "And please, take no note of my changing moods. I do not want you to think that I am some flighty girl who does not appreciate all you have done for her." She stood and came closer, smiling. "I am, in fact, a grown woman, and *very* grateful." Of a sudden, her face was no longer as innocent as its wont, and the Cimmerian was acutely aware of the ripe beauty he had admired upon first seeing her.

"And," she went on, "I *did* say that I would find some way to repay you." She came into the circle of his arms and he crushed her to him as eagerly as she drew his lips down to her own.

Six

The Richest Man in Sicas

Another day in the city, and still no sign of Piris. Conan decided that he had waited long enough. If the strange little man still wished to employ him, he would just have to await his turn to claim the Cimmerian's services.

He had left Brita sleeping blissfully and gone below to lay in his usual substantial breakfast. Afterward he checked with the gate guard, to learn that there was still no sign of Piris. Next he headed for the Square. He now had a sufficient working knowledge of the town, and he knew where to go for information. He idled the morning away among the stalls and beggars, until he saw the person he wanted, standing before a dressmaker's shop.

Delia turned and smiled broadly at his approach. "I knew that you would seek me out."

She was a comely woman, but Conan's night with Brita had left him desirous only of information. For a girl raised in a sheltered home, Brita was most ardent and most eager to experiment. He gestured toward an open-fronted wineshop.

"Have you had your midday meal yet?" he asked.

She threw back her head and laughed lustily. "I just got up! But I'll let you buy me breakfast. Come on." She walked ahead of him, rolling her hips as if her spine had more bones than a snake's. She chose a table next to the low wall that separated the wineshop from the plaza and shouted for a server. The day was cool but a bronze bowl of hot coals stood in the center of the table. The server brought heated wine and returned minutes later with laden platters.

Delia picked up a fowl and bit into it, leaning with her elbows on the table. After swallowing a large mouthful, she spoke.

"Well, what drew you back to me, Cimmerian? Was it my face or my body? Both are unsurpassed in this city."

"Tell me about a man named Andolla," Conan said.

She choked slightly, then looked at him in wide eyed astonishment. "What are you up to now?"

"Business." he said.

"That being the case, I am accustomed to being paid for my services." The Cimmerian placed a handful of silver coins on the table and Delia scooped them up expertly, dropping them into her ample cleavage. Still holding the fowl in one hand, she pointed with the other. "You see that temple?"

Conan looked to where she indicated. The building was an imposing one, set back from the Square by the width of a broad terrace and a ceremonial stairway. Its columns were red and black marble. Smoke from an altar fire seeped through an opening in the roof.

"That's the old Temple of Mitra. People here care so little for the state gods that the priests closed it down years ago. A short time back, this man Andolla came to town and took charge of it. He dedicated it to Mother Doorgah, a Vendhyan goddess with breasts almost as splendid as mine." She shook her shoulders to emphasize her endowments.

"I saw this goddess yesterday, carried in a procession," Conan said. "For the money, I expect more information."

"Don't be so impatient," she grinned. "Don't you want to see if I compare favorably to her?"

He grinned back. "Later, perhaps. Business now. What is this Andolla's brand of knavery?"

She pouted. "Oh, very well. This procession you saw was made up of young people, was it not?" The Cimmerian nodded. "Perhaps you also noticed that they were well dressed. That is because Andolla seeks followers who share three qualities: youth, wealth, and stupidity. He seems to find many such. Once they attend his rituals, they act like his slaves. They squander their inheritances upon him, and some rob their parents, occasionally with violence."

"And do these parents take no action?" Conan asked.

She wiped her mouth with a corner of the tablecloth. "People who raise such children are usually worthless themselves. Oh, a few have gone to the temple to confront Andolla, but his guards expel them, and one or two have died because he cursed them, or at least so he claims."

Conan rubbed his chin as he stared at the temple with calculation. "So this religious rogue has grown very rich, has he?"

"Extremely." She smiled slyly. "What are you planning? You can tell me." She feigned a look of innocent sincerity, causing Conan to laugh aloud.

"Delia, if I have something in my mind that I wish to keep to myself, you are the last person I would inform."

She laughed as raucously. "Be careful of him, Conan. He is most suspicious of people who seem both strong and clever and have no wealth to bring him."

"Know you of a good lever with which I can pry that place open?" he asked.

She picked up a small apple and bit it in two, chewing it slowly, seeds and all, before swallowing. "There is a rich man of this town named Rista Daan, a spice merchant. He has a daughter named Rietta. She has been taken under Andolla's spell and has fled to the temple with a great sum of money. The father wants her back and has tried to hire bravos to go there and take her, but the gang leaders have been paid off by Andolla and refuse to trouble him. That might be a good place to start, whatever you have in mind.''

"Well, well,'' drawled a voice the Cimmerian had heard before. "Look at who is consorting with Maxio's slut!'' Conan turned slightly to see the three thugs clad in red leather whom he had encountered on his first day in Sicas: the tall one, the short one, and the one with the stringy yellow beard. It was the tall one who had spoken. "Still in town, eh, Cimmerian?''

"It would be pointless to deny it,'' Conan answered.

"Barbarians should not pretend to wit,'' said the bearded one.

"Half-wit boys should not pretend to manhood, however long their swords,'' Conan returned. He felt Delia's restraining hand upon his corded forearm.

"Leave us in peace,'' Delia said. "We want no trouble with you.''

"We might have done so,'' said the short one. "But now this savage has insulted us. We do not tolerate such insolence.''

Conan turned to Delia. "These three have baited me since I arrived in town. I think that three times should be sufficient for anyone to endure them.'' His tone was easy and conversational. Her expression was a near-comic mixture of apprehension and excitement.

"Don't be foolish,'' she urged. "There are three of them.''

He shrugged. "That still won't make it an even fight.'' He glanced beyond the three. On the other side of the Square was the temple. A short distance away from it was the house of the rich man named Xanthus. He beckoned to a server, who came running, his expression fearful. The Cimmerian pointed to the platter of hot breads and meat on the table before him. "Fetch a cover for this. I do not want it to get cold while I attend to this matter.'' Then he rose. "I will be back shortly,'' he said to Delia, who goggled at him in disbelief.

The Cimmerian sprang lightly over the low wall and pointed to a spot near the center of the Square. "Let's go over there and fight,'' he suggested.

The thugs stared in amazement. They had lost a little of their

confident swagger. The tall one shrugged. "You may die anywhere you like, foreigner."

Conan walked easily, followed by the three, his hands well
away from his weapons. He did not expect a fair fight, having
seen them kill before, but he doubted that their vanity would let
them cut him down from behind. Even so, he kept far enough in
advance of them to be safe. The slightest rasp of blade unsheath-
ing would be all the warning he would need.

He stopped in a decorative circle formed of colored paving
stones. He was within easy view of the temple, the Reeve's headquarters, and the palace of Xanthus. Word of the impending fight
had spread with uncanny swiftness. People were already coming
out onto stairs, balconies, and rooftops to witness the show.

"This seems a good spot," the Cimmerian announced. "Plenty
of room to fight."

"However you choose to perish, barbarian," said the bearded
one.

Conan turned to face them. The three came forward slowly, the
short one and the bearded one edging away from the tall one,
who stood in the center. Each grasped his sheath in one hand,
the long grips positioned almost vertically. Conan knew that they
would draw straight up and cut straight down, the quickest way
to attack with such a weapon, and the most efficient for three men
standing so close. A horizontal or an oblique cut might foul a
companion's blade.

"How will you have it, then?" asked Conan. "One at a time,
or all at once?" He caught a glimpse of armor among the quickly
forming crowd. It was Ermak, the mercenary leader, come to
judge the new talent.

The three faltered, and the tall one frowned. "I thought you
said you fought only for business," he muttered.

"Now it is business," Conan answered. "Well, don't stand
there all day. My food is getting cold." Still they did nothing,
clearly uneasy at the barbarian's seeming lack of concern. "Will
you laugh as you did when you murdered that man the other day?
I hope so. It is always good to die laughing."

With a muttered curse, the bearded one grasped his hilt. Too swiftly for the eye to follow, Conan snatched out his dirk and snapped its edge against the man's wrist. The arm came up for the expected vertical draw, but the blade did not follow, nor did the hand, which remained where it was, gripping the hilt.

The tall one showed creditable speed, leaping back to give himself both time and distance as he drew, but Conan denied him the latter, springing past the now one-handed man and slamming the dirk upward beneath the tall one's chin, the point piercing the brain in an instant.

The short one had gone dead white, but his blade was clear of its scabbard. With his free hand, the Cimmerian gripped the man's wrist as he jerked his own blade free of the tall one. The short one's eyes widened with horror as he felt his arm held as immovable as if fixed in a vise. He had only an instant for reflection before the dagger crunched through his ribs, piercing the light mail armor he wore beneath his clothing.

Conan released the dirk and stepped back, his eyes wary. The tall one had dropped to the pave like a man beheaded. The short one tottered for a moment, still gripping his sword in one hand as with the other he plucked ineffectually at the hilt protruding from his side. Then the blade clattered to the stone and the man tottered and fell. The third gripped his severed wrist, glaring hate at the Cimmerian.

"Go find a leech with a searing iron and you might yet live," Conan said in disgust. "None of you was truly worth killing."

The bearded man showed more fight than Conan would have given him credit for. With his left hand, he drew his sword straight up and wheeled around to his left, thrusting to his rear, trying to skewer Conan with his point. It was a tricky move, difficult even for an unhurt master swordsman, which the man was not. Conan simply stepped forward and turned along with the man, as if the two were dancing. He reached over the man's shoulder with one hand and gripped his chin. With the other he gripped the back of his opponent's head and twisted violently. The neck bones sheared audibly and the man dropped by the other two.

Before proceeding, Conan looked around. It was foolish to assume that just because he had slain his immediate enemies, there would be none of their friends nearby. The crowd was dead silent, and no man made a hostile move. Conan nodded grimly, stooped and wrenched his dirk free of the bearded one's corpse. He wiped the weapon on the man's red-leather doublet and re-sheathed it, then strolled back toward the wineshop.

Delia tried to stammer a greeting when he resumed his seat, but she could not get the words out. He took the cover from his plate and began to eat, pleased to note that the food was still warm.

"I knew you were strong," Delia stammered at last, "when you hauled me up on the pedestal yesterday. I knew you were mad when you so easily accepted the challenge of those three killers. But I never thought *any* man could be so fast!"

Conan brooded into his cup of hot, spiced wine. "A man of war who treads the world's roads alone, as I do, must be quick. Rarely do I have a trusted comrade to watch my back, or to fight by my side. Long ago I learned to strike swiftly and without scruple. I trouble no man without cause, but one who attacks me had best resolve to die."

"And yet you would have spared the man you unhanded," she said.

"He was no longer dangerous, alone and one-handed as he was. Considering that he was no warrior, he showed some heart at the end. I do not make such an offer twice."

"Uh-oh," Delia said, "here comes Ermak. What does he want?"

"To talk to me," Conan said, tearing open a loaf of bread.

The man in half-armor stopped at the table, his left hand resting easily upon the pommel of his basket-hilted sword. He did not bow or make any formal greeting, but only regarded Conan steadily with chill, gray eyes, the eyes of a professional killer.

"That was a remarkable show, Cimmerian," he said.

Conan shrugged. "It would have been remarkable had they made me draw my sword."

The man smiled grimly. "Aye, it was not a fight. Rather, it was an extermination of vermin. Even so, only a real warrior could have done it so handily. My man Nevus told me of you. Are you seeking work? If so, there is a place for you in my band."

"I am employed just now," Conan answered. "But that may change."

"Then seek me out if it does. I am easy to find." He turned to Delia. "Where is Maxio hiding these days?"

She tilted her head back and lowered her lids as if she were looking down her nose at him. "My man's whereabouts are his own concern. If he wants me to tell you, he will inform me so."

"Good day to you both, then," said Ermak.

Delia shivered slightly as she stared at his retreating figure. "That one is no armored fool with a sword he does not know how to use."

"I can see that clearly enough," Conan said.

She smiled ruefully. "Aye, you hardly need me to tell you such a thing. A man like you knows another warrior when he sees him."

"There is one thing you can tell me," Conan said.

She gave him what was intended to be a coy look. "And what might that be?"

"Do you not worry about what your man Maxio will think when he finds out you have been seen so much in my company?"

"I am neither his wife nor his slave," she said haughtily. "He cannot tell me where to go nor whom to see. I am my own woman."

"I wonder that Bombas has not sent his henchmen to call upon me," Conan commented.

She snorted contempt. "What have you done to cause him any distress? He fears you, because he fears everyone. And he is unsure of why you are here. Be careful that he does not come to believe you a royal spy, sent to investigate him."

Conan emptied his cup and set it on the table. "I had not thought of that. To kill an investigator would merely bring another one in his place. Should he suspect that I spy for the king, he will just offer me a bribe.''

"And if he does that?''

"Why, I will accept, of course!''

Delia laughed raucously again and then rose. "I must be on my way now. If you want to find me, I am usually here in the Square at this time of day. But should you want to see me privily,'' she placed her hands on the table and leaned forward, letting her gown gape open, "I am to be found in the Street of the Woodcarvers. My apartment is just above the Sign of the Sunburst. If I am alone, there will be a white cloth hanging from the window just over the sign.'' She straightened, then added, "White is easy to see at night.'' With that, she turned and left him.

Conan was amused at the brazen invitation, but he had learned to be cautious. He would not take up her offer until he had had a look at this Maxio. He had a suspicion that the man was about to discard his woman and that she was looking about for a replacement. If so, all would be well. If not, there could be trouble.

He rose and left the wineshop. As he crossed the Square, a squad of bored-looking public slaves trundled their wheelbarrow toward the three inert bodies that lay in a widening pool of blood. The slaves carried buckets and bore mops over their shoulders. Nobody came toward him from the Reeve's headquarters, so Conan assumed that he was free from official interference for the present.

He left the Square by way of an alley between the temple and the wall surrounding the house of Xanthus. He was not at all surprised when someone hissed at him from a gate in the wall around the rich man's house.

"You, outlander! Warrior! Come here.'' The speaker was an elderly slave in old-fashioned livery.

"What do you want?'' Conan asked.

The slave leaned out and looked up and down the alley, presumably to ascertain whether anyone was watching. He turned back to Conan. "Come in here. My master craves converse with you.''

It seemed to the Cimmerian that never before had so many people invited him to confer in such a short time. At least this old slave did not try to persuade him with weapons. He ducked beneath the low lintel and entered a courtyard that must at one time have been fine, but now the remains of wilted plants stood in overgrown planters and the wind blew dry leaves over the cracked pavement. Pulped fruit dropped by ornamental olive trees made footing slippery.

The slave closed and barred the gate. "Come this way," he said. Conan followed the shuffling old man through a door in the rear of the house. It opened into a kitchen in which a pair of slave women toiled over a stove. They did not look up as he passed. The slave led him up a flight of stairs and down a hallway and into a spacious room lined with shelves bearing books and scrolls. A fire crackled on a stone hearth.

"Abide here a while," the slave said. "My master will be along presently."

The slave left through a paneled door. Conan strolled to a floor-length window that opened upon a small balcony overlooking the Square; it was no more than fifty paces from where he had slain the red-clad murderers. Anyone who might have stood here, he thought, would have had an excellent view of the proceedings.

"Greetings, swordsman," said a voice behind him. The Cimmerian turned to see an elderly man swathed in thick woolen garments. A mantle of rare white fur draped his shoulders, and atop that lay a chain of massy gold, studded with huge gems. His face was thin and ravaged by time, but his voice had strength.

Conan nodded curtly. "Sir. What would you have of me?"

The old man crossed to the window and gazed out upon the slaves busily plying their mops. The bodies were gone.

"I was in my study when my manslave told me there was about to be an amusing show in the Square. In the past, the rogues of the town slew each other in the alleys of the Pit, and at night. Now they fight pitched battles in the Square in broad daylight. I have come to treasure these little shows. My pleasures have been few of late. I witnessed your slaying of those three fellows in red leather. That was prettily done. Ingas's men are accounted dangerous in this town.''

"I am good at my work," Conan said laconically.

"It is that very thing I wish to speak of. Will you work for me and kill some rogues who need killing?''

Conan suppressed a smile. The man's direct, businesslike manner was refreshing: no offer of dinner or even of a cup of wine, no long, tedious story, just an offer of pay for service.

"What is your offer?" he asked.

"This was once a fine city, with myself as its leading citizen. Now it is a lawless place, dominated by the scum and sweepings of this and all the neighboring lands. It needs a thorough cleansing, and I think you are just the man to do it."

"One man?" Conan asked. "To subdue a town full of outlaws?''

"I will pay generously. You may hire such bravos as you wish. Killers work cheap in this city. But it should not be necessary to exterminate the lot. A few leaders are causing all the trouble. Slay the wolves, and the leaderless dogs will be easy to deal with.''

"I have heard," the Cimmerian said, "that it was you yourself who brought Ermak to town."

"And what if I did? The miners' guild stirred up trouble and required putting down. Then the rogue would not leave town when I ordered him to.''

"Since this is a royal burgh," Conan said, "why did you not appeal to the Crown for help with the miners? Or for expelling the mercenaries?" Conan watched the man's face closely, but the old features displayed only overweening pride and self-confidence.

"My dealings with his majesty, King Numedides, are my own affair, nothing that a barbarian sellsword need concern himself with.''

"As you will," Conan said. "I can do the job for you. I will want twenty thousand golden marks of Aquilonia. Half now.''

To his astonishment, the ancient head nodded. "Done." Xanthus tugged on a cord and moments later the old servitor appeared. The master whispered in the slave's ear and gave him a massive key. Then he turned back to Conan.

"You will have your money presently. You need not render me reports of your progress. When the task is done, come to me for the balance of your pay. I think this concludes our business."

"Not quite," Conan said. He had walked to the window again and stood with his back to Xanthus, staring across the Square toward the Reeve's headquarters. "Will you speak to the King's Reeve and see that he gives me no trouble or interference?" A small looking glass hung on the wall next to the window, and in it he saw the old man wince slightly, his arrogant composure slipping for the first time.

"You are to stay clear of him. I do not want him brought into this matter in any way, and I cannot intercede with him for you."

"I thought you were the richest man in Sicas," Conan said, "and he is a bribe-taker."

"Then bribe him yourself if he troubles you!" Xanthus spat. "By Mitra, I am paying you enough to pass a few bribes! Matters old and ill lie between us, and I'll have nothing to do with Bombas. Now get to your work, swordsman. I expect to hear good things of you in the near future." With that, the old man whirled and stalked out amid floating robes. Conan smiled coldly toward the fur-clad back.

Minutes later, the old butler tottered in, bowed beneath the weight of a leather sack as long as Conan's forearm and as thick as two of those arms held together. The gold coins the sack held were stuffed in so tightly that they did not even clink. Without a word, the Cimmerian picked up the bag and left the house.

With a light heart and a springy stride, Conan sought out the Street of the Woodcarvers. In one hand he clutched the weighty bag as lightly as another man would have held a pillow stuffed with down. He was careful not to give indication of the thing's true weight, for then the practiced eyes of the town's numerous thieves would have discerned that he carried gold.

He saw the Sign of the Sunburst, its gilded rays shining brilliantly in the midday sunlight, but he did not seek Delia. Instead, he went to a joiner's shop and bought a stout wooden casket well mounted with thick iron straps. This he carried to the Street of Locksmiths and purchased the strongest padlock he could find to fit the coffer's hasp.

He bore the coffer, with the bag now safely inside it, upon his shoulder as he returned to the inn. There he added to it most of the money he had received from Casperus. Already he had acquired more money than he could readily carry with him, and he had yet to accomplish a single one of his tasks. He knew that he could not leave his bounty unwatched at the inn, but the strongbox would do until he could cache his new wealth. He all but whistled as he turned the key in the lock. No sooner had he withdrawn the key than the door opened and Brita entered.

"Still no luck, eh?" he said, noting her downcast look.

"None. Oh, a few people have seen girls answering Ylla's description, but who knows if this was her indeed. I myself have seen a score of small, yellow-haired girls her age here." She sat on the room's single chair, knees together and hands clasped upon them. Once again she was the demure, well-bred girl she had at first seemed. Now Conan was not so sure. He knew himself to be less than astute when it came to women, but he was no fool.

Dropping the key into his pouch, he lifted the coffer by its side handles and deposited it upon the foot of his bed. He made the effort seem easy, but the great muscles sprang into prominence along his arms as he did it, earning him an admiring look from Brita. He stretched himself upon the bed, his feet crossed at the ankles atop the coffer, his fingers laced behind his tousled, black-haired head as he leaned back against a pile of cushions.

"Well, I have had a very good day indeed," he said with satisfaction.

She smiled. "I rejoice to hear it. Tell me all about it."

Briefly, he did so. A look of unmistakable jealousy crossed her face when he told her of his luncheon with Delia, followed by a look of horror when he related the challenge by Ingas's three killers. Her hand flew to her open mouth when he told her how he had slain the three. Then he related his summons from the house of Xanthus.

"And you did this just to attract that man's notice?" she gasped, her eyes round with incredulity.

"I would have had to deal with them anyway. They were determined to call me out. Better the three of them before me in daylight than behind me in the dark. I was sure to be seen from the house of Xanthus and the temple both. It was just a question of who would summon me first. Xanthus was quicker." Then he told her of his interview with the old man.

"But surely," she said when he finished, "you do not truly intend to kill or chase out every villain in this hideous town all by yourself?"

"We shall see how it falls out," he said noncommittally. "What troubles me more is the old bandit's readiness to pay. I demanded half on account, expecting him to laugh in my face and offer perhaps one fifth, which I would have accepted. Instead, he agreed upon the half without a word of protest."

"Then he is desperate," she said.

Conan shook his head. "No, it is not that. He is said to be the richest man in Sicas, but the only servants I saw were an old valet of all work and two slatternly women to cook and clean. He has what was once a fine courtyard, yet he has not even a gardener to keep it in order. His house is splendid, but he must have inherited that. Otherwise, the only things splendid about him are his clothes and his jewels, upon which he does not stint. No, the man is a miser as tightfisted as any I have ever seen. Yet he handed me ten thousand gold marks without demur."

"Why would he do such a thing?" she asked.

He grinned without mirth. "Because he expects to get his money back. He is wrong. I will spend my wealth, or gamble it away, or give it away, or just throw it away, but no man takes back what he has paid me when I have rendered him good service."

"And will you do as he wants?" she asked uncomfortably.

"I took his money, did I not?" he said indignantly. Then, smiling, "Of course, all may not fall out exactly as he thinks. But that often happens when one rogue tries to outwit another. I do confess, though, that I wonder what lies between him and the King's Reeve. Bombas is in every man's purse, so why not in that of the man with the biggest purse in Sicas?"

"From the way you have described them," she said, "they do not sound like the sort of men who would let their personal feelings for one another stand in the way of their pursuit of wealth."

"Very true," Conan said. "There is something deeper here, and I will find the bottom of it, be sure of that."

"And yet," she protested, "you have accepted commissions from that man Piris in Belverus, from the fat man Casperus, and now from the rich miser Xanthus. Do you truly intend to carry through for all of them?"

"I do not accept pay under false pretenses," he assured her. "Have no fear. Mayhap a common thread runs through all these things, and when I have found it, I think I will have accomplished all that I have undertaken to everyone's satisfaction, although it may be to their everlasting regret."

"You have much confidence."

"Aye. Tell me, girl, what gods do you worship?"

She was taken aback by the sudden change of subject. "Why, I attend services at the Temple of Mitra, like most Tarantians, and I used to sacrifice to the minor deities of my father's guild, although not lately. Why do you ask?"

"Well, Crom is my god and the god of my people. He is old, grim, and stern. When we are born, he gives us a fierce warrior's heart and the great strength, endurance, and hardihood that are the birthright of every Cimmerian. But he is not a caring god. Unlike the gods of the south, he takes no delight in sacrifice; he gives us no help and we ask him no favors, because he would grant none."

"And so?" she asked, frowning in puzzlement.

"If he were the sort of god men pray to, I would send him a prayer of thanks right now, for sending me to Sicas." Hands still laced behind his head, Conan grinned up at the cracked plaster of the ceiling. "*Everyone* in this town seems determined to make me rich!"

Seven

The Silver Mine

Conan rode from the inn in the light of morning, his iron-bound wooden coffer strapped to the saddle behind him. In the socket that would ordinarily have held his lance, he had placed a spade borrowed from the stable. The hooves of his horse rang loudly on the cobbles as he made his way through the nearly deserted streets, heading southward. If the upper city was but waking as he rode through it, the Pit was as a city of the dead. Not a living soul did he see, although in the alleys he saw a few corpses, soon destined for the river.

Just above the confluence of the rivers, he passed through the Ossar River gate, where the guard merely accepted his proffered coin and did not bother with stupid formalities such as his name, destination, or time of possible return. The bridge he crossed was a good one, made of stone and built upon arches high enough to allow river barges to pass beneath. On the other side was cultivated land, now lying untended after the harvest. The road took him to hilly terrain, first past vineyards but soon into wild country. He guided his horse off the road and into the hills, following no path.

In a wooded dell the Cimmerian dismounted and tethered his mount to a sapling. He stood absolutely still and silent for several minutes, moving nothing but his head as he slowly scanned the skyline and strained his ears for any slightest noise. He heard no sound save those of nature.

Leaving horse and chest, he climbed to the highest ground nearby, his springy hillman's stride making the rugged terrain as easy a traverse as the level pavement of a city. Atop the hill, he found a dead tree, killed by lightning some years before, its leaves gone but its wood sound. This he climbed with the agility of a monkey, and from a convenient limb he enjoyed an unobstructed view of the surrounding countryside. There he sat for an hour, his keen eyes missing nothing, until he was satisfied that no one followed him, that no woodcutter worked nearby, that no rustic lovers in search of privacy spied upon him. Only then did he descend and return to his horse.

He took the chest from his saddle, the spade from his lance-socket, stripped off his armor and set to work. The spot he had selected was far enough from the nearest trees that he was not likely to encounter troublesome roots. First he measured his proposed excavation by eye; then he spread a blanket upon the ground next to it. Kneeling on the grass, he drew his dirk and carefully cut a rectangular outline in the ground. With swift sawing cuts of his blade, he separated the turf from the underlying soil, rolling it up as he cut. When it was fully separated, he lifted it gently onto the blanket. Then he stood and picked up the spade. He dug energetically but carefully, lifting each spadeful of dirt and depositing it upon the blanket, taking care not to heap it atop the preserved turf.

When the hole was about a yard deep, Conan lowered the chest into it. He began to cover the coffer with dirt, tamping it down with his boots after every few spadefuls, so that the ground would not subside over the next few days, leaving a telltale depression. When only about three inches of excavation remained, he carefully relaid the turf, smoothing it with his hands when it was in place.

There still remained a heap of dirt atop the blanket: soil displaced by the chest. This he tied up in the cloth, to be scattered far away from this place. He packed the bundle on his saddle and replaced the spade, then went back to examine his cache. From a few paces away, the site was invisible. Within days it would be indiscernible even to his own eye. Satisfied, he remounted. He did not bother with a treasure map. Conan's sense of direction was flawless. Should he not return for ten years, he would be able to walk unerringly to the spot where he had buried his gold.

That took care of one task. Now he had another. He rode from the wild hills, ever watchful for observers. Near the road he shook the dirt from the blanket, then folded the heavy wool and tied it to his cantle. He headed back toward the town, but just before he came within sight of the river wall, he noted a side road he had passed earlier in the day. It was marked by a gray stone stele carved with the rampant royal lions of Aquilonia, defining what lay beyond as royal property. He reined his horse onto the road.

Ahead of him he saw columns of smoke ascending skyward. As he drew nearer, he began to hear a continuous thudding, clinking sound, and a grinding as of many stones being broken. He rode over a lip of ground and there, spread out before him, was a grimly busy scene. At the edge of a vast, open pit, hundreds of men wielded sledgehammers to break great stones into smaller chunks, while others pushed long poles that rotated huge, vertical stone wheels in endless circles, pulverizing the smaller chunks, reducing them to coarse sand.

The Cimmerian knew this for an ore-crushing operation. Women and children carried baskets of the coarse sand upon their backs to dump them into great iron crucibles that were in turn thrust into beehive-shaped ovens, whence ascended the smoke. Others stood in lines at long handles, monotonously raising and lowering them to power immense bellows.

Somewhere beyond, he knew, would be men toiling with pick and shovel to wrench the ore from the grudging bones of the earth. He surveyed the scene with some disdain. Conan could never understand how freeborn men could blight their lives thus with grinding toil. The fierce excitement of battle was what he loved, and if it was terminated abruptly by a swift, bloody death, so much the better. This sort of toil seemed to be mere degradation to him, and it lacked even the consolation of security and long life. He knew that wounds and early death must be as common among these laboring people as among professional soldiers, but without the compensating loot and excitement.

"Hey, you!" He turned to see a man emerging from a wooden booth by the road. "Who sent you here?" The Cimmerian studied the man. He wore a leather jerkin studded with bronze rosettes, and identically studded wristbands encircled each wrist. He wore a close-fitting steel cap, and in lieu of a sword, a pair of long, slightly curved knives were sheathed at his belt. His weasel face was full of suspicion.

"I came to have a look around," Conan said. The man seemed out of place, somehow. On a sudden inspiration, Conan added, "On orders."

The man's face cleared. "Oh, Lisip sent you, then? I did not recognize you. You must be new. Well, tell the boss that all is well here. The dogs are causing no trouble and work as hard as ever, although sullenly."

"Then why not use the whip?" Conan asked.

"You *are* new, aren't you? Aye, I'd love to stripe their backs, but you don't do that with these half-tamed brutes. They are not like born slaves. It's other threats that keep them in line, if you take my meaning." The man chuckled, smirking with an insinuating familiarity.

"Aye, I know," said Conan, knowing nothing of the sort but determined to find out. "I think I'll ride down there and have a look around. I was told to familiarize myself with the operation."

The man looked at him suspiciously. "I cannot think why, but if that is what Lisip wants, so be it." He gestured toward the mining operation as if offering it to the Cimmerian, who nudged his horse down the hill.

As Conan drew nearer, he began to make out details he had missed. The men wielding sledgehammers to break the rock wore light greaves to protect their shins from stone chips. Many of the men who pushed the millstones or worked the bellows were blind. Rock dust and flying chips of stone took a heavy toll of eyes. The miners wore coarse, heavy clothing, and most of them were gnarled, powerfully built men with massive hands. They watched him with narrow-eyed suspicion.

A short distance from the ore-crushing area was a cluster of huts. Here Conan dismounted near a well and began to haul up buckets of water, emptying them into a trough for his horse. As the beast drank, a group of men gathered around him, gripping tools as they would weapons, their mien sullen and truculent. One came a little forward. He was a squat, square-built knot of muscle, red-eyed from rock dust, his clothes and hair gray with it. He gripped a pick in hands swathed in rags save for his blunt fingers.

"What want you here?" the man growled, his voice little more than a hoarse croak. These people must *breathe* rock dust, the Cimmerian thought. "We have met our quota every day this last turning of the moon. It was agreed that as long as we meet our quota, we are not to be harassed."

Conan took a dipper and drank from the last bucket he had drawn. More people were gathering. There were men and boys of all ages, and some women well past their prime, but he saw no young women, nor did he see any infants. A gray-haired woman pushed to the fore and pointed toward his armored breast.

"This is he, the one I spoke of! Yesterday, when I went to the Square to trade for produce, I saw this one slay Ingas's three killers without even drawing his sword!"

"Good," said the man who had spoken. "Even better had they slain him while he was doing it. Are Lisip's men and those of Ingas at war, foreigner? And if so, why should we care?"

"Why do you think I work for Lisip?" Conan asked.

The man's eyes narrowed yet further. "Who else could it be? Lisip was given the power to— Just who are you, stranger?"

"My name is Conan. I work for none of the gang leaders of Sicas, and it may be that I can be of aid to you."

"Don't trust him!" said a man with a face seamed like the bed of a dry creek. "He must be Lisip's man, sent to spy on us, to see if we are keeping our part of the bargain." He spat. "As if we could do otherwise."

Conan nodded toward the slope he had descended. "Is that man in the shack your only guard? You must be a spiritless lot to let yourselves be controlled by a single thug." The crowd growled at his words.

"He does not guard us," said the first man. "He just watches and reports, as you well know. Lisip has no need to keep guards on us. Now, why are you here?"

Conan could see that these people would not talk to him. He would need to overcome their suspicion. As luck would have it, the opportunity he needed was already on the way. The thug from the guard shack came toward him with stiff, challenging strides. He pushed his way through the encircling crowd of miners and halted before the Cimmerian.

"If you are here to observe the operation," he challenged, "why are you talking to these dogs? You know full well that they are to hold converse with no outsider. Are you truly one of Lisip's men?"

"I made no such claim," Conan pointed out. "You did."

The man's face reddened with rage. "Then begone, or I will kill you!"

Conan set the dipper on the lip of the well. "Try," he said quietly.

Swift as a striking viper, the man drew one of his knives and lanced it toward the Cimmerian's belly, beneath the edge of the brigandine. Moving even more swiftly, Conan grabbed the man's wrist and stopped the point an inch from his flesh. Slowly, he squeezed. Beneath his machinelike grip, the hardened, bronze-studded leather crumpled inward. The bones of the forearm resisted; then they began to grind together. With a brutal twist, Conan snapped the man's wrist, sending the blade flying. Cursing loudly, the thug drew his other knife with his left hand and sent its keen edge slashing toward the Cimmerian's throat. With his free hand, Conan caught the left wrist and did likewise with it, the bones popping audibly. The thug dropped to his knees, his face white and sweaty, nauseous with pain and shock.

The Cimmerian gripped the front of the leather armor and hauled the man to his feet. "Tell Lisip that Conan of Cimmeria does not tolerate being attacked, especially by worthless scum like you. Now go, while I am still in a good mood!" He shoved the man away and the thug began to stagger back up the hill, retching.

The miners looked at Conan in wonder. The one who had spoken first regarded him steadily. The faintest of smiles began to touch the mouth framed by its dust-grayed beard.

"First Ingas, now Lisip. You are a man who is not afraid to make enemies."

Conan shrugged. "Thus far I have encountered only one man worth drawing steel against."

The miner nodded. "Then you've met Ermak." He gestured toward a long, low building nearby. "Come, Cimmerian. We will talk."

Conan followed the man into the building, which proved to be a communal eating place. Two long tables ran its length. At one end of the room, a huge pot bubbled over a fire, sending forth an insipid aroma. The perimeters were lined with shelves, but these were bare. A few baskets of vegetables and roots lay against the log walls. At the miner's gesture, Conan seated himself on a bench at the end of one table. The other took the seat opposite.

"I am Bellas," the miner said. "I am guild chief of the miners of Sicas. Now, who are you and what is your business here?"

"I am a warrior," Conan told him. "And I am about to become a troublemaker."

The man looked at him sardonically. "Sicas has not been lacking in trouble ere now."

"The Reeve and Xanthus and the others have yet to learn about trouble. I will make them curse the day I arrived in this cesspit."

"If you are going to make life hard for them, you are thrice welcome," Bellas said. "I would offer you ale but we drink only water these days."

"I can see that you have fallen upon hard times," Conan observed, looking around at the empty shelves. "That is what I need to know about. How did this happen?"

"It is a long story, dating back many, many years, but recent events are what you want to know. Life was good here, once."

"I cannot see how life could ever be good for a miner," Conan said.

"When silver was first discovered here," Bellas went on, "the ore was rich, and it lay near the surface. In those days the mine was a great, open pit and the miners could at least work beneath the sun. The labor was toilsome, mining work always is, but the pay was good, and our guild stood high in the royal favor. Our guildhall was the finest in Sicas.

"Over the years, the good ore played out and we had to pursue inferior ore that lay deeper, driving galleries far into the bowels of the earth. It was not as good as in the old days, but we maintained a respectable yield. And we miners enjoyed a high reputation. We do the hardest, most dangerous work there is—hardrock mining. We are not slaves or convicts. We are free, proud men."

"And yet you were brought low and now might as well be slaves," Conan pointed out. "How did that come to be?"

"It was Xanthus!" Fury edged the man's voice. "He raised our quota, then raised it again. We protested. It was not just a matter of working harder to dig more ore. If you try to work faster underground, there are more accidents, more rockfalls. Too many men died. We finally marched into the city to confront Xanthus. He would not yield, so we downed tools."

"The mine is royal property, is it not?" Conan asked. "Why did you not appeal to the Crown?"

"The guild sent a deputation," Bellas said. "One morning we came in here to find a bloody sack right here on this table." He thumped the scarred, wooden surface with his fist. "It contained the heads of the men we had sent. This time we seized our tools and went into the town. We found our guildhall burned out and the house of Xanthus surrounded by Ermak's mercenaries. It was useless for us to fight them. We had no proper weapons. But we are not cowards. We have good smiths here, so we returned to our village to have our tools reforged into spears and swords and maces. Ermak's men may be skilled warriors, but we are strong and there are far more of us than there are of them.''

''But you did not confront them,'' Conan said.

''Nay, we did not. When we returned here, we found that Ermak's horsemen had been ahead of us. While we men were in Sicas, they had rounded up our wives and children. We know not where they were taken, but we know they are hidden away somewhere. Any gesture of defiance from one of us and the rogues send us a head, just to remind us whose is the whip hand.''

''I thought it would be something like that.'' The Cimmerian mused for a moment. ''Tell me, where stands the Reeve in all this?''

''That pig-eyed tub of suet! He gets paid for every act of knavery in Sicas, and the villainy of Xanthus is no exception.'' The miner leaned forward, his arms crossed on the table before him. ''You see, the ancient arrangement with the Crown is that the mine factor—the position now held by Xanthus—receives one-fifth part of the refined silver yielded by the mine. In recent years Xanthus has taken more than half. He writes to the palace bewailing the declining yield of the ore while, at the same time, raising our quota so that the royal portion does not grow suspiciously low. Bombas takes his share of this, have no doubt of it. And there is a royal overseer of mines in Tarantia, a nobleman named Coreides. We now know that he must be in collusion with Xanthus. Had we known that from the first, we would never have sent our delegation to the palace. And even if we could get past Coreides—'' he shrugged bitterly and pounded his fist once more upon the table ''—what king would listen to honest workingmen when three of his officials have poured poison in his ear?''

Conan leaned back against the log wall, his thumbs hooked into his studded belt, his fingertips drumming out a rhythm on its polished surface.

"When I came hither," the Cimmerian began, "I sought only information. I thought to find naught but cowed oxen working in this place. Now I have some hope. Tell me; if I were to stir up things in Sicas and bring about there such chaos that the royal authorities would have no choice save to intervene, would you aid me?"

"Foreigner," said Bellas, "if you can but find the place where they keep our women and children, you can leave all the killing to us. Xanthus set Lisip's men to watch us because Ermak's men think themselves above such duty. But the old miser miscalculated there, for Lisip's dogs are too lazy and too stupid to do a good job of it. Mostly they stay up in the guard shack, sodden with drink much of the time. They never bother to make a careful search of the village or of the mine workings. We have been forging every bit of iron we could spare into weapons, and now we have enough to arm every man here."

"Can you use them?" Conan demanded.

Instead of answering, Bellas dipped his hand into a basket behind him and brought it out holding something round, which he tossed to Conan. "This is what we have been living on."

Conan caught the object and examined it. It was a turnip, plain and round and as hard as a stone. He tossed it back. "Poor fare for men who must work as hard as you. And you did not answer my question."

"We have not weakened on this fare," Bellas said, studying the tuber in his hand. Abruptly, his hand tightened into a fist. Near-liquid pulp shot from beneath his fingers for several feet. Conan blinked. He accounted himself among the strongest of men, but this was an astonishing display. "When the time comes," Bellas said, "you will not find us wanting."

"Excellent," Conan said. "I will try to send word ahead, but if not, come when the uproar starts, and come armed. Will you know when things begin to break in Sicas?"

"Some of our old people go marketing every day. They miss little. Tell me something, foreigner."

"What would you know?" Conan asked.

"What is your stake in all this? You are not from here. You are neither guildsman nor royal official, yet you wish to help us. Why?"

Conan rose from the bench. "I am like everybody else in Sicas," he said. "I am here to grow wealthy."

Bellas grinned, but there was no mirth in his face. "You are more likely to be killed, but men die poor as easily as they die rich, and the gods will love you for robbing the likes of Xanthus and Bombas."

"I care nothing about the gods," Conan said, "and those you named are just two among the villains of Sicas."

He rode back to town whistling. This was turning out to be even better than he had hoped. So, the rich man and the Reeve were both skimming from the royal share? Robbing a king was a risky game, even when the king was a weak fool like Numedides. Surely there must be something here that he could turn to account. Now that he knew Bombas and Xanthus were partners in this particular bit of knavery, the question of their enmity became doubly intriguing.

The sun had all but set when he returned to the inn. After caring for his horse, Conan went to the common room and ate ravenously, for he had not eaten that day. He was given much space at his table, for word had spread that he was a dangerous man who made enemies readily.

He examined his quarters but found no further sign of intruders. Brita was nowhere to be seen, and Conan mentally cursed the woman's single-minded determination to locate her sister, no matter the hour or the danger. Still, there was nothing he could do about her at the moment, but he was not through seeking answers for the day. He went down the stairs and out into the street. This time he directed his footsteps toward the Street of the Woodcarvers.

Above the sign of the Sunburst, a square of white cloth was draped from a window. He ascended the stairs and knocked at a stout door. "Who is it?" called a voice from inside.

"Conan," he answered. A small panel slid aside and a blue eye studied him. The panel shut and there was a sound of sliding bolts before the door opened. Delia stood aside and gestured for him to enter.

"Come in, Cimmerian. I wondered how long you would take to come and visit me."

Conan stepped within. The room beyond was a cluttered mess, but its furnishings were expensive. It was illuminated by a dozen candles and half as many oil lamps. On a table stacked with unwashed dishes, a black-and-white cat lapped milk from a silver bowl.

"Welcome to my abode, Conan." Delia scooped a striped yellow cat from a chair. "Sit down and make yourself comfortable. Few men have been honored with an invitation to my home."

Conan sincerely doubted that the woman's favors were as exclusive as she implied, but he accepted the chair vacated by the striped cat and propped his booted feet on a hassock.

"I am honored," he said with a straight face.

She took a pair of silver goblets and a chased pitcher of the same metal and poured both cups full, spilling some wine in the process. Clearly, she had been making inroads on the wine before Conan arrived. He took the offered cup and drank. It was an excellent vintage. The woman was as prodigal with drink as she was with illumination. He wondered what Maxio thought of his woman's spending habits.

"I knew you could not stay away from me for long," Delia said, slurring her words slightly. "Once a man has taken my eye, I will see to it that he comes to me."

"It is not my way to chase another man's woman," Conan said. "What of your Maxio?"

"Maxio!" she said indignantly. "He does not appreciate me. I am too good for the likes of him. Do you not find me beautiful?"

"I'll not deny it," Conan assured her.

"Yet he treats me like some cheap woman of the streets whose looks came from a paint pot and whose hair rightfully belongs to some barbarian woman who sold her yellow tresses to the wig-maker!'' She took a long drink of the wine, as if she needed it to extinguish an internal blaze. ''Why do I waste my love and loyalty on a man like that?'' She finished the cup and poured herself some more, then offered the same service to Conan, but he shook his head.

''You have told me of the enmity that lies between Maxio and Bombas,'' Conan said. ''But there is something deeper between the Reeve and Xanthus. Know you anything of this?''

''What kind of man are you?'' she demanded sulkily. ''Why do you want to talk about those dreary men? Wouldn't you rather talk about me?''

''First the Reeve and Xanthus,'' Conan said. ''Then, perhaps, we shall talk about you and about me.''

''Oh, very well.'' She ran her fingers through her splendid hair, then noticed that her cup was empty once more. Quickly, she rectified the situation. ''I know little of the matter, and I doubt that any do, save the two men themselves. Many years ago, when both were young men, they were close partners. But they fell out, over a woman.''

''A woman!'' Conan laughed. ''Those two?''

''Even old men were once young,'' she asserted, ''and young men value nothing so highly as women, and rightfully so. Anyway, the story is that they both pursued the same woman but were too cowardly to fight for her. At any rate, she died. Perhaps she killed herself. Each blames the other for her death, and black enmity has lain between them ever since.''

''What a pair!'' Conan said. ''Divided by ancient hatred, yet bound together by guilt and villainy.'' He thought over the impli-cations for a while. ''Tell me, Delia, who is the town's main fence? All the thieving hereabouts must mean that there is a re-ceiver for stolen goods. Or do the fences here fight one another as everyone else does?''

A cat sprang into Delia's lap and she stroked it. ''In the Pit

there is an old Temple of Bes, an Ophirian god. Bes has few
worshipers here, but he has the richest temple in Sicas, because
the priest is the town's most prosperous fence. He used to be the
only one, under Lisip's protection, but now there are others.''

"Is the temple near one of the rivers?" Conan asked.

"Yes. It is built against the Fury wall. Why do you ask?"

"I just like to know about these things," Conan said.

"Are you planning a job?" she asked. Her look grew sly, although she was having difficulty in keeping her eyes focused.
"Because if you are, I know of something being planned that you
might get in on. There will be a big payoff, and not much risk."

"I am interested," Conan said.

"Well, Maxio and his boys plan to break into the royal storehouse. It's up near the north end of town, not far from the wall.
It's where the town's tax yield is stored, along with the king's
share from the silver mine. Maxio plans to make a fabulous haul
and get out of town."

"If he robs a royal storehouse, he should get out of Aquilonia
entirely," Conan commented. "Isn't it heavily guarded?"

She laughed. "Oh, aye. By Bombas's men. How much trouble
can they be to deal with?"

"I see. When is the raid to be, and how does Maxio plan to
move his loot out of town?"

She yawned hugely, all but dislocating her jaw. "What did you
say? Oh, yes. I don't know when it will be, exactly. In the next
few days. And he didn't tell me his escape plans. It almost seems
as if he doesn't trust me anymore, the sneaking rat!"

"He is unworthy of you," Conan said.

"That is very true."

"When you know that Maxio is about to make his move, will
you tell me?"

She was not too drunk to remember her greed. "That is the
sort of information I expect to be paid well for. After all, it will
gain you a great deal of loot, and Maxio never gives me anything!"

"I promise to be generous," Conan assured her.

"Well, then, all right . . ." Slowly, her head nodded, her eyelids dropped, and she began to snore.

The Cimmerian rose. Before leaving, he thoughtfully extinguished all but a single candle. Between the woman and her cats, he thought, it was a wonder the block had not been burned to the ground.

EIGHT
Lilac Perfume

When the Cimmerian returned to the inn, all was silent. The last of the late drinkers had vacated the common room, and when he entered the courtyard, his was the only shadow cast by the silvery moon overhead. Swiftly, he climbed the steps to the third floor, and for all his bulk, he ascended as silently as a ghost.

Outside his door he paused. Another man might not have noticed, but his sensitive nose detected a scent of lilacs. Brita had not used scent since he had encountered her. He drew his dagger and thrust the door open. The inside of the room was inky black.

"Come out, Piris," Conan commanded.

"How did you know I was here?" asked the breathy, tremulous voice.

The Cimmerian laughed. "Piris, somehow I just do not need the evidence of my eyes to know you in the dark, even through a closed door." His voice hardened. "Now, tell me why you are in my room hiding instead of calling upon me by daylight, like an honest man."

The little man came out onto the balcony. Even by moonlight, his robes were lurid. "I did not reach town until after nightfall. The gate guard told me where you lodged, and I came hither immediately. Was it my fault that you were out somewhere when I arrived?"

"And who let you in?"

Piris reached into his robes. His hand emerged holding a small ring of tiny tools. "This let me in. These inn locks are childishly simple to open."

Conan had to smile at the man's shamelessness. "And you saw no point in standing outside the door in the dark, eh?"

"There, I knew you to be a reasonable man. You do understand."

"Fetch us a candle, and we will go inside and talk."

Piris ducked back into the room and emerged with the candle, which he carried a few paces to a torch that sputtered dimly in a sconce overhanging the courtyard. The Cimmerian stepped into the chamber and stood silent for a few seconds. No sound came from the next room. Either Brita had left again or she had not returned. The silly fool was probably wandering around in the Pit, calling her sister's name.

Piris returned with the candle and set it into its pewter holder. Conan divested himself of weapons and armor and stretched himself upon the bed. Piris took the room's single chair.

"Now tell me," Conan said. "Where have you been?"

"I would have arrived sooner," the little man said, "but I was clapped into a dungeon in Belverus!" His voice quivered at the injustice.

"How came that about?" Conan asked.

"As I left the city, I was detained at the guardhouse and my belongings were searched. Clearly, someone had told the guards to watch for me. In my baggage they found an exquisite amber necklace belonging to a certain priestess of the city. An enemy had planted the thing on me and tipped the guard!"

"Are you quite certain that it was planted?" asked Conan, skepticism tingeing his voice.

"Sir!" Piris said indignantly. "Credit me with some wit. I

would never leave a town by the main gate while carrying stolen property."

"And just who was this enemy who treated you so treacherously?" Conan queried.

"I cannot be certain, but I believe it was a woman named Altaira, with whom I had dealings. The wench is an accomplished thief and quite capable of such a thing. We had had a . . . a dispute, and she was looking to revenge herself upon me."

"Describe her." Conan said.

"A black-haired bitch who paints her nails and lips the most shocking shade of scarlet. She has the manner of a she-wolf and much the same reputation. She has slain many men who crossed her. Have you seen such a woman here?" The little man shuddered at the thought.

"None like that," Conan said. "How did you get out of the dungeon?"

"When they locked me up, they took everything from me, but I had secreted some valuables, ah, very privily upon my person. With a small jewel, I bribed a keeper to return my clothes, complaining that the dungeon was very cold and damp. This the fool did, not knowing that I had my little ring of tools concealed cunningly within the padding of my sash. With this I let myself out just before dawn, when all were snoring unsuspectingly. I recovered my belongings and left by way of a window, then lowered myself over the city wall by means of a rope. I could not recover my horse, naturally, but I acquired another."

"You are very resourceful," said Conan, who had graced many a dungeon himself, including the one in Belverus.

"And how have you fared here?" Piris asked.

"You were not wrong when you said that this is a wicked city," Conan said. "It is divided among a half-score of rival gangs. Authority is contested between a corrupt Reeve named Bombas and a crooked old miser named Xanthus. The main hangout of the rogues is an area called the Pit, at the south end of town, but now the whole place is wide open. The principal fence is a priest of Bes, whose temple is in the Pit.'' Conan saw no reason to tell Piris of his doings since his arrival.

The little man rubbed his palms together. "This sounds like a place where one can do business."

"Speaking of business," Conan said, "you have yet to explain ours. You said you would tell me when you joined me here. Do so now. I have had a long day, and I must sleep sometime."

"Very well. Know, then, that I come of a very ancient and prominent family of Shadizar. For a hundred generations, we have been counselors to kings and benefactors of the great temples of our land. We are a priestly family, and I myself am an initiate of the Third Order of the Servants of Asura." If he expected Conan to be impressed by this revelation, he was wrong. The Cimmerian yawned.

"At any rate," Piris went on, "as a result of our prominence, my family is the custodian of many famed treasures. Deep within the vaults beneath our palace in Shadizar is kept the vase, carved from a single huge ruby, containing the sacred oil with which every Zingaran monarch is anointed upon accession. Our border fortress in the Kezankian mountains houses the great idol of Sutra, which will cure the afflictions of any petitioner who will but ascend the nine thousand steps up the mountainside upon his knees. Many a bloody-kneed supplicant has found solace at the feet of this god, whose sole priests are members of my family."

"Will you not get to the point, man?" Conan asked impatiently.

"As you will. In my own house in Shadizar is a small temple, dedicated to a god so ancient that none remembers his name. The temple, which lies far underground, is far more ancient than the house, which is tolerably old itself, about seven hundred years. Within the temple crypt reposed one of the family treasures. This treasure was stolen some years ago, and I have pursued it ever since, unable for shame to return to my family. I cannot return to take up my rightful station in life until it is within my hands once more."

"And the nature of this treasure?" Conan asked, sensing where this was leading.

Piris drew a deep breath, as if about to impart something both vital and secret. "It has the likeness of a scorpion with the head of a beautiful woman, carven from a stone like obsidian."

Somehow, Conan was not surprised. He was glad of the flickering, deceptive light cast by the lone candle, for Piris would not be able to read the many expressions he knew to be crossing his countenance in rapid succession, consternation and amusement predominating.

"And what is it that makes this stone insect so valuable?" Conan asked.

"For my family, its value is incalculable. Our fortunes are bound up with it, and it has long been held that should we lose it, our house would surely fall. I shudder to think what may be happening to my kinsmen this very moment, occasioned by its loss. But if I can restore it to its pedestal beneath my house, likewise will our fortunes be restored."

"Then what makes it valuable enough for someone else to steal it?"' Conan demanded.

"The scorpion is a thing of great mystery and magic," Piris said, his voice gone even lower and breathier than usual. "In the hands of a sorcerer, its powers would be immense! And its substance is absolutely unique. The stone from which it is carved is not obsidian, although it has rather that appearance. It was carved from a huge black diamond that fell from the heavens upon ancient Atlantis. It is said that a shadowy priesthood of that fabulous kingdom toiled for many generations to carve the image from the strangely shaped gem, which was even harder than earthly diamonds. During the last century of its shaping, a wonderful temple was built to house the scorpion. When the final stroke of the polishing was done, so was the temple finished, and the image was placed therein.

"Ten days and nights of fearful ceremonies inaugurated the temple, and at midnight of the tenth night, when the moon shone through an aperture in the temple roof upon the last trickle of blood that dripped from the idol's pedestal, the island shook with the blasts of a thousand volcanoes, and Atlantis sank beneath the waves of the ocean, with all of its gleaming cities.'' The voice quivered with awe.

"But the scorpion seems to have survived this untimely wetting," Conan observed.

"Do not speak flippantly of so sacred an object!" Piris admonished. "It is said that the scorpion *walked* from its sunken temple and came thus to Stygia, were it was revered for many centuries until it was given into the keeping of my family in recognition of our mastery of certain religious rites. These rites are of a most esoteric nature and are crucial to the proper ordering of the universe. Terrible cosmic consequences could result from this theft!"

"I see," Conan said. "And what makes you think the scorpion is here in Sicas?"

"It may not be here yet, but in Belverus an informant told me that it was in the possession of a certain caravan master, one Mulvix, and that this man was bound for Sicas. That was why I bade you come hither."

"You think this Mulvix will try to sell the scorpion here?" Conan asked.

"Very likely. I think the man is just a smuggler. As such, the idol must very soon make him most uncomfortable. It is true of all magical objects that the uninitiated cannot bear their presence for long. By now he will be anxious to get rid of it. He may simply try to dispose of it as a valuable art object, or as a unique jewel, but it is more likely that he will seek out a wizard, a very rich one, if there is such a person here in this benighted city."

"There is just such a man," Conan proclaimed, "and I know of a way to ingratiate myself with him."

"Excellent! If we watch both this wizard and the fence you spoke of, we must soon find the scorpion."

"That is how I see it. I shall set about it tomorrow. Now, Piris, just where do you expect to sleep?"

The little man's eyes widened. "Sleep? Why, it is too late to find a room of my own. Surely there is room for me here, even if on a mere pallet on the floor.'' He gestured, as if to demonstrate the spaciousness of the accommodations.

"Piris," the Cimmerian growled, "under no circumstances are you and I going to sleep in the same room. There is a fine stable attached to this inn. The straw is clean."

"The stable!" Piris's voice achieved a near squawk. "How could I endure such a place?"

"Easily, and you will smell the better for it."

"But might I not—"

"Good night to you, Piris," Conan said firmly.

Piris emitted a heartfelt sigh as he walked to the door. "I should have known you were a cruel man when I hired you." He left, shutting the door behind him.

Conan grinned up at the ceiling. In a lifetime spent among the most lawless people in the world, never had he encountered so many villainous schemers in so short a time. Mercenaries, thieves, corrupt officials, religious frauds, would-be wizards, and killers of every stripe were drawn to the town like iron filings to a lodestone. By now he knew better than to trust anything told to him by his employers. Henceforth he would trust only their gold.

Conan rose early and found Piris in the common room. The little man had secured quarters on the ground floor but clearly he resented his night in the stable. Conan ignored the reproach in the doglike protuberant eyes as he breakfasted with his usual gusto.

"This morning I visit the Temple of Bes," the Cimmerian said when he was satisfied. "Do you want to go with me? It is in the Pit."

"That sounds like a worthwhile visit," Piris said. "I would like to . . ." He fell silent as the door opened, and his expression was one of alarm. Conan turned to see a man enter. He was hugely fat, with legs bulging his hose like overstuffed sausages. Greasy black hair framed his jowly face. Conan turned back to Piris.

"What is wrong?" he demanded.

"Oh, nothing, nothing. I but thought for a moment that that man was someone else. Pay it no heed."

Conan grunted as if satisfied. They left the inn and walked southward. As they passed the Square, Conan pointed out Andolla's temple and gave Piris a sketchy account of the man's activities.

"If he is very rich and posing as a mage," the Zamoran said, "he would be a logical buyer for the scorpion." He looked bemused, then spoke once more. "Tell me, Conan; since you have been here, have you encountered a man who is quite tall and very handsome, with wavy blond hair and an easy manner?"

"Not to notice. Why do you ask?"

"He was once an associate of mine, and I thought I might encounter him here. This is the sort of place to attract him. He is a gambler and fancies himself a ladies' man." The latter quality seemed to displease Piris.

"I've met no one like that here," Conan said, thinking that he had not actually *met* such a one. But the description sounded suspiciously like Asdras, whose rat-gnawed corpse he had seen in the alley behind the Wyvern. And, just where was Brita keeping herself?

After much wandering about in twisting streets and blind alleys, they found the Temple of Bes. It was an old and shabby building, much in need of painting. The doorway was flanked by a pair of statues of the grotesque god, who had the body of a bandy-legged dwarf and a lionlike face. His tongue protruded from his comically wide-stretched mouth. The Ophirian god was popular among the lower classes in many lands. He was a god of jollity and good times, a defender against evil spirits and, oddly enough, a protector of women in childbirth. Like most gods, he had a darker side. Bes was also a god of drunkards and thieves.

The Cimmerian and the Zamoran passed within. A priest hurried from the back of the temple to greet them. He wore Ophirian robes, headgear and slippers, and upon his breast was a jeweled pectoral depicting his god.

"How may I help you sirs?" His clothing might have been Ophirian, but his accent was local. "Do you wish to offer a sacrifice? Have you a wife in labor?" He eyed Piris skeptically. "Well, perhaps not the latter. Is it, shall we say, a business matter?"

"Business," Conan said. "We are looking for—" Piris thrust an elbow sharply into his ribs, hard enough for the Cimmerian to feel the jab through his brigandine.

"We are in the market for art objects," Piris said smoothly. "We were informed that you are a dealer in such matters."

"In my small fashion," said the priest. "What sort of art do you fancy? Paintings? Ivory carving? Jewel work?"

"Might we have a look at your stock?" Piris asked.

"But of a certainty! If you gentlemen will come with me, I will show you my inventory." He led them past the altar and to a door that opened upon a flight of stairs. These descended to a room where a pair of slaves guarded a heavy door. The slaves were men of Shem, huge and hook-nosed, with black beards almost concealing the spiked collars that encircled their necks.

From his girdle the priest took a heavy key and thrust it into the door. Massive as the portal was, it opened smoothly on well-oiled hinges. "Bring lamps," the priest ordered. The slaves complied, and moments later Conan and his companion were admiring a fine stock of valuables: jeweled swords, fine portraits, small statues carved from precious materials, jewelry of every description. At the far end of the vault there was a second door. This Conan had expected, and it was the main reason he had wanted to have a look at the temple.

"What lies beyond that portal?" he asked.

"Just the river," said the priest. "Sometimes goods must be moved in and out without bothering the authorities, if you take my meaning. Well, gentlemen, do you see anything such as takes your fancy?"

Piris caressed a ruby-eyed figurine of a rearing lion. "Oh, much of this is most attractive, and rest assured that in time I shall come to make you an offer upon some of these items. However, just now we have a more specific desire. It would be a small statue made of a most curious black stone. It will be quite unlike anything you have ever encountered before. Should this unique specimen come before you, and I think it well might within a very few days, you should find it very rewarding to inform us."

"Ah, a *specific* item!" said the priest conspiratorially. "It is not uncommon for me to be asked to keep watch for a specific item that someone is desirous of obtaining. I have seen nothing thus far such as you seek, but be assured that I shall let you know instantly should it come my way. At one time this would have been inevitable, but business has been greatly damaged of late by all these amateurs who have come to town. Where might you be contacted, good sirs?"

Piris gave the man the name of their inn, and for a while the two conversed professionally upon the subject of property acquired extralegally. While they did so, the Cimmerian examined the vaulted chamber in which they stood. The walls were of brick, curving to form the roof overhead. The bricks did not sweat moisture, which meant that they were well above the level of the river.

As soon as he had heard that the temple abutted the river wall, he had assumed that there would be a river access. In past times, when Sicas had been governed by Reeves more conscientious than Bombas, the priests of this temple would have required a convenient means of moving their nefariously acquired goods.

Conan had long ago learned that it is unwise to enter any house without first noting where all the possible exits lie. The same held true for towns. In a tight situation, it would be good to know that there was a convenient way out of the town that did not necessitate use of the gates.

Their business concluded, Conan and Piris returned to the streets of the Pit. They made a strange pair, the huge, savage-looking Cimmerian and the small, delicate and effeminate Zamoran, but in the Pit they did not rate so much as a second glance from passersby. The inhabitants of the Pit were rarely of the conventional sort themselves.

As they made their way up a winding alley, Conan noticed that they were being followed. This was the Pit, not the Square. He knew that there would be no challenge to an open fight. Without so much as a word, the Cimmerian whirled, his sword hissing from its scabbard. The men behind them halted, unnerved by the abrupt move. Somewhat to Conan's surprise, Piris neither panicked nor ran. He whirled an instant after, drawing a long, thin-bladed stiletto.

"Whose dogs are you?" Conan snarled. One wore the red leather of Ingas's gang, but the rest were nondescript thugs of the Pit. There were six of them, each with drawn sword. Just above and behind them Conan noticed someone watching from a rooftop, but he had no attention to spare for the watcher.

"What matters that?" asked a man whose woolen cap covered holes once graced by ears. "You and your pretty friend will be fish food ere dark."

"It was to deal with such rascals that I hired you, Cimmerian," Piris reminded him. "Please attend to them."

"You heard him," Conan said to the six. "Either begone or attack. I do not want to tarry in this stinking alley."

As one man, the six attacked. The Cimmerian met them halfway, his sword shearing through an unguarded thigh as he ducked past a clumsy blow. He struck a bearded man in the chest with his shoulder, sending him smashing into a wall. The long sword of the man in red leather struck Conan's side, but its keen edge merely split the cover of the brigandine and skittered across the steel plates beneath. Conan's left fist crashed into that one's jaw and the man dropped with a sound of splintering bone. A cutlass glittered toward Conan's face, but he interposed his own blade and the steel rang. The instant the cutlass-wielder's blade halted, Conan grabbed his wrist, disengaged his own blade and smashed his pommel into the bridge of the man's nose. As that one fell, a man with a short sword leaped over the body, his weapon darting for Conan's side. The Cimmerian leaned aside and as the sword went past, clamped the attacker's arm between his own left arm and side. With his pommel, he smashed the elbow joint. Shoving the man off, he placed his back to a wall, his eyes sweeping the alley for more enemies. He was just in time to see the watcher dash away from the rampart of the nearby house. It was only a glimpse, but he had the impression that it was a woman, a woman with black hair and a mouth rouged scarlet.

Conan surveyed the men, who either lay still or groaned and writhed upon the filthy paving stones of the alley. The man he had knocked into the wall and one other, a man of Stygian countenance, lay shivering and jerking, their mouths drawn back in convulsive grins. He looked at Piris.

"I but scratched them," the thief said, gesturing with his stiletto. Its point was stained lightly with blood but heavily with a green substance. He resheathed the weapon.

"Halt, you rogues!" They turned to see Bombas, his bulk almost blocking the alley, fisted hands on his hips. Behind him stood his three close henchmen and a half-dozen of his worthless guards.

"You are a long way from your headquarters, Reeve," Conan said.

The fat man smiled evilly. "And yet I am duty-bound to go forth and arrest those who would defy the law. Your weapons, please."

Conan fumed, but Piris nudged him. "We had best comply, my friend. We have business to conclude in this town."

With ill grace, the Cimmerian complied, handing his weapons-belt to the Reeve. The man took Piris's stiletto and examined it, then looked upon the two men whose heels had ceased to drum upon the stone. He clucked ruefully.

"Did you not know that possession of an envenomed weapon is a violation of royal law?"

The Zamoran's eyes went wide in a parody of injured innocence. "But I bought that weapon believing it to be an honest dagger! Am I an apothecary, to know that its tip was poisoned?"

Bombas did not deign to answer. He looked at the fallen men distastefully and turned to his guards. "Drag this offal down to the river."

"But some of them are still alive," said a guard who carried a bill slanting over his shoulder.

"What of that?" demanded Bombas. "Cut their throats and all will be corrected." Shrugging, the guards drew their daggers.

"Now come with me," Bombas ordered.

Conan and Piris, closely followed by Julus and the two Zingarans, began to trudge toward the Square. Conan said nothing to his companion about the black-haired woman. He was not even certain that he had seen her; the impression had been too fleeting. As they passed through the Square, they drew many looks and some laughter, but Conan decided that most of this was due to the unaccustomed sight of Bombas, out of his headquarters for once.

The Cimmerian knew it was no coincidence that the fat Reeve had just happened to be in the vicinity where the two were set upon, in a part of town that Bombas probably had not visited in years. It was just one more among the multitude of conspiracies that had come to surround Conan. He had no doubt that this, too, would become clear in time.

Within the Reeve's palace, they were marched down a flight of stairs and into a stone-walled cell guarded by an iron-barred door. The door shut behind the two with a resounding clank and the jailer, an oxlike, bald-headed man, twisted a heavy key in the lock.

"Leave us," said Bombas, addressing the jailer and his three henchmen.

"How long are we here for?" Conan asked.

Bombas shrugged. "Perhaps for a short time, perhaps for the rest of your lives. I am always amenable to reason."

"How much reason do we need to get out of here?" the Cimmerian demanded.

"Ordinarily fifty marks' worth of reason is sufficient, but with you two, I am not so sure."

"This is an outrage!" Piris sputtered. "I shall protest to the Zamoran ambassador, who is a personal friend."

At this, Bombas laughed hard enough to set his fat jiggling.

"In the first place, little man, the Zamoran ambassador is in Tarantia, which is quite some way from here. You lack the aspect of a wizard, so I doubt that you can communicate with him from my dungeon. In the second place, I deal with people like you every day, and I think that the last thing you want is to come to the attention of the Zamoran authorities."

"Will we be tried?" Conan asked.

"If I wish. But the next court day is not for many weeks. Even so—" he came close to the bars "—you two need not endure this at all. Tell me what you are in Sicas for. If it is something to my advantage, perhaps we can work out an arrangement. Remember that you are foreigners and have no rights here. I need not try you at all. What is your business?" Neither prisoner said a word. Bombas stepped back, frowning. "Very well, then. I will release you upon payment of five hundred gold marks. Each!"

"Where would we get such a sum?" Piris wailed.

"What concern is that of mine?" Bombas said. He turned and stalked back up the stairs.

"Who set that swine upon us?" Piris asked.

Conan shrugged his massive shoulders. "It's my guess that he was bribed to kill us if the thugs failed to do so. His men took one end of the alley, the thugs took the other. We killed the thugs first. He had not stomach for a fight with me, and he scents riches in keeping us alive. As to who hired him, the field is growing crowded. Incidentally, I think I might have espied your black-haired wench watching the ambush from a rooftop, but I cannot be sure."

"That slut! If she has followed me here—"

"And is she, too, in search of the black scorpion?" Conan demanded.

"Cimmerian, you ask too many questions. My dealings are my own. I have retained your services to aid me, not to be my partner." The little man fretted for a few minutes, then: "By the way, my friend, have you enough gold handy to procure our freedom?"

At this Conan laughed. "You remember my condition when

you found me! You advanced me two hundred dishas, much of which I spent in outfitting and traveling expenses.''

The Zamoran sat on a hard bench depending upon chains from a wall, his every line eloquent of despondency. "Oh. I was hoping that your luck at gaming might have returned, or that you might have, well, acquired a bit of wealth through other means since you left Belverus.''

Conan strode close to Piris and looked down upon him with a thunderous glare. "And what of the rest of the thousand dishas you promised me?''

"I told you that my departure from Belverus was precipitate. I was forced to leave much behind." He looked up and smiled eagerly. "But if we can just recover the scorpion, our fortunes will be restored!''

Conan glanced at the stairway. The oxlike jailer had not yet returned. "Do you have your ring of picks?" he asked.

"Yes," said Piris in a low voice. "But I would rather not use it. We need to be able to move freely about this town, perhaps for several more days. Who knows when the scorpion may arrive?''

Conan went to the door and grasped the bars. He had been clapped in jail many times but he could never become accustomed to the sensation of confinement. His mind worked over the possibilities.

"Something may turn up," he said. Now Piris released an annoying giggle. "What is so funny, little man?" Conan demanded.

"Did you not say that under *no* circumstances would you sleep in the same room with me?''

Conan set his head against the bars and groaned. "Crom has deserted me!''

NINE

The Temple of Doorgah

Conan lay back upon his hard bench, fingers laced behind his head, and pondered the problem of five hundred marks. He had no intention of revealing where he had hidden his gold. He did not want to tap any of his current employers. Piris was already penniless, or claimed to be. Xanthus would have nothing to do with Bombas, and Casperus wished to retain anonymity. Anyway, it might cause them to lose confidence in him if they were forced to spring him from prison. He decided that he needed another employer, one willing to invest five hundred marks to secure the services of a champion swordsman.

He glanced at the next bunk and saw that Piris snored away amid a cloud of lilac fumes. The oxlike jailer was gone, replaced by a younger man who hobbled about on a crutch. The Cimmerian rose and walked to the door. "*Psst!* Would you like to earn some money?" he whispered.

The man looked up from the table where he was carving a model of a river barge. "I'll not unlock you!" he said, then amended, "Not for less than a thousand marks."

"Nothing like that. I just want you to deliver a message. Know you the house of Rista Daan?"

"Who does not?" the keeper said.

"When you get off duty, go to him and say this: 'If you wish to have your daughter back from the hands of Andolla, come to the Reeve's headquarters and buy Conan of Cimmeria out of jail.' Can you remember that? It is worth five marks to you."

The man repeated the message. "Where are my five marks?"

"Do I look like I have money?" Conan said impatiently. "Daan will pay you."

An hour later the lame man was replaced by the bald one. The Cimmerian knew better than to fret or grow impatient. Piris wheedled a gaming board from the jailer, and for a while they killed time playing "King is Dead," at which Piris cheated adroitly. Conan had lost his third straight game when Julus came down the stairs, escorting a man dressed in hose and tunic of sumptuous cloth, over which he wore a coat trimmed with rich white fur.

"Which of you is the Cimmerian?" the man asked.

"Would you mistake me for a savage?" Piris retorted indignantly.

"I am Conan." The Cimmerian stood and approached the bars, making the most of his intimidating size and appearance. The rich man looked him up and down, then turned to Julus.

"I would speak with this one privily." Julus nodded to the jailer, who unlocked the door.

As the Cimmerian followed the others up the stair, Piris called after him, "Conan! Get me out, too!"

Julus led them to a small room off the building's main hall. "My lord," he said, "you had better let me stay in here with you. This one is a savage and has killed several men since coming to town."

"I think not," said the man. "The town seems none the worse off for his activities. Pray leave us."

"As you command." Julus bowed and left, shutting the door behind him.

"Now, explain quickly the meaning of your message. Why should it be worth five hundred marks for me to procure your freedom?"

"How many thousands has Andolla cost you already?" Conan countered. "Are you not Rista Daan?"

"I am, and what know you of me?"

"I was told that your daughter was one of those who have fallen under the spell of Andolla and now spends her days in the Temple of Mother Doorgah."

"And what can you do about the situation?" Rista Daan demanded. His face was lean-fleshed and hard, with deep lines, his silver hair trimmed close. Except for his uncallused palms, he might have been a soldier.

"I have taken this sort of task before," Conan told him. "Frauds like Andolla prey upon the foolish children of the wealthy. They keep the young ones until the money runs out, then kick them into the street."

"I know all that. You say that you can go to the temple and bring her back to me?"

Conan shook his head. "You know that will do no good. She will just get away and run back to Andolla. They always do. No, I will have to destroy his hold upon her."

"And you think you can do this?" Now the man's attitude was less challenging.

"Aye. It will take a few days."

Daan seemed to come to a decision. He nodded curtly. "Very well. If you had claimed that you could restore her instantly, I would have told that fat fool of a Reeve to clap you back in the clink. I think there may be more to you than I had thought."

At a desk near the entrance, Conan collected his weapons and armor while Rista Daan paid for his freedom. That done, they went out into the Square.

"Five hundred!" Rista Daan said as they walked toward his house, which was on the side of the Square exactly opposite Xanthus's. "Why does Bombas value you so highly?"

Conan shrugged. "The swine plays so many games that I think

not even he keeps track of them all. It's clear that not everyone gets jailed in this town just for killing a few men. And I but defended myself. At that, I did not kill as many as I might have. He ordered the deaths of the men I but disabled.''

"He just wants a piece of whatever villainy you are up to," Daan said. "It's no affair of mine. So long as you perform your task for me, I'll not trouble you about whatever else you occupy yourself with."

They entered a spacious courtyard, this one lovingly tended. Roses grew lavishly despite the late season. The house they entered had luxurious furnishings and hangings of precious cloth. The servants wore fine livery and did not appear ill-treated.

"Did they feed you in the dungeon?" Daan asked.

"A few stale crusts and some water," Conan grumbled.

"He pockets even the allowance for prisoners' rations," Daan said. "I am not surprised." He clapped his hands and a servant rushed up. "This man will conduct you to the bathhouse, of which you stand in sore need. When you return, we shall dine and speak of necessary matters."

The Cimmerian followed the servant and soon was luxuriating in an immense tub of hot soapy water as attendants scrubbed him industriously. Afterward he sat before a great looking glass while a barber shaved him and trimmed his dense, square-cut mane. Clean new clothes were brought to him and he dressed, noting that the cut in the leather covering of his brigandine had been expertly repaired with fine stitches. His steel cap had been polished. Even if Rista Daan turned out to be as villainous as the others, Conan thought, he could not be faulted for his hospitality.

The servant now conducted Conan to a dining room, where Rista Daan sat at a heavy-laden table. At the man's gesture, Conan sat and a servitor filled his cup and began to heap the platter before him. For a while the two men ate in silence, Rista Daan sparingly, the Cimmerian ravenously.

When Conan was replete, he sat back and the rich man handed him a small, flat square of wood. In its center was a miniature portrait, exquisitely detailed. It depicted a young girl with straight yellow hair and huge blue eyes.

"This is my daughter, Rietta. She is my only child. I want you to be able to recognize her, because she goes by another name within that foul temple. Andolla gives each of his followers a new name when they join him. It helps to sever their attachment to their families."

"Save those attachments through which money flows," Conan pointed out.

"Exactly. The young fools under his spell constantly send word to their families, begging for money. Sometimes they go home claiming that they have left Andolla forever. Then they raid the family coffers and flee back to the temple."

"How did the girl come to follow the knave?" Conan asked.

A look of pain flitted across the man's face. "I am a spice merchant. I have had to spend much of my life away from home attending to business. As a result, my daughter was in the care of her mother for much of her youth, and my wife was . . . not quite right in the head. This was not noticeable when we were wed, but it grew more pronounced as the years went by. Had I been home more, I might have taken more notice and done something about it." He brooded in silence for a moment. "Well, that is past and there is nothing I can do about it now." He contemplated the depths of his wine.

"Rietta's mother found the state gods very dull, and she was greatly addicted to foreign religions, a taste she passed on to my daughter. As the years went by, my wife became obsessed that she lay under an ancient curse, handed down through the women in her family. She began to perform endless rites to protect Rietta from this imaginary onus. I learned much of this later, from the servants," he admitted. "My wife behaved almost normally when I was at home. In time, though, her sickness became apparent even to me, and I placed her under the close care of trusted retainers. It was no use. One night, in the midst of a terrible storm, she escaped from her room and fled to the roof of the corner turret. From there, she cast herself to the pave below."

Daan was silent for a while, then shook himself and went on. "Rietta was not only grief-stricken, but terrified: The curse had claimed her mother, and now it would descend upon her. At about that time, Andolla moved into the old temple and dedicated it to his foul Vendhyan goddess. Some of Rietta's young and stupid friends told her of Andolla, of what a wonderful man he was, of how he could solve any difficulty of supernatural origin. She went to see him.

"Of course the charlatan had picked up all the town gossip and knew exactly what to say to her. He knew how to protect her from the terrible curse if only she would come stay in his temple. She went, naturally, and has been there ever since. I sought to hire bravos to bring her out, but Andolla has paid off all the gang lords and has protection."

"How does he bleed you?" Conan asked bluntly.

"Before fleeing to him, Rietta raided my strongbox, taking ten thousand marks in gold and far more in jewels. Andolla must have coached her in how to make an impression of my key. She is not strong enough to have carried it all, so he probably sent someone to help her."

"He is thorough," Conan said. "Is there anything at all to his magical claims, or is he pure fraud?"

"That is difficult to say. He claims to be able to slay with curses, and some who have given him trouble have died mysteriously, but that could as easily be from poison. I am most careful of my food and drink these days. And he is not alone. He has a wife named Oppia, and it is my opinion that she is the more cunning of the two."

"This grows complicated," Conan said judiciously, "but I can set the matter aright."

"And what is your fee for this task?" Rista Daan asked.

"My usual fee is one thousand marks," Conan said. "But since you have already paid five hundred for my freedom . . ."

"Five hundred ten," said the merchant, "counting what I paid the jailer for delivering your message."

"Ten!" said Conan. "I told the man five!"

"We have small rogues in this town as well as the great ones." At that, both men laughed. "You'll have the balance of your money when Rietta is back with me. And I am not without influence, both here and in the capital. Whatever charges are against you will be quietly dropped. I like your look, Cimmerian. I think you will render honest service."

Conan rose. "Then I had better be about it. Look to have your daughter back within a few days. After that, Andolla should trouble you no further."

The Square was enveloped in dusk when the Cimmerian left the house. He wanted to call at the temple, but thought it best to check back at the inn first. He had paid several days' advance for his room and Brita's, and he was concerned for her. He looked into the stable to make sure his horse was properly cared for, then climbed the stair to his chamber. As soon as he entered, Brita rushed in from the adjoining room.

"Conan! Where have you been?"

"In jail. Where have you been?" Despite himself, he was relieved to see her.

"Where have I *not* been? I think I have pried into every foul corner of this city, trying to find my sister. She has been seen, but the information is never recent enough to do any good. I fear that she may have fled the city."

"Probably went back to Tarantia," he said. "You'd better do the same."

"Not until I am sure. Why were you in jail?"

"I think I am the only man in town to be arrested for fighting. That was yesterday morning. Where were you two nights ago?"

"I came here as usual," she said, "and I climbed the stair, but I saw a man hanging about on the balcony near our doors, a little man in *very* strange clothes. I was frightened, so I spent the rest of the night in the carriage house below."

Conan laughed shortly. "That was just . . . oh, never mind. Listen to me, girl. I will be away for a day or two. I will contact you if I can, but business calls me elsewhere for a while."

"Surely you are not leaving town?" she said anxiously.

"No, I shall be here. The rooms are paid for. Do nothing foolish. By now, everyone in town knows your mission. If your sister still wants to avoid you, you will not find her. If not, let her seek you out. Take no more foolish risks, because I will be unavailable for help. Do you understand?"

She looked down and clasped her hands. "Yes." He tilted her head back and kissed her.

"Now, stay out of trouble," he admonished. She smiled and he left, feeling uneasy.

The portico of the temple was brightly illuminated by fires burning in bronze baskets, their smoke fragrant with incense. From within came the sound of endless, monotonous chanting. Two hulking young men guarded the doorway, their arms folded across their chests.

"I wish to speak with Andolla," Conan said when he halted before the two.

"Our master does not speak with just anyone," said one of the youths. "He is a holy man, and spends much time in meditation."

"Unclean persons cannot simply call upon him," said the other.

"I just had a bath," Conan told them. "If your master is unavailable, perhaps his wife would speak with me."

"The Holy Mother Oppia is likewise occupied with spiritual matters," said the first.

Conan's patience, never lengthy, had reached its limit. He grasped his hilt. "Would they respond to cries of pain and distress from the entrance?" he growled.

"What is this?" It was a woman's voice. Instantly the two guards turned and bowed as the speaker emerged and passed between them. She was small but well shaped, her hair long and black, her skin dusky. A diamond glittered from one nostril, and a smooth red jewel had somehow been set into the flesh of her forehead.

The guards clapped and chanted, "Holy Mother Oppia, Holy Mother Oppia." She waved a hand and they fell silent.

"My name is Conan of Cimmeria, and I think we have business to discuss."

"I cannot imagine why," she said, "but it is never our way to turn away supplicants. Please come inside."

The guards had given no impression that this was a hospitable temple. Doubtless, Conan thought, the woman just did not wish to be seen speaking with him on the portico. Inside, the temple was illuminated by candles and votive fires burning before idols. The austere Temple of Mitra had been renovated in the overdecorated Vendhyan style. Every surface had been painted to depict Vendhyan deities going about their activities, many of the pursuits bloody, others obscene, most of them incomprehensible. There were as many animal as human figures in the decorations, and small monkeys seemed to have the run of the temple.

The temple proper was a vast room in which at least twoscore worshipers chanted endlessly, clashing tuneless instruments and making what was, to Conan's ears, a hellish racket. The object of their adoration seemed to be an idol of the same huge-breasted female deity he had seen in the procession. The goddess sat crosslegged, her feet atop her thighs, and in her lap sat a man in the same knee-wrenching posture. His eyes were shut and he was motionless.

The woman led him up a flight of stairs to a second-floor gallery that completely encircled the nave below. Skylights above revealed the moon and stars. Oppia wore a single band of sky-blue silk wrapped tightly about her shoulders and descending almost to her ankles. Her feet were bare, their soles stained bright red.

The room into which she led Conan opened off the gallery. It was bare and businesslike, furnished only with chairs and a large desk stacked with parchments. The decoration was minimal, although sticks of incense burned in the hands of miniature idols. The woman seated herself behind the desk and addressed him coolly.

"You are a man of violence, a swordsman," she said. "I have

heard of you. We reject all forms of violence and coercion. Why have you come here?''

"If you will not bear arms," Conan said, "then all the more reason for you to hire someone who is more than willing to do so.''

"We have guards, albeit unarmed," she pointed out.

"Like those two at the door?" Conan all but sneered. "They are worthless, and you know it. What happens when the families of your acolytes hire bravos to come retrieve their young?''

She leaned back slightly, studying him from beneath lowered lids. "Misguided persons sometimes wish to kidnap our followers, but we have arrangements with those who control the men of violence.''

"Then before long, the aggrieved families will go outside of town to hire their strong-arm men." He could see that the thought concerned her. "And are there not times when some of your followers grow reluctant to stay?''

"Sometimes, very rarely, an evil spirit, an enemy of Mother Doorgah's, infects one of the acolytes with an unreasoning urge to leave, but with patience and goodwill, we overcome these sacrilegious compulsions.''

Conan grinned. "I can overcome them very quickly. I am good at that sort of work. Also, while I am sure that you have concerned yourself only with spiritual matters, you may have heard that the gangs in this city are fighting each other more and more. Your agreements with them may not hold for much longer. I am not affiliated with any of them.''

For the first time, she looked him over closely and quite openly. "It may be that we . . . that is, that Mother Doorgah can use a man like you. And if you abide here a while, who knows but that we may be able to bring you to the way of goodness and light?'' A miniscule, secret smile curved the corners of her mouth. "Come, I will show you Mother Doorgah's domain here in the benighted west.'' She came from behind the desk and he followed her back to the gallery.

"Here the faithful chant the daily offices," she said, gesturing toward the nave below.

"How many are there?" he asked. "Faithful, I mean, not offices."

"We now have more than one hundred," she said. "We offer the blessings of Mother Doorgah to all, but we accept only those whose faith and devotion are sincere." By which, Conan assumed, she meant as long as they kept the money coming in. "Great-souled Andolla, my husband, is the conduit through which flows the word of Mother Doorgah."

She led him into a side chapel. Here was another statue of the goddess; this time she was black, her naked body splattered with painted blood. A necklace of human skulls depended from her neck, and she waved a sword as she danced atop a heap of entrails and severed limbs.

"This is Mother Doorgah in her aspect of the Drinker of Blood and Devourer of Entrails. All Vendhyan gods have both the creative and destructive aspects. We worship her primarily in her nurturing, birth-giving persona." She smiled at him frostily. "But we must not overlook her darker side."

"That would be unwise," Conan agreed. He disliked the eastern gods almost as much as he detested the pantheon of Stygia. He came of a dynamic, self-reliant people, and he had only contempt for the apathetic, fatalistic followers of such gods, who held inertia and nothingness as the highest good, oblivion as the only desirable state of existence.

"This," said Oppia as they entered another room, "is where those whose faith falters practice austerities to restore them to the true way." There were shackles hanging from the walls, and in the center of the room was an X-shaped frame fitted with manacles and leg irons. Hanging from one of its arms was a multilashed scourge, each thong studded with brass barbs.

"This should restore their belief if nothing else will," observed the Cimmerian.

"I can see that you are a man of little faith," she sniffed. "That is only to be expected of a barbarian. Still, Mother Doorgah scorns no one, however base. Come."

She showed him the gardens, the workshops, the kitchens and laundries, where all the housekeeping of the establishment was done. The temple owned no slaves. Rather, Conan thought, the acolytes *were* the slaves. They performed all the work. The beauty of the system was that ordinarily one had to pay for slaves. These actually paid to be enslaved. Far from running away, they had to be restrained from running back to the temple.

Behind the temple proper was a large house of four stories, with many rooms. Oppia showed him the large chambers used as dormitories by the acolytes. They were perfectly bare except for sleeping pallets, all of which were neatly rolled against the walls while the acolytes were at services. She described the daily routine of the worshipers, and Conan realized that the wealthy young converts were kept under a discipline stricter than that of military recruits. The offices went on day and night, and the acolytes never had more than two hours of sleep at any time. When they were not chanting, they were working. In the kitchens, he had seen that their diet consisted mainly of boiled gruel. In a state of perpetual starvation and exhaustion, their minds and wills were numbed. Conan was revolted, although he was careful not to reveal his feelings. It made ordinary slavery seem a clean thing by comparison. And yet he was certain that he had not seen the worst of it.

Finally she took him to a spacious apartment on the third floor. "You will lodge here," she said. "I am sure that it is more comfortable than your accustomed quarters."

"It'll do," Conan said. "Where do you live?"

She regarded him coolly. "Why do you need to know that?"

"Times are unsettled, and half of the unhung thieves in Aquilonia are in Sicas. Mysterious people attract rumors, and ignorant men may think you hoard wealth in this temple. If rogues should break into your quarters and you should raise an alarm, I would need to know where to run to your rescue."

"That makes sense," she said. "On this floor, if you turn left in the hall outside your door, then turn right at its end, you come to a red door. Within is our apartment. Never enter those chambers save at my command or that of my husband.''

"I shall not," said Conan, determining to explore their chambers at first opportunity.

"Very good. There remains the question of payment."

"No question about that," Conan said. "My fee is one thousand gold marks. You may pay me half now. Soon your affairs here will be settled one way or the other and you may then pay me the balance."

"What do mean you by that?" she demanded.

Conan shrugged. "Either the gang-fighting will be resolved, with one pack left in control, or you and your husband will leave town."

"Leave town?" Her eyes flashed. "Whyfore should we do such a thing?"

He grinned at her. "Somehow I feel that Mother Doorgah may call you elsewhere soon. I suspect that this has happened many times before. I also suspect that your departure will be sudden and will occur late at night. Be assured that I will notice and will come for the balance of my pay."

She glared at him for a moment; then, abruptly, she chuckled. She reached up and with the long, pointed nail of a forefinger, traced a line down the angle of his clean-shaven jaw. "Cimmerian, I think that you and I shall get on well together." She ran her tongue lightly across her lips, increasing their shine.

"And I think you should pay me five hundred marks now," Conan said.

"Wait here," she ordered, and with a surprisingly girlish giggle, she left the room. He noticed that she turned left in the hallway outside the door. She was going to her apartments. He waited for a few seconds, then looked outside the room. She was nowhere in sight, but from the angle of the hall, he heard a key turning in a lock. So she kept the key upon herself.

When he heard the door shut, he ran silently up the hallway and turned right. A few paces before him was a red-painted door of heavy timbers strapped with iron. The lockplate was a massive thing, but the shape of the keyhole told him that the lock itself, while strong, was of a primitive design. It should prove easy to pick at need.

The hallway was low-ceilinged, illuminated by oil lamps burning in niches. He lifted the chased bronze lid of one and saw that its reservoir was half full. This told him that the lamps were filled once each day, in the morning. He would not have to worry about encountering an acolyte oiling the lamps at any other time.

He listened for the sounds of a strongbox being opened, but the door was too thick to allow any faint noise to pass. Judging that caution would permit him to stay no longer, he made his way silently back to his new quarters. He drew his dirk and was abstractedly sharpening it when Oppia returned.

She held a leather pouch in one hand. Her bandlike garment had become artfully disarranged. It now exposed a narrow spiral of creamy flesh from her armpits almost to her ankles. She held out the pouch and Conan, sheathing his dirk, took it from her. The thin leather was stretched taut and held a satisfying solidity. He had no doubt that the woman would feel equally satisfying. But, he reflected, women were far more dangerous than gold.

"Perhaps I will convert you to the worship of Mother Doorgah after all," she said, coming close.

"She's not my sort of goddess," Conan said.

"Ah, but how do you know? I have told you that she has more than one aspect. Some of them are not for the ordinary acolytes. As Queen of Raptures and Unifier of the Flesh, her rites are such as you might find delight in. I am the sublime instructress in these rituals."

"And the Great-souled Andolla?" Conan inquired. "Does he take part in these ceremonies?"

She stroked his cheek with her fingertips. "My husband is unduly occupied with his magical studies of late. We are not much in company, save when a ceremony of the Holy One requires the presence of us both."

"Is the sanctified Andolla a master of sorcerous arts?" the Cimmerian asked.

"When he is not occupied with his devotions to Mother Doorgah, he seeks a deeper understanding of the supernatural world." Her tone was faintly contemptuous. "To that end he collects sorcerous tomes and other paraphernalia. His studies keep him long hours in solitude."

"You must find that lonely," Conan observed.

"Sometimes," she admitted, "the consolations of Mother Doorgah are not enough. And the male acolytes can be *so* boring." She began to move toward him, but she stopped at the sound of a scream from above. It was a woman's voice, and it was a sound of utter terror.

"Crom!" Conan said, snatching at his hilt. "Someone's being murdered!"

"The Mother curse her!" Oppia snarled. Then she placed a restraining palm upon his heavy arm. "Be at ease. It is one of our female acolytes, and a most troublesome one. She is like this often. Come, she may need restraining."

He followed her into the hallway and to the stair they had ascended before. This time she went up a final, narrow passage to the fourth floor. Though here the layout was the same as on the floor below, Conan noted that most of the doors stood open, the rooms beyond unoccupied. But one room was closed, bolted from the outside. At eye level it had a small window, shuttered so that it opened only from the outside, like that of a prison door.

Oppia opened the shutter and peered inside, then slid back the bar and tugged the door open. Conan went in behind her. As he entered the room, he noticed a smell so faint that it was barely detectable. In a second or two, with a faint outrushing of air, it was gone, but he knew he had not imagined it. Then his attention was drawn to a frail figure huddled in a corner of the room.

It was Rietta, the daughter of Rista Daan. He knew her from the miniature portrait, but she no longer greatly resembled that likeness. Her face was hollow and emaciated, her limbs shriveled. Her once-lustrous hair hung lank and faded. She clearly had not been exposed to sunlight for months. Just now her eyes were wide with panic, staring at the corner of the room opposite that in

that the provocative display of flesh had disappeared. He went back into his quarters, giving the place a closer look now that he was free of distractions. The furnishings, while not lavish, were more than comfortable. Hangings covered the walls, and the floor was carpeted with thick Ophirian rugs. The lamps burned scented oil and this reminded him of something: When he had entered the room above, he had smelled smoke, yet the smell had disappeared almost instantly, and there had been not the slightest source of smoke within. There was not a single brazier, lamp or candle.

More significantly, it had not been any ordinary smoke. He had smelled its like before, and it was made by burning the dried stems and petals of the black lotus. This was used by certain students of the sorcerous arts to induce powerful visions. It was considered far too potent for any but the most advanced of students, and it could be dangerous even for them if the intake were not closely monitored.

He crossed to the window and opened the shutters. Leaning outside, he assessed his position. The window looked out over the pitched roof of the temple proper. The ridge of the lead-tiled roof was about five feet below his windowsill. He craned his head around and looked up. The girl's barred window was just above him. He chuckled. So they were worried that she would cast herself down upon the "pave below"? Rather, they were worried that she might escape.

Beyond the temple lay the Square, now quiet beneath the moon. To his right, a narrow alley separated the temple from the townhouse of Xanthus. To the left, an even narrower path separated the temple from the roof of another building, which, he remembered, was a public theater, and thus probably deserted between performances. It was another of the grandiose structures erected during the city's brief years of prosperity. Lightly, he sprang from his window onto the lead-tiled roof. From the nearby skylights he could hear the monotonous chanting of the worshipers below. Incense smoke drifted up as he walked along the roof, surefooted as the mountain goats of his native Cimmeria.

The alley separating the temple from the theater was no more than a long stride in width, and Conan stepped across it, onto a wide ledge running around the third floor of the theater. The facade of the building was covered with high-relief carvings, and these the Cimmerian climbed until he stood upon the structure's flat roof. Walking its perimeter, he surveyed the prospect beyond. Like the temple, the theater fronted on the Square. To its west side lay the temple. Its rear abutted another building, and along its east side ran the high street of the town. Conan knew that with a running leap, he could vault the high street to the rooftop on the other side. In fact, except for the broad, open space of the Square, he adjudged that he would be able to make his way to almost any part of the town by crossing rooftops. The route would be as easy as using any of the city streets, and undoubtedly a great deal cleaner.

Satisfied with his explorations, Conan returned to the roof of the temple. Looking up, he saw that the window directly above his was the only one on this side of the structure that was barred. Below his own window and the one above ran a narrow ledge that carried around the corners of the building to either side. He stepped onto the ledge outside his window and, pressing himself closely to the wall, began to edge his way toward the western corner. The ledge permitted little more than his toes and part of the ball of each foot, and on this building there was no high-relief carving to provide handholds. Only the rough surface of the stone allowed for a precarious grip. Few men would have been tempted to try such a maneuver, but Conan had been raised amid sheer stone and crumbling cliffs and he had no fear of heights.

The corner presented a problem, since there he could not press himself flat against the wall and would have to lean back slightly as he made his way around it. He was aided somewhat by a drain spout that ran down the facade. The thin bronze creaked slightly beneath the viselike grip of his fingers.

He edged along the eastern side of the building until he came to a tall window. This, he knew, opened to the room with the red door, to the quarters of Oppia and Andolla. With a cautious hand, he tested the wooden shutter. It was latched from the inside, but he could tell by its give that it was held by only a flimsy latch.

At a sound from within, he jerked his hand away and held his breath. It was the rattle of a key in a lock. There was the rasp of a door opening, then a rustling as several people entered the chamber. Nothing was said for a minute, but light began to seep between the boards of the shutter as lamps or candles were lighted within.

"You may go now," said Oppia's voice. There were pious murmurs, and then the closing of the door. She had dismissed the slave-acolytes.

"It is here!" said a voice Conan did not recognize. "It is in the city! I can feel it!" The voice was a man's. It was deep and resonant, like the voice of a trained herald or an actor, but it was full of an almost boyish enthusiasm.

"How do you know?" asked Oppia impatiently.

"Because it is magical and I can feel such things. When one has studied the arts and pried into secret and forbidden things as I have, the presence of an ancient source of great sorcerous power is not difficult to discern."

"Oh, Andolla my husband," Oppia said, "why must you persist in these foolish pursuits? We are rich and powerful as we are. We have wealth and we have slaves to do our bidding. No one ever came to a good end meddling in these things."

"Is what we do so grand?" he asked. "Fleecing young idiots by relieving them of any responsibility for their own lives? I was meant for better things."

"But, my husband," she pleaded, "where have we ever before found such a town? Here we need not be always looking over our shoulders for the king's men."

"At great cost to us," he asserted. "Fully one-third of all we take goes to the King's Reeve alone!"

"One third of our *admitted* take," she corrected. "And a few hundred each month to every gang leader. The rest is ours! I tell you, husband, that we have fallen into a situation richer than those silver mines outside of town. But if you persist in these sorcerous experiments, you will ruin it all. It is the sort of thing that draws notice. And if you buy this . . . this *thing*, the truly great mages may turn their attention toward this wretched little city. Would you attract the likes of Thoth-Amon and the others?''

"With it in my hands," he said haughtily, "I will be their equal!"

"You cannot believe that!" she cried. "A few years of dabbling in forbidden arts, studying a few books of doubtful authenticity, cannot make you the equal of those who have spent many human lifetimes in mastering the arts."

"Nevertheless," he said, "I must have it, and I will have it!"

The squabbling voices faded, and Conan knew that the two had gone into another room. He had heard enough. Carefully, he made his way back around the corner and into his quarters.

He undressed and pulled back the luxurious covers of his bed, but before he lay down, he pulled a chair close to the bed and drew his sword. He set the weapon with its grip slanting toward the bed; his hand could grasp it instantly at need. It was a precaution he never omitted when he slept amid possible enemies. Nor, for that matter, when he slept amid friends.

TEN

The Royal Warehouse

He left the temple in the morning when he could no longer abide the endless chanting, the smell of incense, and the presence of mindless fools. It seemed astonishing to him that the victims could be so happy while being robbed and enslaved. Even sheer stupidity could not account for it. He suspected that there might be a drug at work. If those in charge were willing to use black lotus smoke on just one of their victims, they would not balk at using milder potions to keep the rest in line.

He had a specific goal this day. He now had a working knowledge of the town's streets and alleys. The rooftop routes were there, yet to be further explored, but that project would have to await the fall of night. Most civilized towns had a third means of access, usually unseen and unknown even to the citizenry, and he knew just where to find the information leading to it.

The Pit was, as customary, all but deserted in the early morning hours, but he knew from experience that there was one class of inhabitant that conducted the first part of its business in the hours of darkness and concluded it in the early morning.

At the Temple of Bes he found a deep, shadowed doorway facing the entrance and waited patiently. Within the space of an hour, five men passed furtively within, each bearing a bulky sack. Each left with an empty sack, but the Cimmerian knew that each would have a bulging purse secreted upon his person. The sixth man turned out to be the one he needed. The man was small, and his shoes left damp footprints behind him. The sack he bore over one shoulder clanked slightly. The smell was unmistakable.

When the man emerged from the temple, smiling and stuffing his now-empty sack into the breast of his doublet, he found the towering barbarian planted firmly in his path. Mouth agape, he looked up past the armored chest to the glowering face.

"Wh-what business have you with me, stranger?" he stammered. Conan saw that he was little more than a boy.

"Some information," Conan said.

At this the boy straightened and stuck out his chest in a pathetic show of defiance. "Be you a king's man? I am no informer!" Since he did not add a qualifying price for such dishonorable behavior, Conan's opinion of him went up by a notch.

"You may be the only man in town so scrupulous," the Cimmerian told him. "Nay, lad, I just need a guide. I've but newly arrived in Sicas and am not yet familiar with the town. As you know, there are times when a man needs to get about on matters of business without being seen by the common run of citizens. This is a well-built royal city, and I know that it has sewers and drains. I'll make it well worth your time to reveal to me the secrets of this system."

Now the boy smiled complacently. "Well, outlander, you have come to the right man. No enterprising businessman of this city knows the lower paths so well as Ulf the Unseen." He tapped his bony chest significantly. Then he eyed the Cimmerian's bulk with speculation. "I can show you the main passages. Some of the side tunnels may be too small for you."

"That will be sufficient," Conan assured him. "I just need to know how to pass swiftly and invisibly from one district of the town to another.'' He took a broad gold piece from his pouch and tossed it to Ulf. "Let us be on our way."

"Come,'' said the boy. "We'll start at the river drain.'' They walked toward the confluence of the rivers, which was but a short distance away. Here the low river walls formed an angle, and within the angle was a stone slab set into the pavement. Ulf grasped a bronze ring embedded in the slab and tugged upward. Despite its obvious mass, the slab yielded easily to the frail youth.

"To one who knows not the craft,'' said Ulf, "this slab is very weighty. But it you twist the ring so—'' he showed the Cimmerian how the bronze ring could be moved "—it releases a counterweight inside that does most of the work. This was installed more than three hundred years ago by the legendary burglar Mopsus the Locksmith. It has been a secret of the burglars' guild ever since.''

"Then will you not be punished for showing me the secret?'' Conan asked. "In other towns, the guilds have strict rules and severe punishments.''

Ulf shrugged wistfully. "The days of honorable guilds are long past in this town, stranger. Most of them have been shut down by the outside gangs that have moved in. Maxio's men assassinated all of our guild chiefs last year. Those of us who got away have kept some of our secrets, but there is little point now.''

"Have they not tried to get the information out of you?'' Conan asked.

"What need have they? Maxio's band are a haughty lot and act as if they are too good to be running around in sewers. They get their way by bribery and intimidation.'' He dropped lightly through the manhole.

Conan dropped after him as lightly. "I have not as yet encountered Maxio. What is he like?''

"Avoid him,'' Ulf advised. "He's a smooth little schemer, but as treacherous and murderous as any. The rules of our guild forbid us to carry arms while we are working, and they require that we leave at first sign of a wakeful person, even if it means abandoning rich loot. But Maxio's gang obeys no such rules. Not only have they slain rival burglars, they have even murdered men and women who have come upon them at their work. Shocking behavior!''

Conan surveyed the chamber in which they stood. Its vaulted walls were of brick, forming an arch overhead. It was just high enough for Conan to stand upright. At its southern extremity, morning light came through a rusty iron grating that covered an opening about four feet on a side. At their feet, a narrow stream made its way out through the grate and down to the river, nearly five feet below.

"This is the Great Drain," Ulf informed him. "It runs beneath the high street for its full length. If ever you are lost down here, just determine which way the floor slopes and follow it downward. Eventually it will bring you to the Great Drain."

Conan eyed the grate. "Does the river ever rise high enough to back into the sewers?"

"It happens every few years," Ulf said, "and I would not wish to be here then. Usually there is plenty of warning, though. It happens only after heavy rains in the hills to the north."

"Is it possible to get out through that grate?" Conan asked.

"That is not necessary," Ulf said. He walked to the grate and Conan followed. "Here at the grate you are outside the river wall." He reached upward and pressed a brick that protruded slightly from the others. A section of the brick ceiling swung smoothly downward. Its upper surface was made of molded cement that resembled a part of a boulder. Conan sprang up and gripped the edge of the hole with the tips of his fingers, then pulled himself up to look outside. He saw a rocky slope angling down to the river. Behind him was the angle of the river wall. He dropped back to the damp floor of the tunnel.

"Mopsus the Locksmith again?"

Ulf nodded. "You'll be hearing a lot about him as you tour the deep ways." He took a skin-covered object from his belt and peeled away the cover, revealing a small but finely crafted lamp. With flint and steel he struck a light and closed the crystal window. It cast a strong illumination for a lamp so small, and Ulf proudly displayed the way its beam could be adjusted with a clever shutter.

"This lamp was my father's and his father's before him," he proclaimed. "All of the men of my line have risen high in the guild."

Turning north, they began the tour. Ulf took the Cimmerian through the side tunnels that were large enough to admit the outlander's size, identifying the streets and major buildings above. Occasionally they passed beneath grated drains in the centers of the streets, and when they did, Ulf closed the shutter of his lamp, although the likelihood of observation from above was slight. "Guild rules," was all he would say. "Old habits are hard to break."

Once Conan stopped and had the lad cast his beam toward an odd mark carved into the wall beneath a square hatch of heavy timber. "This looks like the secret writing of the Guild of Poitainian Thieves."

"You are a scholar, I see," Ulf said approvingly. "Yes, it is used throughout Aquilonia as well. This mark identifies that hatch as access to the cellar of the Wyvern."

Traveling northward in the Great Drain, they passed through a heavy stone foundation. "This is the old city wall," Ulf said, "torn down two hundred years ago at the time of the great expansion. Naught but its foundations remain. The Great Drain is the only underground passageway through the old wall; you must remember that."

Farther on, the tunnel was faced with stone instead of with brick and was somewhat more spacious. The smell, however, was no better. Soon they came to a tunnel that was almost as large as the Great Drain. A broad grate in its ceiling admitted abundant sunlight.

"This is the tunnel that runs beneath the Square," Ulf said. "That drainage grate is in its center." He shivered slightly. "These last two years, I've seen blood coming down through that grate some mornings."

"The gangs here are lively," Conan agreed. "Does this tunnel pass beneath the Reeve's headquarters?"

Ulf shook his head. "It was decided not to cut into it. Too much chance of meeting with prisoners tunneling their way *out*, you see. We couldn't very well let dishonorable men learn of our passageways. Besides," he added, "it's all too easy to end up in those dungeons as it is."

Still following the high street, they proceeded up the Great Drain, which was straighter than in the old city. Conan pointed down a tunnel branching to the left.

"Does that run beneath the new theater, the big temple, and the house of Xanthus?"

"You've a good sense of direction," Ulf complimented.

"Aye."

"And are there accesses to all those buildings?"

Ulf shook his head. "Beneath the theater, yes, but not beneath the others. The theater cellar is one of our gathering places. The temple has a drain running from the main altar down through the cellar. That's for the blood of sacrificial animals and the oil and wine that are poured out to the god. Most temples have such a drain, but it is a passage only about a foot square, too small for a man to pass through."

"And the house of Xanthus?" Conan inquired.

"The house of Xanthus is forbidden to us. That family has had dealings with our guild for generations and there is no access."

That made sense. "Show me the way into the theater," he said.

Ulf guided him down the side passage to another ceiling trap, which he pushed open amid much creaking. "The trouble with the new part of town," he said, "is that we have no more of the fine doorways crafted by Mopsus the Locksmith." He shook his head and sighed. "The gods don't make them like Mopsus anymore."

"I want to have a look," Conan said, pulling himself up through the trap. Ulf followed him. The lamp revealed a cavernous room full of props: masks, backdrop paintings, old benches, ropes, curtain weights, racks of stage lamps, and all the miscellaneous debris of a theater that has been in operation for a good number of years.

"What do you want here?" Ulf asked. "There is little worth stealing in a theater. Besides, theater people and thieves usually get on well together, having much in common."

"I am more interested in the location than in the contents. Do you know the inside of the building well?"

"Intimately," the lad said. "As a boy, I explored the whole place when my father and uncles came here for guild meetings."

"Show me how to get to the roof," the Cimmerian said.

They went up a flight of stairs to a backstage chamber. The floorboards echoed softly beneath their feet. Behind the curtains, the stage surface was littered with rotting fruit. Apparently the last performance had been unsatisfactory and the company had departed without cleaning up.

In the wings beyond the stage, Conan followed Ulf up a wooden stair that zigzagged its way up to a catwalk from which the curtains were controlled. Another stair led from that to a cupola set atop the roof. Ulf opened the cupola's door and gestured outside. Both men squinted through the bright light at the lead-sheathed roof. Conan saw the parapet and the roof of the temple beyond.

"This is what I wanted to see," he pronounced, shutting the door. "Let's go back."

They resumed their tour, always traveling up the Great Drain, occasionally going off into side tunnels, where Ulf identified their location when they reached various prominent sites of the city. Most of the accesses were marked with the enigmatic sigils of the Poitainian thieves' guild. The tunnel ended at a blank wall.

"We are now just below the main gate of the landward wall," Ulf said.

"There is no passage to the other side of the wall?" Conan asked.

"No. I do not suppose that escaping from the city ever occurred to the guild. If one had to do that, the river hatch is a better way. There is seldom a watchman stationed on the river wall."

"It is sufficient," Conan said. "You've been an excellent guide." They walked back to the angle of the river wall, taking only a few minutes to traverse the length of the city. When they emerged, Conan tossed Ulf another coin.

"Here. You've served me better than I had hoped. And be of good cheer. I think that soon things in this town will settle back into the old ways and your guild can resume its former customs. Do not worry that you have revealed the secrets of the underground passages to me, for I'll be long gone."

Ulf favored him with a gap-toothed grin. "You look like one who can truly stir things up, but I cannot believe that a single man can set things aright in this city."

"Have no fear," Conan told him. "I will not be alone when things began to happen. The next few days may be a good time for you to lie low. Keep clear of the Temple of Bes, and watch out for Maxio's crowd. They may grow short-tempered very soon."

The boy gaped. "You have this all planned, do you?"

"Not entirely," Conan told him. "But things are shaping up nicely. With men as foul as those who run roughshod over this town, trouble is never far away. To bring everything down, it is only necessary to provide a lot of trouble all at once."

Ulf shook his head. "Well, it escapes me how you propose to do this."

"Leave it to me. By the way, I have heard that Emrak's men rounded up the miners' wives and children and hold them hostage someplace to guarantee the miners' good behavior. Know you where they might be?"

"Nay. The whole incident is a matter of rumor and whispers. The miners have kept to themselves, and they used to be the rowdiest men in the district. These days you see only a few of the old people from the mine settlement. No one speaks openly of it."

"I'll find out," Conan promised.

"I think you will," Ulf said, nodding. "Well, farewell, outlander. I've had a long day's work and it is past my bedtime. I think I'll sleep for ten days or thereabout, keeping your advice in mind.''

They parted, and Conan walked back toward the center of town. He took a detour into the Street of the Shoemakers to buy a new pair of boots. His sojourn in the sewers had ruined those he had on his feet. The way people stood back from him reminded the Cimmerian that he had better remove the aftereffects of his subterranean exploration before returning to the temple. He found a public bathhouse.

After turning over his clothes to the laundresses, he luxuriated in a deep wooden tub of near-scalding water, pondering his next move. He wanted a look at Maxio. He had yet to encounter Lisip or Ingas, but he had seen enough of their men to have a low opinion of the pair. He had been inclined to favor Ermak's men, who at least were professional fighting men like himself, until he learned of their abduction of the women and children of the mining community.

There was a knock at the wooden partition next to the tub. Conan's hand went to his sword-hilt; as always, the weapon was ready to hand. Then the panel slid back to reveal a familiar face and a good deal of the body below it. The sliding partition separated the men's and women's sides of the establishment. As in most such places, the necessity of separation was interpreted liberally, hence the movable divider.

"Good day, Cimmerian," said Delia. Droplets of condensed steam clung to her hair, which she had piled on top of her head. She leaned back on her elbows, apparently perched on one of the deep tub's steps, for the water lapped only to her navel, which, Conan noted with interest, contained a very fine star sapphire.

"Greeting, Delia," he said. "Is it just a coincidence that we chose the same bathhouse today?"

"Don't be ridiculous," she said. "I saw you ducking in here and decided that I needed a bath as well." A pearl necklace with a ruby pendant decorated her neck and the deep valley between her breasts, which were, as she had boasted, nearly as spectacular as Mother Doorgah's. "After all, we don't want to be seen too much in company publicly."

"Do we not?" he asked.

"Well, it wouldn't be wise . . . not just yet, that is." There was a conspiratorial edge to her voice, a tone he was growing weary of, having heard it so often in this town.

"And what about later?" he asked.

"Well, that depends upon what you do with what I am about to tell you," she said, looking up at the ceiling with an expression of innocence that was utterly foreign to her handsome face.

"Out with it then," he said impatiently. "Be assured, you have gained my attention."

"Getting a man's attention is easy," she said wistfully, trailing her hands downward over her voluptuous body, from collarbones to hips. "Keeping it is another matter."

"Trouble with Maxio, eh?" the Cimmerian inquired.

"He is tiring of me," she replied, "and his eyes wander toward women not half as beautiful as I. He is bored with me. Can you imagine ever becoming bored with me?" she demanded, her lovely eyes flashing.

"I could not think of it," Conan muttered. In truth, the woman was certainly difficult to ignore.

"You are a better man than Maxio," she said. "You know how to appreciate a woman like me. And for that reason, I will favor you with that bit of information we spoke of the other night."

Conan was amazed that she had any memory of the evening at all. "You mean Maxio's job?"

"Exactly. I now know when it will take place."

"Then tell me," he urged.

"Not so fast," she chided. "A woman must look out for herself, you know. You are a splendid figure of a man, and I think you and I may have a great future together, but suppose that you and Maxio kill each other. Where would I be then?"

"How much?" Conan asked.

"Two hundred marks," she said. "Gold."

He laughed. "Twenty would be more like it!"

"Do you take me for some petty informer?" she demanded, splashing the water petulantly. "One hundred fifty, no less."

"Seventy-five," he said, "and I expect full details."

"One hundred twenty-five, and it is only because you are so handsome that I even consider so low a sum!"

"One hundred," Conan countered. "Just imagine me as being ugly."

She sighed. "Done, but it is only because I burn for the touch of your hands upon me. It is to be tonight."

"What time?" Conan demanded.

"Three hours after the fall of night. Do you know where the royal storehouse is?"

"I have seen it," Conan answered.

"There are two floors, with no windows on the ground floor and only small, barred windows on the second. The roof is flat, made of heavy timbers covered with lead tiles. The walls are very thick." She had put aside her flirtation, and her voice became brisk and businesslike.

"How does Maxio propose to get in?"

"For several months now," she said, "Maxio's men have been going up on the roof. They've detached certain of the lead tiles, and they've been sawing away quietly at the timbers with a special, very thin blade. While one saws, another sucks up the sawdust with a copper tube covered at one end with gauze. They're down to the last half-inch now, and tonight they'll go in."

"How many of them?"

"Five besides Maxio to go inside. Three to carry the loot to their cart, and one in the cart."

"How do they gain the roof of the storehouse?" Conan asked.

"Behind the storehouse is an alley and beyond that, the Temple of Anu. They've bribed the priest of the temple for use of an upper room, supposedly to hide out from other gangs, but really because you can get from there to the roof. In the room, they keep a plank bridge for crossing the alley. Tonight they'll have their cart hidden in a side courtyard next to the temple. They'll cover the loot with canvas, and on top of that goes a load of dung.

When the gate opens in the morning, it will be just another dung-gatherer's cart heading out to sell fertilizer to the local farms.''

Delia leaned back and raised water in her cupped hands, tilting it to cascade over her body. "Maxio says that he will lie low, that the theft may not even be discovered for days, but I do not believe him. I think he will leave with the loot tonight, and abandon me here.''

"He is a treacherous wretch indeed,'' Conan said.

"Well, do you not think that is worth a hundred marks to you?''

"Surely you don't think that Maxio would let me in on a feat that he has been preparing for months?'' he asked.

She smiled slyly. "A man of your wit will find a way to turn this information to advantage.''

"No doubt,'' he answered. He took his belt pouch from where it lay by his sword and separated the requisite coins, which he placed in her damp palm.

She surveyed her bare, voluptuous form. "Now where am I going to put this?'' she asked, coquettishly.

"That is your problem,'' Conan replied, sliding the partition firmly shut. From beyond it, he heard her full-throated laughter.

Treacherous bitch, he thought, but he was unable to summon up much rancor toward her. There was something robustly innocent in Delia's amorality. She was, indeed, a lone woman among predatory men, and who would blame her for selling one to another, especially if that one was about to abandon her? She was an experienced woman, and Conan did not doubt that she was correct on that point. It must have happened to her with some frequency in the past.

A laundress brought in his clothes, newly scrubbed of their sewer effluvium and dried by the cellar furnace that heated the water for the baths. He had himself shaved by the establishment's barber, buckled on his brigandine, resumed his weapons, and went out to see what else the day had to offer.

In a stall on a side street he saw an old woman selling silken scarves. On impulse, he asked her if she had seen Brita. The crone eyed him sourly.

"That poor, mad lass who runs all over town seeking her sister? I see her nearly every day lately. If you are her man, you had best lock her up before she's killed, or worse. How she has stayed alive and free in this town is a mystery. I hear that she even roams about at night. She must be under the special protection of some god."

"And her sister?" Conan asked.

"Could be any of a hundred girls around here." A cunning gleam came to her eye. "P'r'aps she's just angry with you and that's why she's away from you all day and all night. A present might win her favor back. A silk scarf, perchance?"

He shook his head and left the old woman cackling behind him. A random check of gossipy shopkeepers confirmed that Brita was still engaged in her futile search. He was beginning to doubt her sanity. She needed a caretaker, but that was not a task he wished to assume. He was a free man, subject to all of the risks inherent to that state. He no more wanted to be tied down by a madwoman than by a wife.

Cloaked and hooded, the Cimmerian appeared at the headquarters of the King's Reeve with the fall of night. The rickety guards gaped at him from the doorway.

"I must have words with the Reeve," Conan told them.

"But he is still at table," said one.

"Then he can invite me to share supper with him," said Conan. "I have information that he greatly wishes to hear. Tell him that it is a matter of which we have spoken before."

Shaking his head and clucking, one of the guards disappeared into the interior. Conan hoped the man would be able to retain the message in his aged mind. A few minutes later the hulking Julus appeared.

"My master will see you now. Do not waste his time."

Conan did not bother to answer; he merely followed the guard to a spacious room, where Bombas sat at table. The table was heaped with viands, but there was only a single setting. Numerous plates of bones and other devastated foodstuffs already littered the broad surface. Still biting into a joint of meat, the Reeve raised bleary eyes toward the intruder.

"What do you want?" he demanded past a mouthful of venison.

"You bade me come to you should I have certain information you desire." Behind him, Julus lounged against a wall, arms folded casually across his broad breast.

"Say on." Bombas set down the joint and wiped his fingers on a napkin.

"Do you still want Maxio?" Conan asked. "I can give him to you, this very night."

The bloodshot eyes sharpened and the Reeve almost smiled. He gestured to a seat opposite him. "Sit you down, foreigner. Have something to eat."

"I have already eaten," Conan said, taking a chair. The Reeve signaled and a slave girl filled a cup, which the Cimmerian took.

"Now, tell me what you know."

Briefly, Conan outlined what Delia had told him. The Reeve chewed and nodded. He drank heavily, but his eyes never lost their cunning gleam. When the recitation was done, he wiped his mouth.

"Very good, very good, my friend. You shall be richly rewarded for this." He leaned forward. "*If* what you say proves to be true."

"What do you mean?" Conan demanded hotly. "Do you think I would lie?"

"Easy, man. Curb your tongue," the Reeve cautioned. "Your words have the sound of truth, but I must be cautious. How came you by this information?"

"I have made friends in the Pit," Conan said. "You understand, I would never learn anything if I let my sources of information be known."

"Aye. I see that you know the rules of this game. Well, no matter. Nothing counts but that I have my brother's slayer in my grasp." He closed a chubby fist as if squeezing something. "Tonight we'll bag the lot."

"Very good," Conan said. "And my reward?"

"Not so fast," Bombas cautioned, chuckling. "That comes only after I have Maxio."

Conan shrugged. "That suits me. I will come by for it on the morrow." He made as if to leave, knowing that he would not.

"Just a moment," Bombas said sternly. "Sit down. I want you to go with us this night."

"Wherefore?" asked Conan.

"Because I am yet uneasy about you. I want you to stay close by me until this business is done. Now tell me, barbarian, why a man like Rista Daan was willing to pay so well to have you out of my dungeon."

"That is between him and me," Conan answered. "However, if the very wealthy and distinguished Rista Daan wishes to inform you, you need only ask him."

Bombas shifted uneasily in his seat. "Oh, well, I suppose it is of no account." He turned to Julus. "Get the men together," he ordered. The big man smirked slightly at the word "men" but went to do is master's bidding. When Julus was gone, the Reeve turned back to face the Cimmerian.

"What sort of man are you, Conan?" he asked. "You are handy with weapons, but you haven't sought to join any of the gangs. You interest me."

"I work for myself," Conan said, not taken in by the Reeve's suddenly friendly tone. "Sometimes people hire me for a particular service. I prefer that to long-term employment."

"A mercenary, eh? Just pay, no oath of fealty for you, is that the way of it?"

"Something like that," Conan agreed.

"Well, perhaps after tonight you'll wish to take service with me. I'm a generous master, just ask any of my men." He chuckled merrily, apparently in the best of spirits.

"I did not think you hired men who were sound of limb," Conan said, enjoying the way the fat face went red.

"I can always use a good man," Bombas said, "as long as he knows how to curb his tongue."

They waited in silence for a few minutes; then Julus returned to report that all was ready. From the dining room they went to the armory, where Bombas's contemptible force was assembled. Conan noted that all were now equipped with crossbows, the only weapons with which they could possibly be of menace to sound, experienced fighting men. The two silent Zingarans were there, and these two, along with Julus, were the only men to whom the Cimmerian accorded a second thought.

From the Reeve's headquarters they passed through back alleys unseen. In this better part of the town, all were indoors early, the doors barred and their windows shuttered. Honest citizens wanted nothing to do with a band of armed men moving about the city after dark. Conan thought wryly that in daylight, this group would provoke more laughter than fear.

Near the royal warehouse, Bombas stationed men in doorways and dark alleys on three sides of the building, leaving untended the side fronting the Temple of Anu. Last of all, he went into the small shrine of a local god. From it, one could see both the temple and the storehouse. The moonlight dimly illuminated the strip of sky between the two buildings. According to Delia, that strip would soon be bisected by the burglars' plank bridge.

"Now we wait," announced Bombas. The fat Reeve, the bulky Julus and the two slight but deadly Zingarans, together with Conan, crowded the little shrine to capacity.

For more than an hour, no one spoke. The Cimmerian forced himself to the patient, but the task was not easy. The Reeve smelled sourly of wine, the others of the sweat of tension. Bombas's nerves began to play on him.

"Barbarian," he hissed, "have you brought us—"

"There!" Conan whispered. He pointed to the grayish strip of sky before and above them. Something slid across the space like the tongue of a dragon. "The bridge."

Moments later they saw stealthy forms crossing the plank, making no sound. Within the shrine all was gloom, but enough moonlight penetrated for Conan to see the shine of the Reeve's teeth as the man grinned triumphantly.

"You did not speak idly, foreigner," said Bombas. "We will wait here now. Let them busy themselves within. Let them feel comfortable. We do nothing until I give the signal."

For several more minutes they waited. By straining their ears, they could just hear faint rustling sounds from above. There were some muffled cracks, undoubtedly signifying the completion of the rooftop passageway into the storehouse.

"Soon now," said the Reeve. Then, when a number of minutes passed without further sound, he turned to Conan. "Barbarian, I want you to go in there. Go up to the roof and drop through their hole. Tell them to surrender themselves and I will show them mercy."

"Why should I do that?" Conan demanded.

"Because I order it," said the Reeve. Then, in an almost wheedling tone: "There will be no danger. You are a warrior, fully armed, and they are just burglars, probably not even carrying weapons."

"But you have a key to the front door," Conan protested. "Why not just go in and shout up the stairs?"

"They would scatter," said Bombas. "You can block their exit from the hole they've made while we come in from the front."

"Why not use one of your own men for the purpose?" Conan asked.

"They would make noise. I've always heard that Cimmerians can climb like mountain goats. You can do it easily and silently. Go now. There is no danger, and I will increase your reward. How sounds a thousand golden marks?"

"Half as good as two thousand," said Conan.

"Two thousand then!" said Bombas, fuming. "Now go!"

The Cimmerian stepped from the shrine and walked around to the front of the Temple of Anu. There was a cheerful spring in his step because he had enjoyed making the fat Reeve sweat. It amused him that Bombas had bargained, fully aware that he would pay nothing. Conan decided that meanness was so much a part of the man's character that he could not even feign generosity in order to tempt a victim to his death.

The front of the temple was plain, but the facade had been ornamented, some of the stones protruding a few inches from the others in pleasing patterns. These provided adequate finger-and toe-holds for Conan, who scaled the wall easily. At the parapet, he raised his head slowly until he could see across the roof. It was deserted.

He swarmed over the parapet and crossed the roof. The plank bridge was still in place. Before crossing, he went to the side of the building where Delia had said there was a courtyard. The cart was there, barely visible, its black-garbed driver clucking quietly to the draft ox, keeping the beast still.

The Cimmerian crossed the roof and walked across the bridge as easily as if he strode the stones of the Square. The roof of the royal warehouse was not truly flat, but had a noticeable slope for purposes of drainage. The dull lead tiles sucked up moonlight so efficiently that they were all but invisible, yet Conan could see a faint light gleaming through a ragged hole a few paces ahead. He strode to the hole and looked down. Below, voices spoke in loud whispers. It seemed to him that they also spoke in anger. He dropped through the gap and hung for a moment by his fingertips, then dropped the final few feet to the floor. Men turned to gape at him.

"Who are you?" demanded one.

"No time for that," Conan said. "You're betrayed! Bombas and his men are out there, and they intend to kill you all. If you would live, you had better get away at once. Which of you is Maxio?"

A wiry man of medium height came up to him. He wore dark clothes and a close-fitting hood with a long tail that dangled down his back. Like the others, he held a dagger, drawn at the sudden apparition of the huge barbarian.

"I'm Maxio, and just who are you?" He held his blade angled toward Conan's throat.

"No time for that," Conan said again. "They'll be storming through the front door in a moment, and Bombas has a grudge against you."

A seam-faced man spat on the straw that was ankle deep on the floor. "What have we to fear from Bombas or his men? I'd relish carving the fat toad myself!"

"Ermak's men are with them," Conan said. Instantly, the men grew pale and staring.

"Ermak!" said Maxio, mouthing the name like a curse. "That villain will take any man's pay!"

There was a crashing sound from below as the great front door swung open and smashed against a wall. "Kill them!" bellowed a voice up the stairs. "Up, and kill them all! No mercy!" It was Bombas.

"Do you believe me now?" Conan said.

A form appeared at the top of a stair to the lower floor. It was one of the Zingarans, and he had his crossbow leveled directly at Conan's breast. It was a powerful weapon, easily able to pierce the Cimmerian's light armor. The snap of the string's release and Conan's lightning-swift dodge occurred at the same instant. The bolt whizzed past him and made a sickening thud as it struck a hapless burglar. Even as the man fell, Conan snatched the dagger from the nerveless fingers, whirled and flung it with unerring accuracy and tremendous force. It pierced the Zingaran's throat and crunched through the vertebrae to protrude a handbreadth behind the man's neck. He pitched back down the stair, spraying blood. Between the snap of the string and the impact of the dagger into the man's throat, scarcely two heartbeats had elapsed.

Maxio gave a low whistle of appreciation. "You know your business, stranger." Then, to his men, "Out!" he snapped. They piled bales and began to climb out, but the first through fell back, a bolt in his chest.

"They're on the temple roof," Conan said. No more faces appeared at the stair, but something more ominous did: smoke.

"The warehouse is afire!" cried one of the burglars, his voice rising with panic.

"Then it's burn or be skewered," Conan said. "Here, grab some of these bales of cloth and push them out ahead of you. They may absorb the bolts while you make a run for it." The men faltered; then the sound of crackling came from below. At that there was a sudden burst of activity. Men snatched up thick bundles of cloth and scrambled up the improvised ladder. Most of them made it through, and the Cimmerian and his new companion could hear a commotion outside.

"Floor's getting hot," Conan commented. "Time for us to leave." He all but ran up the piled bales and through the hole, then reached back and drew Maxio out. "You know the rooftops better than I do," he said. "What's a good way out of here?" Dead men lay on the roof of the storehouse, and on the roof of the temple other men were struggling. The plank bridge had been knocked away. Nobody was shooting at them, and someone was raising a fire alarm. A lurid glare began to pulse through the ragged hole in the roof.

"This way," said Maxio. They crossed to the side of the roof opposite the shrine from which Conan and the Reeve had watched the alley. Here a lower building abutted the storehouse, and the two men sprang down to its roof. They ran across and Maxio dropped from there onto a balcony, the Cimmerian following close behind. They sprang onto another balcony across a narrow street, then ran through the upper floor of what seemed to be a deserted building. From there they exited a ground-floor doorway onto an empty street.

"The old town is better for this sort of thing," Maxio said. "You can get anywhere without ever coming down from the roofs. We're far enough away to be safe now. Let's not hang about here, though. I am more comfortable in the lower city."

"To the Wyvern, then," said Conan. The two made their stealthy way until they reached the old town, where the near-black streets and the indifference of the inhabitants made stealth unnecessary.

At the sign of the Wyvern, they descended the stair to the door and stood upon the landing, surveying the scene. The tavern entertained its usual villainous clientele, who surveyed the newcomers in turn. The two elicited only a passing interest before they descended to the main floor and secured an empty table in a corner. A large bloodstain on the wall behind one of the chairs identified the table as the scene of a disagreement earlier that evening. A candle guttered in a holder carven in the form of a naked Stygian dancer.

At their order, a server brought wine for Maxio, ale for Conan. The two men clinked their vessels together and drank. Maxio was first to speak.

"I do not believe we have met, and you are not the sort of man I would readily forget. Who are you, stranger?"

"I am Conan of Cimmeria." He took a long drink. The autumn brewing had just been broached, and it was excellent ale.

"I have heard of you. You've made a reputation for yourself in a short time. So tell me: How did you happen to drop through our hole in the storehouse roof just in time to warn us of the ambush?"

"Your woman Delia got wind of it and asked me to go warn you before Bombas laid his hands on you."

"Delia!" he said, amazed. "Well, perhaps the wench is not as worthless as I had adjudged. She's a beauty, but she drinks like a public drain and talks far too much. And I cannot abide her cats. I half expected her to sell me to Bombas. How did she find out about the ambush?"

Conan shrugged. "I've no idea." He would not complicate matters by inventing a story for her. Doubtless the woman would dream up one of her own.

"Why did she choose you to send?" Maxio asked.

"She saw me kill those three men of Ingas's the other day. Tonight she needed a man of courage and skill and so she sought me out, knowing that I am not working for any of the gang lords. And I expect to be paid."

"Be assured of it," Maxio said. "I would not let such a service go unrequited." He gazed into his wine cup. "I will pay you . . . that is, as soon as I have restored my fortunes."

"Did you get away with nothing from the royal storehouse?" Conan asked.

"There was nothing worth the stealing in the place," Maxio

said, sounding mystified. "Just bulk goods, no precious metals or jewels."

"I thought I heard the sound of voices arguing before I dropped in," Conan said.

"Aye. The men wanted to hold me responsible for the dearth. But the royal warehouse should be full at this time of year. The king's share is taken to Tarantia at the beginning of the new year, which is not far off."

Conan smiled to himself as another piece of the puzzle clicked into place. "Tell me, why was there no watchman at the storehouse?"

"Because he was long gone ere you arrived," Maxio said. "He's just another of Bombas's drunken old beggars. I'd been paying him for months to hold his tongue, and tonight I gave him his final payment. He was to flee town with it." Maxio nodded and stroked his chin. "It was probably that old sot who tipped Bombas."

"Perhaps," Conan said. "But doesn't it seem strange to you that the King's Reeve would set fire to the royal storehouse just to smoke out some burglars?"

"I didn't think of that in all the excitement," Maxio admitted. "The way the place was going up when we left, it must be naught but glowing embers by now."

"And no way of saying what was in it before the fire," Conan pointed out.

A look of sudden comprehension suffused Maxio's lean features. "That fat, scheming pig! He's looted the place himself! Now he'll report that he went there to catch the thieves and that they set the fire to aid their escape." He glared and called for more wine. "Bad enough to be thwarted after so much work. Far worse to do Bombas such a good turn. Who would have thought that hog-eyed barrel of suet could be so clever?"

"It does not pay to underestimate men just because they look stupid," Conan said.

Maxio drank deep of his second tankard of wine and slammed it to the scarred table. "And Ermak! He's always hated me, but to work for Bombas just to catch me! That's it, then. From now on, it's to the death between me and Ermak!''

"Brave speech," Conan said, "but he is a professional, with a pack of trained killers. You probably lost half of your band tonight, and your men are just second-story burglars. How do you propose to deal with Ermak?''

"I will think of something," Maxio said. He dipped his fingers into his wine and flung a few drops to the floor in token of a vow. "There are many in this town who would aid me in ridding ourselves of those strutting bandits who call themselves soldiers.''

"Good fortune, then," said Conan, "and do not forget that you owe me for tonight." He began to rise, then remembered something. "By the way, what know you of a man named Asdras?''

Maxio's eyebrows rose slightly. "You mean the man who was dirked out back in the alley a few nights ago? I diced with him a few times, as did nearly everyone in the Wyvern. Just another second-rate gambler and would-be adventurer, from what I saw, getting by mainly on looks and luck. Why do you ask?''

"I am not truly interested in him," Conan said, "but he is supposed to have come here in company with a young woman, little more than a girl, named Ylla. She is small and fair-haired. Have you seen aught of such a lass?''

Maxio shook his hooded head. "Neither seen nor heard." He considered the question further for a moment. "Asdras didn't talk much about himself, but from what he did say, it seemed to me that he was *waiting* for a woman to arrive. Once I heard him say that she was a beautiful black-haired wench, and as dangerous as a viper.''

"Did he speak her name?" Conan asked.

"Alta? Altena? I think it was something like that. I paid little heed at the time. There's small profit to be had in another man's problems with women. I've enough troubles with my own.''

"So you have," Conan affirmed. He rose and bade Maxio farewell, then left the Wyvern. Stretching and yawning, he made his way through the deserted streets of Sicas. As he passed the Square, the moonlight glinted silver upon the marble monuments. To the north, a reddish glow proclaimed that the fire was not yet extinguished.

In the temple, he passed the nave by way of the second-floor gallery. Below, a handful of acolytes kept up their chanting before the statue of Mother Doorgah. As the Cimmerian returned to his quarters, he entertained himself with the thought that very soon now, all that chanting would stop for good.

ELEVEN
The Tavern Of The Iron Skull

He awoke with light streaming through the single window of his room, but it was the light of late day. He rose and stretched, then crossed to the basin of water that stood in a corner. He splashed his face and toweled vigorously. Through the window he could see a large part of the Square beyond the temple roof. The stall-keepers were dismantling their tables and awnings. From a distance, he heard the great bell toll above the city gate. It would ring thrice, at intervals of about half an hour, and upon the third ring, the gate would be closed for the night.

He did not regret having slept the day away. In fact, he decided, it might be the best thing to avoid moving about in broad daylight for a while. He was acquiring enemies at a great rate. The Cimmerian armed himself and left his room. As he passed along the upper gallery, his attention was drawn to the service in progress in the temple below.

The crowd was larger than usual, and he noticed that not all those present wore the robes of an acolyte. There were about twenty newcomers. They were of both sexes, and all of them were

richly attired in silks and velvets. Here and there he saw the furs
of marten and sable.

The air was thick with smoke, and a group of acolytes sat
cross-legged behind the huge idol, making a clangorous, tuneless
music with flute, drum, cymbal, and stringed instrument. Andolla stood before the idol, at his feet a golden basin, steaming
over a green flame. With hands raised, Andolla sang in a wailing,
high-pitched voice and in a language that Conan had never heard.
When the priest turned to face the worshipers, his face bore a
sheen of sweat and a rictus of ecstasy.

Just below the statue's dais, Oppia clapped her hands rhyth-
mically, leading the acolytes and the newcomers in their chant.
Andolla turned and took a great two-handled cup from the lap of
the goddess and held it high. Instantly the music, clapping and
chanting ceased. He bent low and dipped the massive silver vessel
into the steaming pot. Once more he raised it, white drops falling
from it back into the cauldron.

"Behold the milk of Mother Doorgah, with which she nour-
ishes her children! Drink of this, and gain enlightenment!" Andolla drank from the cup; then Oppia ascended the dais and took
it from his hands. She drank likewise before carrying the weighty
vessel to the worshipers below. She took the cup from one to
another, giving it to the newcomers first. As the vessel was passed,
the music resumed, now quieter and at a slower tempo. Twice
Oppia returned to the dais and refilled the cup as Andolla, now
facing the idol once more, resumed his high-pitched song. Conan
noted that the newcomers drank with some trepidation, making
faces at the taste, while the acolytes snatched eagerly at the cup,
as men dying of thirst will snatch at a cup of water. On more
than one occasion, Oppia had to pry the vessel away from an
acolyte with some force.

When all had drunk of the potion, the chanting resumed again.
Conan set his back to a wall, stood in the shadows, and waited.
Nearly an hour passed without incident, but he did not lose pa-
tience. He had a feeling that he was about to see something cru-

cial here, the secret of these people's hold over their all-too-willing victims.

A shriek pierced through the chanting. The Cimmerian saw one of the newcomers, a young woman, pointing upward, toward the idol's face. He felt the hair at the back of his neck prickle. The closed eyelids of the goddess had opened, and the exposed orbs glowed as if from an inner fire. In fact, now that he looked closely, he saw that it *was* an inner fire. Low flames burned within the idol's head, behind the glass eyes. From somewhere in the temple, lights trained on the idol's countenance were being shifted, causing shadows to move, giving the semblance of changing expressions flickering across the face.

Conan looked back to the worshipers and saw that their eyes were raised ecstatically, tears running down the cheeks of many. A slight creaking announced another change in the idol. Slowly, the arms raised from the sides and swung forward, as if in benediction. From his vantage point, the Cimmerian could see that there were lamps placed in wells beneath Andolla's feet. These lamps, invisible to the worshipers, began to wobble subtly. The effect was to make the huge breasts above seem to tremble.

It was an elaborate and fairly impressive display, Conan thought, but it should not have convinced a child, or even the sort of fools who thronged the temple . . . unless the fools were drugged. He knew that there were many drugs that could bring about illusions. With the tedious, mind-numbing chants to soften the audience's mental resistance, a clever magician, using a bit of impressive stage managing, could easily control the suggestible minds of onlookers and assure that they saw the visions he wished to bring about.

Either Andolla and his wife were immune to the effects of the drug or they had only feigned drinking from the cup. Neither shared the glassy-eyed stare of the others. After a few more minutes of the show, the idol resumed its wonted posture and the lights returned to normal.

"Mother Doorgah blesses you, her children!" Andolla cried. "All things are possible to Mother Doorgah. There is no earthly difficulty that she may not solve. You need but bring your sorrows before her and she will take them unto herself. Give thanks and obedience to Mother Doorgah. Make your offerings of the worthless material goods of this passing, ephemeral world to Mother Doorgah, and she will . . .''

Conan was not about to waste any more of his time listening to the priest's mindless drivel. He made his way to the kitchen. He found it deserted, since the acolytes were all in blissful communion with Mother Doorgah. He ignored the pots of bland gruel intended for the novitiates. Obviously, Oppia and Andolla did not live on such.

He found a separate pantry containing the private stock. It was not locked; mere acolytes would never violate so holy a place. On a cutting board lay several roast fowl and a large joint of beef. He helped himself to a roast duck and carved off a generous slice of the beef. Beneath a cloth he found fresh-baked loaves, still warm from the oven, and appropriated one. He helped it all down with a flagon of the excellent golden wine of Poitain.

Appetite satisfied and in excellent spirits, Conan went back into the temple. Andolla still led his flock in their endless chants, but Oppia was no longer among them. He found her in the vestibule, speaking to one of the newcomers, who was making an unsteady departure. The young man's over-refined face was filled with rapture and near-worship for Oppia. When the wealthy youth was gone, she turned and saw the Cimmerian.

"What have you been doing?" she demanded. "You were away all night and then you snored the day away."

"I have been looking out for your interests," he said, "as you hired me to do. A good thing for you, too. Last night, in the Pit, I heard talk of this place."

"Oh?" she said. "And what was the nature of this talk?"

"It seems that Rista Daan is hiring men to make a raid on the temple and fetch his daughter back to him."

"I told you, we have arrangements with all the gang leaders here. They are well paid to leave us alone."

"Apparently one of them thinks he is not paid well enough," Conan said.

"Which one?" she demanded.

"Ingas."

"Him! I settled with him just last week, and he has raised his already extortionate rates three times this year! I detest that robber! Well, if there is any more to this than mere talk, I know just how to deal with a man who refuses to stay bought. I had hoped to avoid such trouble, but other hard men have crossed me to their regret."

"This temple is a maze, and it is hard to get from one place to another quickly," Conan said. "I think you should give me a room on the same floor as the girl, so I can keep a closer eye on her."

"I think not," Oppia said. "I want no one on that floor save her. The . . . the evil spirits are especially strong near her, and you would not be able to sleep. You might even come to harm."

"As you will," he answered. "But I feel that I cannot guard her properly where I am. I go now to see what I can learn in the Pit."

"See that you do not stay absent for long," she ordered. "You are away from the temple too much. When you are not here, you are of little use as a guard . . . or for any other use I might have for you."

"Be assured, you are always in my thoughts. You'll not regret you hired me." He turned and left the temple, descending the steps to the pave below.

The broad, monument-studded Square was almost devoid of people at this late hour, but there was a lively commerce beneath the colonnaded portico, where the ladies of the evening plied their ancient trade. Sconce-held torches provided light by which the women paraded their wares and lesser merchants peddled the goods that always seemed to go with such traffic: drink, trifling gift items, medications and potions guaranteed to restore flagging powers. A few dancers postured and pirouetted for tossed coins. Fortune-tellers offered their services to the gullible.

Feeling in need of a little diversion before getting down to the deadly serious business of the night, the Cimmerian ambled across the Square toward the colonnade to watch the human parade. As he neared, he saw a familiar form standing on the steps of the portico talking with a pair of gaily dressed women, their overused features disguised by heavy cosmetics and flattered by the soft, flickering torchlight. It was Nevus, his acquaintance from Ermak's troop. The man smiled when he saw the Cimmerian approach.

"Conan! Come join me. These two ladies would very much like companionship for the night. I confess that I have reached an age at which two women present a challenge that two swordsmen would not. Join us."

"I regret to tell you that I have business to attend to this night," Conan said. "Another time, perhaps. But I would speak with you."

Nevus turned to his companions. "I will return presently, my lovelies. Seek no lesser company in the meanwhile." He left amid soft laughter from the women.

"I thank you," Conan said as the two stepped into a shaded alcove provided with a stone bench where citizens could take refuge from the sun in the broiling days of summer. "Tell me, Nevus, where do Ingas's men disport themselves of an evening?"

The soldier gaped. "You want to stay well clear of that place! The redbirds harbor little love for you since you slew three of them just a few paces from this spot. I wish I could have seen that. Ermak spoke highly of the feat, and he is a man sparing of his praise."

"Nevertheless," Conan said, "I wish to call on them."

"It is upon your head, then," said Nevus. "Most nights they keep to a dive called the Skull. It is in the Pit."

Conan nodded. "I've seen the sign. Tell me, Nevus, what do you know of your leader's dealings with Xanthus? I heard a rumor that he raided the miners' village for Xanthus and took away the women and children."

The man would not meet his eyes. "I know little of that. It

was before I came here and joined the band. The others will not speak of it.''

"Little wonder," Conan said. "It is not worthy of a warrior to act so. That is work for slavers.''

"Well, I had nothing to do with it!" Nevus insisted.

"I rejoice to hear it," Conan said. "Thank you for your aid.'' He turned to leave when Nevus spoke.

"Conan. You should not go down to the Skull alone. Do you want me to go along?''

"No, but I thank you for the offer. Nevus, you seem to be a an honorable warrior. I advise you to break your connection with Ermak and leave this town. Things are about to get very bad here.''

"I do not know what you mean, Cimmerian. Bad times are when a warrior prospers best. And when I take service with a man, I stay by his side until he is dead or fails in his side of the bargain. Ermak has not yet failed to pay his men on time." It was a mercenary's highest commendation, and there was no arguing with it.

"Farewell, then, Nevus.'' The Cimmerian turned to leave.

"Good luck at the Skull,'' said the mercenary.

"And good luck to you with those women," Conan said. "You'll need it more than I.''

He wandered down the dark streets into the lower town. He recalled that in his explorations, he had passed a sign shaped like a human skull, curiously wrought from strips of blackened iron. It was but a few streets' distance from the Wyvern, and as Conan approached it, he saw that lights burned in the eye sockets of the skull sign, providing the only illumination to be had on the street. Salts of copper had been added to the flames, for they burned ominously green.

Unlike the Wyvern, which was below street level, the Skull stood higher than the street, and Conan ascended a short flight of steps to its porch, beneath the skull sign. The door was closed against the chill of the night, and he grasped the massive bronze ring to pull it open.

Within, it was a far smaller establishment than the Wyvern, with only a scattering of tables. Besides a few women, all of its inhabitants were men dressed in red leather. At his entrance, they stared at him as if seeing an apparition. There were about a dozen of them, and as soon as they were over their astonishment, they began to rise from their tables, snatching at their long swords.

"Hold!" barked a stern voice from the rear of the room.

Conan ignored them all as he crossed from the door to the bar. He displayed a slight unsteadiness as he moved, as though he were well into drink. He leaned on the bar and snapped his fingers at the woman behind it.

"Wine!" the Cimmerian called. It was delivered and he drank. His ears told him that no one drew near. With his tankard half emptied, he turned and leaned back with his elbows on the bar. Every eye in the room glared at him. At the rear, a man sat alone at a table. He was older than the others, with a clean-shaven face and a dissipated mien, but he bore the unmistakable stamp of the Poitainian nobility. He dressed in red leathers, like his men, but his were elaborately tailored, and richly embroidered with silver and gold wire. The left breast was embroidered with the crest of a high family of Poitain, but the emblem was slashed with the jagged, horizontal bar that signified the bearer had been disinherited. The man seemed to wear the symbol as a sort of defiance.

"You are a bold one to beard us in our very den," said the man whom Conan knew could only be Ingas.

"A brave hunter beards lions," Conan sneered. "It is not necessary to beard jackals." There was another stirring among the thugs, and another calming gesture from their leader.

"Who are you, Cimmerian?" Ingas demanded. "Who has hired you to defy me? Who has paid you to slay my men?"

"I work for none of your rivals," Conan said. "As for those three fools, it was they who set upon me. They behaved insolently from the time I arrived in this town. Finally they challenged me in public as I sat at dinner. That I do not tolerate."

"Aye," Ingas said. "They acted on their own, not upon my orders, wherefore I have let the matter rest and have not sent my men for your head. I might have let it stand at that, but now you have come to my own territory to cast your defiance in my teeth, and that *I* do not tolerate!''

"Am I to tremble at the threats of a Poitainian outcast?'' Conan demanded, deliberately slurring his words. All the while, he kept his eyes upon the two men standing closest to Ingas. Both of them were somewhat older than the rest of the gang. One was a tall, saturnine man whose nose had been cut almost in half at some time in the past. The other was a squat, barrel-shaped lump of muscle, with huge hands.

Ingas sat back, smiling. "No, you are not going to provoke me just yet. Even a drunken Cimmerian would not come here and behave like this without a reason. Someone has hired you to do this, foreigner. Which one? Ermak? Lisip? That fat scoundrel Bombas? Do their men await without?'' Nervously, his men eyed the door, fingering their hilts.

Conan snorted. "You are a coward, just as I thought." He drained his tankard and slammed it down on the bar. "I'll pay you and your effeminate redbirds no more heed. Farewell, Poitainian. I came here expecting a good fight, but you have disappointed me."

Weaving slightly, he left the Skull. Once outside, he lost his drunken walk and began to head for the high street. From behind, he heard the door of the Skull open and shut again. Now he resumed his slight stagger, which he continued affecting as he made his way back toward the new town. He was careful not to overdo it, as Ingas's men would grow suspicious were it an obvious ploy. He kept to the middle of the street.

Conan was certain that the killers would not attack him in the lower city. Ingas was now convinced that he was working for a rival. The men he had sent to follow the Cimmerian would be under orders to find out where he was going before they were to kill him.

When he reached the Square, he stopped by a fountain and splashed water in his face, as if trying to clear the wine fumes from his head. As he did so, he scanned the plaza. All was now deserted, the ladies gone from their portico. From a sconce along the front of the portico he took a low-guttering torch and carried it across the pave. He did not go to the temple. Instead, he went to the theater.

At the top of the steps he passed between the massive pillars. Ignoring the large main-entrance doors, he went to a small, shuttered window to one side, where admissions to the performance would be sold. With a powerful wrench of his hands, he snapped the shutter's latch and opened it. Thrusting the torch ahead of him, he passed inside.

From an entrance hall he passed into the main floor of the theater, where ranks of benches faced the stage. Above was a balcony where the more fashionable members of the audience could sit in comfort, aloof from the common rabble. The sides of the auditorium were lined with the sumptuous private boxes of the wealthy.

Walking slowly so that his followers would have no difficulty, Conan ascended the steps to the stage. At its rear was a stack of ladders for the use of the stagehands. He appropriated one and carried it up the many steps to the catwalk above. Gazing down over the rail, he could just make out two stealthy forms crossing the stage, following the light of his torch. When he could hear their feet upon the steps, he crossed the catwalk, then went up the final stairs to the cupola. He moved out onto the roof and carried the ladder to the parapet. He did not need the ladder to cross to the temple roof, but he used it anyway, leaving it in place in case the men following him lacked his head for heights. He walked to the center of the temple roof and halted just before his own window. Then he stood there, waiting.

He did not need to wait long. The two stalkers emerged from the cupola and scanned their surroundings. Conan heard them conferring in low whispers. The moonlight leached away all color, but he could see that one was tall and lean, the other squat and barrel-shaped. This was what he had expected. By now, Ingas knew better than to send his inexperienced young thugs.

One of them saw the ladder and pointed to it. Almost tiptoeing, they went to the parapet and surveyed the roof beyond. Conan withdrew into the deep shadows against the wall beside his window. After a brief consultation, the men crossed the ladder, stepping gingerly, clearly nervous about the drop below. They then turned and squinted over the temple roof.

Conan stepped from the shadows. "Are you looking for me?"

Two long Khorajan sabers slithered from their scabbards. "What sort of chase have you been leading us, barbarian?" said the squat one. "First the theater, now the temple. Surely the fraud and his woman have not hired you to trouble our master?"

By way of answer, Conan drew his own sword. "No, but I have other uses for you."

"You do not seem so drunk as you were but a little time past," said the saturnine man, his voice heavy with the accent of Poitain's mountain province.

"Why have you followed me?" Conan asked.

"Our master decided that you had troubled him more than enough, even to insulting him to his face. He wishes you dead, foreigner, but he wants to know which of his enemies hired you."

"That is a matter he will just have to wonder about," Conan said, "since the two of you will not be reporting back to him."

"Enough of this," said the taller, coming toward Conan in the flat-footed glide of an experienced swordsman.

Abruptly, Conan shouted: "Villains! What is your business here?" The two killers were disconcerted for a moment. The shorter man rushed in, swinging his sword horizontally. The Cimmerian blocked neatly with his own blade, then fended off an oblique cut from the taller man. He swung two blows in return, making them wide and forceful but a little slow, so that the attackers would be able to block them. He wanted to ensure plenty of loud sword-clashing.

When he was sure that everyone was awake within, the Cimmerian began to fight seriously. These two were not as inexpert as the three he had fought in the Square, and it would be folly to play with them further. In the dark, on the uncertain surface of the roof, the two were having a difficult time of it in just keeping out of each other's way, but that would not last much longer.

Conan maneuvered the shorter man between himself and the taller, then lowered his guard, inviting a high cut. The man seized the opening, making a swipe at the exposed neck. The Cimmerian ducked and felt the other's sword tick slightly on the top of his steel cap. As he ducked, he straightened his sword arm, running the man through his barrel chest. Drawing his blade free, Conan simultaneously placed a foot against the man's body and shoved him backward, sending him stumbling into the taller man. That one fell back a step, his arms flying wide in an attempt to retain his balance.

The Cimmerian vaulted across the squat man's body, bringing his sword down in a terrible slash against the exposed shoulder. The man was wearing a lightweight shirt of mail beneath his red-leather doublet, but it availed him little against Conan's sword, which crunched through flesh, bone, and mail indifferently.

Even as the man fell, Conan rushed to the parapet and grabbed up the ladder that spanned the alley between the temple and the theater. He carried it across the temple roof and placed it just in front of his window, slanting against the wall below the window above.

"What's happening out there?" called a voice. A light flickered in his own room, and he could make out a number of forms crowding through the door. The voice belonged to Oppia.

"Come look," Conan said. "They came for her, just as I told you they would."

With the aid of an acolyte, Oppia climbed out through the window. Several acolytes followed her, bearing lamps and torches. She stooped low and examined the two bodies, then straightened and faced Conan.

"Ingas! He shall pay for this! How did this come about?"

"I went to the Pit, as I said earlier I would. There I spoke with some contacts I have made here in the city. I learned from them that the kidnapping attempt would probably come tonight, so I rushed back and waited for them. I knew it would be far easier for them to reach her room by the rooftops than by coming up through the temple. They would have to come right here to my window, so I awaited within. As soon as they set up their ladder, I challenged them.''

She studied the bodies. ''How did they expect to get through the bars?''

Mentally, Conan cursed himself. He should have thought of this and brought a crowbar or other tools to scatter around. Thinking fast, he pointed at the corpse of the squat man.

''That one was said to be the strongest man in Sicas. Look at the size of those hands. He must have planned to wrench the bronze bars from their settings bare-handed.''

''No doubt,'' she said. Then she turned to the wide-eyed acolytes and pointed at the burly young men who had been guarding the doors. ''Take this carrion down to the river. See that you dispose of it before daylight.'' They began to drag the corpses toward the window. ''No, you idiots! I don't want my floors bloodied. Just toss them to the alley below and collect them there.'' Obediently, the men dragged the corpses to the parapet, lifted them over it and dropped them. A second later came a sickening duo of thuds.

''What is happening?'' asked a male voice. Andolla climbed through the window.

''Ingas has reneged on his bargain with us, my husband,'' Oppia reported. ''He sent two of his men to steal back Amata and return her to her father. This Cimmerian warrior, whose services I have engaged, has already earned his keep. He slew the kidnappers before they could reach her window.''

The priest glanced at Conan. ''Oh, good. Ingas, eh? I shall prepare a mighty spell for him. He shall regret this.''

''As you will, my husband,'' she murmured.

Conan studied the man. It was the first opportunity he had had to examine Andolla at close range. He was a tall man of middle years and dignified bearing, even standing upon the uncertain footing of the temple roof. Like his well-modulated voice, his bearing carried the unmistakable stamp of theatricality, as if he were not a priest, but rather, an actor playing the role of a priest.

"Has this petty altercation drawn any notice?" he asked.

"The Square is as quiet as usual for this time of night," Conan reported. "If the guards at the Reeve's headquarters noticed anything, they've been careful not to show any interest."

"Well, then," Andolla said, "I must return to my thaumaturgical labors. See to this, my dear."

"I already have, husband," Oppia said through delicately gritted teeth. She turned to a pair of whey-faced girls who stood by. "Fetch mops and buckets and clean this up," she ordered, pointing to the broad pool of blood that glinted black in the moonlight. In addition, two broad smears of blood made a trail, marking where the bodies had been dragged to the parapet. "When that is done, go to the alley and wash down the bricks. I want no trace of this night's happenings visible when the sun rises in the morning." The girls clapped their hands and bowed in ritual obeisance. They followed Andolla through the window, and soon Conan and Oppia were alone upon the temple roof.

"This was splendidly done, Cimmerian," she said. "Think you he will try again?"

"It is very likely," he told her. "Or perhaps Rista Daan will approach one of the other leaders. If Ingas betrayed you for gold, why not the others? Next time there may be more than two to contend with."

"Curse them all!" she said. "I long to be away from this place. It was a fertile field before, but now it is like some savage beast that has gone mad and has begun to devour itself. All these mobs of predatory men, banding together to prey upon the carcass of this town, no longer content to share the meat of the kill. Now they will turn and rend each other." She looked up at the towering barbarian. "But you are different. Though you are a man of blood and violence, you are not a mindless pack animal. You are like a lion among hyenas."

"I am like them, Priestess. But I am a better fighting man than they."

"I think it is more than that. Continue to give me loyal service and you may be destined for better things, just as the holy Andolla and I are so destined." There came a commotion from behind. The female acolytes were maneuvering their mops and buckets out through the window.

"I must supervise this," she told the Cimmerian. "Our devoted followers have perfect faith, but they cannot even do something as simple as cleaning up blood or disposing of bodies without someone to watch over them." She paused. "You were right, Conan. Tomorrow I shall have another room prepared for you, a room directly across the hall from Amata's."

He nodded, satisfied. "Very good, Priestess. I think I shall be able to accomplish more that way." He looked up at the girl's barred window, wondering whether she had taken any notice of the night's doings.

TWELVE

The Demon and the Curse

The day was blustery, with the fitful wind blowing sheets of rain across the Square. Conan left the temple swathed in his great cloak, its hood drawn over his head against the weather. Thus attired, he was distinguished by nothing except his size and tiger-like gait, and in this town there were no few men of his size, men who moved dangerously.

He knew that things were about to erupt in Sicas and that he could accomplish nothing if he remained aloof in the temple. He had a need to know what was going on in the town. To that end, he turned his steps toward the Pit. There were yet several places in the lower city where his presence was unlikely to precipitate immediate violence.

Just beyond the line where the old city wall had once stood was a small tavern called the Bear and Harp, and he had heard that it was frequented by the storytellers and minstrels, both those of the city and those just passing through. These were men and women whose livelihoods depended upon their knowing all about what was going on, and he could think of no better place to inform himself.

As he entered the tavern, he heard a woman's voice proclaiming a new poem, verses by the mad Tarantian poet, Caprio. It was well known throughout Aquilonia that Caprio only feigned madness, so that he could get away with his outrageously scurrilous verses defaming various highly placed personages of the kingdom. There was an ancient tradition that mad poets were under the special protection of the gods; therefore, there was little the authorities could do about the man, who in their eyes had earned death many times over.

In the entranceway the Cimmerian divested himself of his cloak, shook the worst of the rain from it, and hung it on a peg by a half score of similar garments. As he went into the common room, the patrons turned from the singer to study the newcomer. All were armed, as was only prudent in times like these, but they were not, for the most part, the professional fighters and criminals such as thronged the town. He saw two or three whose armor or general look of furtiveness identified them as part of the rougher element, but they had probably come for the entertainment.

He went to the bar and ordered mulled ale. The barkeep took a pitcher from the hearth, where a crackling fire of well-seasoned hardwood logs gave forth a cheering warmth. As the Cimmerian drank from the tarred leather tankard, the woman singer's place was taken by a storyteller, who began to tell of events in the far provinces of the land. From all indications, Aquilonia was breaking up as the feudal lords, disgusted with King Numedides, reverted to their old ways and set up as independent suzerains, neglecting to send their annual tribute to Tarantia. Some defied the king openly; others were being more subtle, testing the power of the throne without risking an open breach. Only the frontier provinces of Bossonia and Gunderland remained firmly loyal. Those two provinces, although not populous, contained some of the best fighting men of the kingdom.

Conan listened with interest. He would be finished in this town soon, and for a professional soldier, news of impending civil war was the finest of music. The civil strife in Ophir had been going on for years and the land was a picked-over carcass. Aquilonia was matchlessly rich and had been at peace for many decades. The loot of a city such as Tarantia would be incalculable. And that was just the largest of Aquilonia's many rich cities. Even the harrying of a minor province could give a common soldier wealth enough to retire from the wars. Not that Conan was ready to retire just yet.

"Let me stand you to your next tankard," said a man next to him. This one was a small one, dressed in colorful hose and doublet. Atop his head was a long velvet cap, with several drooping feathers forming a somewhat bedraggled cockade. Slung over his shoulder was a small harp in a bead-decorated leather cover.

"Gladly," said the Cimmerian. The harper beckoned to the barkeep, who hurried over with the pitcher.

"You are the northerner who has the hard men of this town chasing their own tails with perplexity. You must have a fine story to tell."

"I am just a humble warrior, minding my own business," Conan said solemnly.

The harper guffawed. "And I am the long-lost prince of Khitai, about to return home to reclaim my rightful throne. I expect more than that for a tankard of this exceptionally fine mulled ale, flavored as it is with exotic spices of the east."

"Story for story, then?" Conan inquired.

"It is a bargain. What do you want to know?" the harper asked, his eyes glowing with curiosity.

"I have been keeping out of sight all day. What has been happening among the gangs these last hours?"

"Well—" the man leaned close "—Maxio has let it be known that he is after Ermak and will kill him, even if he has to use poison to do it. The King's Reeve says it was Maxio who burned down the royal storehouse to escape after he'd looted the place. Something has Ingas's men all worked up, and they go about glowering, their hands on their hilts as if they want to cut anything that moves. Ermak says he will be happy to fight anyone who feels that he and his men should be run out of town. All the little gangs are hiring themselves out to anyone who seems to feel the need of reinforcement. Lisip is growing worried that all this chaos is apt to bring the royal troops down upon the city, and he is calling for a peace conference, to settle matters without open war in the streets.''

"Is there any word that royal forces are on their way?" Conan asked.

"Not so much as a breath, but who can say? There may be royal spies in town. There are some who think that you are one such." The harper raised his eyebrows and angled his head as if expecting to hear an admission from the Cimmerian. He got no such confession. "Anyway," he went on, "you heard that last minstrel. The royal authority is in such disarray that it might be a very long time before the king takes note of this little corner of his domain. Now, what is your tale?"

Conan leaned close. "You understand that you must not let it be known where you heard this." He did not make it a question.

The man reached into the breast of his doublet and brought out a tiny image that he wore around his neck on a chain. It was a medallion bearing the likeness of a god with a harp. He bestowed a kiss upon the image.

"I swear by Ilas of the Golden Fingers, patron god of all harpers." He tucked the medallion away.

"Very well. I have been sent by one whose name I cannot reveal, even in the strictest confidence, to learn which way the wind blows here." The harper nodded, hanging upon the outlander's every word. "Bombas is looting the royal tax revenues, and has been at it for years, in league with Xanthus, the royal mine factor. To break the Miners' Guild, Xanthus brought in Ermak's mercenaries. They abducted the women and children from the mining village and hold them hostage for the miners' obedience. It was Bombas who set fire to the royal storehouse to destroy evidence of his theft."

The harper's mouth dropped open. "And I thought *I* was good at gathering news."

Conan clapped a hand upon the man's shoulder. "You gather information with your ears. I do it with my sword arm. My way is faster, and it gleans many facts that men will not yield in ordinary conversation.''

"Such information," the harper said, "is worth more than a single mug of ale. Allow me to buy you another.''

The two drank and talked for a while, but the harper's look grew abstracted, and from time to time his lips moved silently. The Cimmerian knew that the man was working this new information into a song. When the harper soon departed, Conan sat at a table, drinking mulled ale and listening to the singers and storytellers. He was well content with his work just accomplished. In the strange, swift way that minstrels had, this news would be all over Tarantia sooner than a swift horse could have borne it there. It was another stir to the boiling-over pot that was Sicas.

The rain had tapered off by the time Conan left the Bear and Harp. The wind blew less gustily as he made his way through the dim streets. The weather was depressing, and it seemed to have damped the fighting belligerence of the gangs. He knew it was but temporary. The gangs were, at most, unsettled and disoriented by the sudden changes and betrayals. Soon they would be ready for rampage, and then the blood would flow plentifully.

"Conan!" The voice was an urgent hiss, and he turned to see a cloaked, veiled figure in a doorway. At first he thought it was Brita, but then he saw that this woman was far too large for that. "Come here," she urged.

"Good evening, Delia," he said, smiling. The woman all but hauled him through the door as she drew aside her veil. Inside was a perfumer's shop. At a glare from Delia, the elderly proprietor retired discreetly to an inner chamber.

"You treacherous dog! What have you done! Maxio is alive and free. He is hiding out from Bombas and Ermak, but he will come out soon!"

"Yes? But what of that? Surely you did not expect me to kill him for you?"

She looked around as if afraid of being overheard. "I thought we had an agreement!" she hissed. Her face was a mask of terror.

"We did," Conan said. "I agreed to pay you money for information. I was to use that information however I saw fit, and I did."

"But now he will kill me for betraying him," she wailed.

"Nothing of the sort," Conan assured her. "He thinks that Ermak learned of the job and sold him out. I told him that you had got wind of it and sent me to warn him."

She closed her eyes and almost fainted with relief. After a few deep breaths, she regained her composure and then glared at the big Cimmerian as if her beautiful eyes could set him aflame.

"What game are you playing, you scheming wretch? I've all but cast myself at your feet and you use me to further some plan of your own."

"What did you expect?" he countered. "You sold your lover to me for your own purposes."

"Of course I did," she said, bewildered. "But I put him in your hands because *I* wanted to be in your hands. It is not as if I turned him in to the authorities for a reward. I would never stoop to such a thing!" She seemed honestly indignant.

"I did not mean to impugn your honor," Conan said.

"Well, you could at least have warned me," she said, her anger dissipating with relief.

"I have been very busy, and also trying to keep out of sight."

"I can well believe that you have been busy. Ever since you arrived in town, the place has been in turmoil. All the gangs had worked out agreements, and things went along with only a little brawling and an occasional murder. Now nobody knows where anybody stands; they are all suspicious of one another. What are you doing?"

"Nothing that will endanger you," he assured her, "so long as you are careful."

"Very well, I believe you," she said, somewhat mollified.

Another question occurred to him. "Delia, what know you of a black-haired woman, newly in town and most likely searching for someone, or some thing. She may be calling herself Altaira."

"That one!" she said. "I have seen her in the Pit, where she goes about alone after dark as fearlessly as a pack of warriors armed to the teeth. And none dare molest her, either. I never saw a man who looks half so deadly as that woman. What want you with her?''

"Nothing. I but want to know what she is doing. I think she may be looking for someone or some thing, and possibly it is a matter with which I am concerned.''

"I heard that she is waiting for Mulvix,'' Delia said.

"And who is Mulvix?'' Conan asked, remembering where he had heard the name.

"He is a caravan master who visits Sicas once or twice a year. Like many such, he is a smuggler. I've no doubt that he and the woman have some sort of smuggling business together.'' Her boldly flirtatious look returned. "Do you want me to find out what I can about her? I can get close to her as no man in this town can. She would not see me as a rival in some scheme.''

"No!'' Conan said. "Stay away from that woman, and do not even ask questions about her. She has a way of disposing of anyone who arouses her suspicions.''

Delia pouted. "Oh, very well, if you scorn my help . . .'' She left him an opening to protest, which he refused to exploit.

"You would be best advised to patch up matters with Maxio,'' he said.

She stamped her expensively shod foot. "I do not understand you at all!'' She stormed from the shop.

A sweet aroma reminded Conan that this was a perfumer's shop, and he summoned the proprietor from the rear. He asked the old man if Brita had been in.

"Aye, near every day,'' the man answered. "She was in just this morning, asking about that sister of hers. Seems a decent, well-bred girl, although I think she is a little mad on this subject of her sister.'' With a bony finger he tapped his gray temple portentously.

Conan nodded, musing. The presence of the black-haired woman Altaira and the imminent arrival of the caravan master Mulvix tied in with Piris's story. Whatever other truth his tale might contain was doubtful at best. These musings supplied another inspiration.

"Have you any lilac scent?" he asked the perfumer.

"But of course, sir." The man went to a shelf and took down a small flask. "The very finest pressings from this year's harvest in Khemi, where the richest lilac blossoms are grown. Is it for the . . . ah . . . the lady who was just here with you?"

"No," Conan said. "It is for another friend. I will want it delivered."

"That is no difficulty," the shopkeeper said, taking quill and parchment from a desk. "The recipient?"

"Piris of Shadizar," Conan said.

"And this person's lodgings?"

"The city dungeon," answered the Cimmerian.

The poised quill faltered in its plunge toward the parchment. "Eh? Did I her you aright, good sir? I almost thought that you said 'the city dungeon.' "

"That is indeed what I said," affirmed Conan.

The old man shrugged philosophically. "As you will. Any message?"

"Just say, *'Conan has not forgotten you. This is the very least I can do. It is almost in my hands.' "*

"What is almost in your hands?" asked the old man.

"He will know what I mean." Conan paid for the costly scent and left the perfumer's.

As he crossed the rain-washed Square, the Cimmerian all but ran into a fat figure waddling in another direction. It was the Reeve, who gasped as he recognized the face within the cowl.

"Cimmerian! You are alive!"

"Aye, no thanks to you!" His hand went to his .hilt. He had wished to avoid the Reeve, and he disliked the idea of cutting the man down in full view in the middle of the Square, but he might have no choice in the matter. Amazingly, the man's fat face registered what might only have been called delight, even though he was, for once, not backed by his remaining henchmen.

"But I thought that Maxio and his men had slain you! We saw

you cross the bridge to the storehouse, and then there was nothing, no call from you and no sounds of a fight. We were sure that Maxio or one of his men had dirked you in the back as you dropped into the storehouse, so I resolved to show the villains no mercy. I rejoice to see you alive!''

"And well you should," said Conan, "considering that you set fire to the storehouse while I was in it.''

The Reeve looked around as if to see whether anyone stood near enough to hear his words. "That was an accident. One of my blundering men knocked over an oil lamp with the butt of his glaive. The oil poured onto a great heap of the woven wicker we use to bale the wool for transport. The fire was out of control in seconds. Of course, in my official report I said that the burglars had set the fire to cover their escape. You understand these things, do you not? They were truly at fault, anyway. Ah, my friend, did Maxio escape?''

The Cimmerian grinned. "He was very much alive when last I saw him.''

"The gods curse the man! Conan, we have matters to discuss. Come back with me to my headquarters and we will talk.''

"I think not," Conan said, unwilling to step into a trap. "Over here.'' He stepped into a small kiosk that housed a statue of a long-dead benefactor of the town.

The Reeve followed closely. "Conan, my friend, things in this city are getting far out of hand. You may have heard that Lisip has called a peace conference in hopes that things may be sorted out before the whole town is aflame.''

"I've heard," he affirmed.

"I have agreed to the conference and will be present. Will you attend as well, as my bodyguard?''

"You have your own men," Conan pointed out.

"I can neither trust nor depend upon them," Bombas said. "But you are now the most feared swordsman in the city. Your presence will ensure the good behavior of all toward me. I will make it well worth your trouble.''

"All right," Conan said. "You need not pay me money. Just release Piris."

"Agreed. I will turn him loose as soon as we return safely from the conference."

"No, release him when we leave for the meeting. Who knows whether either of us will return alive from it?"

The fat shoulders shrugged. "Have it as you will. The man is nothing to me, in truth."

"When is the conference to be held, and where?" Conan asked.

"The time and place are not yet agreed upon. Thus far, Ermak and Ingas have not assented to it, and who knows what Maxio will decide? The place will probably be the Wyvern, which is neutral ground to most of these scum. I will give you word as soon as it has been decided. Where do you lodge these days?"

"Never mind that. I will be in touch with you. If that is all, I must be going now." Conan turned and left the kiosk without further words. As he did not want Bombas to see him enter the temple, he walked past the temple and the theater and traveled north along the high street.

He went to the inn to see how Brita fared, but she was not there. The innkeeper affirmed that she came and went at all hours and said further that a young man who wore two swords had been asking about the Cimmerian. Conan was not interested in meeting with Casperus just yet. The innkeeper promised to keep safe any messages sent to Conan; none would be delivered to the Cimmerian's rooms. The last thing Conan wanted was for Brita to be prying into his doings.

It was fully dark when he returned to the temple. An acolyte conducted him to his new room, directly across the hall from Rietta's chamber. The shuttered window of this room opened onto a stone-paved courtyard three stories below. He knew that the kitchen gave into this courtyard. Even as he watched, a female acolyte emptied a pail of hot water out the back door, further wetting the rain-dampened stones.

Below his window was a narrow ledge, and by leaning back and looking up, he saw that the roof was an easy climb from the ledge. He was beginning to consider this city more in terms of rooftops and sewers than of streets and buildings.

There was no one else on the floor save himself and the young woman across the hall. He peered through the door-window into her chamber and saw that she lay unnaturally pale and still, only the slightest rise and fall beneath the blanket drawn up to her chin proving that she still lived.

He looked into the rooms on both sides. One was featureless, unoccupied and unfurnished. The other had a window set into the adjoining wall, separated from the girl's room by a pane of thick glass. On the sill of the window burned an oil lamp, which provided the sole illumination for Rietta's chamber. The glass pane was not perfectly smooth, but he could see through it into the chamber tolerably well. He climbed out the window and pulled himself up onto the roof, then crossed to the other side. Swinging his legs over the low parapet, he dropped to hang by his finger-tips. The balls of his feet just touched the ledge outside his window. He reentered his room, satisfied that he could pass from one room to the other unseen from the hallway. With no further business for the evening, he lay on the bed, still fully dressed. He wanted to be ready to take action without having to scramble into his clothes in the dark.

He awoke dizzy and disoriented. To Conan, who always awoke fully alert, this was distressing. Ordinarily, only a strong blow to the head caused this sensation. Then he was aware of something else: the very faint odor of a pungent smoke. It was the same smoke he had scented before, in Rietta's room.

Swiftly, he rose and rushed to the window. Daring the effects of his unwonted dizziness, he went out onto the ledge and pulled himself up to the roof. He breathed deeply of the cold night air. The stars overhead appeared unnaturally bright, and they seemed to shift their position and color. The illusion lasted for only moments; then all returned to normal.

Apparently the black-lotus smoke was quicker in its effect than the drug given to the worshipers below, and the influence dispersed as soon as the victim was free of the smoke. Whatever the mechanism for injecting the smoke into Rietta's chamber, enough had leaked across the hall to mildly affect the Cimmerian. His clarity restored, he decided that it was time to see what was going on in the girl's chamber.

When he entered the room next to hers, he saw that the lamplight had grown feeble. No acolyte had entered to trim the wick in several hours. He saw a faint glow from the other room. Before peering through the glass separating the chambers, he extinguished the flickering flame, both to see more clearly and to prevent it from casting its glow upon his face.

In a corner of Rietta's room, near the door, something was taking shape. He felt that familiar prickle at the back of his neck, the crawling revulsion he always felt in the presence of sorcery. For he saw that this was true sorcery, not a mechanical illusion such as the frauds had produced with the statue of Mother Doorgah.

It was a shambling, unstable shape, its form vaguely manlike. Its legs were short and stumpy, but so large was it that the top of its spherical head touched the ceiling. It was greenish in color, glowing faintly, not as if from within but rather as if the sun of another world shone upon it. Its eyes were deep pits, and its wide mouth worked as though it strove to speak. There were neither nose nor nostril openings that Conan could discern. Its mouth was lined with hundreds of needlelike teeth. Its form was hideous to him, and he could only imagine what it must seem to the poor, drugged girl on the other side of the wall.

The shape stretched forth an ape-long arm, a taloned finger at its end pointing toward a corner of the room, where Conan assumed the girl must be huddling in terror. Its mouth continued to work, and now a voice seemed to emanate from it.

"I come for thee, girl," it said. The voice was deep, the words slurred. Also, it was oddly familiar. "I come for thee," continued the demon, "and soon your protectors' spells will be for naught. The curse of your mother, and of your grandmother, and of all your female ancestors, has fallen upon you. The spell that surrounds you grows weak, girl. Soon I shall break through, and then you are mine! Perhaps even now . . .'' It shambled forward, and the girl began to scream. It was a wailing shriek that jarred even upon the Cimmerian's hardened nerves.

He heard the sound of feet upon the stairs and decided that he had seen all that was needful for the moment. Quickly, he was out the window, across the roof and back within his own room. He was about to go out into the hall when he remembered that it might rouse suspicion were he to appear fully dressed. He tugged off shirt and breeches, then drew his sword and stepped into the hall, dressed only in a loincloth.

A pair of acolytes turned, their eyes gone wide at his appearance. "Open!" he ordered.

"Not until the Holy Mother Oppia or the Great-souled Andolla tell us . . .'' The voice terminated in a strangled squawk as the point of the Cimmerian's sword went under the acolyte's chin and forced his head back against the door. The other acolyte scrambled to throw back the bar.

Pushing past the two trembling novitiates, Conan entered the chamber. There was the faintest tinge of smoke lingering, and he heard the same outrushing of air as he had heard the first time he had entered the room. The girl was twisted into a trembling knot in a corner. He laid his sword on the floor and gently took her by her arms.

"The phantom is gone, lass. Look at me.'' The girl could hardly help doing so, so wide were her eyes. But now the unreasoning terror faded, replaced by a look of bewilderment. He was aware that he presented a spectacle scarcely less daunting than that of the demon, but at least he was human.

"Who are you?'' she asked, her voice weak and shaky but sounding sane enough.

"What are you doing in here?'' The question came from one in the doorway.

"What was I hired to do,'' replied the Cimmerian, standing, his sword now back in his grip. He turned to face Andolla. He glanced past the man's shoulder to the corner in which the demon had appeared. Now he saw a small, square opening in the wall, covered by gauze. The voice of the demon had been Andolla's voice, distorted but recognizable. Conan knew that the hole in the wall led to a speaking tube; such were sometimes used in wealthy households for the summoning of servants.

"You have no business in here!" the priest said. "You were engaged to protect the girl from those who would kidnap her. These matters of the Spirit World must be left to me and to the Holy Oppia. Leave now."

"When I am satisfied that she is safe from those kidnappers you mentioned." He looked past Andolla to the gaping acolytes. "Bring lights," he ordered.

"What for?" demanded Andolla as the acolytes brought forth lamps and candles.

Conan went to the window. "I want to see if anyone has been working at these bars," he answered. "If the girl saw faces at the window, it might have touched off this panic."

"Fool!" Andolla said. "Can you not see that the shutter is still latched from the inside?"

It was a good point, but Conan was not about to let him get away with it. "And did you not know," he sneered, "that accomplished burglars can easily unlatch and relatch any fastening to conceal evidence of their passage?"

"What now, husband?" said Oppia's voice. Conan did not turn around. Holding a candle, he carefully studied the sill by the bronze bars. Here he found another hole. Bending low and pretending to examine the base of the bars, he could smell a powerful aroma of old, stale smoke. This was how the smoke was injected into the room, and probably evacuated as well. A large blacksmith's bellows would likely do the job nicely. He straightened and turned.

"No, the bars are sound. It was the demon again, I suppose."

"This one is high-handed for a mere hireling," protested Andolla. "There is no place for an unbelieving, naked savage in our household."

"Allow me to see to him and to the girl, Holy One," Oppia said. "These are trifling matters for one with your heavy duties of study and ritual. Please, husband, return to your devotions and allow me to handle these matters.''

The tall priest reassembled his wounded dignity. "As you say, my dear. But see if you cannot curb this disbelieving barbarian. His very presence offends Mother Doorgah.''

"Mother Doorgah has a use for every living soul,'' she reminded him. "I will attend to the matter.'' Nodding and grumbling, the priest left. She looked at the acolytes. "You may go as well.''

When they were gone, she took Rietta by the shoulders. The look of panic returned to the girl's eyes and Oppia slapped her several times, leaving scarlet finger marks on the wan cheeks.

"You have allowed it to come again!'' Oppia said. "By your weakness and lack of true faith, you have allowed it to come. The Great-souled Andolla and I exert ourselves with rituals and spells night and day to keep it in the Spirit World, where it belongs. How can you be so selfish? I despair of you, child. Soon, Mother Doorgah must despair of you as well. Unless you can furnish her proof of your devotion, our spells of protection will be futile, for only Mother Doorgah's love for you gives us the power to protect you. Forget about yourself and show Mother Doorgah how great is your love for her! Only tribute of gold or jewels will move her, for those substances are sacred to Mother Doorgah. To us, on this trifling, temporal plane, they are worthless trash, but in the higher world of the gods, they are magical. Bring us these things that we might give them in turn to Mother Doorgah and you might yet be saved, the curse that has plagued your ancestresses for generations broken!'' She released Rietta's shoulders and stood, her face twisted with disgust as the girl collapsed into hysterical tears.

Conan pushed past Oppia and picked up the girl. She weighed next to nothing. His hand would almost span both of her thighs together. She was dangerously emaciated. Gently he put her on her bed and covered her with the thin blanket.

"Enough,'' he said. "Let us talk outside.''

In the hallway, he shut the door to Rietta's prison and closed the viewing-window. As he did this, Oppia studied him with great interest. His near-naked body was heavily muscled and seamed with old battle scars. The marks of blade and beast were all over him. More than size and scars, however, the sureness of his movements proclaimed his dangerous presence. He moved as a tiger moved, with absolute mastery of every muscle and bone, with a total awareness of where each body part was in relation to every other. There were many powerful men in the world, but it was this coordination, combined with the Cimmerian's bewildering swiftness, that made him a matchless fighting man. All this the woman read in her frank, intimate appraisal.

"She will not last long like this," Conan warned.

"Never has one offered such resistance," Oppia said. "I do not know whether she is stubborn or merely stupid. Surely, in her terror she can find a way to get more out of her father."

He favored her with an evil grin. "Leave her to me. I'll bring her around."

"My husband would never stand for that," she said.

"You are the one who handles matters here," he said. "Give me a free hand with her and you'll soon see action out of her father."

"Very well," she said. "You have my leave. Think you that you can bring her around soon?"

"I must," Conan said. "This town is about to erupt. Either it will burn to the ground or the royal troops will arrive to restore order. Either will be bad for you. It is time to grab what you can, pack up your trick idol and go."

She gave him a smile of complicity. "We have the drawings for the idol and can always craft another. You saw through that quickly enough."

"It's obvious to one who isn't drugged. What do you use on those fools?"

"A special decoction of blue lotus root that I purchase from Stygia. It is horribly costly but it does bring in the donations." She drew closer and felt of his arms, as one would test the muscles of a racehorse.

"The demon she sees," Conan demanded. "Is it real?"

"Aye. My husband summons it through his thaumaturgical arts, but it is a mindless, voiceless thing, as insubstantial as smoke. Andolla is convinced that with stronger sorcery, he can make it real. But let us not talk of these things. I have more pleasurable matters in mind." She ran a hand across his chest and raised her lips toward his.

Oppia was a beautiful and desirable woman, but the Cimmerian was sure that once he put his hands upon her, he would squeeze her beautiful, swanlike neck until the breath ceased to pass between her lips. He stepped back.

"What disturbs you, Cimmerian?" she breathed.

"If he can summon demons," Conan said, "he can set one against a man who displeases him. A man who traffics with his wife, for instance."

She laughed deprecatingly. "Surely you do not fear phantoms, you who are so brave in combat."

"I fear no man, and I do not fear fire or steel. But any man may fear supernatural things. It is no disgrace."

"You disappoint me. I had thought you an experienced man of the world. Now you speak like a childish barbarian."

"I am a barbarian. And I know that things of the Spirit World are not to be trifled with. What good is steel against a phantom that can strike through walls and armor?"

"And am I not a prize worth the risk?" she asked.

"You are a beautiful woman," Conan said. "And you are strong-willed. If you can put an end to your man's magical doings, then nothing would stand between you and me."

She stepped away from him. "We shall see. I must think upon this. You would have to prove that you are very, very valuable to me." She glanced at the door to Rietta's prison. "I think you know how to prove that." She turned and walked toward the stair. "Good night, Cimmerian."

When she was gone, he returned to his chamber. Reflecting that living in this temple had much in common with living amid the crags and cliffs of his native Cimmeria, he went out the window once more. This time he descended from ledge to ledge until he stood in the deserted courtyard. He entered the kitchen through its back door and found the place deserted. The embers of the banked fires give him the light he needed as he gathered meat, cheese, fruit, and bread and wrapped them in a napkin. He filled a gourd flask with milk from a pitcher and stoppered it. This accomplished, he rescaled the wall and reentered his room. He took two candles from his table. One was for light. For the other he had a different purpose.

At Rietta's door he knocked, then opened. The girl sat up, alarmed to see this near-naked savage in her room, illuminated by the sinister, flickering light of a single candle. She pressed against the backboard, her knees drawn up to her chin, arms wrapped tightly around them.

"Who are you? And why are you here?"

"I am Conan," he said. He placed the candle on the floor and the bundle on her bed and left the room, returning seconds later with a chair. He sat and unwrapped the bundle. "I am here to aid you. You are very weak and sick. This will help."

"What is it?" she asked.

"An old Cimmerian remedy. It is called food. Eat it."

"But the Holy Ones have commanded me—"

"Oppia has put your cure in my hands," he said, silencing the protest. "Eat it all, but eat very slowly, or it will make you even sicker than you are. Start with the fruit, then try a little of the meat or cheese. Dampen the bread with milk, or you may not be able to swallow it. If you've had nothing but that watery gruel for weeks, your body may have forgotten how to handle real food."

She was puzzled, but by now she was so accustomed to submitting that she obeyed. While she applied herself to the food he had brought, he took the unlighted candle to the window. He drove the hard wax down into the smoke-hole, then pounded it out of sight with the pommel of his dagger. When he had cleaned the last traces of wax from the rim of the hole, he sat by the girl's bed. She watched him with apprehension, but she ate as ordered.

"Stop now," he said when about half of the food was eaten.

"Let us see if you can keep that down. If so, you will finish the rest. Now, tell me about this curse that so plagues you."

"It is the inheritance of the women of my line," she said dolefully. "Generations back, we were cursed for sacrilege, and the gods send demons to torment us until either the demons take us or we take our own lives to escape them, as my mother took her life to escape the demon that haunted them. Now it is coming for me."

"And your mother told you all this?" Conan asked.

"Some of it. The rest was explained to me by the Holy Ones, along with the things I must do to purge the curse from my soul."

"Child, your mother was sick in the head, and the curse she told you of existed only in her mind."

"But the demon!" Rietta protested.

"Did you ever see it before you came to live here in the temple? Before you were put in this very room?" he asked.

"Well . . . no." Her eyes grew vague, and the Cimmerian knew that he was pressing her too much and too quickly.

"Rietta." She looked surprised to hear her own name spoken. "Rietta," he repeated, "I swear to you that from this night hence, you will feel better, and that the demon will not come back to you. It is only an insubstantial wraith. It could never harm you, and it will trouble you no more. If all I say is true, will you trust me?"

Slowly, she nodded her head. He hoped that it was because she meant it and not because her spirit was so shattered that she would agree with anything said to her.

When she had finished eating, he gathered up all traces of what must to her have been a feast and carried them back to his own chamber. Then he lay on his bed to rest. Previously he had wanted simply to return the girl to her father, as he had contracted to do. Then he had resolved to expose and destroy the religious fraud perpetrated by Andolla and his woman. Now he wanted to raze this place to its foundations.

THIRTEEN
The Smuggler

When the Cimmerian entered the Wyvern, all conversation ceased. Scarred, branded, and tattooed faces turned toward the landing, where the barbarian stood shaking the rainwater from his cloak. The one-eyed, slit-nosed, and earless watched with close interest as he folded the garment. He would not hang it upon the row of empty pegs set invitingly at the landing. In this place, it would be stolen the instant he turned his back on it.

He descended the stair and looked about for a table with a vacant seat. He saw one near a corner, where he could sit with his back to a wall and enjoy a clear view of the room. The three men who sat at the table looked no more verminous than did the rest of the patrons in the place. He walked to the table and looked down upon its occupants, who paused in their dicing.

"Do you mind if I join you?" he asked. Even the big Cimmerian would not violate the rules that governed such a place, where any lapse of manners could earn swift death. Unless, of course, he deliberately wanted to provoke a fight. A man with a black spider tattooed on his brow and one with a copper nose strapped over the gaping hole where once there had been a nose of flesh and cartilage looked at him; then they looked to the third man.

This one was even more colorfully mutilated than the others. One of his legs protruded stiffly, its knee mangled beyond use. One arm ended in a wrist stump that was neatly patched and cauterized. Conan judged that it had been lopped for theft in some land where that punishment was favored. The man was also wry-necked, his head canted at a permanent angle so that his right ear almost touched his shoulder.

"Join us, warrior," he said in a surprisingly deep, rich voice. "We are honored to have the new terror of Sicas at our table. Barkeep, ale for the Cimmerian!" He chuckled. "I hear that you have a taste for strong drink. I saw a few Cimmerians up in the Bossonian Marches, but they were dull company; morose water-drinkers who always looked as if they were attending a funeral."

"I share few tastes with my countrymen," Conan said, "else I would have stayed in Cimmeria." He took the ale mug brought him by a server and raised it to the wry-necked man. "I thank you."

The man with the tattoo rattled a dice cup. "The game is Shemitish Suicide," he said curtly. "Are you in?" It was a quick came, where money was won or lost on a single roll. The Cimmerian tossed a few coins into the center of the table.

"In," he announced. The cup was passed. Each man shook and upended it once. Conan rolled three stars and a dagger; a middling roll, but the others rolled lower. He raked in his winnings, leaving his next wager on the table.

"That is Spider," said the wry-necked man, managing an angled nod toward the tattooed one, "and that is Copper-nose," indicating the other. "I am called Falx the Lucky."

Conan looked at the man skeptically. "To my eye, you have seen more than your share of misfortune."

The man grinned and tapped his twisted neck. "Had you been hanged and lived to tell of it, you would count yourself lucky, too."

"So I would," Conan said, shaking the cup and slamming it down on the table. He lifted it to reveal four eagles, the highest of scores. The others groaned. "The goddess!" he proclaimed triumphantly, using the traditional name of that throw. It seemed a good omen, so he broached his real reason for coming to this place.

"Tell me, my friends: If a man wished to speak with Lisip, how would he go about it?" The others studied him with close evaluation.

"For one thing, he would attract attention," said Falx the Lucky. "You have done little else since arriving here in Sicas. I think that the old boss would be willing to grant you an audience."

"Could you arrange that?" the Cimmerian asked while Spider rattled dice in the cup.

"I think so. Hold the game for a while." Falx rose and limped away from the table. Obediently, the others let the dice rest, although they seemed little inclined to engage their new companion in conversation. That suited Conan well. He had not come to this place to consort with the likes of these. He sat back and drank his ale, a thumb hooked into his studded belt.

The rest of the clientele of the Wyvern paid him no heed after their first surprise at his appearance in their den. He saw no red leather identifying Ingas's followers. None of those present had been among Maxio's men on the night of the raid on the royal storehouse. There were a few armored men who might have belonged to Ermak, but he did not recognize any faces.

After a few minutes, Falx the Lucky came dragging his stiff leg back across the floor, which was sticky with spilled blood and wine.

"Lisip is upstairs," he said to Conan. "He will see you now."

Conan rose, and many eyes watched as he crossed the floor and ascended a stair, following Falx's slow pace. There was danger here, but he was confident in his ability to carve an escape through Lisip's men, who were even less competent than Ingas's, and nothing like Ermak's.

His guide came to a door strapped with iron. Set into it was a small viewing-window; even that was covered with an iron grate. The window opened and a suspicious eye studied them both. The two stood well back so that the watcher could see that no one was with them. The door opened and they went through.

"In with you," said the watchman, a burly lout with long, tangled hair and a vest made of woven leather straps, liberally studded with bronze nailheads. He wore an iron-shod club thonged to his belt, over which a hairy belly sagged. He shut and barred the door behind them.

"What do you want of me?" said a voice from the dim rear of the room. The speaker sat behind a broad table. He was a huge man, both powerfully muscled and rotund. His massive, bald head was set squarely atop his sloping shoulders, obviating any visible neck. Old scars streaked the bare face and scalp, and the immense hands that lay atop the table were gnarled and much weathered. Except for the net of wrinkles that intersected the scars on his face, his age was difficult to judge. He looked like an ancient tortoise, and his black eyes were as expressionless as a reptile's. His lipless mouth was set in a straight, horizontal line.

"A few words privily," Conan said.

"You may go," Lisip said to Falx. "Umruk stays," he continued, indicating the watchman. "He cannot hear." Falx bowed his way out and Conan took a chair facing the old tortoise, making sure that Umruk could not see his lips move as he spoke.

"You injured my man out at the mines," Lisip said without preamble. "What were you doing there?"

"Xanthus hired me to sort some things out for him," Conan said. "I went to have a look for myself. Your man spoke insolently to me. I could have killed him. He has nothing to complain about."

"What sort of business?" Lisip inquired.

"That is between Xanthus and me."

"There has been much talk of you since you arrived here," Lisip said. "You slew three of Ingas's men in the Square. Two nights ago, another two were sent to follow you from the Skull. They were not seen again. Was that your doing?''

Conan shrugged. ''What are Ingas's men to you?''

''Nothing at all. But I want to know where you stand as far as I am concerned. There is too much trouble in this town as it is, without some Cimmerian wild man running about making more. I used to have things here operating to my satisfaction. All the rogues of the town worked for me, and I saw to it that the respectable citizens were never bothered, save by the occasional burglary. And the burglars only stole; they never harmed anyone. Now all is changed.''

''The change happened long before I got here,'' Conan pointed out. ''It may be that things can return to normal.''

''How?'' Lisip asked. The reptilian eyes narrowed slightly.

''Ermak and Maxio are at war. One must kill the other soon. With either of them gone, things should cool down. If Maxio dies, Bombas will cease being overly distracted and begin to concentrate on the business that has been so profitable to everyone. If it is Ermak who perishes, his men will drift out of town or hire out to other gangs. They are nothing without him. Either way, you should be able to handle the survivor.''

''Aye,'' said Lisip. ''But I do not think much of Maxio's chances. If it is Ermak who lives . . .''

''Very true,'' Conan said. ''In this city, only I am a match for Ermak in an open fight.''

''Are you saying that you will go to work for me?'' Lisip demanded.

Conan leaned back in his seat. ''I am saying that I am not your enemy. Just now, I do not work for you or for any of the gang leaders. I have other matters to attend to. Later, who can tell? Let us say that should it come down to just you and Ermak, my sword may be for hire.''

''And in the meantime, you will stay out of this business?'' The tortoise face grew as hard as stone.

''If I can. Much depends on how well I can stay clear of the troubles here. My plans will keep me in Sicas for some days more. I may need a hiding place, a bolt-hole where I can stay out of sight for a while.''

''Is that all? I can supply you with that. There are cellars here in the Wyvern—''

Conan shook his head. ''Your former associate, Julus, now works for the Reeve. I'll wager he knows every hiding place in this city. No, I need something more secure. I have heard that you have a stronghold somewhere near the city, a place where the brats and women belonging to the miners are held to keep their menfolk sweet and docile.''

''Aye, you'd be safe there. But you must keep this to yourself. No telling what sort of foolishness those rock-eaters might try if they knew where the sluts and cubs were.''

''Your secret is safe with me,'' Conan said. ''After all, it's my neck, too.''

''South of here, about a half-day's ride, there is an ancient fort on the east bank of the river. It was a border fort once, back before the Ophirians were pushed beyond the Tybor River. Been abandoned for centuries, but still sound. That's where they're kept, under close guard.''

''If I need to go there, how will I let the guards know I have your permission to hide out in the fort? I won't have time to send word ahead.''

Lisip opened a drawer and drew out a flat medallion of lead, its surface stamped with a figure of a wyvern. ''This is my seal. Show this to the man at the main gate and he will admit you.''

''Just the gate guard?'' Conan asked. ''No sentries posted at the approaches?''

''My men?'' Lisip said. ''Are you serious?'' That was just what Conan wanted to hear. He took the seal and placed it in his pouch.

''Very well. I'll not move against you or your men as long as they do not molest me. When the situation has changed, we will speak further.'' He rose to go, then turned back to Lisip. ''Oh, I have heard that there is to be a peace conference.''

"Where did you hear that?" The words came out between lips that scarcely seemed to move.

"Bombas told me. He does not trust his own men to provide him with adequate protection. He wants me to come along as his bodyguard."

"Aye, there is to be such a conference, if I can persuade enough men to attend. Will you be there?"

"It is a paying job," the Cimmerian said. "But it is just for that one night. It does not mean that I have thrown in with the pig."

"Very well. You'll have no trouble from me. The swine has naught to vex him, anyway. Nobody here is insane enough to attack the King's Reeve, no matter how much we would like to."

"Did Maxio truly slay Bombas's brother? I heard that it happened here in the Wyvern."

The massive shoulders moved slightly in a shrug. "It was Maxio's dagger. What care I which hand wielded it? Burdo was as worthless a swine as his brother, Bombas. He thought that because we have an arrangement with the Reeve, he was entitled to disport himself without payment and that he was safe from harm down here in the Pit. He was wrong on both counts, most especially on that last one."

"I shall keep that in mind," Conan said. "No man is truly safe here."

"No man," Lisip affirmed.

The Cimmerian took his leave and left the gang leader's sanctum. The common room seemed to hold the same crowd as before. The street outside was as black as always during the nights. He walked slowly toward the upper town, hand on hilt, stopping frequently to listen for following footsteps. He heard and saw nothing, but that did not cause him to relax his vigilance. This had been a dangerous town to begin with. Now his situation was more perilous than ever.

He made his way to the inn and called for ale at the bar. With a leer, the barkeep handed him a folded sheet of paper. "It came for you this afternoon,'' he said. "Brought by the jailer.'' The paper smelled faintly of lavender.

Conan opened it and read. In a delicate, Zamoran hand was written: *"It was, indeed, the very least you could do. When will you buy me out of here?"* Laughing, The Cimmerian tossed the note into the fire.

He finished his ale, then went to the courtyard, where he found a torch and set it alight. As he ascended the stair, he noted something amiss. Stooping low, he held the torch a few inches above the steps to discern whether he had seen aright. Drops of blood newly stained them. Slowly, he resumed his climb. The spattering of blood continued along the gallery; then there was a small puddle of it outside the door of his chamber.

Silently, the Cimmerian drew his sword. With a jerk, he snatched the door open and thrust the torch within, keeping his wrist well outside lest a sudden descending sword unhand him. Inside, all was quiet. Huddled on his bed he saw Brita, ashen-faced and wide-eyed. For a moment he thought her dead, and the blood hers. Then, with relief, he saw the form stretched on the floor.

"Is anyone in there besides the dead man?" he asked, sword still at the ready. She looked up, as if noticing for the first time that he was there, and shook her head. He sheathed the weapon and entered the chamber closing the door behind him.

"Are you hurt?" he asked. Again she shook her head. "Then what is wrong with you? It's just a dead man. They do not cause near as much trouble as the live ones." He rolled the corpse onto its back. The man had a long, bony face, its length emphasized by a sandy, pointed beard. His heavy cloak and long boots were of the sort worn by caravanners.

"How came he to be here?" Conan asked.

"Just a while ago," she began, stammering, then gathering strength and firmness, "there came a knock at the door. I opened, thinking it to be you. This man stood in the doorway, his face like that of a man dead already, the front of his clothes soaked with blood. Oh, Conan, he was ghastly. He staggered inside, clutching a bundle to him. He said only: 'For the Cimmerian,' then collapsed there as you see him. I tried to turn him over, but he was too heavy, and his life had already fled. I have been here ever since, terrified. I did not know what to do, thinking that his murderer might be just outside.''

Conan stooped and examined the man. Someone had nearly eviscerated him with a dagger. The weapon was not present.

"Must have been a bull of a man to climb those stairs cut like that," he pronounced. "Where is this bundle you spoke of?"

"There." She pointed to a corner where something lay wrapped in bloodstained cloth. "It rolled there when he fell. I have been afraid to move."

Conan straightened. "We don't want him found here. All is quiet below. I will carry him to an alley near the Square and leave him there. He'll be found tomorrow, and maybe his comrades will want to give him burial. You clean up here. Get a bucket of water from the kitchen. Can you do that?" Wordlessly, she nodded.

"There is blood outside the door, also, and on the stairs. If you miss some, at least it will not look so much like someone died here. If anyone asks tomorrow, say that I staggered in drunk early in the morning, bleeding from a head wound."

"You think of everything," she said.

"I will be back presently." He lifted the corpse and draped it over a shoulder, ignoring the blood that smeared him in the process.

No one was stirring in the inn when he carried his inert load down the stairs, and the street without was too dark for any watcher to see him as he bore the body toward the center of the town. He left it in an alleyway, then went to one of the public fountains and washed off as much of the sticky blood as he could manage. It disappeared readily from the oiled-leather covering of his brigandine. As for his clothes, he could always buy new.

He returned to the inn and found Brita industriously scrubbing at the floor like any housewife. It seemed that performing this homely chore had restored her usual serenity.

"I have already cleaned the gallery and the steps. I do not think I missed much."

"No one in this town makes a great fuss about spilled blood," Conan said. "But until I know what this is all about, I do not want that particular corpse associated with me."

Now he crossed to the corner of the room and picked up the cloth-wrapped package. It was astoundingly heavy for its size. He turned it over and over, examining the wrappings. Broad, bloody handprints stained the cord bindings, as well as the cloth beneath them, so he knew that the wrappings had not been tampered with.

"But how could he know to bring it to me?" Conan mused aloud.

"What did you say, Conan?" Brita asked, wringing pinkish water into the bucket.

"Nothing. I must decide what to do with this."

"What is it?" She stood and came closer, but he would not let her take the thing from him. The less she knew, the better.

"You need not concern yourself. But you have seen that it is something men kill for. I must conceal it until I know where it should go."

"Where will you hide it?"

"That is another thing you need not concern yourself about," he said. Noting her downcast expression, he added, "I do this only for your own good. This is an evil thing; the less you have to do with it, the safer you will be."

"Oh, very well," she said, pouting.

"I must be away. Soon it will be light. I will come back before long. Have you everything you need?"

"Yes. My wants are few. I wish that you were more in my company, though. Have I displeased you?"

"No, but who can keep up with you, the way you disappear for days on your mad quest? I have many things to do, and many enemies to avoid, and I cannot be lumbered with a woman."

"Lumbered!" she said hotly. "Is that what I am now, a mere impediment? Something that might get in the way of that sword arm of yours? Well, I can care for myself!"

"I've no time for this. Farewell until the next time, Brita." He left, muttering imprecations against women and their too-easily hurt feelings.

In the high street, Conan paused. This was one mission that had to be kept absolutely secret. He found a street grate and lifted it. Returning to the inn's courtyard, he took a torch from a bundle by the stable door and returned to the street. He waited by the grate until he was certain that he was unobserved. Then he dropped into the Great Drain. Reaching overhead, he slid the grate back into place.

At least the recent rains had washed the drainage system clean. The air was dank, but it was not foul. He walked a few paces from the grate, then set the heavy package upon the damp stones. Sitting upon the bundle, he took flint and steel from his belt pouch and from his tinderbox he drew a bit of charred cloth. Striking a light thus, working entirely by touch, was a tedious business, but he had patience. After several minutes of striking, a spark took hold in the tinder, and its glow began to spread as the Cimmerian blew gently upon it. He pressed it into the oil-soaked tow that wrapped the end of the torch, blowing all the while. Soon he had a flame sufficient to illuminate his way through the Great Drain.

He emerged from the sewer into the theater and ascended to the roof, whence he crossed to the roof of the temple, taking great care, for the thing he carried was weighty. He did not go to his chamber; rather, he descended the rear wall of the temple, his burden lashed to his back by his sword belt.

He entered the deserted kitchen and from it took the stair that led to the cellar. The cellar of the temple was cavernous, containing storage bins full of wood for the sacrificial and warming fires, unused furniture, offerings accumulated over the years, and much other debris. Here were also the furnaces, used for warming the water for ritual baths and for heating the entire temple by a system of flues. A fire was kept burning at all times in one of the furnaces, and Conan first made sure that no acolyte was in attendance before he crossed the floor. He swung the furnace door wide, and by the light of the fire within, he unwrapped his parcel and tossed the bloodied bindings into the flames. Then he held up and admired the object of so much greed, intrigue, and bloodshed.

Despite the lurid red of the flames, the thing was blacker than the blackest night. It seemed to gleam brilliantly, yet at the same time it seemed to suck up all light and cast none back. Its body was that of a scorpion, so realistically portrayed that he would not have been surprised had it begun to crawl upon its six legs and snatch at him with its pincers. The tip of its stinger glistened as if with a special liquid blackness.

Its head was that of a woman, her beauty as serene as the insectile body was grotesque. Her eyes were open, black within black. They showed neither pupil nor iris, yet they gazed keenly, and he did not like to think what they might be seeing. Whatever its true origin, whether the image of Selkhet carved by the sculptor Ekba, as Casperus had said, or the nameless Atlantean idol carved from a diamond that fell from the heavens, as in Piris's tale, or something else entirely, he could not deny that the object had great magical force. Conan was sensitive to such things, and he hated them. The image's very weight was unnatural. It could not have weighed more had it been made of pure gold.

At least, he thought, he had a perfect place to hide the thing, right here in the temple. He carried his prize to the great chamber that lay beneath the nave. Near one end was a solid, rectangular structure of masonry that reached from the stone-flagged floor to the ceiling. It was a pedestal, and when this had been a Temple of Mitra, it had supported the colossal stone statue of the god that had stood in the temple above. Now it supported the trick statue of Mother Doorgah.

Once, many years before, Conan had performed a very special service for a renegade priest of Mitra. In gratitude, the man had revealed to the Cimmerian a secret of the ancient priesthood, from which he had been expelled. In every Temple of Mitra, he had said, there was a place concealed within the pedestal of the god's statue where treasures, or even the priests themselves, could be hidden in moments of extreme danger. Then he had explained how one might enter such a crypt.

Conan went to the rear of the pedestal. Once more he looked around to be sure that he was unobserved. Counting carefully from the floor, he pressed certain stones; each moved a fraction of an inch. These stones were in appearance identical to all the others, and only one who knew the formula with which to find their positions, and who also knew the proper order in which they had to be pushed, could open the secret crypt. At Conan's final push, a section of the stones, almost man-high, swung smoothly, noiselessly, inward.

He stooped and went inside. Within, he groped at the wall to the right of the doorway until he found a niche in which were stacked a number of candles. He took one over to the furnace and lit it, then returned to the crypt. The chamber within was empty. Its walls were lined with niches, but nothing now stood in them save for the one reserved for candles. There were unobtrusive ventilation slots in the floor and ceiling. Otherwise, it was completely sealed except for the doorway.

A small stone pedestal rose from the center of the floor to waist height. In the old days, a small statue of Mitra, identical but for size to the colossus above, would have stood on the stone post. Now the Cimmerian set the black woman-headed scorpion in its place. The thing gleamed balefully in the light of his candle. He blew out the candle, replaced it in its niche and reentered the cellar. Then he reached back and touched a single stone near the opening. The stone portal swung shut. In an instant, it was undetectable. For the first time since finding the dead man in his chamber, Conan breathed easily. He would be supremely happy when he had this treasure off his hands.

He left the cellar, and as he passed through the kitchen, he did not forget to appropriate some viands for Rietta.

FOURTEEN
The Rogue's Conference

He had come to an agreement with Lisip, and Bombas wanted him for a bodyguard at the peace conference, should that ever take place. Maxio was neutral for the moment, as was Ermak. That left only Ingas and his gang as immediate enemies. Conan decided that he might as well go out in daylight.

The blustery, rainy weather of past days had given way to bright skies and warm sunshine. The Square was thronged, for most of the townspeople had not ventured out in the rain and now needed to replenish their larders, as well as to trade the latest gossip. Conan found the Square abuzz with talk of a number of killings that had taken place the night before. He asked a stall-keeper for details.

"Sometime after midnight, Maxio and his men staged a raid on Ermak's headquarters and killed three of Ermak's men. They missed Ermak, though."

"Maxio?" Conan said. "But his men are burglars, not warriors."

"They went in fast, when everyone there was asleep. Burglars are good at that sort of thing. Killed a few and ran. Sometime later, a pack of Ingas's men caught five of Lisip's in an alley in the Pit and cut them down. Then there was a caravaneer found dead this morning not far from here, but nobody knows if that was a part of the gang-fighting.''

The Cimmerian wended his way to the inn and took his horse from the stable. He rode out through the city gate to give the beast some exercise and make sure that it was sound of wind and limb. He planned to be using it in the next day or two. Before riding back into the city, he stopped by the pasture where the recently arrived caravan had picketed its beasts and unloaded its goods for the local merchants to bid on. He noticed several caravanners sitting around a camp fire and dismounted.

''Is this the caravan of Mulvix?'' he asked.

''Aye,'' said one, looking up at the big foreigner. ''But Mulvix is dead. We buried him this morning.''

''How came he by his death?'' Conan inquired.

The man shrugged. He wore a dirty cloth knotted around his head and he scratched in his beard. ''Mulvix was a man who carried many a dangerous cargo. I think that this time his luck deserted him. He took his latest treasure into the town last night, but he did not come back. Most likely somebody decided to kill him and take the thing instead of paying.''

''What was it he carried?'' Conan asked.

The man shook his head. ''Mulvix was never one to let on about his little secret burdens. And we all knew better than to ask.''

''We are sorry to lose Mulvix; he was a good man,'' said another. ''But we are happy to have that thing gone from our midst. I think it was no honest smuggler's load.''

''How so?'' Conan asked.

''Ever since we left Belverus,'' he said, ''we've had bad luck. Accidents. Animals lost. And every one of us has had trouble sleeping, and we were plagued by bad dreams.''

''That is true,'' said the man with the rag around his head. ''And the beasts have been all but uncontrollable; biting, kicking, running away, and fighting their loads every morning as we packed up. And since last night, look at them!'' He pointed to where about fourscore mules placidly munched grass. ''Like little lambs, just as they were before we stopped at Belverus.''

''Mulvix trifled with something he never should have touched,'' said a gray-bearded muleteer.

''He said nothing about who was to receive this thing?'' the Cimmerian asked.

''Not a word,'' said the first speaker. ''Mulvix never spoke of such things.'' He looked Conan over suspiciously. ''Why do you ask?''

''I am working for the Reeve,'' Conan said, half-truthfully.

''When did that fat rogue ever care for aught save his payoff?'' asked the gray-bearded one. ''We've always paid him the king's share plus his own payment, to keep him happy. What does he want now? Is there a tax to be paid for dying in his cursed town?''

''If so,'' said the one with the headcloth, ''he can try to get it from Mulvix, or from whoever slew him. Not a coin more will he get from us. We may never come this way again. This town lies under a curse worse than the one on whatever it was that Mulvix bore hither.''

Conan smiled. ''Come back next time your path brings you close,'' he advised. ''I think you will find a different, and much quieter, town.''

''Eh?'' said the graybeard, but the Cimmerian had already remounted and was riding back toward the city gate. As he rode, he fell in with a group of forty or more men with the same destination. All were hard-looking specimens. The faces of some were deeply stamped with villainy. Others wore battle armor and were clearly mercenaries. Conan reined in beside a man who wore city clothes but whose sword and dagger looked well used.

''How is it that such a company rides into Sicas?'' Conan asked.

''Word came to Shamar that Sicas is a lively place, and that any man with a sword to hire out can find good employment there. All the prominent leaders are hiring, and the pay is high.''

Conan turned to a little group of mercenaries. "Do you come to join Ermak?"

"Aye," said one. "We were here until last year, when things grew too quiet to support so many good fighting men. We rode out for the wars in Ophir, but now Ermak sends word that we are needed once more."

"How are things in Ophir?" asked Conan with professional interest.

"Bad," said a man who wore a high-spired Zingaran helm. "The war has gone on too long. There is plenty of fighting, but nothing left to plunder."

Conan decided that when he left Sicas, he would not ride to Ophir. While the newcomers were paying their gate duties, he rode on into the city. It seemed that the night's excitement had extended into the day, for there was a street fight in progress before the inn. Two bands of men were having it out with steel, battling in earnest. At the courtyard entrance, the inn's male workers blocked the way with sword and stave.

He saw Brita striving to press herself into a wall as the men fought just a few steps from her, their flailing weapons passing within inches of her. Conan cursed and spurred his horse forward. Could the woman not stay clear of trouble? He snatched a club from one of the stablemen and hefted its three-foot, knotty-headed length, waving it as easily as another man might handle a willow wand. He rode among the brawlers, flailing like a madman. The club rang on steel cap or cracked into bare pate indifferently. The result was always the same: a man stretched senseless on the cobblestones. Soon the standing men backed away, bewildered by this unexpected fury.

"Take your fight elsewhere!" the Cimmerian shouted. "This inn is under the protection of Conan of Cimmeria. Are there any of you who wish to challenge me?" He dropped the cudgel and drew his sword. "Speak up, dogs! I've not slain a man all day and my blade is athirst!" There were a few mutters, then the hiss of weapons being resheathed. Men stooped to lift their wounded comrades, and the whole crowd, so fierce minutes before, turned and made its way down the high street.

"Why, sir," said the innkeeper, "I thank you for this."

Conan dismounted. "Well, let the scum curse me for a spoilsport, but a man must have *one* place in this town where he can find some quiet." He went to Brita. "Are you well, girl?"

"I am unhurt," she said, brushing at some flecks of blood that decorated her mantle. "None of this blood is mine; it flew from their weapons. I might have been killed, though, had it not been for you. I never saw a single man put an end to a fight like that!" Her eyes shone with admiration. "Once again, I must thank you for rescuing me."

"That is because I was the only *man* in the fight." He turned to the innkeeper. "Who were those dogs? I have not seen them ere today."

"Two of the smaller gangs," the man told him. "One group has thrown in with Lisip. The others were old rivals, and now the first pack feels strong enough to attack them."

"Well, things are about to get worse," Conan said. He nodded toward the upper end of the street, where the newcomers were riding toward them.

"Mitra, be our aid!" the innkeeper moaned. "More of them!" He summoned a slave. "Go to the Square. Purchase extra fire buckets. Until I say otherwise, the men will sleep in shifts, with some on watch at all times for fire and riot."

They passed into the courtyard and Conan handed his mount over to a hostler. He turned to enter the common room. "Come, Brita, you can tell me of your . . ." but she drew back from the door.

"We will speak later," she said. "I have learned of a place where my sister may be hiding. I must go there now. I will rejoin you before long. Farewell, and thank you again for my rescue."

He was about to call out to her when he was accosted by a man who stood just inside the common room. Within the dimness he could make out the figure of a young man wearing a brigandine belted with a matched pair of swords.

"I would have some words with you, Cimmerian," Gilmay said.

"Make them brief," Conan said. "I've much to do."

"Aye, you have been doing much these past days, but little of it seems to be the service for which my master engaged you."

"I've not eaten today and am famished nigh unto death," Conan said. "If we must talk, then let's eat while we're at it. Even the sight of your face cannot spoil my appetite." He saw the youth's countenance darken.

"You'll not provoke me into fighting," Gilmay said. "I know better than that."

"Then you've more brains than ere now I credited to you," Conan answered, taking a seat. "Now, what is your business?"

Gilmay sat across from him. "After so many days, you have not yet tendered a single report."

"I've nothing to report yet," said Conan.

"But my master *knows* the thing is now in the city! Through his arts, he can detect its presence."

"Then will his scrying glass not tell him where it lies?" the Cimmerian inquired.

"If it could do that, would there be any need to hire a barbarian lout to find it?" Gilmay asked hotly. "The thing's sorcerous nature makes it immune to such spying."

"That is unfortunate," Conan said, reaching for a platter of meat pasties. "Casperus will just have to wait until I have something to report to him."

"He grows impatient," Gilmay said. "You have been swaggering all over this town, getting into fights, making a nuisance of yourself, and doing us no good at all. Sometimes you stay here at this inn, other times you disappear. Where are you hiding out, Cimmerian?"

"If I told you that, I wouldn't be hiding, would I?" Conan took a pull at his ale, eyeing the youth warily through the glass bottom of the pewter tankard. He could see that he had pushed Gilmay as far as was advisable and that it was time to relent, just a little. He set the tankard on the table.

"Listen, Gilmay. There is soon to be a peace conference, and the King's Reeve has asked me to attend him there as bodyguard. Nobody, not even I, can make a decent search of this town until things quiet down. Everyone is too nervous and wary. Tell your master that I have made arrangements with the priest of Bes, who is the town's main fence, and I have ingratiated myself at the Temple of Mother Doorgah, whose priest fancies himself a sorcerer. If either of them lays hands upon the idol, I will know of it."

"That is better," said Gilmay, somewhat mollified.

"Now it is your turn to speak," said Conan.

"What would you know?" Gilmay asked.

"What know you of a beautiful, murderous, black-haired wench who may call herself Altaira?" He watched the youth closely.

"I know nothing of such a woman!" Gilmay said, too quickly and far too emphatically.

"Yes you do," Conan said. "You will need many more years and much more experience before you can lie to me with success, lad. Now tell me what you know of a strange little man who dresses like a Shadizar harlot and favors lilac scent." To his surprise, Gilmay's face flushed scarlet and he sprang from his bench.

"Just concentrate on finding the thing you were hired to find, barbarian!"

"Tell your master that he has little chance of seeing the idol he wants so badly until I know more of these two. Tell him also that a smuggler named Mulvix was found dead this morning, knifed by someone who relieved him of a small parcel. Now run along and inform Casperus. Tell him also that I want no interference, and no games."

Gilmay whirled and stalked away. Conan was satisfied that he had given the bubbling pot another stir. He reapplied himself to his meal, but it seemed that he was not to be allowed even this to enjoy in peace. Another man came to stand before his table and he looked up to see the hulking shape of Julus, the Reeve's henchman. The brutish thug sat without waiting for an invitation.

"The Reeve would speak with you," said Julus.

"About what?" Conan asked.

"That is not for me to say," Julus maintained.

"You are his dog and you know everything he does," Conan said. "Is it about the peace conference?"

Julus studied him with small, shrewd eyes. "Aye. It is set for tonight. Why he wants you there is beyond me. I am all the protection he needs."

Conan grinned at him with a predatory baring of teeth. "Perhaps he does not trust you. I do not trust you myself. Tell me, Julus; the other night at the royal storehouse, was it Bombas who bade the Zingaran shoot me with his crossbow, or was it you?"

The man's expression betrayed nothing. "We thought you dead already. If the Zingaran aimed at you, he must not have known at whom he aimed. It was dark."

"Aye, the light was poor until the place was set afire. Whose doing was that?"

"A clumsy guardsman," Julus said, his face as bland as ever.

"That is what the Reeve told me," Conan said. "I wondered whether you would have a different story."

"Why should I?"

The Cimmerian could see that he would get nothing this way. "Why the sudden decision to hold the conference tonight? Does this latest round of killings alarm even the headmen of this town?"

"That is a part of it," Julus admitted. "But there is another matter. There are scurrilous, lying tales making the rounds. They are in the mouths of every minstrel and storyteller in the district. Those vagabonds are saying that the Reeve has been stealing from the king and that he himself set the fire at the royal warehouse." The man's deep-set eyes were steely. "Now where would they get ideas like that?"

"Ask them," Conan said. "Anyway, as you say, they must be lying."

"More men have been hung because of lies than were ever condemned for a truthful accusation," Julus pointed out.

"That is so," Conan allowed. "Perhaps it is time for you to seek a new employer."

Julus rose. "Be at the headquarters at nightfall, Cimmerian." He turned and left.

Conan released his grip on his dirk. He had thought that Ermak was the only truly dangerous man in the town. He had been wrong. He had allowed himself to be deceived by Julus's apish look and loutish manner to think the man was stupid. He had known many men to die for such misjudgments. The man was shrewd and dangerous, and like nearly everyone in this town, he was playing a game of his own.

When his meal was finished, Conan went to the Square and idled about until he saw Delia making her usual rounds. She smiled at his approach, but it seemed to him that the usually ebullient woman was wan and nervous.

"Conan! Where have you been?" she demanded.

"I have been active, but mostly in the hours of darkness," he said. The two wandered into a dark corner of the portico to speak.

"Delia," Conan went on, "there is to be a peace conference tonight. I will be there, acting as the Reeve's bodyguard. He no longer trusts Julus. Will Maxio be there?"

"I do not know! He acts so strange lately. One minute he says that there must be peace, that things have gone too far, and the next he swears that he will kill Ermak on sight, or that he will slay Bombas. Twice today he has said that he will go to the conference to reason with the others, and twice he has said that he will not. I do not know what to tell you."

"Tell him this for me: I will be there tonight, but I have undertaken to guard Bombas for only this conference. As long as Maxio does not threaten the Reeve, I care not what else he does. I do not as yet take sides in any of the goings-on here in Sicas."

"Perhaps you do not take sides," she said, her voice gone hard, "but you are involved in them up to those blue eyes of yours. I think there would not be half so much chaos here were it not for you."

"What is the matter, Delia?" he asked cheerfully. "Do you not like excitement?"

"If you were with me, I think I could enjoy all this," she said forthrightly. "As it is, I am frightened."

"Just be careful and you will come to no harm," he said. "And relay to Maxio what I have told you."

"I will," she said. "Now go. I am beginning to think that it is not a good thing to be seen in company with you. Leave me and I will go on in a little while."

He bade her farewell and left the niche. He had one errand yet to perform. He wandered among the vendors in the Square until he found what he was looking for. In a corner of the market, among the poorest and pettiest of the hawkers, an old woman sat on the pavement, her aged back against a stone wall. Before her was spread a blanket bearing clay pots and bowls for sale. It was the woman from the mining village, the one who had seen him slay Ingas's three men. Casually he walked over to her, then squatted and pretended to examine her pitiful wares.

"Greeting, Grandmother," he said in a low voice.

"Greeting, Cimmerian." Her sharp old eyes darted about to search out observers.

"I have a message for Bellas. Will you deliver it, exactly as I give it to you?"

"Tell me!" Now her eyes glittered with hope.

"Tell him this: In the hours before dawn tomorrow, all the ablebodied men of the mining village must arm themselves and travel southward, down the riverbank, until they are well out of sight of the town. I know where the women and children are being held, and if Bellas will follow my instructions exactly, you will have your families back before sundown tomorrow."

"I will tell him!" she said, her eyes shining with tears. She repeated his instructions word for word.

"Very good," Conan said. "Now, someplace within a halfday's march downriver, all must cross to the east bank of the river. Is there a bridge or a ford, or a ferry?"

"Aye, there is a small bridge, about five miles to the south.

There is no true road; the bridge is used only by herders to move cattle from one pasture to another.''

"Perfect!" Conan said. "Stone or wood?"

"Wood atop old stone pilings. It falls into poor condition if nobody uses it for a few seasons.''

"Then tell Bellas to bring along tools in case we need to repair the bridge.''

"I will do it," she said. "Go with the blessings of all the gods, Cimmerian.''

"Do not bless me until I return with your menfolk and the wives and bairns tomorrow night,'' Conan cautioned. "You could have cause to curse my name.''

"A man who even tries to aid us earns my prayers,'' the old woman maintained stoutly.

Conan made his way back to the temple. He was glad that he knew the bridge might be in a ruinous state. He had known sizable military operations to founder because no one had thought to bring a spade, or a rope, or any of a thousand mundane items that could prove to be crucially necessary. There was more to war than men, horses and arms.

Oppia saw him as he entered the temple. She was upset, and for once it was not because of his lengthy absences from the place.

"Come," she said. 'Look at this!'' She took him by the hand and tugged him toward the nave. Inside were the acolytes, as well as some of the newcomers who had been there the night Andolla had performed his statue trick. The hall shook with loud chanting and the orchestra played as before, but now something was different. A dense, crimson glow hovered shapelessly above the head of Mother Doorgah. Andolla chanted with arms outspread. He sat cross-legged, but this time, instead of sitting directly upon the lap of the goddess, he hovered two or three feet above it.

"How is he doing it?'' Conan asked. "Wires?''

"No, you fool'' she hissed. "The glow began to form during the morning offices. This afternoon my husband attempted the spell of levitation, and this time it worked. His magical powers have increased tenfold!''

"Perhaps Mother Doorgah smiles upon him," Conan said. Oppia favored him with a withering glare.

"This is probably harmless," she said, "but I fear that his success may tempt him to try some truly dangerous work of wizardry."

"Would that not attract even more worshipers, with yet more generous donations?"

"The risk is too great. I fear that my husband does not truly understand the powers he toys with. Something terrible could come of this."

"That would be a great pity," Conan said. "Oppia, I must be away for part of this night."

"It is good of you to tell me, for once," she said in a voice that might have drawn blood.

"This is important business," he went on imperturbably. "There is to be a peace conference tonight, with most of the town's gang leaders in attendance. Bombas will be there as well, and he has asked me to go with him as his bodyguard. He no longer trusts his own men."

"What makes him think he can trust you?" she demanded.

"We Cimmerians are known to be true to our word," he said.

"All sorts of men have that reputation," she said bitterly, "but I have never encountered one of them."

"Even so, the happenings at the meeting might be of interest to you," he pointed out.

She thought about it for a while. "Yes, you are right. It would be good to know whether there is to be peace here, and if not, how the battle lines are to be drawn. Go then, and report to me when you return."

"You may be asleep when I get back," he pointed out.

"I rarely get any rest now," she said. She stared at the bizarre spectacle in the temple. "And it looks as if I will be getting even less."

Conan went to the upper floor and looked in upon Rietta. She was in deep and, for once, peaceful sleep. She was no longer as pale and listless as she had been, and she was putting on a bit of flesh. Soon, he judged, she would be strong enough for him to carry her away from his place without her dying from the shock.

When he arrived at the Reeve's headquarters, Julus and the remaining Zingaran eyed him without favor. Conan returned the look. Both men were heavily armed. None of the knock-kneed and feeble guards seemed to be present. Soon Bombas came from within his chambers, muffled in a heavy cloak.

"Do we go to the Wyvern?" Conan asked.

"No," the Reeve said. "Ingas will regard that place only as Lisip's territory. All finally agreed to the Guildhall of the Gold-smiths. It is but two streets south of the Square. It is a small place, only two stories, with no other buildings adjoining and grounds all the way around. We will meet on the upper floor. Each of us is to be accompanied by no more than three followers. Only one may accompany each leader upstairs. The others may stay downstairs or, if we wish it, on the grounds outside."

"I've seen peace conferences between warring nations carried out with less caution," Conan said.

"The stakes here are the same," Bombas rejoined. "Death for one who walks into a trap unprepared."

They left the headquarters and crossed the Square. The public area contained its usual evening population, but nobody spared a glance for the four hooded, arms-clinking men who walked south-ward. They entered the maze of side streets and in a few minutes stood before the goldsmiths' guildhall. This had once been a town-house and was surrounded by handsome gardens, where now armed men paced. Julus spoke to the Zingaran, and that one joined the milling men in the gardens.

"He will warn us if a body of men tries to steal close, Excel-lency," said Julus.

"Come along," said Bombas, and the three men entered the hall.

The ground floor was well appointed, intended for the entertainments held periodically by the wealthy guild. Just now a number of men sat in the lavishly upholstered and carven furniture, their feet propped upon the fine dining table. Some had laid aside their rivalries and were dicing.

"Wait you here," Bombas said to Julus. Then, to Conan, "Attend me, Cimmerian." Conan followed the Reeve up a broad, curving stair to the upper floor. They entered a long room, where the guild conducted business. It was as well appointed and highly decorated as the room below, but its only furnishing was a single long table, lined with massive chairs. Here sat the men they were to meet with.

"It is about time you got here," said Ingas, his gold-embroidered, red-leather costume glowing richly in the light of many candles.

"I am the King's Reeve, and I hurry for no man who is not my better in rank. I see none such present."

"What is that rogue doing here?" Ingas demanded, pointing at Conan.

"He attends me," Bombas said. "Each of us was to bring one guard, and he is mine. Has anyone an objection to that?" He stared haughtily down the table.

"I've no problem," said Lisip.

Ermak shrugged armored shoulders. "You may come attended by a dancing bear for all I care."

These three Conan recognized. There were others, leaders of minor gangs, but they kept silence in the presence of their betters. The Cimmerian made a circuit of the room, looking out of each window.

"Where is Maxio?" he asked when he had completed his survey.

"He has not arrived yet," said Lisip. "I doubt that he will show himself. Something has him acting like a madman lately."

"Let's kill him and be done with it!" said Ermak, pounding a gauntleted fist upon the table. "His little band are just burglars; they contribute nothing to our wealth." He turned to Bombas, and his neatly trimmed beard was split by a narrow smile. "Save the percentage of their takings that they share with his Excellency.''

"We do not come here to speak of killing, but of an end to killing," Bombas said. He spread his hands in an appeal to calm and reason. "At the very least, let us keep the slaying down to a sensible level, as we did in the old days. The bloodletting confined to the Pit, perhaps a throat-cutting or two, and the bodies in the river before daylight . . . who will take notice of such small matters? Certainly not I or my fellow royal officials. But pitched battles in broad daylight in the Square and in the high street? These things cannot but draw attention.''

"What will draw the king's attention," said a loud voice from the doorway, "is your plundering!"

"I wondered when you would show up, Maxio," said Ingas. "Now you and Ermak can have it out right here on the table.''

"I'd be as happy to cut that one's fat throat," said Maxio, pointing at Bombas.

"Any who threatens the Reeve is a dead man," said Conan. "He is my charge for the evening. How you and Ermak want to settle things is up to you.''

Bombas looked at the Cimmerian with annoyance. "Do not provoke them.'' He turned back to face down the table. "Now, how shall we settle this? First, I urge an immediate cessation of all hostilities. These raids and ambushes are worse than disruptive, they are unprofitable! Who gains from such tactics?''

"You," said Maxio. He took a chair and propped his feet insolently upon the table. A gaunt, hollow-eyed daggerman took up station behind Maxio's chair. "Every battle weakens us and stuffs money in your purse. As you grow more frightened, your greed increases. Once we paid you ten percent of our takings to stay out of your dungeon. Then it became fifteen. Now, so terrified are you that you want twenty-five! I can see the tallow oozing out of your pores at the prospect that the king will take notice of you. How long before you want the whole of it?''

"Is that all?" Bombas asked. "Very well. For the sake of

restoring peace to my city, I am willing to accept ten percent once again. Now I ask you: Could I be more fair than that?''

"Just as I thought!" It was another voice from the doorway. All turned to see Xanthus standing there. "You scoundrels now conspire to divide up my city in secrecy!"

"*Your* city!" shouted Bombas, his face crimsoning. "*I* am King's Reeve here, not you. You are a mere lowbred merchant, no better than a slave trader! What business have you here, *mine factor*?"

"You suffer from the delusion that you are a nobleman, you baseborn heap of lard," said Xanthus with withering contempt. "You earned your rank through treachery, flattery, and your unfailing obsequiousness to your superiors. Do not strike haughty poses with me, Bombas. You are merely the richest thief in Sicas"

This, Conan thought, was even better than the bickering of the gang chiefs. Then Ermak spoke.

"Nay, that would be you, Xanthus. I keep the miners sweet for you, else you'd not have a head on your shoulders. You squeeze their blood and steal the king's silver. A gilded thief is still a thief."

"We are all thieves here." The monotone voice of Lisip cut through the banter. "Let us get back to our business in this place. I did not come here tonight because I relish the company of this lot."

"Aye," said Ermak, "let us settle things and be done with it."

"Will you all," Bombas said, "agree to the immediate cessation of hostilities?"

After a few moments of sullen pondering, answers of "aye" began to make the rounds of the table. Maxio kept his silence.

"You do not speak, Maxio?" Eramk prompted, his sardonic smile in place.

Pointing at Ermak's armored breast, Maxio spoke not to him, but to the others. "I will not trust this rogue's word. A murdering plunderer who pretends to be a soldier is not to be believed."

"Now, Maxio," said Bombas, veins standing forth on his brow

with the effort of speaking calmly. "Why must you persist in this hostility toward Ermak?"

"Probably," said Conan, "because Ermak has called in reinforcements from Ophir. They rode into town yesterday."

"Cimmerian!" hissed the Reeve. "Will you not be still?"

"And who knows who comes into town better than you, Bombas?" jeered the aged Xanthus. "It is your dogs who guard the city gates, although there is not a diseased cur in the town that is not better off than your guardsmen!"

"That settles it for me!" shouted Maxio. "If Ermak is bringing more of his mercenaries into town, he does not mean peace!"

"Try to use such addled wits as you have left, Maxio," said Lisip. "Ermak must have sent for those men many days ago, long ere the peace talks were even proposed."

Maxio whirled on the old gang leader. "You are in league with him! I see it now! The two of you would squeeze the rest of us out and have the city all to yourselves!"

A shouting match erupted, and as it roared on, Xanthus sidled over to the Cimmerian and whispered urgently. "Slay Bombas for me, barbarian! Do it tonight and you will have the rest of your pay. You need do no other service for me."

"If the murder of a royal official were easy or safe," Conan said, "you would have done it yourself years ago. Besides, are you not afraid that when he dies, your own guilty deeds will become known?" With a snakelike hiss, Xanthus turned away.

"I am leaving!" Maxio shouted. "Let none seek to follow me. I will observe the peace for the rest of this night, but after that, look to yourselves!" Followed by his gaunt companion, the burglar chief stalked from the room.

"I believe things would be much quieter," Lisip said, "if Maxio were out of the way."

"I have no objection," Ingas said boredly.

"You all know how I stand on the matter," said Ermak.

"Very well," Bombas said. "Any of you may slay Maxio, no questions asked. He is a mad dog. He slew my brother, and I think I showed great forbearance in speaking to him so courteously this night.''

The talks continued for another hour, and all agreed to the cessation of hostilities, but Conan was confident that their words meant nothing. These were not the sort of men who could ever abide by such conditions. They were predators and scavengers, always eager to attack one they thought to be weaker. He saw Xanthus draw Ingas aside privily and speak with him. Then the man did the same with Ermak. The Cimmerian guessed that he was offering support to each man against the other.

''Are we agreed, then?'' Bombas asked, rising. ''I think we shall have a quieter town now. Once Maxio is out of the way, there will be no need for further conflict, and you may all renegotiate your agreements with me. Now that you will not be needing your surplus men, it will be a good idea to dismiss them. I will not even charge them an exit duty at the city gates.''

''You are a greedy fool, Bombas,'' said Xanthus. ''Your grasping blindness will be the ruin of us.'' He stalked out, his face looking as if he had eaten something exceedingly sour.

''I do not think that Xanthus means you well,'' remarked Conan to Bombas as he followed the Reeve from the upstairs room.

''Pay him no heed,'' said the Reeve. ''He does not dare move against me, with so much of the king's lawful silver in his coffers.''

Julus and the Zingaran rejoined them in the gardens, and the four men made their way back to the Reeve's headquarters.

''Farewell, Cimmerian,'' the Reeve said. ''You gave me good and honest service this night. I may wish to call upon you again.''

''Next time,'' Conan said, ''I will want gold in payment.''

''I know that it is gold that buys men's loyalty,'' said the Reeve with a sigh. ''And little enough loyalty does it buy at that. Go, Cimmerian.''

Conan left the Reeve's headquarters, the apelike Julus glaring at him all the while. He was not halfway back to the temple when a touch of lilac on the evening breeze told him that he had company. Piris rose from her seat on the lip of a fountain.

"Why did you leave me in there so long?" Piris asked.

"I have a better question," said Conan. "Why did I not leave you there for the rest of your life?"

"Because you took service with me," Piris said, "and you Cimmerians are known to be men of your word."

"I recall no vow to keep you out of prison," Conan said. "I undertook only to find your scorpion goddess."

"Have you found her?" Piris demanded eagerly.

"Aye," Conan said.

"Where is she?" Piris's voice broke into a frustrated squeal.

"Better you should ask yourself where you are going to find the remaining eight hundred dishas you agreed to pay me for finding it for you."

"But, but . . ." Piris sputtered. "If I but had the image in my hands, I could pay you."

"Pay me, and then you get your scorpion," Conan said firmly. "If you do not want it, there are others who would like very much to have the thing."

Piris's eyes bugged. "What? What are you saying? Who wants my scorpion?"

"I will tell you nothing more until you come up with the balance of the pay we agreed upon back in Belverus." He swept an arm, taking in the city around them. "In a place of such opportunity, a man of your skill should have no trouble finding the money. Good evening to you, Piris."

Conan turned and left the little man sputtering behind him. He did not want Piris to see him enter the temple, so he walked past it and turned down the alley between the temple and the theater. When he reached the wall around the temple's rear courtyard, he vaulted to the top and stretched his length upon it. Moments later, Piris came down the alley, looking this way and that, but never upward. When he was gone, the Cimmerian dropped to the courtyard and walked toward the kitchen door.

Abruptly that door burst open and a man came stumbling out, his eyes staring in terror, his mouth drawn back in a wordless scream. It was one of the male acolytes, a burly youth who sometimes stood guard at the door. Conan grasped the front of the young man's robe before he could dash past.

"What is it?" Conan demanded.

"Demons!" the youth shouted. "Things with wings and claws. They came for me! Let me go!" For all his size, his struggles availed him nothing in the Cimmerian's iron grip. Conan could smell smoke on the robes he held. This was not the milk of Mother Doorgah.

"Just breathe deep, boy," Conan commanded. "It passes quickly." He slapped the panicked face lightly to get the youth's attention and repeated his instruction. Within seconds, the terrified expression began to fade and the young man looked to be halfway lucid.

"Now tell me, lad," Conan growled, his face an inch from the other's and looking twice as deadly as any demon's, "what was it? Was it by any chance a little accident with a *bellows*?" He snapped out the last word and shook the acolyte hard enough to make his bones rattle.

"Yes!" the youth all but shouted. "Holy Andolla brought the censer from his thaumaturgical study and connected it to the bellows. I placed the bellows to the wall pipe and began to work it. I do this every three or four evenings. But this time something went wrong. Smoke gushed back from the wall pipe. Then, then . . ." The eyes widened once more at the horror of the memory.

Conan pointed at the rear gate. "Go! If you ever come back here, the demons will surely take you!" With a strangled cry, the youth dashed for the gate and snatched it open. He did not pause to close it in leaving.

"What is happening out here?" Oppia stood in the back door, a harried expression on her face and her hair in a wild snarl.

Conan scratched his head, gazing at the rear gate. "I was just coming in when one of your acolytes ran past me, screaming as if all the demons of hell were on his trail."

"Doubtless he thought they were," she said. Then, sharply: "And what were you doing, coming in the back way?"

"I left Bombas but a few minutes ago," he answered. "I did not want him to see me coming into the temple."

"Oh," she said. "Yes, that is the wisest thing." Distracted, she turned to reenter the door.

"Do you not want to hear what happened at the peace conference?" Conan asked.

"Later," she said. "Tomorrow, perhaps. There has been an accident here, and I must set things aright."

"Andolla has summoned mischievous spirits," Conan said solemnly. "They will make a shambles of all your undertakings if he cannot control them."

"Aye, I believe that to be true," she said, weariness in her voice. "Go to your chamber, Cimmerian. I will call if I need you."

Grinning, Conan climbed the stairs to his lodging.

FIFTEEN

The Border Fort

At morning's first light, Conan awaited the opening of the river gate. The guard who opened the gate was not the same one who had been there when first the Cimmerian had ridden forth to bury his treasure and visit the mining village. This guard, a nearsighted fellow with a scraggly beard, brought out an official tablet.

"Name?" he said. He looked up, and his bleary eyes sharpened at sight of the golden coin that glittered between the fingers of the big barbarian.

"Are you fond of gold?" Conan asked.

"What man is not?" replied the guard.

"This is yours if you will make no note of my passing."

The guard snatched the coin from him. "I see no man. If you ride forth quickly, no one else will, either." He pushed the gate open and Conan rode through. He crossed the bridge and turned south on the narrow dirt track that paralleled the river. He was out of sight of the city walls before the light had grown bright enough for him to be observed.

The morning was peaceful, and the song of birds accompanied

him as he rode. The low ground near the river was forested, which suited his plans perfectly. A large number of men could travel this path without being seen.

He found the miners in a clearing by the path. There were about a hundred of them, strong and determined-looking. All were armed in one fashion or another. Iron-headed maces and spiked wooden bludgeons predominated. Powerful men, accustomed to the pick and sledgehammer, would be able to use such weapons with efficiency. A few had crude shields. Against Ermak's professionals, their lack of armor and discipline would be a terrible handicap, but Lisip's thugs would present no such difficulty.

Bessas came forward. "Lead us to them, Cimmerian," he said. The iron head of his mace bore a circle of pyramidal lugs; the weapon's handle was four feet long.

"South of here, on the other side of the river, there is an old border fort," Conan told them. "Do any of you know it?" No one had been there. He had expected as much. Most peasants and workmen like these had never traveled five miles from the place of their birth.

"Then I will have to scout it out when we get there," Conan said. "Come, let us not waste time."

The men rose to their feet and followed him. They did not look the least afraid, but they were silent and grim. Even among the younger men there was none of the banter he usually saw in soldiers about to go into battle. These were men whose lives were hard, brutal, and lacking in any cause for optimism. They would not celebrate until the fight was over and they had their women and children safely back at home.

An hour's march brought them to the bridge. Conan dismounted and walked across it, examining every inch along the way. The abutments on the banks and the pilings that rose from the bed of the river were ancient, but they were solidly made of well-cut and dressed stone. At one time, he deduced, this must have carried an important road. The bed was crudely made of timber; the road itself was of rough-hewn planks, now rotted in places.

"Cut wood and repair these bad spots," the Cimmerian ordered.

"It's no trouble to cross if you're careful where you step," protested Bellas, who was plainly impatient to get to the fort.

"When we come back this way," Conan pointed out, "we may be running, it may be dark, and we may be carrying wounded men or your women and children."

"Hadn't thought of that," Bellas admitted. He led a work party into the woods, bearing axes, saws, and adzes. Soon the sounds of woodcutting echoed through the morning air and men returned bearing sap-sticky lengths of wood. These men were used to fashioning mine timbers, and they shaped the wood to fit the bridge gaps swiftly. Ere long the bridge was sound and the men crossed to the eastern bank. Here another small dirt road paralleled the course of the river.

"I will ride on and find the fort," Conan said to Bellas. "March in haste, but do not run, and keep close watch. If anyone comes riding southward, do not let him pass you and thus bear word of your approach to the fort."

"We will be sure of it," Bellas said.

The Cimmerian rode onward. Before he had gone far, another road angled in from the northeast to join the one he traveled. This road bore signs of frequent traffic, and Conan surmised that the men in the fort took it when going back and forth to Sicas.

He dismounted when he smelled smoke. Tying his mount in a copse of trees, he took to the bush, staying away from the road as he approached the source of the smoke. Within minutes he lay belly-down on a ridge overlooking the fort, which lay on low ground in a bend of the river and occupied no strategic advantage that Conan could discern. He decided that it had been a garrison post for troops ranging the old border and was abandoned as soon as the border shifted to the southeast.

It was a small place, laid out in a rough rectangle. Its lower walls were sound, but the upper battlements were in ruin. This made no difference in its current employment, which was as a pen for human livestock. Two stone towers flanked the gate, and smoke rose from one of the towers. More smoke came from fires built within the yard surrounded by the walls. A few ramshackle sheds were built against the inner periphery. He guessed that Lisip's men were quartered in the towers, while the prisoners sheltered in the sheds.

With his practiced soldier's eye, he measured the defenses and turned over in his mind various means of storming the place. Its walls had lost a good six or seven feet from their original height. The miners had tools, and there was abundant wood nearby for making scaling ladders. Had he been leading well-trained and drilled soldiers, he would have gone for a simple assault with scaling ladders, attacking two or three of the low walls simultaneously. But that was a tricky job even for professional soldiers.

The gate lay between the two towers, each of which rose perhaps ten feet higher than the flanking walls. New conical roofs had been erected over these towers, which had once themselves been topped with battlements. There were arrow slits in the towers, but the Cimmerian doubted that any of Lisip's men were armed with crossbows. This place had been renovated as a prison for keeping hostages in, not as a castle for repelling assault from without.

The gate itself was made of massive timbers. They fit the opening none too well, and to Conan's initial amazement, they appeared to be barred on the outside. He realized that it made sense when he recollected that this was nothing but a glorified cattle pen. He decided that entry would have to be made through the gate.

People moved about listlessly in the surrounded courtyard, but he could tell little about them save that all seemed to be women and children. A few men paced along the walls. These were likewise obscured by distance, but he saw no glint of armor on them, just the occasional metallic glint from the hilts and pommels of belted weapons. Then something different caught his eye.

A man came from one of the towers, not ambling casually, but striding with purpose. Iron reflected a hazy silver light around his form, and as he made a circuit of the wall-walk, he slapped or punched or otherwise improved the alertness of the others. Conan cursed to himself. As he had feared, there was a leavening of Ermak's men among Lisip's thugs. How many might there be?

No matter. He and his group would have to fight whoever was here with what they had. The miners wanted their women and children back, and they were willing to accept many of their troop slain to accomplish it.

He examined the terrain to determine how close the miners could approach the front gate without being seen. There was a curve in the road where it rounded a low hill about three hundred paces from the gate. He could find no means that would allow them to come closer. Conan knew that he could get the gate open. The question was: Could he keep it open long enough for the miners to storm through?

An hour later, the men arrived. Conan was waiting for them by the road.

"The fort is a little way farther down this road," he told them. "The prisoners are there. I could see them from above. Lisip's scum guard them, but I saw one of Ermak's men, and there may be more of those. I have Lisip's pass to get me through the gate." He held up the leaden seal the old gang boss had given him.

"When I get the gate open," he continued, "you must attack immediately. The gate cannot be pushed shut from within. They must come out and pull it shut, and for that reason alone, I have a chance of holding it until you get there, but do not tarry along the way." Whatever these men were, he thought ruefully, they were not foot-racers.

"Just get the gate open," Bellas said. "After that, you may stand back and let us do the rest."

"Do not be too confident," Conan cautioned. "I do not know how many of Ermak's men are in there."

"They will die like the rest," Bellas said.

"They may take more killing, though," said Conan. "Do not try to fight them single-handed. If one shows himself, let two or

three of you together attack him. Move fast, attack from mor
directions than he can defend, and do not get in each other'
way.'' They nodded at the advice. He hoped that they woul
remember it in the excitement of battle.

"I go now," he told them. "Be ready to come running as soo
as you see the gate open."

He mounted his horse and set out at an easy gait. His weapon
rested loose in their sheaths. The saddle beneath him gave fort
a soft creaking of leather and wood. The midday sun shon
brightly. It was deceptively peaceful, and for all his relaxed mien
the Cimmerian was ready for the sudden, furious outburst of vi
olent action soon to come. He was a warrior, and he lived fo
battle. That this fight would present difficulties only made life
more interesting.

He reined in before the gate, and a man thrust a dirty, shaggy
head over the ruined battlement. "Who are you, and what do you
want?" he demanded.

"Lisip sent me," Conan said, holding high the lead medallion
"Let me in."

The man squinted his bloodshot eyes. "Throw it up here."

The Cimmerian tossed the seal and the man managed to catch
it on the fly. He did some more squinting. "Looks like Lisip's,"
he finally pronounced. "Let yourself in. I'm not coming down
there to help you."

Conan dismounted and began to tug on the gate bar, making it
seem far more of a struggle than necessary. "What kind of fort
is barred from the outside?" he asked.

"This is no fort," the man answered. "This is a slave pen. It's
a damned nuisance, too. When we want to go out, one or two of
us must go down a ladder to unbar the gate."

"What goes on here?" A bearded face, framed by a steel
casque, thrust over the wall. "Who is this man, and by whose
leave does he unbar the gate?"

The thug showed him the seal. "The chief sent him. This is
his pass. I know my master's seal."

While the armored man studied the thing, Conan hoisted the

bar clear of its retaining brackets. He began to stagger back as if the weight of the iron were too great for him, then he stumbled and dropped it, managing to cast it a few paces farther from the gate. The mercenary looked toward him sharply.

"You clumsy oaf!" the man shouted. "Must you botch a task so simple?"

"What of it?" Conan shouted up at him as he tugged the gate open, hoping to distract the soldier for a few crucial seconds. "I will bring my horse through and then climb up there and come back down here by your ladder, then rebar the gate, then go back up the ladder and pull it up after me. I never saw such a fort!"

"Why, you . . ." Now the soldier looked up, his jaw dropping as he saw what was coming down the road toward them. The head jerked back behind the rampart, and an alarm bell began to clang.

Hastily, Conan tugged the heavy gate fully open. He heard shouting from within, and his sword was naked in his hand as the first defenders reached the portal.

Suddenly he faced four men who stood almost shoulder-to-shoulder in the gateway. They were Lisip's thugs. All were armed with swords, and for several seconds the Cimmerian had his hands full just defending himself from the licking, glittering blades, with no time to counterattack. He managed to deal one of the attackers a cut on the sword arm and to stab another in a too-advanced thigh. The wounded men merely backed out of the fight and their places were taken by two other thugs.

The Cimmerian retreated from the gateway as if he were being driven back. As he had anticipated, one incautious man advanced ahead of the others. With a little more room in which to maneuver, Conan beat the other's sword to one side with his own blade and ran him through the chest. As the man fell, he caused another to stumble, and Conan clove that one through the shoulder before the man could regain his balance.

The Cimmerian strode forward and re-engaged the defenders of the gateway. Moments later a pack of the miners rushed past him, swinging their crude weapons with terrible effect. They

seemed not to care if they were wounded, so long as they coul
deal death in return. In seconds the gateway was gained and th
fighting spilled into the courtyard beyond.

His part of the attack was finished, but the Cimmerian coul
no more desert a battle well commenced than he could sto
breathing. Amid clashing weapons and roaring, smiting men, h
passed beneath the lintel. He saw the armored man who had chal
lenged him descending a stair and rushed to meet him.

Grinning, his bloodied sword at the ready, the Cimmerian me
the soldier at the bottom step. He blocked a chop to his head an
parried a swift thrust toward his throat, sending back a series o
lightning jabs in return. These the mercenary parried, but he wa
forced back up the stair, whence he tried to take advantage of hi
higher position to slash downward at Conan's head and shoulders
As he blocked one of these blows, Conan leaned forward an
grasped the man's ankle, tugging it off the step. The mercenar
lurched sideways and as he did so, Conan thrust his point int
the man's neck just above the gorget. The soldier toppled off th
stair with blood in his scream.

The Cimmerian dashed up the stair to the wall-walk. Two o
Lisip's men attacked him, but he merely knocked them from th
walk into the struggling mass of men below. He surveyed th
scene in the courtyard and was satisfied that the miners woul
have no difficulty in mopping up the rest. Lisip's men were fallin
everywhere. There were three or four of Ermak's still fighting
but they were being mobbed. The women and children wer
cheering and crying excitedly.

Sword still in hand, Conan went into the nearest of the gateway
towers. The interior was foul-smelling. This one had housed Lisip's men. A quick check of all three levels disclosed no skulkin
enemies, nor anything of interest.

He crossed the walk over the gateway to the other tower. This
one had been used by Ermak's men. The ground floor was an
armory-and-supply room. The second floor had been their sleeping quarters. He ascended the stair to the upper room. This one
was full of chests. He whirled at sounds coming from behind.

then relaxed as he saw Bellas, holding a child in one arm and leading a pretty young woman with his other hand. A huge grin divided the man's beard, and it struck Conan that this was the first time he had seen one of these people smile.

"I take it that the fighting is over?" Conan said, slamming his sword back into his sheath.

"All done," Bellas affirmed. "None of the dogs escaped to bear word of this to Sicas." More of the miners came up behind him.

"Excellent. Some of you with maces break these chests open. I want to see what Bombas was hiding up here."

Gleefully, amid much boisterous jesting, the miners did as he had bid them. They were in the highest spirits, and Conan learned that they had taken but few casualties in the brief, vicious battle. Lisip's men had been surprised, terrified, and outnumbered, and the miners fought with no trace of chivalry. Their own few dead and numerous wounded they accounted a small price for getting their women and children back.

"We lose more in a single cave-in," Bellas said, shrugging off the butcher's bill.

As the Cimmerian had suspected, many of the chests contained silver, some of it in the form of coin, but more in bullion, still bearing the inspector's stamp from the mine. There were other valuables as well.

"You must bear all this back to your village and hide it," Conan said.

"We did not come here for loot," Bellas said, holding up his woman's hand as proof of what really mattered.

"This is not loot," the Cimmerian told him. "Unless I am much mistaken, most of this belongs rightfully to your king. He may even prove grateful if you keep it safe for him." Conan had little faith in kingly gratitude, but these people would need whatever leverage they could muster when royal forces finally arrived to set the district in order. Then he noticed a cabinet standing in a corner.

"What is in that?" he asked, pointing. One of the miners

turned and with a casual sweep of his mace, smashed the padlock, hasp and all, from the cabinet doors. He opened it and looked inside.

"Just some books," the man said, shrugging.

Intrigued, Conan went to the cabinet and drew out a stack of large, heavy tomes bound in fine Shemitish leather. He opened the top volume and saw that it contained scant writing, but many columns of numerals.

"What are they?" Bellas asked.

"I am no scribe," Conan said, "but I have stood before many a paymaster to collect my wages and I know an accounting ledger when I see one. I will wager that these list how much treasure Bombas has taken in and how much he has paid out, and for what. And I would wager just as much that he has another set of these books in his headquarters, one that he shows the royal treasurer. Those books will show that he took in far less and paid out far, far more. You must take these and hide them as well. With these books, you can assure that Bombas will hang."

"We will keep them safe," Bellas vowed.

"Somewhere in there," Conan said, "will be his military accounts. He receives pay and rations for a hundred men, together with their mounts, quartering and stabling and all other expenses paid by the Crown. With that, he hires a score of half-dead derelicts and they probably do not receive half-pay. It is paltry compared to what he must be skimming from the mines, but no opportunity to steal is too small for a man like Bombas."

"What will you do now, Cimmerian?" Bellas asked.

"Return to Sicas. I have a number of other matters to occupy me just now."

"You play a dangerous game, my friend," the miner said.

"That is the only kind worth the playing," Conan told him. "It is also the most rewarding."

"Why not come back with us to the village?" Bellas urged. "When the time is right, you can lead us into Sicas to finish this work."

Conan shook his head. "No, I have much to do in the city

before the time is ripe for that. There is great gain to be had there. Why let Bombas enjoy it all?''

''I think you are mad, but know that for this day's deeds, you are our friend for life. When you need us, do not hesitate to call upon us.'' It was simply said, and Conan knew that it was meant.

He parted company with the miners as they were finishing their work at the old fort. The chests were being carried away on the strong backs of some of the men as others fired the fort. The sheds and the wooden interiors of the towers were torched, and a great heap of lumber and brushwood had been heaped in the courtyard as a pyre for the corpses of the enemy dead. Their own dead would be buried in the village after the customary rites. Conan rode northward until he lost sight of the great column of smoke that ascended to the heavens behind him.

He did not hurry, but rode at a leisurely pace. Although the sun was down, darkness had not yet fallen. Near the town, he rode through the campground where the caravanners pitched their tents and built their fires. There were few traders at this time of year, and he saw that the party with which Mulvix arrived had departed.

He passed through the city gate with the usual bribe and rode to the inn. The stableman wore an odd look as the Cimmerian walked his horse into the near-dark of the stalls. Conan was about to ask the man what was wrong when he felt something very solid crash against the back of his head.

The Cimmerian dropped bonelessly, not quite unconscious, but completely unable to make his limbs function. He could feel ropes being tied around his wrists and ankles, and he could do nothing about it. Then a heavy blanket was wrapped around him. The last thing he heard before drifting into unconsciousness was a man's voice.

''Take him to the dungeon,'' said Julus.

SIXTEEN
Chaos Descends

He awoke feeling as if a volcano had erupted in his head. Only savage instinct kept him from groaning aloud. Sounds of pain and helplessness might draw predators. He shifted, and straw crackled beneath him. It was not the first time he had awakened lying on a cold stone floor covered with straw, a ferocious pain rending his skull.

Slowly, he raised a hand and felt the back of his head. He touched the stickiness of drying blood. Grimly, stoically, he pressed his fingertips against the scalp, then tightened them as hard as he could, sending spears of blinding agony through his whole body, causing lurid lights to flash behind his eyelids. He ignored the pain. To his great relief, he felt no shifting of bone beneath the skin. His skull was not fractured. His steel cap and dense black hair had been sufficient to spare him a crushed skull.

Now that he knew he would not die of the injury, he struggled to a sitting position. Dizziness washed over him for a few moments, but he willed it away. He had been injured far worse in his time, and he knew that those who had cast him into this place had far worse in store for him. He heard footsteps approaching.

"Well, our prize lives, after all." He looked through the bars and saw the hulking form of Julus. The man's image wavered, doubling for a moment; then it coalesced into sharp focus.

"Did you think you could kill me?" Conan asked.

"Assuredly, I did not want you to die," Julus said. "I gave Atchazi strict orders that you were not to be killed, but he is still full of resentment that you slew his friend, and he struck harder than intended. Think how our fun would have been spoiled had you died."

"It was the Zingaran?" Conan asked. "He must have a better arm than I thought."

"You will see soon enough," Julus said.

"Why have you dragged me here?" the Cimmerian demanded. "I have done nothing that is forbidden in this town."

Julus broke into roaring laughter. "Do not speak like a fool, foreigner! What care I what you have done or have not done? I want to know what you *plan* to do. I brought you here to get some answers!"

"That would be a man's task, and I see no men besides myself in this place," Conan sneered. Apparently they did not suspect him of the events at the fort. Perhaps they did not even know of the raid yet.

"Get in there and chain him up!" Julus commanded. Men crowded into the cell and dragged the Cimmerian from it. He tried to struggle, but simply sitting up had demanded all the strength he could summon. Even such men as these could handle him easily.

A rope was passed between his bound wrists, then passed through a ring set into the stone ceiling. Men hauled on the rope, and soon the Cimmerian's body was stretched painfully, only the balls of his feet touching the floor. Julus approached, an evil grin on his face and a short wooden club in his hand.

"This way," Julus explained, "we do not have to pick you up when you fall." The club flashed out, and pain bloomed in Conan's side. A backhanded swipe smashed into his jaw. Even through the haze of agony, he knew that he would live, and he set himself to wait out the ordeal. Either blow could have splintered bone, but Julus had stopped just short of the necessary force. The man did not intend to beat him to death.

"Why are you here, barbarian?" Julus demanded. He punctuated the question with several blows of the club to Conan's knees, elbows, kidneys, and beneath the arms. He knew where the nerves were to be found to cause the greatest pain.

"Who sent you? Are you a king's man?" he persisted.

For a long time the Cimmerian said nothing as the stick drew ever greater levels of pain from his body. The punishment was agonizing, but as yet, he had felt nothing of importance give way in his body. A blow landed across his nose and blood gushed out over his face and chest. He could taste it in his mouth as well. At least the brute avoided damaging his jaw and throat. He wanted Conan able to speak. A flurry of blows to his kidneys wrenched a gasp from the Cimmerian.

"I am here to get rich, like everyone else in this town, curse you!" He knew he could take more punishment, but there was no point in it. To speak sooner would arouse the man's suspicions. To wait longer would be to invite crippling injury. Above all, he must avoid that. The Cimmerian could endure pain that would drive a civilized man to death or madness, but his body had to be sound enough for an escape when the opportunity came.

"I do not believe you," Julus taunted, but now his blows came less forcefully. "What sort of bargain did you make with Lisip, Cimmerian? And what is your game with Maxio? You seem to be sharing his woman. That bespeaks something more than friendliness. Where do you hide of nights, when you are not at the inn?"

"I carouse in the Pit," Conan said, spitting a mouthful of blood onto the floor, "and I seek better ways to loot this place, same as you, dog." His nose was swelling, his eyes blackening. He hoped that his eyelids would not swell shut. A blind man had little chance of escape.

Julus struck him across the calf muscles of both legs. Instantly the rocklike muscles knotted into vicious cramps. "The truth,

Cimmerian!" Julus bawled. "I will have the truth from you!" He rained a shower of blows on Conan's unresisting body.

Conan faded in and out of consciousness. From time to time he managed to mutter words, always sticking to his insistence that he worked alone, to enrich himself.

"I think you like this, Cimmerian," Julus said, striking him again on the ribs. The man was sweating from the exertion. "I think you enjoy this as much as I do. The gods have been kind to throw us together this way, have they not?" A commotion behind him caused Julus to turn. A man came running down the stair.

"What is it?" Julus demanded. "You had best have good reason to thus interrupt my sport."

"The Reeve says come!" the man said urgently. "We must all mount and ride at once! Make haste!"

"Now what is this all about?" Julus muttered. "We will finish this later, Cimmerian." With a casual backhanded swing, the club crashed against the side of Conan's head. Crimson light flashed before him, then darkness descended.

When he awoke, he could not feel his hands. He was still as he had been, his arms stretched above him, his feet barely touching the floor. His whole body was a mass of agony, except where it was numb. As near as he could determine, though, nothing was seriously damaged. He had not been cut badly, there were no broken bones, and he did not think that he had sustained any internal injuries, although he might need time to know that for certain. He had great faith in the healing powers of his rugged physique and knew that he would be hale within a few days. But first he must get out of this place, before Julus came back. Slowly, favoring a neck that had gone stiff, he raised his head, finding that his chin had stuck to his chest with dried blood.

For a minute he thought he had gone blind. He could smell the burning wick of an oil lamp, but he saw no light. Gradually he realized that his eyelids were likewise stuck together with dried blood. With much facial contortion, he managed to get one eye partially open and saw the lamp, burning in a sconce. In a chair tilted against a wall sat a jailer, dozing. He was a potbellied, shaven-headed man the Cimmerian did not recognize from his earlier stay. A ring of keys hung at the man's belt, and a knife was similarly attached.

Conan groaned loudly. The jailer's eyes opened slightly.

"Water!" Conan cried. "Bring me water, for the love of Mitra!"

"Why should I bring you water, scum?" the jailer asked. "I love neither you nor Mitra."

"I die of thirst!"

"You'll not live long enough to die of thirst," the man assured him. "Julus will be back soon, and then he will resume his sport. That is what you will die of."

"I will pay you," said the Cimmerian.

"With what?" The jailer gestured toward a heap of clothing and arms in a corner. "We already have your belongings. The money in your purse has long since been divided, though I got none." The man's tone was resentful, and Conan saw a place wherein to drive a wedge.

"I have more, much more," he said.

"Where?" the jailer demanded, his face animated with greed.

"First bring me water."

Grumbling, the man left. He returned a few minutes later with a pail of water and a dipper. He filled the dipper and held it to the Cimmerian's mouth. Conan drank thirstily. Two dippers satisfied him.

"Now pour the rest over my head," he instructed. Shrugging, the jailer did as he was told. The water sluiced over the matted black locks, washing away some of the blood from Conan's eyes and reviving him somewhat.

"Where is this money?" the jailer demanded.

"One more thing," Conan said. "Lower me to the floor. I am nigh dead from the pain in my arms."

"You said money for water. Do not play games with me."

"Lower me, or I will not tell you," Conan said.

"One more chance," the jailer warned. He went behind Conan. Seconds later, the rope went slack and Conan dropped to the cold stone floor. There he writhed, all but howling with the renewal of the torture. The jailer prodded him with a booted toe, then grasped a handful of the black mane and jerked Conan around to face him.

"Now, dog, the money! Julus is not the only man here who can make you scream."

"He did not make me scream, and neither did you!" Abruptly, Conan's bound legs lashed sideways, kicking the jailer's feet from beneath him. The man fell with a thud, squalling. He tried to get up but the Cimmerian's bound legs slipped over his head and the knees locked around his neck. Slowly, inexorably, the barbarian squeezed. The jailer flopped like a beached fish, but he could neither get loose nor make an outcry. He gave up his futile attempt to pry the iron legs from his throat and snatched at his knife. But already the man was weakening. Before he could cut, Conan slammed him against the floor with a violent wrench. The knife flew through the air.

The jailer lay inert. Just in case it was a ruse, Conan increased the pressure and held it for a few minutes longer. Then he released the neck and lay still for a while. Coming on top of the beating, this exertion had drained him. But he knew that it was no time to tarry. He crawled across the floor in search of the knife.

He pawed at the weapon, but his numbed fingers would not close around the grip. He managed to get the butt of the knife between his teeth and brace its point against the floor. By sawing his wrist bindings against the edge of the blade, he contrived to cut through his bonds with a few minutes' exertion. When his hands were free, he waved his arms in circles, forcing blood into the extremities. Now the agony was even greater than what had gone before. Gritting his aching teeth, he waited it out. The pain threatened to go on forever, but in time it passed. With his hands now functioning, the Cimmerian quickly cut his ankle bindings and stood. He was shaky and weak, but he could stay upright after a fashion.

He redonned his clothing and armor and belted on his weapons. This made him feel immeasurably better, although he was aware that he could not wield arms with anything approaching his usual power. He needed to rest and recover.

Slowly, he climbed the stair, leaning against the wall as waves of dizziness swept over him. Before entering the headquarters' main floor, he waited and listened. All was quiet. He saw no guards flanking the front door. Apparently Bombas had taken even his worthless guards on his expedition. Conan had no doubt that they had ridden out to the fort to survey the carnage. He must be in safe hiding when they returned.

From Julus's questioning, the Cimmerian knew that they were unaware of his presence in the temple. He guessed that Rista Daan was too important a man for them to interrogate, so they knew nothing of his own mission to rescue the man's daughter. Even in the midst of his pain and peril, Conan felt a stab of concern for the girl. He had been too long away from the temple.

He staggered outside and stood within the shadow of the doorway. The night was dark and he saw no one in the Square. He did not walk across the plaza, but kept to the shadows of the buildings surrounding it. He was unmolested except for stray dogs that approached him hopefully, then slunk away at his unpromising look. When he passed the house of Xanthus, he went into the alley that separated it from the Temple of Mother Doorgah. In the rear of the temple he found the gate unbarred and passed through into the court.

Crossing the kitchen, he went into the main temple. There the acolytes chanted. Something seemed different about the chant, as if it were somehow deeper, more resonant, sending a vibration throughout the spacious structure. He decided that the ringing in his head was confusing him. Disoriented, he finally found a stair and ascended. He stepped off a landing and found himself before a door.

"Conan!" He turned to see Oppia standing there. She wore a

filmy nightdress and an expression of consternation. "Where have you bee—what has happened to you?" The Cimmerian realized that in his addled condition, he had come to his former quarters, on the same floor as the apartment of Andolla and Oppia. She hurried to his side and studied him by the light of her lamp.

"You look more dead than alive! Who has done this? These are not the marks of a brawl!"

"The henchmen of Bombas," he said, belaboring his sluggish brain to come up with a story that would convince her to keep him hidden. "The Reeve wants to know what goes on in this temple. He thinks that you hoard treasure. I would tell nothing. Some alarm called them all away and I managed to escape."

"Come, we must get you cleaned up and bandaged." Her voice sounded somehow different, lower and more vibrant. He decided that his hearing was still defective from the beating.

"I just need to lie down and rest for a day or two. I will heal by myself."

"Nonsense," she insisted. "If nothing else, I do not want you bleeding all over the temple. Come with me." She tugged at his hand and he followed her around the corner to the red door. Not only did she sound different, but it seemed to him that she appeared different as well. She had been a comely woman before, but now her beauty was in some way enhanced. As she walked before him, her hips seemed to have a fuller rondure and she swayed enticingly. Her already-slender waist looked even smaller. He shook his head; perhaps his vision had been affected also.

She unlocked the door and led him within. The anteroom held images of the goddess festooned with precious gems. The floors were covered with costly carpets, and the walls with hangings of equal value. The lamps were works of art. Conan saw no sorcerous paraphernalia. Apparently, Andolla kept all such materials in his study below. He followed the woman into a small room with a floor of green tile in which was sunk a deep tub of purple marble. Hot water gushed from the mouth of a golden dolphin at one end and drained from another into a catch basin.

"Get in there," Oppia ordered. She began to tug at his clothing. Feeling no special inclination to resist, the Cimmerian stripped and climbed into the tub. With a grateful sigh, he lowered himself until the hot, steaming water lapped at his shoulders.

"All the way under," she ordered. Obediently, he submerged himself. When he came back up, she scrubbed at his scalp with a coarse sponge. He winced as it scraped over the lacerations, but he knew that he would heal the swifter for the cleansing. Oppia sat on the edge of the marble tub and laved industriously at his shoulders.

"Do not flatter yourself," she warned. "I am not your bath attendant. I would send one of the acolytes for this task, but I do not want an acolyte to see you looking thus. I want no tongues wagging. I had thought you a fine figure of a man, but just now you are something with which to discipline children. You are so bruised that your body is as black as a Kushite's, and your face is so swollen I would not have recognized you save for that black thatch and your armor."

She shifted herself to his front to sponge his chest, and he studied her. The steam had caused her thin nightdress to cling to her every curve, and she might as well have been naked. Her breasts looked larger and fuller than before, and her belly, despite her tiny waist, was gently rounded. Impossibly, her face seemed to have broadened, without losing any of its beauty. The look reminded him of something, but he could not bring to mind what it might be.

"I want you to recover quickly," she said. "Strange things are happening here, and I grow afraid. My husband's spells have gained great strength, I know not why. Things are not as they were, and I want a strong man close at hand to deal with trouble. Even I . . ." She stopped herself, perhaps fearing to reveal too much.

"Just keep me hidden away for a day or two," Conan said. "I shall be as good as new, and you need fear no enemies."

"Wait here," she said, rising. She swayed from the room and Conan relaxed in the water, letting the hot bath draw some of the sting from his wounds. She returned a few minutes later, bearing a large cup.

"Drink this," she ordered. "It is watered wine with herbs. It will help your injuries heal." He took the cup and drank. For once, he did not suspect drugs or poison. When he had finished the potion, she signaled for him to stand. She helped him dry himself, then rubbed unguents into his cuts and abrasions.

"There," she said. "That is all we can do now. Get dressed and return to your quarters, if you think you can negotiate the stairs."

"I can do it," he said. "I've been hurt far worse than this."

"I will send acolytes to check upon you from time to time. Tell them if you need anything."

"I thank you," Conan said. "Are you sure that Andolla does not mind you bathing hired swordsmen in his private bath?"

"My husband," she said, "is too busy of late to pay much heed to what I do. Go now. I will visit you in the morning."

Dressed only in his loincloth, the rest of his belongings bundled beneath an arm, he left the apartment and walked to the stair. He ascended to his floor and went into his quarters, which seemed to be as he had left them. Leaving his clothes and arms, he crossed the hall and entered Rietta's chamber. She was sleeping peacefully, and she looked far less frail than before. There was mo smell of smoke in the room.

It seemed that the new developments had caused Andolla and Oppia to neglect their charge. He went to the window and determined that the wax plug had not been tampered with. He left, closing the door silently.

He went into his own room, fell upon his bed and slept like a corpse.

He awoke feeling as if his body were carved from wood, stiff and unyielding. Groaning, he pushed himself to a sitting position and swung his legs off the bed. He forced himself to stand, then stretched his limbs until he had worked some of the stiffness from his joints and muscles. As agonizing as the effort was, he knew that he would be fit the sooner for it. There came a knocking at the door, and he placed a hand on his sword hilt.

"Come in," he said. An acolyte entered, his eyes widening at the sight of the near-naked, massively bruised swordsman.

"My mistress bade me see if you were awake and had need of aught, sir," said the youth, bowing over clasped hands. The Cimmerian wanted nothing more than sleep, but he had someone else to look after.

"Bring me food," he demanded. "Bread and meat and some strong broth, and whatever fruit the kitchen has." The acolyte bowed again and left. Truly, he was not very hungry, but he knew that Rietta had not eaten decently in at least two days. When the viands arrived, he dismissed the acolyte and crossed the hall.

"Conan!" Rietta was sitting in her bed. The eyes that widened at his appearance were bright and clear for the first time. "Where have you . . . what happened to you?"

"I grow tired of that question," he said, setting the tray on the bed before her bare toes. "Here, you need some of this after two days of gruel."

"Yesterday they forgot even the gruel," she said, snatching at a loaf and tearing into it.

"I would have been here, but I spent the day in a dungeon." He watched as she ate. Her appetite had returned and she absorbed the food swiftly. He nodded, satisfied.

"Now," he said, "get up and walk around the room." She obeyed and he studied the way she moved. She was not yet fully recovered by any means, but her steps were firm and steady. He knew that he could not wait until she regained full strength. Strange things were happening in the temple, and he had a feeling that they would soon become even stranger.

"You cannot stay here longer," he told her. "I will take you to your father's house tonight. Be ready."

"Tonight?" The smile that spread across her face was the first sane expression of joy he had seen in this place. Then the smile faded. "Oh, but how can I face him? I stole from him and let these dreadful people use me like a puppet. How could I have allowed them to do such things?'' Her face flushed with shame.

''They took advantage of your grief at your mother's death,'' he told her. ''Then they weakened you with their accursed drugs, until you had no will of your own. The fact they had to isolate you and starve you and drug you heavily shows that you were far stronger than the others here. Your father will forgive you, girl, else he would not want you back.''

''I hope you are right,'' she said. ''I will be ready when you come for me.''

''It will be very late,'' he told her. ''Perhaps not until just before dawn.''

''I will be ready,'' she promised.

The Cimmerian returned to his own room and fell upon his bed. When he awoke again, it was almost dusk. Again he rose and stretched. Already his body was mending itself. He touched his face and knew that the swelling was almost gone. The rugged northland-bred people could suffer terribly and heal swiftly.

He smiled at the thought of catching up with Julus. Though the man had shrewdness, he lacked foresight. At the very least, he should have thought to cripple the Cimmerian's sword hand, but the lackey was too arrogant to anticipate the outlander's escape. He would have cause to regret it.

Armed and muffled in his cloak, Conan left the temple. With the light fading, people were scurrying from the Square, as if afraid to be caught in the streets after dark. In this hardened place, their haste seemed unusual. In return for some information, Conan assisted a stall-keeper in disassembling and folding his booth.

''Have you not heard?'' the man said. ''There is full-scale war in town now! This morning Lisip's men invaded Ingas's headquarters in the Iron Skull. Ingas and every one of his men were slain! There will be battles in all the streets tonight!''

''Excellent!'' Conan said.

''What's that you say?'' The stall-keeper looked, but the big foreigner was gone.

Conan made his way through the streets until he reached an imposing house, where he went up the outside stair to the second floor. There he rapped at the door. Gilmay opened, his hands going to his hilts. Conan ignored him and walked inside.

"Where is Casperus?" he asked.

"Cimmerian!" the fat man cried, waddling from a back room. "I did despair of ever seeing you again! I have been plunged into a mood most melancholy, sir, most melancholy. And now you must at once render me the fullest accounting of your doings anent the scorpion. You will apprehend, sir, that I do not ask for an account of *all* your doings, for I fear, sir, that I might not live long enough to hear it out! For I suspect, sir, I deeply suspect, that you have not devoted the entirety of your time and efforts upon my behalf."

"You said you wanted the scorpion," Conan told him.

"Indeed I did, sir."

"I have it."

"Splendid! I cannot help but notice, however, that you have omitted to bring it hither, sir. Where might it be?"

"I have it hidden, in a very safe place. It is extremely heavy for its bulk, and just now it would be unwise for me to go about the streets of Sicas carrying it. At any moment I may need both hands for fighting."

"Indeed, sir, indeed," Casperus said, his jovial mask slipping, allowing his seething anger to show through. "You have been most busy, have you not? These pitched battles between the street gangs have been your doing, not so?"

Conan shrugged. "They never needed my encouragement to kill one another."

"And there is word in the town of a veritable storming and massacre at a fort near here. Do I detect your warlike expertise in this incident?"

"It is of no consequence to our business," he answered.

"Oh, but it is, sir, it is! This town, which was merely disorderly when you arrived, is now chaotic! No one may move about freely save, perhaps, an expert warrior like yourself. I have no

choice save to trust your word, sir, since I may not go out and
see for myself what you are up to.''

''You may always trust a Cimmerian's word,'' Conan growled

''Oh, aye, sir, that I may. I had expected integrity from you
and courage, and perhaps a certain species of low cunning, but
never, sir, *never* did I expect subtlety!''

''I choose not to be insulted. I will send for you within two
days, at which time I will lead you to where the scorpion is hidden. Bring the rest of my money.''

''Sir, you are an impudent scoundrel!'' Casperus proclaimed.

''I shall be called many names far worse ere I die,'' the Cimmerian said. As he turned to go, he found Gilmay blocking his
way.

''There must be a reckoning between us soon, barbarian,'' the
youth said.

''Aye,'' said Conan, pushing past him. ''Pray that you do not
have to pay it.''

SEVENTEEN
Things In The Temple

The moon was setting when he returned to the temple. He had spent much of the night prowling the town's taverns, collecting information. Screams, shouts, and the clash of arms seemed to come from every alley. There was a reddish glow in the sky above the Pit, where a number of fires burned. There was no longer any talk of peace. Every gang was at war with every other, and the Reeve huddled in his headquarters, completely unnerved. For years he had robbed the king of warriors' wages, and now he was paying for his greed. He had no men worthy of the name to call upon to restore order.

At least the Reeve's flunkies were not combing the town in search of the Cimmerian. Bombas had greater fears now. In a way, Conan found this disappointing. He truly wanted to encounter Julus again.

There was no sign of Ermak or of his men. Conan judged that they were holed up in their headquarters, waiting out the chaos. As battlefield soldiers, they had little taste for skirmishing in the dark streets.

There was also no sign of Brita. He told himself that her troubles were none of his affair, that he had warned her repeatedly to give up her mad mission here and go home. Even so, he feared the worst.

Piris seemed to be lying low as well, a fact that suited the Cimmerian. Undoubtedly the little man was trying to raise the rest of the money in payment for the scorpion. It was equally certain that he could accomplish this by illegal means, whatever that meant in this place.

He climbed the steps to the temple, briskly at first, then slowing as he neared the entrance, from which came decidedly strange sounds and flickering lights of many colors. To his ears came the monotonous chants. He had grown so accustomed to the sound that he scarcely heard them anymore, but now there was a new intonation to them. There were deep, growling notes, unlike the product of human voices, and high-pitched wails of equally inhuman origin, seeming to squeal up past the threshold of hearing. The lights flashed green, red, purple, and other colors so nacreous that Conan had difficulty putting a name to them.

As he entered, something at his feet made him stop and stare. A procession of scorpions passed before his booted toes, their ranks equally spaced, as solemn and stately as a hieratic parade. Who ever heard of scorpions coming out in winter? he thought wildly. And these looked like the fat black scorpions of Stygia, not the small brownish scorpions common to the Aquilonian summer months.

Gingerly he stepped across the arthropodan procession and passed within, one fist clamped around his sword, his jaw clenched as tightly. He felt as if his hair were standing on end like the fur of a fighting tomcat.

An acolyte passed him, favoring the Cimmerian with an idiotic smile. The face had somehow grown prolonged and snoutlike, and his arms, covered with hair, dangled almost to his knees. A stumpy tail protruded from the rear of the man's robe. He looked, Conan thought, remarkably like the monkeys sculpted on the facades of Vendhyan temples.

"Where are Andolla and Oppia?" the Cimmerian demanded. Despite the bizarre transformation, the acolyte did not appear in the least threatening. He raised a hairy arm and pointed into the nave. Conan ran past him and stopped just within the cavernous room, gaping at the sight looming ahead.

The crowd of acolytes chanted ecstatically, and every one of them was undergoing some sort of transformation. Many had the monkey aspect; others were sprouting insectile appendages. One stout acolyte had developed gigantic ears and a long prehensile trunk. After gawking at them for a few moments, Conan raised his eyes to the dais.

Andolla sat cross-legged as always, but he sat twenty feet in the air, unsupported. He was surrounded by a crimson aura, and light seemed to fall in drops from his fingertips. His voice boomed above the chants with the volume of a volcanic eruption.

Below him, Oppia stood on the colossal lap of the goddess. With eyes closed, she led the chant in a shrill voice. Her robes had slipped down, and she stood bare from the hips upward except for her jewels. She, too, had undergone a shocking transformation.

Her breasts were huge and perfectly hemispherical, unaffected by gravity. Above the exaggerated rondure of her hips, her waist appeared no more than a hand's span in circumference. Even her face was different. She had become identical in aspect to Mother Doorgah.

Then he noticed that the statue itself had altered. It's color was almost black, and the majestic face was no longer that of Mother Doorgah, nor did it bear the features of Vendyah. Something cold and aquiline now inhabited the countenance, which was far more beautiful than before. With dismay, the Cimmerian recognized the face of the scorpion goddess.

He ran to the nearest stair and climbed. The higher he ascended, the less uncanny grew his surroundings, although there was still something unnatural about the light, and the angles of the walls seemed to be tilted out of proper alignment. By the time he reached the living quarters, all seemed to have returned to normal. As he went up the last flight of stairs, he saw someone climbing ahead of him.

"Out of my way," he growled, reaching up for a shoulder. The other spun to face him.

"Crom's bones!" Conan cried, leaping back two steps and snatching out his sword. A greenish, shambling monstrosity stood on the steps above him, staring at him from eyeless pits in a misshapen face, its gaping mouth lined with slimy, needlelike teeth. It was the demon of Rietta's curse, given substance by Andolla's unwitting use of the power of the scorpion goddess, who now dwelled in the crypt below the colossal statue of Mother Doorgah.

The thing hissed and lunged at him. Instinctively, Conan thrust upward, leaning his shoulder into the action. The monster made a squealing sound as the blade sank deep. Swift as lightning, the Cimmerian withdrew the blade and thrust again, and yet again, sinking steel into the foul body repeatedly, trying to find a vital spot. The blood that poured from the wounds was partly green, partly red. Even as its talons scrabbled for his throat, Conan understood that this was yet another acolyte transformed by sorcery. The priest could not make something out of nothing, but his will had shaped an acolyte into the form of the insubstantial demon with which he had terrorized Rietta, and now the mindless thing climbed toward her room to follow its master's will.

Realizing that the creature must have some remnant of a brain left, Conan left off stabbing and instead brought the edge of his sword downward onto the scaly skull, cleaving it almost to the humped shoulders. Another blow cleft it further, and a third nearly hewed away the cranial remains. The thing moved about blindly for a while, then slowly collapsed, continuing to twitch for some time with unnatural life. Conan flattened himself against a wall and breathed hard, watching it die. The brief effort had left him drenched in sweat.

When he was sure that the demon was fully dead, he bounded over the monstrous corpse and dashed the rest of the way up the stairs. He hated to think what might have happened had he been just a few minutes slower. At the very least, Rietta would have been driven truly mad by the sight of the creature he had convinced her was but the vaporous construction of petty magic, drugs, and her imagination.

He first went to his own quarters, and with a sheet carefully cleaned the blood and ichor from his sword and garments. He saw nothing there that he needed to take with him and so he crossed to Rietta's room. He found her sitting on the side of her bed, her fingers clasped in her lap. She looked up with an affrighted face; then relief spread across her features when she saw who it was.

"Conan! Oh, how glad I am to see you! Since nightfall, the sounds from below have been hideous, and when an acolyte came to look in on me, she did not seem . . . exactly human."

"Strange and unnatural things are afoot," Conan confirmed, "and we must be away from here. Are you ready?"

"More than ready!" She stood, dressed only in her shift. "I certainly have nothing to gather up. Let us go!"

"You'll not freeze between here and your father's house, girl. Come with me." He took her hand and led her across the hallway into his own quarters. He had no intention of leading her down the stair past the demon's corpse and then through the temple. He climbed out his window and hung from its sill.

"Now," he ordered, "come on out and cling to my back."

"What if I fall?" she asked, her eyes huge.

"You probably won't die, falling from this height. It's better than staying here. Hurry up!" Taking a deep breath, the girl scrambled out and climbed down to wrap her arms around his neck and her legs about his waist, managing not to dislodge his grip in doing so.

Slowly, his toes finding minute purchase and his fingertips gripping tightly, he descended the wall. Within a few minutes they stood on the flags of the courtyard.

"You can let go now," the Cimmerian said. She did so reluctantly. "Come. Stay close to me." They went out through the back gate, then down the alley between the theater and the temple. When they were halfway across the Square, well away from the temple, she began to breathe a little easier.

"What is happening back there?" she asked. "You said that they were frauds, but there is real sorcery in that place."

"Something unexpected strengthened Andolla's paltry spells, and now he is no longer in control. It was not what I had planned, but those two are about to receive what they deserve."

"What *you* had planned? You mean that you have had something to do with all this?"

"Strange things happen sometimes," he told her. "I needed to return you to your father, and I needed somewhere to hide out for a while, and the temple seemed a good place in which to do it. Then I needed to secrete something I had been hired to find, and I knew of a good place in the temple to that end. And all of that has led to this." He turned and looked back toward the temple. It presented a deceptively tranquil aspect. He shook his head.

"Let's go talk to your father," he said.

An hour later, Conan left the house of Rista Daan. A fat purse, pleasantly stuffed with four hundred and ninety marks, was tucked beneath his belt. The merchant's thanks had not been effusive, but they had been heartfelt.

Darkness still spread its mantle over the city, and the Cimmerian pondered his next move. He could not return to the temple. Bombas's men might come seeking him at the inn. Then he remembered one place in the town where he had an open invitation to call at any hour. He headed for the Street of the Woodworkers.

The brawling seemed to have died down, and he heard no more sounds of combat as he walked cautiously through the streets. Twice he had to step over bodies, but he was unmolested. Within a short time he stood across the narrow street from the sign of the Sunburst. Above the sign, the shutters were open and light poured out. The woman's fondness for nocturnal illumination was as extravagant as ever.

From a long habit of caution, Conan waited, dividing his attention between the apartment above and the street below. He did not expect Maxio to be there. Surely the man had more sense than to go where his enemies would be looking for him. Still, the Cimmerian knew better than to take anything for granted.

He had been watching for a few minutes when he realized that he was hearing something that was out of place. It was a common enough sound, but it was coming from the wrong direction. It was the piteous wailing of a cat, and it emanated from the windows above.

Conan strode across the street and up the stairs. The door to Delia's apartment was slightly ajar, and light streamed from it. His sword was in his hand when he entered. Inside, he stood and scanned the room, which was as cluttered as he remembered it. Cats were everywhere, prowling restlessly, and the many candles had burned to mere stumps. The sound of wailing came from another room, and Conan approached it slowly.

Within, a single white cat crouched keening upon a wardrobe, staring down at something on the floor. The Cimmerian stepped over to see what it might be, already knowing what it was.

Delia lay with sightless eyes staring up at the cat. Just below her left breast protruded the hilt of a dagger.

EIGHTEEN
The Black-Haired Woman

The Temple of Bes was deserted in the morning hours. The whole of the Pit was quiet, bracing itself for the day's inevitable bloodshed. When Conan entered the temple, the two Shemite guards came from behind an improvised barricade, spiked clubs in their hands.

"Summon the priest," he told them. One stepped past him and peered out into the street to make certain he was unaccompanied. Satisfied that the Cimmerian planned no raid, he went in search of the priest, who arrived a few minutes later.

"Ah, my Cimmerian friend of a few days ago. Welcome, sir. I must apologize for these warlike preparations, but I no longer feel safe. It is as if everyone here has gone mad and all the violent men of the city rend one another like wild dogs!"

"I don't blame you," Conan said. "It will all be over in a day or two, I think."

The priest raised both hands, palms outward, toward the image of Bes. "For this I pray to my god daily. Now, my friend, how may I help you?"

"First, have you seen my companion of a few days ago, the small man?"

"Ah, he of the singular clothing and the lilac scent. Yes, he has been here with some frequency, most recently yesterday evening. I fear that I have not been able to give him just recompense for his . . . offerings, as it were."

"Why is that?" Conan asked.

"If you will come with me, I will show you." The priest led him down the steps to the crypt and pushed the door open, then gestured for the Cimmerian to enter. He did so, then surveyed the scene.

"Mitra!" he said with wonder. "The thieves of this town have been busy indeed!"

"I prefer to think of them as worshipers," said the priest. The crypt was stacked almost to the ceiling with loot. Chests of jewels and plate, fine lamps, inlaid tables, art objects of every description, spices and incense, all were crammed into every available corner.

"With the troubles proliferating in the town," the priest said, "many men wish to liquidate their holdings and transform their variously acquired valuables into ready cash, easily transportable should their leave-taking be precipitate. As a result, the temple is rich in valuables but cash poor, and for that reason, I have not been able to pay your friend proper value for what he has brought hither."

"Considering what it cost him to get the goods," Conan said, "he should have little cause for complaint. Left he any message for me?"

"None, I fear," the priest admitted.

"Well, then. Here is something I require of you. I wish free access to your river gate—" he pointed at the portal in question, to which only a narrow path through the loot allowed access "—at any hour of day or night. I want your guards to admit me and let me through instantly, without question, and to be silent about it afterward." From the pouch at his belt he drew a smaller bag of cloth and handed it to the priest. "Here are a hundred silver marks."

"I thank you, my friend. Bes thanks you. Bes is the most merciful of gods, and does not like to see men endure the sufferings of the rack, the scourge, and the noose. And these, I think, would be your inevitable fate in this town before very long. I can see that you have endured some rough treatment already."

"Nothing I cannot pay back in kind," said Conan, whose bruises were still livid.

He left the temple and thought about how to reach the other end of the town. There was always the sewer system, but he had tired of skulking about. If any man thirsted for his blood, let him come openly. The Cimmerian walked up the middle of the street in full daylight.

The town through which he passed was a place at war. The respectable citizens stayed behind their locked gates, barred doors, and closed shutters. The gangs roamed in steel-bristling packs. Whenever such a pack approached the big Cimmerian, his snarl drove them to the wall, letting him pass in peace. He was in no mood for trifling this morning. Delia's murder had wiped out the pleasure he had felt at returning Rietta safely to her father. Any man who wished to shed a little of Conan's blood had better be willing to lose quite a bit of his own in return. Men could read this in his bearing and therefore gave him wide berth.

He reached the inn without incident. The common room was nearly deserted. The servers sat at a table talking among themselves for want of customers.

"Has the woman I was with been in?" he asked the innkeeper.

"Not for two days," the man said. "In this town, that probably means she is dead." His look was reproachful. "You should have taken better care of her, an innocent, gently bred girl like that."

"I wonder," Conan muttered. "Have there been any messages for me?" Wordlessly, the man reached beneath the counter and brought forth a folded piece of paper, sealed with wax and reeking of lilacs. Conan broke the seal and read.

"Meet me at dusk in the upper room of the Wyvern," the delicate script bade him. *"I have the rest of your pay."*

Conan wondered whether this was a trap. The Wyvern was Lisip's territory. But how could the gang lord know that he had led the raid on the old fort? No one had escaped, and surely the miners would not have betrayed him. Most likely, Piris had merely arranged a local contact. As Conan had chosen the temple for a place to hide out, Piris had found quarters in the Wyvern's labyrinth of rooms.

Satisfied, he went to a table and ordered breakfast. He was impatient for the evening. It was time to collect his pay and be away from this place, before the royal authorities arrived. They would hold everyone who fell into their net, and many men would spend years in the dungeons, or at breaking rock in the royal quarries, or at rowing royal barges, while the investigations proceeded at a glacial pace. This was a fate Conan was most eager to avoid.

He was deeply troubled by Delia's murder. Who had done it? Maxio was the most likely candidate. In a fit of jealousy or pique, he might easily have slain her. In spite of her many glaring flaws, Conan had liked the big raucous beauty. He much preferred an honest trollop to any sort of hypocrite, and Delia had not had a hypocritical bone in her voluptuous body. Who else might it be? Ermak, possibly. He might have questioned her about Maxio's whereabouts and then killed her, but there had been no signs of torture or struggle. Truthfully, he had no idea of how many enemies the woman might have had. She relished playing with dangerous men, and those who shared that taste seldom enjoyed long life. The Cimmerian determined that whoever it might be, that one would pay for the deed.

He spent a few hours in the stable, caring for his horse and going over every inch of his harness. The damp winter weather was deadly for fine leather, and he scoured away every trace of mold and carefully oiled every bit of his riding gear, paying special attention to girths and other straps. Nothing was more embarrassing than, with pursuit but a few paces behind, to leap into the saddle only to have it all tumble ignominiously to the ground because a neglected surcingle had parted.

When he was satisfied with his horse trappings, he gave equal attention to the animal's hooves, examining each in turn, testing the condition of the hoof and that of the shoe, then every nail of the shoe. Dissatisfied with one shoe, he had the smith across the street replace all four shoes, under the watchful eye of the rider.

With that done, he gave similar attention to his weaponry, cleaning and oiling it scrupulously, going over each edge with a fine whetstone, testing hilt and grip for any slightest hint of movement. Age and climate could cause a grip made of bone or wood to shrink, robbing the blade of support at the crucial juncture of blade and hilt, thus weakening the whole weapon.

By the time all was to his satisfaction, it was late afternoon. He had dinner in the common room, then went out into the street. His steps led him south, past the Square and into the Pit, where he was to meet Piris. At one point he was forced to make a detour around a block where the narrow street was crowded with fighting men.

The Wyvern was not heavily populated as the Cimmerian entered. Of the men who sat drinking at the tables, many were bandaged; other men lay groaning on the floor. He went to the bar and called for ale. The barkeep brought him a jack of tarred leather, slopping foam as he set it on the ancient, nicked counter.

"Is Piris here yet?" Conan asked.

"I saw him go upstairs an hour ago," the man said.

Conan decided that there was no rush, that Piris could wait until he finished his ale.

"He must be a popular man this evening," the barkeep said.

"How so?"

"Well, just before you arrived, a woman came asking for him and I told her where he was. She went up after him."

Conan all but choked on a mouthful of ale. "What woman?" he demanded, slamming the jack upon the bar. "Which room?"

"A black-haired wench with a dangerous look in her eye. What other kind would come into the Wyvern unescorted? As to what room, it is on the third level, with a cockatrice painted on the door. It's—'' But now he was addressing the Cimmerian's back. "Aren't you going to finish your—" Already, the big barbarian was leaping up the stairs. The barkeep shrugged and finished the ale himself.

The Cimmerian fairly flew up the steps, jostling aside trollops and their customers in the process. At the third level, he looked around frantically. He saw a door with a dragon, one with a serpent, one with a lion. At the far end of the hallway, he saw a yellow door with a red cockatrice painted on it. He moved toward the door swiftly but silently, his weapons held close against him lest they make a betraying clatter. By the time he reached the portal, he was balancing on the toes of his boots. There he stopped and listened. He heard the sound of squabbling voices but could make out nothing of what they were saying. Taking a deep breath, he thrust the door open.

Inside, two figures stood facing each other across the length of a table. Each held a dagger extended toward the other. The black-haired woman stood with her back to him. Piris faced him. The little man looked up at his entry, and relief flowed across the effeminate features.

"This is she!" he said in his odd, breathy voice. "This is Altaira, the treacherous wench who betrayed me into the dungeon of Belverus! Slay her!" He held forth his envenomed weapon as if he had little trust in the Cimmerian's ability to protect him from this virago.

"Turn, woman," Conan said.

"Not while this vile little catamite holds his poisoned steel!" she hissed.

Conan's own sword slid from its sheath. "I'll not let him stab you in the back, and if I wanted you dead, you would be dead already. Turn."

Slowly, the woman turned to face him. The face was heart-shaped beneath its mass of black locks, the mouth a crimson slash, the eyes boldly outlined in cosmetic. The skin was as white as the purest snow. She seemed a stranger, yet there was something familiar about her features. Then he knew.

"Brita!" Never had he seen such a transformation. Except for the shape of the facial bones, there was no similarity to the shy, well-bred girl he had aided. Even the color of the eyes was different.

"This is your Tarantian girl?" Piris asked with a squealing giggle. "You have been gulled, my barbarian friend! But do not be too ashamed; she has taken in men far more experienced than you."

"So," Conan said. "Many things become clear now." His sword point was level with her throat. Ordinarily he never drew steel against a woman, but he had never encountered one as uniquely deadly as this one. "No wonder those bandits I rescued you from were so well mounted. Their job was to present a sham ravishment, then get away as fast as they could."

"Of course," she said, her voice colder than any steel. "I followed you and Piris from that tavern in Belverus, and I eavesdropped upon your meeting. I knew instantly that you were one of those foolish men who would go out of his way to rescue a woman, and then feel himself to be her protector."

Conan laughed hollowly. "As if you ever needed a protector. So it was you and Piris and Asdras who stole the scorpion from Casperus?"

"No!" Piris insisted. "The scorpion is mine!"

"It belongs to whoever can keep it," Altaira said. "And we had it for a while. Yes, I planned to get the scorpion from the fat man. I sent Asdras ahead to Sicas, but Piris, who is far cleverer than you, Conan, would not leave my side and was too cautious to give me a chance to kill him. So I passed the idol to Mulvix, who was headed to Sicas with his caravan. He did not know what it was and always went by the smuggler's code, that a smuggler does not pry into the cargo he has agreed to deliver. He delivered it to me here as promised."

"And she planted false evidence on me to have me thrown into the dungeon before I could chase her down!'' Piris said indignantly.

"I should have known,'' Conan said ruefully. "All the way here, and after we arrived, you kept getting word of this 'sister' of yours, but never when I was with you.''

"That is because your brain is in your sword arm, Cimmerian,'' she said. "A more intelligent man would have noticed.''

Conan shrugged philosophically. "I have ever been a fool where women are concerned. That you gulled me I do not hold against you. It is every man's duty to look out for himself. But I take it amiss that you took advantage of my better nature.''

"What do you mean?'' she asked, clearly perplexed.

"It would be useless to explain it to you. The miners who live near here understand these things better.''

"I think you have gone mad,'' she said.

"That first night,'' Conan said, "when you brought me here to the Wyvern . . . you had been down here first. You summoned Asdras outside and stabbed him. Then, all innocence, you dragged me down here so we could 'discover' him. One less with whom to share the scorpion.''

"And when we went to the Temple of Bes,'' Piris said, "she followed and set her hired rogues upon us. And just in case that should not be enough, she set the Reeve to arrest us and clap us in the dungeon here.''

"But you could not foresee,'' Conan said to her, "that the rich spice merchant would buy me out of jail to rescue his daughter from the Temple of Mother Doorgah.''

"Ah, is that what happened?'' she murmured. "Truly, I could not keep track of everything.''

"You acted strangely,'' Conan said, "when I told you of my interview with Casperus. It was the only time you allowed your mask to slip with me. When you realized your mistake, you seduced me to distract my mind from your mistake.''

"Seduced you!'' she said. "Does a mare need to seduce a stallion?''

"I would never have let that happen,'' sniffed Piris.

"That I do not doubt one whit," Conan said. Then, to Altaira: "And when Mulvix came to our rooms at the inn, he was not dying as he climbed the stairs, was he? You had left him word of how to find you, and he came straight to you, and to your dagger. Then you took some of the blood and left it on the walk and on the stairs so that it would look as if he had trailed it all the way up. Why did you not take the scorpion then?"

She made an eloquent movement of her beautiful white shoulders. "Piris was here, Casperus was still here. I had yet to deal with them, and when you hold the scorpion, it is not easy to manage anything else. I knew that you were trustworthy and stupid. You would hide it for me until I should want it back."

"And hide it I did," said Conan, grinning. "Have you any idea where?"

"Wretch!" she cried. "Where is it?"

"Why should I tell you?" he asked.

"Well," she said, her voice turning conciliatory, "I can see that I was wrong about you, Conan. I had thought you a simple, brainless savage. But, truthfully, you do have a brain in that head of yours, and you have been playing games in this town as subtle as my own. In fact, you and I could prosper mightily together."

"Too late, Brita, or Altaira, or whatever your real name is," said Conan. "I know too much about you now, and no man who values his life would come near you. But tell me this: What is *your* story about the scorpion?"

"I suppose that this fool and the fat man have told you about what a great, magical idol it is?"

"They did," Conan affirmed, "each in his own way."

"Well, they both lied," she said. "You have held it. How did it feel?"

"Heavy," replied Conan.

"Of course it is heavy. Nothing is weightier than gold, and of all gold, the heaviest is white gold!"

"White gold!" Conan exclaimed. The metal was all but legendary. White gold was to silver what silver was to lead. Its brilliance was incomparable, and it was esteemed by goldsmiths as the noblest of metals. Most commonly, its value was pegged at ten times the worth of an equal weight of the finest gold.

"Aye," she said. "It is no ancient idol, no black diamond fallen from the heavens. It was cast no more than five hundred years ago as tribute from the king of Keshan to the priest-king of Stygia. In those days, Selkhet was the preeminent goddess of Stygia, the patroness of the royal house, and the king of Keshan, wishing to curry favor, gathered the white gold from the royal treasury and had it cast into this image and sent to Khemi, the capital.

"Not long after that, it was stolen. It has turned up over the years, and early in this time it acquired its present guise. It was coated with a black enamel, an amalgam made from powdered obsidian."

"Not a magical talisman, eh?" said Conan, thinking of the very odd happenings in the temple of Mother Doorgah.

"Not at all," she said. "But what it is, is the most valuable single object on earth. Its value is incalculable, and it could make both of us rich beyond our wildest dreams."

"She lies!" Piris shrieked. "It belongs to my family! And it is unthinkably ancient and magical."

"Oh, be quiet, both of you," Conan said. He brandished his blade and the two stood back. "I no longer care what the damned thing is. I want nothing to do with it, though it be made of white gold and give the owner eternal youth to boot."

"But you promised to deliver the scorpion to me," Piris squeaked. "You accepted my pay!"

"So I did," Conan said, "although I assuredly would not have undertaken the task had you given me the full story of your 'treasure.' Not for a mere thousand dishas, at any rate," he amended.

"That is immaterial," Piris protested. "You gave me your word!"

"I did that, to my regret," Conan said. "And lead you to it I shall." He turned to the woman.

"Tell me one thing: Did you kill Delia?"

"Delia?" she said. "You mean Maxio's slut? I did not even

know she was dead." As near as Conan could judge, she was telling the truth.

"What?" exclaimed Piris, his eyes gone wide in mock amazement. "You mean there is someone in this town she *hasn't* stabbed?"

"Listen to me, you two," Conan said. "I have matters to attend to. I am leaving you now. If you would have the scorpion, meet me at noon tomorrow in the Square, before the theater."

"You will leave me here alone with this she-demon?" Piris asked indignantly.

"I did not undertake to be your bodyguard," Conan said. "You two may kill each other for all I care. But if it is advice you want, I suggest that you come to an agreement. And now I bid you both good evening." He backed through the doorway and shut the door. From the other side of the painted cockatrice, he heard the two voices resume their squabbling.

As he descended to the common room, something occurred to him. He went back to the bar and summoned the barkeep.

"Were you here a bit more than a month ago, when the Reeve's brother was stabbed upstairs?"

"Aye," said the barkeep, wiping out a jack with a filthy rag. "I think that was the only time Bombas ever showed his fat face in the Pit, when he came down to claim the body, surrounded by his worthless men."

"Who discovered the body?" the Cimmerian asked.

"It was Julus," said the barkeep. "That was just after old Lisip drove him out for skimming. He went to work for Bombas right after Burdo was murdered."

"Aye, I thought it might be something like that," Conan said.

"What's that?" said the barkeep, but once again he was addressing Conan's broad, armored back.

From the Wyvern the Cimmerian made his way through the dark streets to the Temple of Bes. When he presented himself, one of the Shemitish guards conducted him to the crypt and opened the river door for him. He stepped out onto the riverbank and made his way around the confluence of the rivers to the bridge. He climbed the abutment to the roadbed and set out at an easy walk.

He reached the ridge overlooking the miner's village in less than two hours. Despite the late hour, he saw several high-burning fires around the perimeter of the village. He walked down to the nearest blaze and three men, armed with crude spears, stepped forward to challenge him.

"Who goes . . . it's the Cimmerian!" Grinning, the rest came forward.

"Is Bellas here?" Conan asked.

"Nay, but he shall be," said one. A boy was sent to fetch the head man. A few minutes later, he arrived.

"Ask what you will of us," the man said simply.

"Would you see an end to all this business?" Conan asked.

"Aye, with every breath I draw, I would like to see that."

"Then come all of you to the Square tomorrow, a little past noon. Come armed."

"That we shall!" said Bellas, and the rest cheered.

"Do not celebrate just yet," said Conan. "It will be a hard fight this time. Ermak's men."

"Good," said Bellas. "The last fight but whetted our appetite for revenge."

"Then you'll have your fill tomorrow," Conan promised. "Remember, wait until just a little past noon, then come into the town. Force the river gate if you have to, but if you move swiftly enough, the dodderer on guard will have no time to shut and bar it."

"We shall do as you say," Bellas said.

"I will see you tomorrow, then," said Conan. Moving like a ghost, he disappeared from the circle of firelight.

The Cimmerian walked back toward the town, but when he reached the river, he did not cross. He had no doubt that he could scale the low river wall easily, but he had no wish to do so. He had run out of safe havens in the town, some lair where he could enjoy a night's uneventful sleep. Instead, he walked into a nearby copse of trees and rolled himself into his cloak. He adjudged from the height of the moon that he had a good two or three hours before daylight. The morrow promised to be a busy day, and he knew that he would need to be fully alert. Within minutes, he was asleep.

NINETEEN
The Final Battle

He crossed the bridge as the sun rose on what promised to be a fine, clear day. The gatekeeper was surprised to see a traveler waiting without as he opened the portal on creaky hinges. This was a man Conan had not seen before, younger than most of them but graced with a peg leg, and bearing a hook where his left hand should have been.

"If it were you, stranger," the man warned, "I'd not come into this town on this day."

"Why not?" asked Conan, passing through. He tossed a coin, which the man caught adroitly with his remaining hand.

"Because there's a big fight brewing today. The gangs've sulked all night, and I hear they're going to have it out once and for all in the Square."

"That should be a fine show," Conan said. "I must go find a good place from which to watch."

"As you will," the man said. He took a tablet from his belt and opened it, balancing the thing on his good knee and extracting a stylus from its resting place behind his ear. "Name and business?"

Conan tossed the man another coin, which was caught just as adroitly as the first, though the hand was burdened with the stylus. The guard shrugged and put away the tablet.

"And now I have advice for you, friend," said Conan.

"What might it be?" the man asked.

"Start looking for a job. You will need a new one soon."

The man shrugged resignedly. "I can always go back to begging."

Conan walked through the Pit's deceptive early morning quiet. He passed into the newer part of town. The Square was entirely deserted. For once, no one had come to set up a stall. Word was all over the town that it was a day for battle and that this time it would not be merely an amusement for spectators.

When Conan entered the common room, the innkeeper gaped and hurried to his side.

"Cimmerian, you must be careful! Julus has been here a number of times, seeking for you. I think the Reeve wants to clap you in his dungeon."

"Bombas and his dogs will be far too busy this day to trouble over me," Conan assured him. "What concerns me now is not the Reeve or his lackeys, but breakfast!"

The innkeeper shook his head. "You are mad, like everyone else in this town, but have it as you will. Seat yourself and eat your fill. It may be your last meal, if the town gossip is to be believed."

Conan sat at a table where a newly arrived lot of caravanners made way for him. He laid in a substantial breakfast, not because he thought it might be his last, but because he was hungry and because he knew that soon he might have to flee the town, and he had no idea of when he would eat again. When his appetite was satisfied, he beckoned a serving boy to his side.

"What would you, master?" asked the boy, eyeing the Cimmerian's stalwart frame and gleaming armament with envy. Conan gave him directions to the house where Casperus was staying.

"Tell the fat man," Conan instructed, "or the ill-favored lout with two swords, these words: 'Conan of Cimmeria has what you want. Meet him before the great theater on the Square at noon and he will lead you to it. If you do not come as instructed, our agreement is at an end.' Now, lad, repeat that to me.'' The boy repeated it accurately, twice. ''Good,'' Conan approved, tossing him a coin. ''Be off with you.''

The boy left upon his errand, and Conan passed some time trading stories with the caravanners. He was most interested to learn of the doings in the other areas of Aquilonia, where the barons were defying the king.

He went to his room and found his belongings as he had left them. These he packed; then he went to the adjoining room, where Brita had stayed. There was no trace that said she had ever been there.

''I wonder,'' he said to himself, ''how the wench managed to change the color of her eyes.''

Carrying the saddlebags, he descended the stairs and went to the stable, where he saddled his horse and tied the bags behind the cantle. He rolled up his cloak and tied it there as well.

''Do you ride out today, sir?'' asked the stableman.

''Not just yet,'' Conan said. ''But soon. I want the horse to remain saddled thus, and tethered here, just inside the doorway. Will you see to that?'' He handed the man a coin.

''Oh, aye, sir. You are not the first to stay here who wished to be ready to leave at a second's notice. The lady will not be going with you?''

''No, she will not. Has the horse had water and grain?''

''Aye, early this morning.''

''Good. Give it no more.'' A foundered horse would be of no use to a fleeing man.

He left the stable and stood in the courtyard, studying the sun. It was almost noon. He walked out into the street and began to walk toward the Square. The street was deserted, but many eyes observed him from behind shutters. People stood on balconies and on rooftops, and all watched the Cimmerian silently. He walked with easy confidence, his only sound the occasional click-ing of a massive bracelet against sword or dagger hilt. He walked slowly, for he had no wish to arrive betimes and have to hang about the Square, where he could not remain unseen for long.

When he rounded the corner of the theater, he did not proceed into the Square but, rather, climbed its steps and stood within the gloomy shade of its portico, watching the events. The far end of the square, where the Reeve had his headquarters, was already swarming with men. Fighting had not yet commenced, but men stood about in groups of varying size, waving their weapons and shouting.

Ermak's men massed in a compact formation before the headquarters of Bombas. The Reeve must have bribed them to support him, Conan thought. Then he espied Casperus and Gilmay as they came into the Square from a side alley. They looked to be apprehensive and indignant, but the fat man radiated greed that could be felt even at a distance. Soon they were before the theater, looking about, but they did not glance up the steps to where the Cimmerian stood.

People crowded the rooftops of the buildings ringing the Square; no one was able to resist the prospect of such a spectacle. They would regret their eagerness to see blood flow, Conan thought, should those buildings be set afire. Then he saw two people come across the Square from the direction of the Pit. One was a black-haired woman, the other a small man who wore luridly colored clothing. Conan could almost smell the lilacs. Gilmay was first to catch sight of them.

"You two!" he cried. "How came you here?"

"We came at the Cimmerian's invitation," said Altaira with a withering curl of her scarlet lip. "As, I have no doubt, did the two of you."

"Ah-h," said Casperus, smiling. "Now we are all together again, except for our poor dear Asdras, who, as I am given to understand, has escaped the sufferings of this transitory life for the undoubted pleasures of the life to come."

"He will soon have much company in that life," said Conan, descending the stair. They all turned at the sound of his voice.

"Ah, what a clever fellow you are, sir," said Casperus. "Now you expect us to bid against each other for the idol, not so?"

"No," Conan said. "I have come to lead you to it, as I agreed. How you decide who is to have possession is your affair."

"Then lead on, sir, lead on!" said Casperus, chuckling. Conan began to walk toward the temple and they followed. At the far end of the Square, the screaming climbed to a crescendo; then sounds of clashing steel filled the air.

"The rogues of this town do seem bent upon mutual massacre," said Casperus with a sigh. "It is so sad. How we shall miss them all."

They paused before the steps of the temple. "I will warn you," Conan said, "that there is great magic loose in this place. Casperus, if you have any of the sorcerous skills you claim, you may need them."

The fat man looked concerned. "Why? What has happened?"

"The priest in here thinks that he is a wizard as well. When I hid the scorpion here, his spells grew in power."

"What are you talking about?" asked Altaira. "I told you that the image has no sorcerous power!"

"No power?" said Casperus, chuckling. "My dear lady, how wrong you are!"

As they entered, their ears were assailed by the hideous, discordant chanting of inhuman voices. They walked gingerly toward the nave, from which poured a frightful, unnatural glow.

"Mitra preserve us!" said Casperus. "What has happened here?" They gazed upon the fearful spectacle within. Around the colossus, the remaining acolytes chanted and howled, but they were no longer even remotely human. They were either scaly or hairy, and fanged, pincered, even tentacled. Some had transformed into shapes without description. The statue was no longer that of Mother Doorgah, but was half-metamorphosed into the semblance of a gigantic black scorpion with the face of a woman.

Upon its back danced Oppia, now fully transformed into the form of Mother Doorgah, but she was not the beautiful, benevolent goddess of the earlier statue. This was Mother Doorgah in her aspect of Drinker of Blood and Devourer of Entrails. From the ghastly mess of human remains upon which she danced, she had done exactly that to her husband, Andolla.

"Quickly," Casperus urged. "You must lead me to the place where he worked his sorcery." His face was pale and sweaty.

"No!" Piris insisted. "The scorpion! Take us to the scorpion!"

"Aye," said Altaira. "To the scorpion! It has nothing to do with this. It is not magical."

"I think we will do as Casperus says," Conan told them. "I do not want whatever is happening here to get loose in the city."

"And get loose it will, soon," said Casperus. "We will never get away from here alive unless I put a stop to this."

Quickly, Conan led them along a gallery flanking the nave and into the rooms below. Soon he found the chamber where Andolla kept his sorcerous impedimenta. Swiftly and efficiently, Casperus studied the instruments and the books that lay open.

"The fool!" he said. "He managed to assemble some powerful talismans, and even more powerful tomes. Only a wizard of the first rank should touch these! This is what happens when an amateur dabbles in sorcery." With sure movements, incredibly fast for a man of such bulk, he began to rip parchments that bore strange symbols and to scatter sand paintings. With great precision, he altered geometrical patterns chalked upon the floor and tossed certain waxen effigies into a brazier, where they flared and melted.

"There," he said when he was done. "That may just contain the damage. Let us go."

"We go to the cellars," Conan said, taking a lamp from a table. "Get lamps or candles and follow." They did as he said and were very subdued as they walked down the steps behind him.

All was quiet in the vaulted chambers below the temple. There was no indication of the chaos above. Conan led them to the great support pillar and began to press the keystones.

"The big statue is directly above," he told them. "I think that may have something to do with the way the thing reinforced Andolla's spells.''

''I have no doubt that it did,'' said Casperus.

''You talk like fools!'' hissed Altaira.

''Master,'' said Gilmay, who was getting over the shock of the spectacle above. ''Why not let me kill this vicious strumpet?'' He half-drew one of his swords.

''No killing,'' Conan warned. ''There will be no killing until I give you the scorpion, as I promised. After that,'' he shrugged, ''you may kill and eat each other for all I care.''

''My dear Altaira,'' said Casperus, ''you have only greed, whereas I have greed and scholarship. You refer to the scorpion of white gold, do you not? I, too, know of that one. Did you think that was the one we had?''

''Is it not?'' she said, paling.

''I fear not. That was a relic of a far later age. Once there was civil war in Stygia, and a contestant for the throne thought to have the copy made and substituted for the original, thinking that it would give him power. He used white gold because only that metal could duplicate the weight of the original. Many legends grew around it later, due to of its unique value. You must have heard one of them. I fear that the copy was melted down centuries ago. What our resourceful friend has secreted within this pedestal is the true idol.''

''But . . . but . . .'' She got no further, for now the door began to open. Their eyes shone with a combination of fear and avarice as the stone moved aside. Then the scorpion stood before them, just within the aperture.

''It has moved,'' said Conan, the words almost freezing in his throat. ''I set it on the pedestal in the center of the chamber, and it has moved to the door.'' His scalp crawled as he backed away, hand on hilt.

''Ah, is she not beautiful?'' said Casperus, ignoring the Cimmerian's words. ''And now she is mine again!''

''Never yours, and not yours now!'' Altaira said, drawing a dagger from within her sleeve and plunging it into the fat man's

back. The huge bulk collapsed across the scorpion and she tried
to push it aside. With a strangled shriek, Gilmay drew his swords
and aimed a great double blow at the woman's body.

Unthinkingly, Conan drew his own sword, and with a lightning
slash, he sheared away the youth's head. Even as the corpse collapsed atop the other, Altaira withdrew her dagger and favored
Conan with an evil smile.

"You just cannot get out of the habit of protecting me, can
you, barbarian?" Catlike, she whirled and plunged her blade
through Piris's throat. The little man's eyes bugged as he staggered back, hands at his throat, blood spurting between his fingers.

The woman gasped and stared with horror at a deep gash that
ran the length of her forearm. The slender dagger in Piris's hand
was stained with her blood, and with a darker substance.

"The scorpion is all yours," Conan shouted, "and I wish you
all joy of it! Never did four people deserve each other more!" He
went back up the stairs in a series of bounds that quickly brought
him to the nave of the temple. The hellish noise had ceased, and
the unnatural glow was gone. The light admitted by skylights
illuminated a floor covered with writhing, groaning people, who
seemed to be regaining their human aspect. The huge statue had
collapsed to a heap of fragments. He saw Oppia lying atop the
heap. If she was alive or dead, he neither knew nor cared.

After the temple, the bright sunlight and the cheerful sounds
of battle seemed wholesome indeed. He saw that the miners had
arrived, and now the whole Square was thronged with shouting,
struggling men. Bodies lay everywhere amidst a little of broken
weapons. From the rooftops, onlookers cheered the fighters on,
without discrimination.

Conan worked his way around the periphery of the Square until
he stood before the Reeve's headquarters. The steps leading up to
it were ringed by a double line of Ermak's men. Conan passed
behind them and went up the stair. On the third step from the top
stood Ermak, directing his men. He was too busy to take notice
of the Cimmerian, who passed within the headquarters.

Just inside the door, two men were screaming at one another. Conan was not surprised to see that the two were Bombas and Xanthus.

"Fool!" Xanthus screeched. "It is all over now! Your greed has brought the royal forces upon us!"

"*My* greed?" yelled Bombas, his face gone scarlet. "It was *your* idea to skim the royal silver!"

Julus spotted Conan and came forward. "What are you doing here, barbarian?" The other two broke off their argument and stared at the newcomer.

"I've come to collect the rest of my pay," Conan said.

"What pay?" Bombas demanded.

Conan pointed to Xanthus. "The pay he promised me for cleaning up his town. I have done it, and I want my pay."

"What do you mean?" screamed Xanthus.

Conan jerked a thumb over his shoulder in the direction of the Square. "That is my doing. By the time the royal forces arrive, they'll be able to hang any surviving rogues with a single short rope. When the noise dies down, this will be a quiet town once more. Pay me."

Xanthus's face convulsed with near-apoplexy. "But I did not . . . I did not . . ." He was unable to finish.

"By the way," Conan said to Bombas, "you will be one of those gracing that rope. I found your real account books in the fort when I led the raid there. They are in safe custody and will soon be in the king's hands. He is not much of a king, but he is enough of a sovereign to hang a thieving official." Bombas's hand went to his throat as if he already felt the hemp.

"So all this is your doing, eh?" said Julus, coming forward with a sword bare in his hand.

"Aye, it is. And in a moment I am going to pay you for that beating. I am not tied up now. But first one thing: It was you who killed Delia, wasn't it?"

The brute smiled as if at a pleasant memory. "That I did. How did you guess? The wench threatened to spread tales about me if I did not pay her. Slaying her was so much easier."

Conan looked at Bombas. "Do you know what she threatened to tell you about your henchman?"

"Do not listen to him!" Julus barked.

"She was going to tell you," Conan went on, "that it was Julus who slew your brother, using a dagger he stole from Maxio. Lisip had just expelled him for stealing, and he wanted to curry favor with you. So he killed Burdo, then went to you to say that Maxio had slain your brother, letting you know that he was just the right-hand man you needed to replace your brother. But Delia saw it, didn't she?"

"She guessed," Julus said. "She kept it to herself as a trick to keep Maxio sweet. When she gave up on keeping him, she came to me with her threat." Abruptly he whirled and thrust his sword through Bombas's belly. Quick as a thought, he had the sword back out and turned to face Conan with a grin. "The king will be grateful to the man who slew his thieving Reeve. Do you not think so?"

"He will not have the chance!" Conan said, hewing at the thug with even greater swiftness. Julus backed across the room, fending away blows with a confident look. Then his look was alarmed, then terrified as he knew that he would not be able to strike a blow in return. He began to bellow for help, but all sound was drowned by the racket from without.

"This is a little different from torturing bound men, is it not?" said Conan, not allowing his words to interfere with the deadly rhythm of his blows.

Eyes wide with horror, Julus abruptly leaped back, simultaneously hurling his sword at the Cimmerian. Conan expected the move and ducked below the hurtling steel. He felt the tick of the blade as it nicked his steel cap in passing; then he was running after the fleeing Julus. Three bounds and a lunge, and his blade spitted the man from back to front, a handsbreadth of steel standing out before the thug's breast. Conan withdrew his blade, and bright blood pulsed out of both wounds.

"A coward always dies like a coward," Conan commented. He turned and walked back toward Xanthus. The old man stared at the corpse of Bombas with satisfaction. Then he looked up at the approaching barbarian.

"I—I cannot pay you just yet, Conan! I must assemble the money, but I promise you, I shall."

"You'll do nothing," Conan said, "not even live much longer. Your name is on those books as well."

A figure dressed in half-armor entered the doorway. It was Ermak, his blade stained as was Conan's. "It is finished! Pick-swinging miners have broken my men and they flee!"

Xanthus pointed at Conan. "Ermak, kill that man! I will make you rich if you will slay him for me!"

"Aye, I'll slay the rogue," said Ermak. "But not for your money, you foolish old skinflint. You're a dead man if ever there was one, with the king's men on their way, as they must be by now."

"I will see both of you hanged!" screeched Xanthus. Then he looked down with alarm. A hand gripped his robe. The hand belonged to Bombas, and the fat Reeve began to pull the old miser inexorably downward. "Let go of me! Julus slew you!"

"Because of you," Bombas wheezed, "my Lorinda died! Now I am going to kill you!"

"That was *your* doing. Yours!" Xanthus protested.

"Who is Lorinda?" Ermak asked.

"A woman they both loved, long ago," said Conan. "There is no need for us to fight. It is all over here. We are professionals, you and I."

"Oh, but we must," Ermak said grimly. "This was the sweetest situation a warrior ever encountered. A whole town to loot without battle. And you ruined it. I do not know how you did it, but it was all your doing. From the moment you arrived, everything began to go sour. Guard yourself!" He gave the Cimmerian that much courtesy, then he attacked.

This was not like fighting Julus. Conan found himself defending his life with desperation. Ermak was strong, swift, and highly skilled. He was better armored than Conan as well, and did not have to pay as much attention to defending his body, for the fine steel of his cuirass was proof against even Conan's blows, while Conan's brigandine might be pierced by a hard and well-aimed thrust.

For the first moments of the fight, the Cimmerian concentrated on defense, analyzing his enemy, and plotting his own strategy. He found himself enjoying this. It had been far too long since he had felt himself fully tried in single combat with a worthy opponent. He lived for mortal combat, and now the fierce joy of it began to suffuse him, and this was his true edge. Ermak was a cold, hard, professional warrior, but Conan was a barbarian.

After his fierce initial attack, Ermak shifted to a more calculating strategy. His armor was heavy, and he knew better than to tire himself too quickly. Now Conan began his assault. Twice his blade rang from the other's casque, but without real force. The basket hilt of the other's sword prevented an attack to the hand, and the man guarded his sword arm well.

The half-armor ended partway down the thigh. Conan launched a flurry of high attacks, drawing Ermak's guard upward, then abruptly slashed low, gashing the man's leg just above the knee. Ermak did not waste time in seeing how badly he was hurt, but instantly took advantage of the low position of Conan's sword to slash at his opponent's face. The Cimmerian avoided the attack only by leaping backward, and only a man of his extraordinary swiftness could have accomplished the adroit move.

Ermak pressed the onslaught, forcing the Cimmerian to give ground, for once momentum has been lost in a fight, it is hard to regain. But the gang lord's leading leg was weakening from its wound, his high boot filling with blood.

"Damn you, barbarian!" he growled. "Why?"

Conan did not answer. Instead, he lowered his sword slightly. Ermak exploited the opening and thrust at the Cimmerian's throat. Conan parried the blade, not with his sword this time, but with the massive bracelet on his left wrist. He let the blade slide high past his left shoulder while he lunged with his whole body behind his weapon. His point caught Ermak just beneath the cheekbone. It passed upward through the rear of the eye socket, through the brain, and halted at the back of the skull. Conan needed a forceful wrench to free the blade. Ermak continued to stand for a few seconds, then toppled as stiffly as would a falling tree, the clash of his armor ringing loudly on the marble floor.

"That is how a warrior should die," said Conan, cleaning his sword on a wall hanging. "On his feet and facing his enemy." He resheathed the weapon and went to inspect Xanthus and the Reeve. The features of the miser were twisted and empurpled, Bombas's fat beringed fingers buried in the flesh of his scrawny neck.

"So those soft hands were good for something after all," Conan said.

He left the headquarters and walked out into the Square. It was carpeted with bodies, and citizens stood around surveying the carnage. An eerie silence reigned. He walked the length of the great plaza, noting in passing that Maxio lay dead, clutching his belly, his look of perpetual anger still upon his countenance.

He made a leisurely progress back to the inn. It seemed that there would be no rush after all. He went to the stable and claimed his horse. As he mounted in the courtyard, the innkeeper came up to him.

"What has happened?" the man asked.

"I think that this will be a quiet town now," the Cimmerian answered.

He rode out into the street and contemplated which way to turn. He could ride southward through the Pit to the river gate and cross the river, there to dig up the substantial loot he had buried. But that would be weighty burden to carry and guard. He had a well-stuffed purse, and the treasure was safe where it lay. It was never a bad idea to have such a cache against hard times. He might someday need to raise a force of fighting men, and the cache would make a useful first payment for their services. He turned toward the landward gate.

He ignored the gate guard, who sat outside his booth, despondently gazing at the ground, undoubtedly contemplating a return to the begging bowl. It was a fine day, and the Cimmerian nudged his horse to a brisk canter.

Before he had ridden far, he passed a royal force riding the other way. It was a hundred strong, and at its head rode a royal official. Just behind him rode a royal executioner. Conan doubted that they would have much to do when they reached Sicas.

At the juncture with the high road, he encountered four armored men, grim of mien and glowering at him. He recognized Nevus and three of the mercenaries he had met riding into Sicas a few days before.

"I see that a few of you escaped with your lives," Conan commented.

"Aye," said one. "We waited here to see if Ermak would join us."

"He will not join you," Conan informed him. "Ermak is dead."

"Only you could have slain him," said Nevus. "That means it is our task to avenge him." The four began to ready their weapons. Conan did not touch his own.

"It was a fair fight. There is nothing to avenge."

"You spoiled one of the softest berths I ever had," said another. "We should slay you for that."

"Then I'll ask you the old mercenary's question," Conan said. "Who's the paymaster?"

The four looked at one another for a while. Then, one by one, they put away their weapons. "Aye," said Nevus. "What's the sense of fighting without pay?"

"Good," Conan said. "Let us all be friends." He looked at the bulging purse each man wore at his belt. "I see that each of you came away from Sicas with a full purse. So did I. Listen to me. I have been conversing with travelers. Numedides totters on his throne, and the barons are breaking away from him. There will be war soon, and the recruiters will be all over Tarantia. Let us go there and spend our money. By the time we've drunk and wenched and gamed it all away, we'll have a pick of good fighting positions."

"Aye" cheered the four. They wheeled their mounts and took up the royal high road toward Tarantia. After they had ridden for a while, Nevus turned to Conan.

"Cimmerian," he asked, "back there in Sicas . . . how did you do it?"

Conan thought for a while, then turned to his new companion with a hard grin. "That was a town of rogues, my friend, and I am the greatest rogue of all!"

Nevus shook his head in admiration. "That you are, Conan of Cimmeria!"

THE MIGHTY ADVENTURES
OF CONAN

☐ ☐	55210-5	**CONAN THE BOLD** *John Maddox Roberts*	$3.95 Canada $4.95
☐ ☐	50094-6	**CONAN THE CHAMPION** *John Maddox Roberts*	$3.95 Canada $4.95
☐ ☐	51394-0	**CONAN THE DEFENDER** *Robert Jordan*	$3.95 Canada $4.95
☐ ☐	54264-9	**CONAN THE DEFIANT** *Steve Perry*	$6.95 Canada $8.95
☐ ☐	50096-2	**CONAN THE FEARLESS** *Steve Perry*	$3.95 Canada $4.95
☐ ☐	50998-6	**CONAN THE FORMIDABLE** *Steve Perry*	$7.95 Canada $9.50
☐ ☐	50690-1	**CONAN THE FREE LANCE** *Steve Perry*	$3.95 Canada $4.95
☐ ☐	50714-2	**CONAN THE GREAT** *Leonard Carpenter*	$3.95 Canada $4.95
☐ ☐	50961-7	**CONAN THE GUARDIAN** *Roland Green*	$3.95 Canada $4.95
☐ ☐	50860-2	**CONAN THE INDOMITABLE** *Steve Perry*	$3.95 Canada $4.95
☐ ☐	50997-8	**CONAN THE INVINCIBLE** *Robert Jordan*	$3.95 Canada $4.95

Buy them at your local bookstore or use this handy coupon:
Clip and mail this page with your order.

Publishers Book and Audio Mailing Service
P.O. Box 120159, Staten Island, NY 10312-0004

Please send me the book(s) I have checked above. I am enclosing $ _____
(please add $1.25 for the first book, and $.25 for each additional book to cover postage and handling.
Send check or money order only—no CODs).

Name _____
Address _____
City _____ State/Zip _____
Please allow six weeks for delivery. Prices subject to change without notice.

THE BEST IN
SCIENCE FICTION

☐	54310-6	A FOR ANYTHING	$3.95
☐	54311-4	*Damon Knight*	Canada $4.95
☐	55625-9	BRIGHTNESS FALLS FROM THE AIR	$3.50
☐	55626-7	*James Tiptree, Jr.*	Canada $3.95
☐	53815-3	CASTING FORTUNE	$3.95
☐	53816-1	*John M. Ford*	Canada $4.95
☐	50554-9	THE ENCHANTMENTS OF FLESH & SPIRIT	$3.95
☐	50555-7	*Storm Constantine*	Canada $4.95
☐	55413-2	HERITAGE OF FLIGHT	$3.95
☐	55414-0	*Susan Shwartz*	Canada $4.95
☐	54293-2	LOOK INTO THE SUN	$3.95
☐	54294-0	*James Patrick Kelly*	Canada $4.95
☐	54925-2	MIDAS WORLD	$2.95
☐	54926-0	*Frederik Pohl*	Canada $3.50
☐	53157-4	THE SECRET ASCENSION	$4.50
☐	53158-2	*Michael Bishop*	Canada $5.50
☐	55627-5	THE STARRY RIFT	$4.50
☐	55628-3	*James Tiptree, Jr.*	Canada $5.50
☐	50623-5	TERRAPLANE	$3.95
☐		*Jack Womack*	Canada $4.95
☐	50369-4	WHEEL OF THE WINDS	$3.95
☐	50370-8	*M.J. Engh*	Canada $4.95

French policemen try to hold back hordes of exuberant Parisians who filled streets, crowded onto tricolor-draped balconies and perched precariously on rooftops as General Charles de Gaulle formally ended four years of German occupation with a victory parade along the Champs-Elysées on the 26th of August, 1944.

LIBERATION

Other Publications:
THE KODAK LIBRARY OF CREATIVE PHOTOGRAPHY
GREAT MEALS IN MINUTES
THE CIVIL WAR
PLANET EARTH
COLLECTOR'S LIBRARY OF THE CIVIL WAR
LIBRARY OF HEALTH
CLASSICS OF THE OLD WEST
THE EPIC OF FLIGHT
THE GOOD COOK
THE SEAFARERS
HOME REPAIR AND IMPROVEMENT
THE OLD WEST
LIFE LIBRARY OF PHOTOGRAPHY (revised)
LIFE SCIENCE LIBRARY (revised)

For information on and a full description of any of the
Time-Life Books series listed above, please write:

Reader Information
Time-Life Books
541 North Fairbanks Court
Chicago, Illinois 60611

This volume is one of a series that chronicles in
full the events of the Second World War.

WORLD WAR II · TIME-LIFE BOOKS · ALEXANDRIA, VIRGINIA

BY MARTIN BLUMENSON
AND THE EDITORS OF TIME-LIFE BOOKS

LIBERATION

Time-Life Books Inc.
is a wholly owned subsidiary of
TIME INCORPORATED

Founder: Henry R. Luce 1898-1967

Editor-in-Chief: Henry Anatole Grunwald
President: J. Richard Munro
Chairman of the Board: Ralph P. Davidson
Executive Vice President: Clifford J. Grum
Editorial Director: Ralph Graves
Group Vice President, Books: Joan D. Manley

TIME-LIFE BOOKS INC.

EDITOR: George Constable
Executive Editor: George Daniels
Director of Design: Louis Klein
Board of Editors: Dale M. Brown, Thomas A. Lewis,
Robert G. Mason, Ellen Phillips, Gerry Schremp,
Gerald Simons, Rosalind Stubenberg,
Kit van Tulleken, Henry Woodhead
Director of Administration: David L. Harrison
Director of Research: Carolyn L. Sackett
Director of Photography: John Conrad Weiser

PRESIDENT: Reginald K. Brack Jr.
Senior Vice President: William Henry
Vice Presidents: George Artandi, Stephen L. Bair,
Robert A. Ellis, Juanita T. James, Christopher T. Linen,
James L. Mercer, Joanne A. Pello, Paul R. Stewart

WORLD WAR II

Editorial Staff for *Liberation*
Editor: William K. Goolrick
Picture Editor/Designer: Raymond Ripper
Staff Writers: Dalton Delan, Malachy J. Duffy,
Brian McGinn, Tyler Mathisen,
Teresa M. C. R. Pruden
Chief Researcher: Frances G. Youssef
Researchers: Michael Blumenthal,
Loretta Y. Britten, Josephine Burke,
Christine Bowie Dove, Jane Edwin,
Frances R. Glennon, Oobie Gleysteen, Pat Good,
Catherine Gregory, Chadwick Gregson,
Clara Nicolai
Copy Coordinators: Patricia Graber, Victoria Lee
Art Assistant: Mary Louise Mooney
Picture Coordinator: Alvin L. Ferrell
Editorial Assistant: Connie Strawbridge

Editorial Operations
Design: Anne B. Landry (art coordinator);
James J. Cox (quality control)
Research: Phyllis K. Wise (assistant director),
Louise D. Forstall
Copy Room: Diane Ullius (director), Celia Beattie
Production: Gordon E. Buck, Peter Inchauteguiz

Correspondents: Elisabeth Kraemer (Bonn);
Margot Hapgood, Dorothy Bacon (London);
Miriam Hsia, Susan Jonas, Lucy T. Voulgaris (New
York); Maria Vincenza Aloisi, Josephine du Brusle
(Paris); Ann Natanson (Rome). Valuable assistance
was also provided by: Janny Hovinga (Hilversum,
Netherlands); Judy Aspinall, Lesley Coleman
(London); Carolyn T. Chubet, Christina Lieberman
(New York); John Scott (Ottawa, Ontario); M. T.
Hirschkoff (Paris); Mimi Murphy (Rome).

The Author: MARTIN BLUMENSON, educated at
Bucknell and Harvard, served in the U.S. Army in
World War II as historical officer with the Third
and Seventh Armies in the European Theater of
Operations. Later, he commanded the 3rd Histori-
cal Detachment in Korea and was the Historian of
Joint Task Force Seven during atomic weapons
tests in the Pacific. He has been a visiting professor
at Acadia University, The Citadel, and the Army
and Naval War Colleges. Among his books are
*Breakout and Pursuit; Anzio: The Gamble That
Failed; Kasserine Pass; Salerno to Cassino; The
Patton Papers, 1885-1940* and *1940-1945;* and *The
Vilde Affair: Beginnings of the French Resistance.*

The Consultants: COL. JOHN R. ELTING, USA
(Ret.) is a military historian and author of *The
Battle of Bunker's Hill; The Battles of Saratoga;* and
Military History and Atlas of the Napoleonic Wars.
He edited *Military Uniforms in America: The Era
of the American Revolution, 1755-1795* and *Mili-
tary Uniforms in America: Years of Growth, 1796-
1851,* and was associate director of *The West Point
Atlas of American Wars.*

CHARLES B. MACDONALD is the Deputy Chief
Historian for Southeast Asia in the U.S. Army Center of Military History. He served as a rifle company commander in the 2nd Infantry Division during World War II, and was awarded the Silver Star
and the Purple Heart. His books include: *The Siegfried Line Campaign; The Last Offensive; Company Commander; The Battle of the Huertgen Forest; Airborne* (a history of airborne operations in
World War II); and *The Mighty Endeavor: American Armed Forces in the European Theater in
World War II.*

Library of Congress Cataloguing in Publication Data

Blumenson, Martin.
    Liberation.

    (World War II; v. 14)
    Bibliography: p.
    Includes index.
    1. World War, 1939-1945—Campaigns—France—
Normandy. 2. World War, 1939-1945—France—Paris. 3.
Paris—History—1940-1944. I. Time-Life Books. II. Title.
III. Series.
D756.5.N6B57   940.54'21   78-21967
ISBN 0-8094-2512-2
ISBN 0-8094-2511-4 lib. bdg.

CHAPTERS

PICTURE ESSAYS

CONTENTS

PARIS UNDER THE SWASTIKA

Led by a spit-and-polish military band, German security troops strut down the Champs-Elysées at noontime in a daily ritual most Parisians deliberately ignored.

GALLIC ESPRIT VS. THE THIRD REICH

By the summer of 1944, when the Allies were attempting to break out of their Normandy beachhead, France had been under the German yoke for four years. The Occupation was oppressive in every region of the country. Germans searched houses and arrested innocent civilians, rationed food and fuel, carted off valuables and deported young men to work in German war industries. But nowhere was the German presence more acutely felt or bitterly resented than in Paris—the country's capital and the city that symbolized France to most Frenchmen.

An occupation force of more than 30,000 administrative and security troops moved into the city, took over 500 hotels and hung huge swastikas from public buildings and monuments. The Germans reserved the best restaurants for their officers and set aside cinemas and brothels for their soldiers. They outraged Parisians by parading troops and bands through the city, by naming streets after German heroes and by melting down 200 of Paris' statues for bronze.

In addition to flaunting their victory with banners and bands, the Germans intimidated Parisians with hundreds of humiliating regulations and restrictions. Displaying the national tricolor or singing the "Marseillaise" was forbidden. Anyone who insulted a German soldier, defaced a propaganda poster or listened to BBC broadcasts was subject to arrest and imprisonment. Public gatherings and demonstrations were controlled, and a strictly enforced curfew kept Parisians at home from midnight to 5:30 a.m.

In their daily contacts with Parisians, the Germans were ordered to behave correctly and courteously. They usually were careful to pay for everything they bought. They used German-French phrase books to try to engage the French people in friendly conversations. But their efforts made little difference to most Parisians, especially those whose husbands, brothers, sons or fathers were among the two million French prisoners of war in Germany. When a visiting German wondered what had happened to the city's gaiety and *joie de vivre*, a Parisian bitterly responded: "You should have come when you were not here."

German road signs, located at major Paris intersections such as the Place de l'Opéra, guided drivers to military headquarters and support units.

Under a giant poster of Marshal Pétain, head of the French puppet government at Vichy, Parisians read clippings from a German-controlled newspaper.

Accompanied by a smartly dressed friend, Luftwaffe officers study the odds at the Auteuil race track, where underfed horses ran during the Occupation.

At a Paris bookstall, a soldier finds a German title among the French and English ones. Newsstands sold a daily paper and dozens of magazines in German.

German soldiers jostle past civilians to inspect the wares at the Paris Flea Market. Merchants routinely overcharged the Germans for perfumes and trinkets.

Outside a military barracks in Paris, German soldiers and band members await a formal inspection.

Oblivious of a nearby cinema for German soldiers, Parisians crowd around a street peddler's table.

From his headquarters in the swastika-bedecked

TURNING A COLD SHOULDER TO THE ENEMY

Using the ancient strategy of dividing and conquering, the Germans turned French against French and created an atmosphere of fear and suspicion among Parisians. The chief architects of this policy were the Ge-

Hôtel Meurice, the German military commander of Paris issued orders to his garrison and controlled every detail of the daily lives of three million Parisians.

stapo and SS, which recruited waiters, servants and concierges into a network of informers and offered cash rewards for reports of hostile actions or attitudes. Some Parisians took advantage of the offer to settle grudges against former business associates or lovers, and a daily stream of anonymous denunciations flowed into Gestapo headquarters on the Avenue Foch.

Thousands of Parisians were dragged out of their homes in the small hours of the morning and whisked away by the Gestapo. Some were guilty of nothing more than an anti-German remark. Some were tortured and released with a warning that worse would follow if they talked about their treatment; many were deported to prison camps and never heard of again.

To protect themselves from this reign of terror, Parisians repressed their feelings and hid their true opinions with noncommittal comments or complete silence. No one discussed politics in public, and the people went to such lengths to avoid eye contact that the Germans nicknamed Paris *la ville sans regard* (roughly, "the city that never looks at you").

At the Berlitz language school, the Germans opened an anti-Semitic exhibit entitled "The Jew and France" in September 1941. Indoors, a bust with exaggerated racial features illustrated how to recognize Jews, graphic displays chronicled Jewish "misdeeds" and posters depicted the Jews' allegedly pernicious influence on French politics and culture.

THE SIGNS OF HATRED

In addition to the restrictions and privations imposed on their fellow Parisians, the 160,000 Jewish residents of Paris were subjected to the brutal excesses of Hitler's racial policies. French Jews were virtual prisoners in their native city. Their businesses were confiscated, their homes looted of valuables, and many were forbidden to practice their professions. They were forced to wear yellow stars on their clothing and were banned from restaurants, markets, parks and phone booths.

Stateless, foreign-born Jews living in Paris suffered a more brutal fate. They were the targets of frequent SS-organized roundups, and more than 30,000 were deported to concentration camps. Of the almost 13,000 non-French Jews arrested in July 1942, only 30 survived the horrors of Auschwitz.

Wearing the required yellow star with the word "Juif" (Jew) in the center, a Jewish

woman grimly goes about her business. Non-Jewish Parisians ridiculed the German regulation by wearing stars with such inscriptions as "Buddhist" and "Zulu."

1

When the Allied armies landed in Normandy on June 6, 1944, they expected to make rapid progress once they were safely on shore: Preinvasion plans called for the British to take the critical road junction at Caen and push inland 20 miles the first day. At the opposite end of the line, American forces were supposed to cut across the Cotentin Peninsula, turn north and take the great port of Cherbourg by D-plus-8. In the area between these two critical objectives, American troops were expected to push southward into Normandy and establish themselves on an east-west line running through Saint-Lô and Caumont—approximately 16 miles inland—by D-plus-9.

Once these objectives were attained, the plan called for Allied forces to sweep through the entire Brittany peninsula, capture the port of Brest and seize a large area between the Loire and the Seine Rivers. By the end of three months, an avalanche of supplies, weapons and troops would be pouring into the beachhead, and the Allies would be in possession of a giant springboard for a massive drive across northern France toward Germany. Meanwhile, plans were afoot for a large-scale invasion of France's Mediterranean coast; the Allied forces landed there were to drive north up the Rhone Valley and join with the eastbound forces from Normandy, thereby trapping all the German troops in southwestern France in the jaws of a giant pincers and completing the liberation of France. Then the final defeat of the German armies and the end of the War might be within the Allies' grasp.

But by the middle of June, the expansion of the Normandy beachhead had fallen behind the timetable set by the planners. Caen was still in German hands, and Allied forces were nowhere near Cherbourg. They had pushed isolated salients down to Villers Bocage and Caumont, but they were stymied on the way to Saint-Lô, and along most of the rest of the front the offensive had slowed to a crawl.

There were two major reasons why the Allied advance had bogged down: the tenacity of the Germans and their skillful use of the terrain. As the Germans faced north toward the sea, they could see that the mortal threat to their forces lay in the Caen area at the eastern end of the front. The country was wide open there, ideally suited for tank operations. Beyond Caen, gently rolling hills led toward Falaise and the heart of France. A breakthrough in this area

BATTLE OF THE HEDGEROWS

could spell disaster for the Germans, posing the threat of encirclement of all their divisions in Normandy and undermining their whole defensive position in the West. Accordingly, the Germans deployed the majority of their forces in the area of Caen and ferociously resisted every attempt by the British to capture the city and break into the plains that lay beyond.

West of Caen the terrain was made to order for the defense, and the Germans could afford to spread their forces more thinly. This was the hedgerow country, or *bocage* as the French called it—a patchwork of thousands of small fields enclosed by almost impenetrable hedges. The hedges consisted of dense thickets of hawthorn, brambles, vines and trees ranging up to 15 feet in height, growing out of earthen mounds several feet thick and three or four feet high, with a drainage ditch on either side. The walls and hedges together were so formidable that each field took on the character of a small fort. Defenders dug in at the base of a hedgerow and hidden by vegetation were all but impervious to rifle and artillery fire. So dense was the vegetation that infantrymen poking around the hedgerows sometimes found themselves staring eye to eye at startled Germans. A single machine gun concealed in a hedgerow could mow down attacking troops as they attempted to advance from one hedge to another. Snipers, mounted on wooden platforms in the treetops and using flashless gunpowder to avoid giving away their positions, were a constant threat.

Most of the roads were wagon trails, worn into sunken lanes by centuries of use and turned into cavern-like mazes by overarching hedges. These gloomy passages were tailor made for ambushes and were terrifying places for men on both sides. "In a sunken road," Corporal John Welch of the Seaforth Highlanders later said, "the tension left me feeling like a wet rag."

The sunken lanes were also deathtraps for tanks. Confined to narrow channels, they were easy marks for German *Panzerfausts*—antitank rocket launchers—camouflaged in the hedgerows. A tank that ventured off the road and attempted to smash through the thicket was particularly vulnerable. As it climbed the mound at the base of the hedgerow, its guns were pointed helplessly skyward and its underbelly was exposed to fire from antitank guns in the next hedgerow. Dennis Bunn of the Scottish 15th Recon-

naissance Regiment, who fought in the hedgerows, described what it was like to drive through them in a heavy armored car. "Inside the car was intense heat and darkness, outside brilliant sunshine. I sweated and gripped the steering wheel with damp hands as I peered through a small aperture at the ground in front, the high hedge on the right, the ground sloping away to the left, at the trees, the bushes, seeing or suspecting danger in every blade of grass."

The mental and physical strain were so exhausting that discipline was affected. There was a great deal of drinking—this was Calvados country—but with or without the assistance of alcohol, many men seemed to be in a stupor. "Over a stretch of time," said an American platoon leader, "you became so dulled by fatigue that the names of the killed and wounded they checked off each night, the names of men who had been your best friends, might have come out of a telephone book for all you knew. All the old values were gone, and if there was a world beyond this tangle of hedgerows you never expected to live to see it."

The weather compounded the soldiers' miseries. Through much of June and the first half of July, a cold, clammy rain fell, turning the earth into a quagmire. Fighting from field to field, troops crawled and slogged through pelting rain and ankle-deep water. The sickly sweet smell of death assaulted their nostrils. And every so often they came upon the grim spectacle of hastily improvised graves topped with crude wooden crosses, boltless rifles or steel helmets.

The Germans fought with great stubbornness and skill in the hedgerow country, although weeks after the landings Hitler and his generals were still not ready to concede that this was the main Allied attack. They persisted in their belief that the major effort would come in the Pas-de-Calais area, up the coast of France from Normandy. And while the fighting raged in Normandy, they kept the Fifteenth Army —some 200,000 men strong—guarding the Calais coast against an attack that would never come.

Nevertheless, the Führer viewed the Normandy invasion as a threat that must be eliminated at all costs. He told his top subordinates in the West—the respected Field Marshals Gerd von Rundstedt, the theater commander, and Erwin Rommel, the commander of Army Group B—that "every man shall fight and die where he stands." Even though the units in the Pas-de-Calais area remained untouchable, Hitler directed that seven other divisions be transferred to the battle area from Brittany, the Bay of Biscay area, central, eastern and southern France, and from as far away as the Eastern Front. If the Allied armies could be confined to a small area close to the English Channel, he believed that a decisive counterstroke could still be launched. The beaches could be regained, and the Allies could be sent reeling back into the sea.

Meanwhile, the Allies were concocting a plan of attack of their own that called for a one-two punch against the Germans. The British under Lieut. General Sir Miles Dempsey would strike at Caen and attack the bulk of the enemy's forces. And while the British Second Army "got the enemy by the throat," as General Dwight D. Eisenhower, the Su-

preme Allied Commander, put it, the American First Army would push north to take the port of Cherbourg.

The Caen attack had to be put off because of a shortage of ammunition, but on the 14th of June, American troops set out to capture Cherbourg. The U.S. First Army commander, Lieut. General Omar N. Bradley, planned the offensive in two basic stages, using the VII Corps under Major General J. Lawton Collins as his spearhead. Collins would drive westward 20 miles from the road junction at Carentan to the west coast of the Cotentin Peninsula. Then the American force would change direction and push northward toward Cherbourg.

Collins, who had earned his spurs as a division commander on Guadalcanal, launched the attack with two of the U.S. Army's most reliable divisions, the 82nd Airborne and the

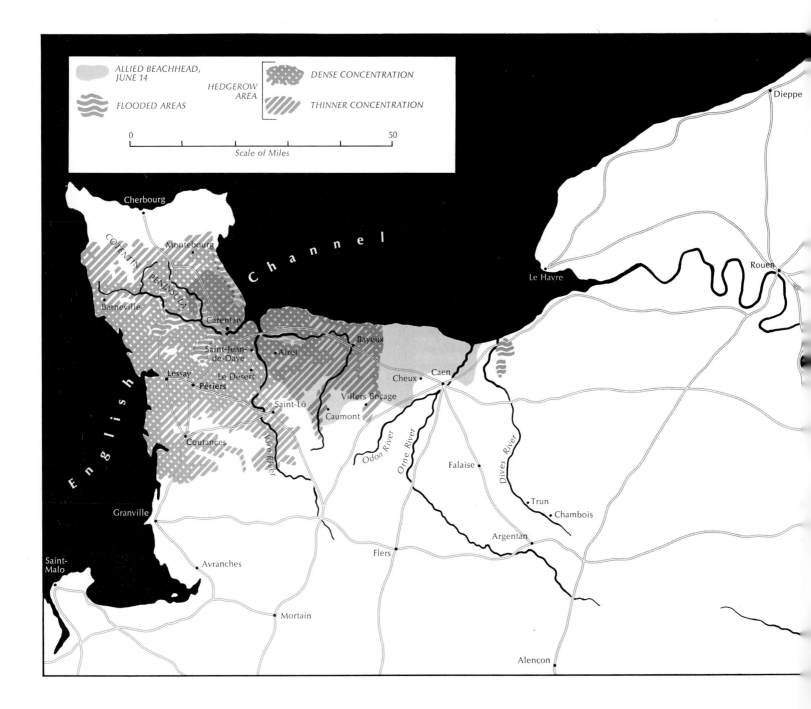

9th Infantry. As they headed westward from Carentan they had to cross the Merderet and Douve Rivers, both of which were flanked by huge marshes. Normally, most of the area drained sufficiently in the summertime to be used as grazing land for cattle, but by mid-1944 the Germans had constructed concrete dams that kept the fields flooded, which restricted all movement to causeways and footpaths. The American troops had to force their way along these narrow passages under heavy enemy fire.

But the Germans had their own problems. They were short of ammunition, and the only tanks available to them in this sector were obsolete French models that had fallen into German hands after the debacle of 1940. As Collins delivered a series of sharp infantry jabs on a narrow front, the Germans pulled back. In the process they split their forces, most of them turning south on the coast road, and the rest retreating north to help defend Cherbourg.

Near Barneville-sur-Mer on the morning of the 18th of June, American artillery caught part of the southbound force, a column attempting to escape down the coastal highway, and methodically destroyed it, littering the road with wrecked vehicles. The Cotentin Peninsula was now cut off, and the stage was set for an attack to the north to capture the port of Cherbourg. Before this attack could get under way, American forces were regrouped and reorganized. Collins was given the 4th, 9th and 79th Infantry Divisions for the attack to the north. The recently activated VIII Corps—with the 90th Infantry Division and the 82nd and 101st Airborne Divisions—was given the assignment of holding a defensive line across the peninsula to protect the rear of Collins' troops.

As the men of Collins' VII Corps started for Cherbourg, they were held up briefly by enemy troops dug in along a railroad embankment in the Montebourg area. But the opposition was merely a gesture. The commander of the Cherbourg garrison, Lieut. General Karl Wilhelm von Schlieben, was under orders from Hitler to carry out a fighting withdrawal, then to hold Cherbourg at all costs. Schlieben just wanted to show that he was obeying the Führer's command. That night he drew his forces back into a system of forts and strong points protecting the port from the landward side.

On June 20 the three American divisions ran into this defensive complex, a belt of steel and concrete fortifications arranged in a semicircle four to six miles south of the city. Massive blockhouses were spotted along the perimeter; they had underground ammunition storage bunkers connected by trenches, and the area around the blockhouses was interlaced with barbed wire and crisscrossed by antitank ditches. Bristling with automatic weapons and covered by artillery, the bunkers commanded every approach to the city. It quickly became clear that there would be no easy entry into Cherbourg. When one battalion attempted to move past a crossroad on the edge of the city, machine guns opened up from houses all around. A deluge of artillery shells from nearby hills struck the command group, mortally wounding the battalion commander, injuring his staff and driving the whole unit back. Another battalion, attacking a suburb of Cherbourg, was hit by small-arms fire

Before the Allies could break out of the Normandy beachhead and liberate France, they had to overcome a stubborn German defense in some of Western Europe's most difficult terrain, the hedgerows of Normandy. Varying in concentration as indicated by the density of the lines on the map, the hedgerows provided ideal defensive positions for the enemy. The Germans made Allied progress all the more arduous by flooding large areas through the manipulation of dams they had built for this purpose. But by the middle of July, American forces had reached Saint-Lô and, with British troops near Caen, the Allies were poised for the major offensive that eventually would drive the Germans from France.

and shellfire; within just a few minutes 31 men were dead and 92 injured.

Inside Cherbourg, notwithstanding the spirited defense encountered by U.S. troops on the outer fringes, all was not well. Schlieben had about 25,000 men at his disposal, but they were of doubtful fighting quality. Included were policemen, Naval personnel assigned to port duties, clerks, antiaircraft gunners and slave laborers from all over the Continent who had been brought in to work on fortifications and V-1 missile sites. Of the combat troops, one fifth were non-German: Poles, Russian and Italians swept into the German war machine as a by-product of conquest and occupation. The defenders were further handicapped by a shortage of weapons and supplies. Though the garrison had been doubled since before D-Day, the Cherbourg area had never been adequately provisioned for a siege. Now there was not enough time to correct the shortages of food, fuel and ammunition.

Hitler himself was apprehensive. "Even if worse comes to worst," he informed Schlieben, "it is your duty to defend the last bunker and leave the enemy not a harbor but a field of ruins." Schlieben replied forlornly that his garrison was totally exhausted, had been trained poorly and included too many older men.

Collins had hoped to avoid a frontal assault against the city. But he was growing more and more impatient—a restless figure in a trench coat stalking the front lines. On June 21 he directed that an ultimatum be broadcast to the defenders in German, Polish and French, threatening them with annihilation if they did not surrender by 9 o'clock the next morning. But with Hitler breathing down his neck, Schlieben was in no mood to capitulate. Instead, he gave his troops a terse order. "Withdrawal from present positions is punishable by death," he said. "I empower all leaders of whatever rank to shoot at sight anyone who leaves his post because of cowardice."

When his ultimatum expired without an answer, Collins called for an "air pulverization" of the fortifications. On the afternoon of June 22, four squadrons of RAF Typhoons —rocket-firing fighter-bombers—spewed their deadly ordnance into the fortress. Six squadrons of RAF Mustangs then strafed the German defenses, and 375 U.S. fighter-bombers attacked in waves at five-minute intervals, bombing and strafing the area for an hour. The result was a spectacular show, but not an unmixed success. The fortifications were a long way from being pulverized, and some American troops were strafed by their own planes. But the bombing did further sap the garrison's already weakened morale, and in ground attacks on June 23, all three U.S. divisions made significant headway against the main German defenses.

Schlieben now reported to Rommel and Hitler that the fall of Cherbourg was only a matter of time. Pointing out that there were 2,000 wounded troops in the city who could not be cared for adequately with available medical supplies, he asked whether the destruction of his force was really necessary. He was told to keep fighting.

On June 25, as the Americans tightened their grip on Cherbourg, troops of the 79th Division came up against Fort du Roule, the strongest of all of the city's defensive positions. Built into the face of a promontory, the multilevel fort afforded protection against attack by sea or land. Heavy coastal guns, under the edge of a cliff, commanded Cherbourg's harbor, while machine guns and mortars in concrete pillboxes atop the promontory pointed in the opposite direction to stave off attackers from the landward side. The approaches to this bristling complex of fortifications were covered by a large antitank ditch, barbed-wire entanglements and bunkers. On the sloping ground at the base of the promontory, infantrymen were deeply entrenched.

As the troops of the 79th struggled forward, they came under heavy machine-gun and mortar fire from the top of the promontory. German artillery zeroed in on them, and a hail of small-arms fire poured down from the infantry entrenched on the slope.

While an artillery battalion of the 79th Division took the fort under fire, all of the machine guns of two infantry battalions were trained on the German infantrymen. Inch by inch the attackers worked their way toward the fort, covering each short advance with small-arms and machine-gun fire, blasting gaps in the wire with Bangalore torpedoes, planting demolitions in pillboxes and blowing them up. To flush out the defenders, they combined pole charges —demolitions attached to the ends of long rods—with "beehives," packets of explosives covered with an adhesive substance that stuck to pillboxes and other fortifications.

A MOSAIC OF FORTIFIED FIELDS AND DEATHTRAPS THAT STALLED AN ARMY

An aerial photograph reveals the Normandy countryside as a mosaic divided by hedgerows into hundreds of small, tightly enclosed fields.

Normandy's hedgerows, compact earthen mounds covered with thornbush and trees and encompassing an average of 500 small fields per square mile, stretched before the Allied invaders like a never-ending obstacle course, 60 miles long and 25 miles wide. Intended originally to mark property boundaries and to shield crops from violent sea winds, the hedgerows afforded near-perfect concealment for German rifles, mortars, machine guns and antitank weapons. And they were all but insuperable barriers for Allied tanks.

Armored units began a desperate search for a device that could blast or cut its way through the obstacles. The breakthrough was achieved when Sergeant Curtis G. Culin Jr. of the U.S. 102nd Cavalry Reconnaissance Squadron welded pointed steel blades cut from German beach obstacles to a tank, enabling it to plow through the hedgerows with guns blazing. Culin's invention worked so well that General Bradley had "hedgerow cutters" mounted on three of every five tanks in the First Army. General Eisenhower later wrote that these ingenious devices "restored the effectiveness of the tank and gave a tremendous boost to morale throughout the Army."

Armed with steel blades, a light tank prepares to slice through a hedge.

Searching a hedgerow for snipers, soldiers advance past a dead comrade.

In one area of the front, Corporal John D. Kelly and his platoon of the 314th Infantry Regiment were pinned down by fire from a pillbox. Kelly crawled back to the rear to get a pole charge. Then he advanced up the slope under fire to the base of the pillbox, set the charge and exploded it at the end of the pole. But the explosion had no effect; machine guns in the pillbox went right on firing. Kelly slithered back down the hill as bullets whined around him, got another charge, crawled up the slope again and managed to blow off the ends of the machine guns that were sticking out of the pillbox slits. Still the pillbox defenders refused to yield. Kelly went back down the hill and repeated the whole process. This time he blew the rear door of the pillbox open. Then he flung some grenades through the doorway, and the survivors came out and surrendered.

By midnight on June 25, men of the 79th Division had cleared the upper defenses of Fort du Roule. The following day, tanks and tank destroyers fired armor-piercing shells at the face of the promontory. A demolition team lowered charges from above the fort, and an assault team finally climbed the promontory to rout the last of the defenders.

The end was now clearly in sight at Cherbourg. Schlieben tried to bolster the sagging spirits of his troops by handing out Iron Crosses that were dropped in by parachute. But he could see that the garrison was doomed. "I must state in the line of duty," he radioed to Rommel, "that further sacrifices cannot alter anything." Rommel reminded him of the Führer's order to fight to the end. Schlieben took over personal command of the fighting around his command post. Forced finally to retreat to his underground bunker headquarters, he radioed his last message: "Documents burned, codes destroyed."

From a prisoner the Americans learned where Schlieben was holed up. On June 26 two rifle companies worked their way toward the command shelter and sent a prisoner in through the tunnel entrance to demand the German commander's surrender. When Schlieben refused, tank destroyers were summoned to fire into the tunnel. A few rounds flushed out some 800 defenders, including the commander. Four hundred Germans preparing to defend the city hall gave themselves up once they were convinced that Schlieben had been captured.

The surrender of Cherbourg threw Hitler into a rage; he had expected Schlieben to defend the city until he and everyone else was killed. Schlieben later blamed the troops. Their "fighting ability," he wrote, "can only be described as inferior." He added: "You can't expect Russians and Poles to fight for Germany against Americans in France."

By the last day of June, two weeks behind schedule, Cherbourg was in American hands, and the 9th Division was mopping up the remaining enemy defenders on nearby Cap de la Hague. But for the time being the coveted port was an empty prize. The Germans had surrendered, but they had effectively denied the Allies the harbor. The architect of the destruction, Rear Admiral Walther Hennecke, was captured with Schlieben, but he was awarded the Knight's Cross by Hitler, who called the admiral's feat "unprecedented in the annals of coastal defense."

The port was a shambles. Mines were everywhere. Sunken ships blocked all the basins. The harbor's electrical system and dock machinery were destroyed. Quay walls were damaged, cranes were toppled and twisted, the breakwater was so heavily cratered that the sea washed through it. Three weeks of intensive clearing would be needed before the port could begin to operate. Not until September would all the obstructions be removed. Meanwhile, the bulk of supplies for the Allied troops on the Continent must continue to come in over the Normandy beaches.

On June 20 Hitler ordered the first move in his campaign to drive the Allies back into the sea. He called for a massive counterattack at the end of June aimed at Bayeux, near the hinge between the American First and the British Second Armies. In the attack the 2nd Panzer Corps, consisting of two seasoned armored divisions from the Eastern Front, would combine with two other divisions in reserve and two already in line in Normandy.

There was only one problem: the 2nd Panzer had to get there. Allied fighter-bombers and the French Resistance had so crippled the transportation network that the panzer corps—not to mention critically needed supplies—was prevented from reaching the front. Before it could arrive, the British beat the Germans to the punch.

Two days before Hitler issued his attack order, General Sir Bernard L. Montgomery, Allied ground forces commander, had written his own directive for an attack on Caen, code-named *Epsom*. General Dempsey's Second Army was ordered to encircle the city; the main effort would be made by the VIII Corps, under Lieut. General Sir Richard O'Connor, a veteran of the fighting in the North African desert who had been captured by the Italians in Libya in 1941 and released a few days after Italy's capitulation in September 1943. The attack was to involve 60,000 troops, 600 tanks and 300 guns, plus the support of 400 artillery pieces from adjacent corps areas and additional backup from naval gun-

fire and air power. O'Connor's mission was to cross the Odon River and take the high ground south of Caen.

The troops committed to *Epsom* were largely untried, but they went at it with a vengeance. Part of the attacking force was the 49th Division, whose men had served as an occupation force in Iceland and were known as the "Polar Bears." The division jumped off early on the morning of June 25 in a heavy mist. Machine-gun and tank fire from the Germans mowed down many attackers, but the survivors closed with

After surrendering to an officer of the U.S. 9th Division, Lieut. General Karl Wilhelm von Schlieben (center), commander of Cherbourg, and Rear Admiral Walther Hennecke (in visored cap, right), Naval commander in Normandy, are escorted to American Army headquarters on June 26, 1944. Although later denounced by Hitler as a poor commander, Schlieben held off U.S. forces long enough for Hennecke to demolish the city's port facilities. Schlieben turned himself over to the Americans in order to save the lives of some 300 wounded soldiers who shared his underground shelter with him and were suffocating from noxious artillery fumes.

the enemy and fought with such fury that they later were called the "Butcher Bears."

The British attack inched ahead as O'Connor unleashed an entire armored division on a narrow front. The tank column was supposed to punch through to the corps' objectives across the Odon River. But the tanks got stalled in the wreckage of the heavily bombarded town of Cheux, and German artillery forced the supporting infantry to dig in. A heavy rain started to fall, miring both the British and the German armor.

During the next couple of days, the VIII Corps managed to seize a bridgehead across the Odon and to get some tanks onto high ground beyond the river. But Montgomery and Dempsey had begun to worry about concentrations of German armor reported by aerial reconnaissance and about plans for the Bayeux counterattack found on a captured SS officer. They decided to break off the British offensive and consolidate their positions in readiness for a German blow. It proved to be a wise decision.

The blow fell on June 29, and the British were prepared. Six German panzer divisions spearheading the attack were blasted by British antitank guns and by a tremendous sea and air bombardment. Even the near misses from 16-inch naval shells knocked out Panther and Tiger tanks, blowing them over on their sides like toys. Heavy bombers struck the town of Villers Bocage, creating such rubble that German tanks could not move through it for the attack.

Under the ferocious British pounding, the force of the German effort spent itself in a single day. Rommel's headquarters recorded a "complete defensive success"—the attack on Caen had been stymied—but that was not what the Führer had in mind. The German Seventh Army had expended the forces being assembled for the climactic thrust at Bayeux that was supposed to knock the Allied troops back into the sea.

Rundstedt and Rommel were convinced in any case that the Germans could never regain the initiative. On the day that O'Connor launched his attack, they had recommended going over to the defensive as a matter of policy, "no matter how undesirable this may be," as Rundstedt phrased it. When Hitler met with his top commanders at his Bavarian mountain eyrie at Berchtesgaden on June 29, Rommel proposed that a new defensive line be established along the Seine. He noted that the latest British offensive had been stopped only by the commitment of the force allocated for the Bayeux push.

Hitler responded with a harangue: the panzers should have "Dunkirked" the British. Coupled with the onslaught of V-1 missiles then in progress against London, the attack could have forced the British to sue for peace. The Germans were still capable of offensive action, the Führer declared—dependent, of course, "on when troops and supplies can be brought up." In any event, the Allies seemed incapable of breaking out of their beachhead, and no ground must be yielded to them under any circumstances. There was to be no thought of strategic withdrawal. "We must not allow mobile warfare to develop," Hitler said, "because the enemy surpasses us by far in mobility. . . . Therefore everything depends on fighting a war of attrition to wear him down and force him back."

Depressed by the Führer's rantings, Rundstedt and Rommel returned to France. The situation was now deteriorating rapidly, with German casualties outnumbering replacements. German vehicles needed 200,000 more gallons of fuel per day than were available. Other supplies also fell far short of the need. Only 400 tons of supplies were reaching the front every day through the crippled transportation system; 2,250 tons were required.

On July 1, with a steady rain falling and Allied fighter-bombers grounded, the German Seventh Army launched another attack in an effort to wipe out the British salient across the Odon River. The attack was stopped cold—mainly by massive concentrations of artillery. Rundstedt saw the failure as further evidence of the futility of the German effort. He called Field Marshal Wilhelm Keitel, chief of the OKW, the German Armed Forces High Command, and explained the situation to him.

"What shall we do? What shall we do?" asked the distraught Keitel.

"Make peace, you fools," Rundstedt answered. "What else can you do?"

Keitel reported the conversation to Hitler, and the next day the Führer's adjutant arrived at Rundstedt's headquarters in Saint-Germain-en-Laye, just outside of Paris, and gave Rundstedt the oak leaf cluster to the Knight's Cross and a polite handwritten message from Hitler that removed him from command.

Rundstedt was supplanted by Field Marshal Günther von Kluge. Valued by Hitler as a general who obeyed orders and kept his mouth shut, Kluge had led the German drive to the Channel in 1940 and had served on the Russian front before taking over in the West. In assuming his new command, he announced his commitment to an "unconditional holding of the present defense line."

Available for this assignment were the Seventh Army under General Paul Hausser and the Panzer Group West led by Lieut. General Heinrich Eberbach. Together these forces comprised six corps and nearly 500 tanks. The bulk of the men and all but about 70 tanks were positioned south of Caen, organized in depth along three defensive lines to protect the Falaise plain. The remainder guarded the American sector south of the Cotentin Peninsula, where the combination of hedgerows and marshes favored the defense.

On July 4, Dempsey launched an attack aimed at taking Caen once and for all. The battle opened with the Canadians of the 3rd Infantry Division—supported by flamethrowing tanks, 428 field guns and the 16-inch guns of battleships in the Channel—driving for the airfield at Carpiquet, next door to Caen. On the first day the Canadians took the village of Carpiquet and the hangars on the northern edge of the airfield. The southern half of the field remained in enemy hands. The 12th SS Panzer (Hitler Jugend) Division, a unit of teenagers who made up for their youthfulness by the fierceness with which they fought, launched a series of counterattacks on July 5. Some of the Canadian positions were penetrated, but the enemy attacks were beaten off by artillery and RAF fighter-bombers.

The airfield was still in German hands on July 7, when the main attack on Caen was set in motion. Three divisions, 115,000 men, pushed off toward the northern suburbs of Caen after an overwhelming air and artillery preparation.

Pinned down amid the rubble of La Bijude, two and a half miles north of Caen, members of the British I Corps' 59th Division protect their comrades with rifle fire as they dash for a doorway. Delayed by street fighting that cost the 59th Division more than 1,000 casualties, the drive on Caen took the Allies 33 more days than D-Day planners had expected.

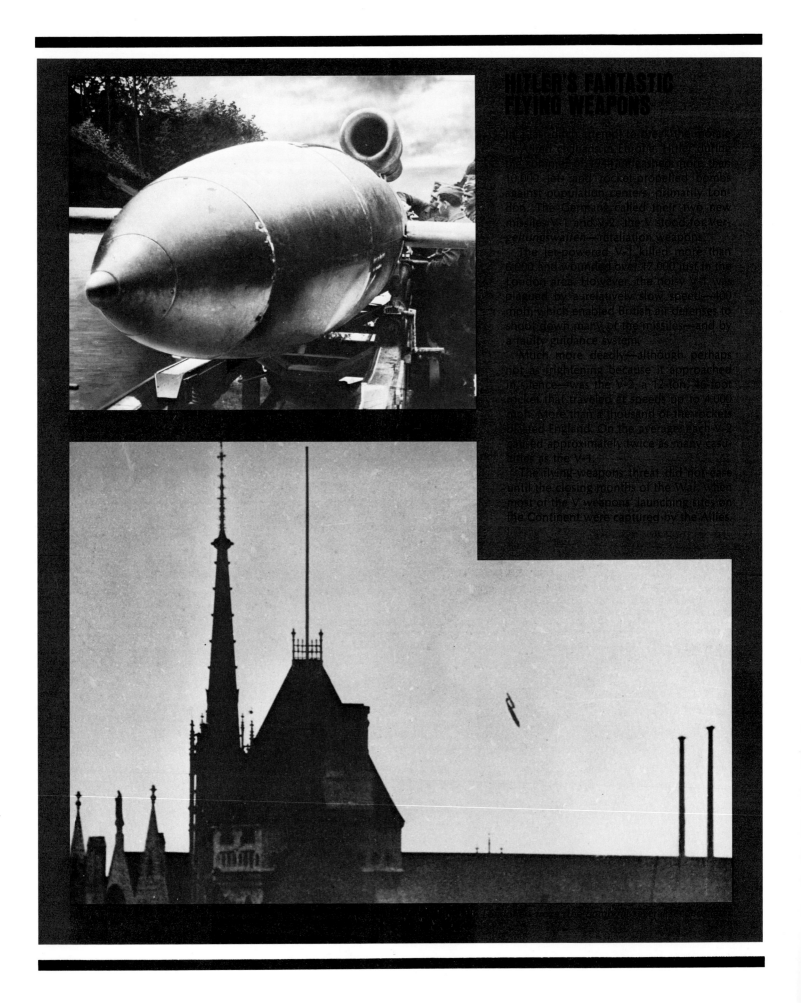

HITLER'S FANTASTIC FLYING WEAPONS

In a belated attempt to turn the morale of World War II against Europe, Hitler during the summer of 1944 unleashed more than 10,000 jet- and rocket-propelled bombs against population centers, primarily London. The Germans called their two new missiles, V-1 and V-2, the V stood for *Vergeltungswaffen*—retaliation weapons.

The jet-powered V-1 killed more than 6,000 and wounded over 17,800 just in the London area. However, the noisy V-1 was plagued by a relatively slow speed—400 mph, which enabled British air defenses to shoot down many of the missiles—and by a faulty guidance system.

Much more deadly—although perhaps not as frightening because it approached in silence—was the V-2, a 12-ton, 46-foot rocket that traveled at speeds up to 4,000 mph. More than a thousand of the rockets blasted England. On the average, each V-2 caused approximately twice as many casualties as the V-1.

The flying-weapons threat did not ease until the closing months of the War, when most of the V-weapons' launching sites on the Continent were captured by the Allies.

A few minutes before 10 p.m., some 500 four-engine bombers flew over the British units waiting to jump off and dropped 2,500 tons of bombs on the edge of the city. The bombing backfired on the Allies. Relatively few Germans were in the target area; instead, they were manning a network of elaborate fortifications that was too close to the British lines to be bombed. Most of the Germans, therefore, were unaffected by the bombing; the might of the attack fell largely on the city's population. Moreover, the bombs left such mountains of rubble and such enormous craters that later attempts to get through the town quickly and exploit its capture were frustrated.

In spite of the air and artillery preparation, the Germans fought back savagely when the attack was launched. Casualties were high on both sides. Some German strong points held out until flamethrowing tanks moved in to blast them at point-blank range.

Early on the morning of July 9, SS General Kurt Meyer, commander of the Hitler Jugend Division, after deciding to defy the standing order to "hold fast," started to evacuate his units across the Orne River. "We were meant to die in Caen," he later said, "but one just couldn't watch those youngsters being sacrificed to a senseless order." A little later, Rommel and Eberbach authorized the withdrawal. Troops of the Canadian 3rd Infantry Division completed the occupation of the Carpiquet airfield that morning at 11:15.

British and Canadian troops entered Caen early that afternoon and found the streets choked with huge blocks of stone. From the ruins came faint groans. About 6,000 men, women and children had perished; thousands more were injured. "The dead lay everywhere," recalled one witness, "not corpses, just the remains, fingers, a hand, a head, and pathetic personal belongings, a bottle of aspirin, rosary beads, torn and mud-soaked letters. . . ."

The capture of Caen cost the British about 3,500 men killed, wounded and missing, along with 80 tanks. The tanks could easily be replaced, but the infantrymen could not. Britain had been at war nearly five years now and had provided three quarters of the troops for the European campaign up to this point. Britain was running out of men. Much the same was true for the Germans, who had lost 6,000 soldiers in the Caen battle.

Bitter as it was, the battle for Caen served an invaluable purpose for the Allies. Montgomery succeeded in drawing the bulk of the German divisions into action against the British Second Army and away from the Americans to the west. It was clear from the ferocity of the German defense, however, that there was little immediate hope of cracking the enemy defenses in the Caen sector. If the stalemate in Normandy was to be broken, Bradley's First Army would have to break it.

After the fall of Cherbourg, Bradley had turned all of his forces to the south. Two critical objectives lay in the path of the American First Army. One of them was Coutances, located on the coastal road 40 miles to the south. Three major roads and two secondary routes met at Coutances; one led southward along the coast through Granville to Avranches, the gateway to Brittany and the heart of France. The First Army's other critical objective lay 15 miles to the east of Coutances at Saint-Lô, where four major roads and four secondary ones converged.

The attack to the south would lead directly through the worst of the hedgerow country, and much of the terrain over which Bradley's troops would have to move had been flooded by heavy rains in recent weeks. But Coutances seemed to be not as waterlogged as elsewhere, and Bradley placed his heavyweight VIII Corps under Major General Troy H. Middleton in that sector. The VIII Corps now contained four divisions: the 82nd Airborne, the recently transferred 79th, the 90th and the newly arrived 8th.

In the center Bradley placed Collins' VII Corps, with one untried division, the 83rd, and two seasoned ones, the 4th and the 9th. Their mission was to take the road junction of Périers and then move southeast to cut the Coutances–Saint-Lô highway.

On the left Bradley positioned the XIX Corps under the command of Major General Charles H. Corlett. Initially, the corps would have only one division, the 30th, but the 29th and the 3rd Armored would later be added. Corlett's objective was to get astride the Vire River, attack down both sides and capture Saint-Lô.

The attack began on July 3, when the men of the VIII Corps jumped off, full of confidence and optimism, believing that the Germans were worn out and would withdraw. But they encountered heavy rain and stubborn enemy resistance. Crack troops of the 82nd Airborne moved forward easily at first, then ran into fierce opposition; they ground out a total of four miles in three days at a cost of approximately 1,200 casualties.

To the east of the 82nd, the 90th and the 79th Divisions lost more than 4,000 men between them as they pushed four miles through the hedgerows. Attacking in the rain, the 90th lost over 600 men on the first day and suffered even heavier casualties the following day.

The newly committed 8th Division also had its troubles. The division was regarded as one of the best-trained outfits in the U.S. Army, but it had to learn the hard way to slip around enemy units and methodically make its way through the hedgerows.

In 12 days of fighting, the four divisions of the VIII Corps advanced seven miles at a cost of 10,000 casualties. Meanwhile, in the VII Corps sector, the 83rd Division attacked toward Périers on July 4 over soggy ground enclosed by still more hedgerows. Almost everything went wrong from the start. The attackers were plagued by deadly but invisible enemy fire. Infiltrating German infantrymen seemed to be everywhere, and the hedgerows frequently proved almost insuperable obstacles. Tanks chewed up telephone wires, commanders and their units lost communication with one another, a regimental commander was shot and snipers picked off engineers who were trying to clear minefields. By an enormous effort, the division pushed forward 200 yards, taking six prisoners and losing 47 killed, 815 wounded and 530 missing. (As if he knew how badly his opponents were faring, the commander of the German troops in the area—an elite parachute regiment—returned American medics he had captured.)

But the Germans could not be everywhere; the battle was grinding them down, too. The XIX Corps found this out on July 7, when it uncovered a weak point in the Germans' defenses. One of the 30th Division's early objectives was the little crossroad hamlet of Saint-Jean-de-Daye, straddling the north-south road to Saint-Lô. To take the village, the troops of the 30th had to cross the Vire et Taute Canal from the north and the Vire River from the east. The crossings were opposed, but resistance was so light that the commander of the corps, General Corlett, concluded that he might make a swift stroke to the south. Bradley gave him the 3rd Armored Division, and Corlett ordered its commander, Major General Leroy H. Watson, to cross the Vire River at Airel and make a "power drive" to the south. The objective was a 300-foot hill known as Hauts-Vents, three miles down the road, dominating the Vire River bridge and the main road leading into Saint-Lô from the northwest.

The spearhead of the armored division, Combat Command B under Brigadier General John J. Bohn, had to cross the Vire at the same point where 30th Division infantrymen had already crossed. That meant putting a column more than 20 miles long, with 6,000 soldiers in 800 vehicles and trailers, across the single bridge at Airel—on a piece of ground that was already bursting with 30th Division troops and equipment, and under continuous enemy attack. All of this had to be accomplished with inexperienced troops and officers and with no time to coordinate the movements of the armored division through the territory occupied by the infantry.

Bohn's combat command was originally scheduled to follow the main road after crossing the Vire River bridge. The tanks would dash down the highway, secure the bridgehead and then turn south to provide a spearhead for a further advance. But the 3rd Armored Division's commander, General Watson, was fearful that this route would expose the tanks to flank attack by the Germans. He decided, therefore, that Bohn should turn left immediately after crossing the bridge and follow some unimproved roads and trails that would bring him out three miles below Saint-Jean-de-Daye.

This decision was to lead to an almost unbelievable succession of blunders, misfortunes and delays that would cost the luckless Bohn his future with the Army. The first thing that went wrong was that the unimproved roads and lanes proved to be so narrow that the tanks were forced to fan out over the countryside. The tanks got hopelessly bogged down among the hedgerows, and demolition teams and bulldozers had to be called up to clear a route for them through the thickets.

On the first day, Bohn's task force made only a mile and a half. Behind them eight infantry battalions, four tank battalions and three artillery battalions were jumbled together in the maze of hedgerows. In the confusion, tankers of the 3rd

The gaunt remains of the cathedral of Notre-Dame rise from the ruins of Saint-Lô, a strategic Normandy crossroads town that was almost 95 per cent destroyed before troops of the U.S. 29th Division captured it on July 18, 1944. The devastation brought about by more than a month of Allied bombing and shelling was intensified by a two-day German artillery and mortar barrage. So great was the destruction that many U.S. troops fell into an awed silence upon entering the rubble-choked streets. Said one soldier: "We sure liberated the hell out of this place."

Armored and infantrymen of the 30th Division fired at each other and 16 men were shot.

In an effort to unscramble the mess, Corlett put Major General Leland S. Hobbs, commander of the 30th Division, in charge of all the troops of the bridgehead. On July 9, Hobbs sent Bohn an ultimatum: take the objective at Hauts-Vents by 5 p.m. or be relieved. Corlett then fired off a separate message to the same effect. Bohn finally managed to get some of the tanks unsnarled and sent eight of them off in the direction of Hauts-Vents. But they were slowed by the swampy lowlands and the narrow, sunken roads and trails in the hedgerow country.

At this point, a new threat to the troops in the bridgehead suddenly loomed. Corlett and Hobbs learned from aerial reconnaissance that heavy German reinforcements, including elements of the 2nd Panzer Division and the Panzer Lehr Division, were on their way to this sector of the front. Rumors ran through the ranks, and fears mounted when a

force from the 2nd SS Panzer Division struck the 30th Division near Le Désert. With strong artillery support, the 30th beat off the attack, but later a company of the 743rd Tank Battalion was ambushed by German armor with the loss of a dozen tanks and more than 40 casualties.

Reports circulated that whole battalions were being surrounded. A supply party of about 200 men on the main road south of Saint-Jean-de-Daye panicked and began running back toward the intersection in small groups.

In the meantime, Bohn's missing eight tanks started down a narrow lane and got lost among the hedgerows. When the tanks finally emerged on the main road to Saint-Jean-de-Daye, instead of turning left, as they were supposed to, they turned right.

This proved to be a fatal mistake. It brought them directly into range of the 823rd Tank Destroyer Battalion, an American outfit that had deployed its guns on both sides of the main road to protect Saint-Jean-de-Daye from the south.

The tank-destroyer gunners were edgy because they had been getting reports that German tanks were in the area. When the silhouette of a tank appeared at the top of a rise 3,000 yards away, they thought it was German. But they double-checked by radio to headquarters to ask whether any American armor was in the area. The answer was no—any tanks in the vicinity must belong to the enemy. By now several tanks had come into view, turrets rotating as they fired machine-gun bullets and occasional high-explosive shells into the hedges and fields bordering the road.

The first round from the tank destroyers, fired at a range of 600 yards, slammed into the lead tank and wounded the commander. At that moment Bohn, who was trying to get in touch with the eight tanks on the open radio channel, clearly heard the stricken tank commander say, "I am in dreadful agony."

The lead tank and one other were knocked out, and in the exchange of gunfire, 10 tank and tank-destroyer crewmen were wounded. The six remaining tanks quickly turned around and headed south toward Hauts-Vents.

At this point, Hobbs decided that the tanks were getting overextended. He sent an order to Bohn to halt the tanks where they were and have them button up for the night. Bohn tried to reach the six tanks by radio but was unable to get through to them.

The little advance force went rumbling down the road to Hauts-Vents and arrived there shortly after dark. They were just in time to be strafed by U.S. planes, which were supposed to have attacked Hauts-Vents much earlier but had been delayed by bad weather.

By now Bohn had suffered through an almost incredible series of frustrations and snafus. His orders had been switched before his tanks crossed the bridge, and as a result the armor had become entangled with the infantrymen of the 30th Division. The eight tanks that had finally managed to unscramble themselves had become lost, had taken the wrong road and had been shot up by their own side.

That night Hobbs relieved Bohn of his command. "I know what you did personally," Hobbs said, "but you are a victim of circumstance."

The fired general was understandably bitter. Hobbs had ordered him to take Hauts-Vents or be removed, then had told him to call off the tank attack on that objective. Bohn had tried his best to reach the tanks, but had been prevented because their radios were out of order. The tanks had proceeded to take the objective, only to be strafed by American planes. "You spend your whole life preparing for combat," Bohn said, "and the whole thing goes down the drain in three days."

Bohn may have been well out of it, however. The worst was still to come.

The Panzer Lehr Division attempted to launch a counterattack in the early hours of July 11, but the effort merely proved that the hedgerow country was no better place for German tanks than it was for Allied tanks. The German division managed to penetrate U.S. positions in two areas, but troops of the combat-wise 9th Infantry Division, which had fought in Tunisia and Sicily, worked their way around through the hedgerows and closed in behind the attacking enemy tanks. The infantrymen then sealed off the Germans' escape routes, and American tanks, tank destroyers and bazookas mauled the enemy armor. Heavy casualties were inflicted; one unit that had started the counterattack with six officers, 40 noncoms, 198 men and 10 tanks was reduced to seven noncoms and 23 men—without tanks or officers.

With the German counterattack stalled, the American XIX Corps resumed its advance, but exhaustion forced it to stop near the Lessay–Périers–Saint-Lô highway. In the meantime, farther west, the VIII Corps, after battling its way through seven miles of hedgerows, also halted within sight of that road. At this point, Coutances, only 14 miles ahead, seemed as unreachable as Berlin. The VII Corps, sloshing around in the muck south of Carentan, was forced to stop four miles short of Périers.

The fighting among the hedgerows had now proved to be

so costly that Bradley's original objective—the Coutances–Saint-Lô highway—seemed unattainable. Just to reach the line from Lessay to Caumont, the First Army had suffered 40,000 casualties, 90 per cent of them infantrymen. Bradley knew that the American offensive was bogged down badly. He needed to do something decisive soon. By now most of the attacking units of the First Army had arrived at the Lessay–Périers–Saint-Lô road. That road was only partway out of the murderous hedgerow country that the men had been fighting through for the last couple of weeks, but it would have to do as the platform for the next offensive.

That offensive was already taking form in Bradley's mind. But before he could do anything else he had to capture the road junction at Saint-Lô and secure his flank on the left.

Once charming and serene, Saint-Lô had been a favorite leave spot for the German occupiers before June 6, but Allied bombing had turned it into a pile of rubble, and 800 civilians lay dead in the ruins.

The assignment of capturing Saint-Lô fell to the 29th Division. The Germans held out stubbornly on Martinville Ridge, east of the town, until the 2nd Battalion of the 116th Regiment, under Major Sidney V. Bingham, found a weak spot and advanced to within 1,000 yards of Saint-Lô. Bingham's battalion was cut off, but he reported by radio that he thought he could hold out.

Early the next morning, the 3rd Battalion, under Major Thomas D. Howie, moved out under cover of heavy mist to relieve Bingham's isolated group. Combat-wise Germans, knowing that the mist could conceal just such a movement, stepped up their artillery fire and poured machine-gun bullets into the murk. Howie's men crept forward and held their own fire. After several hours they worked their way through to Bingham's men. Both units were then supposed to move on and enter the outskirts of Saint-Lô, but Bingham's battalion was no longer fit to make the effort. On the radio the commander of the 29th Division, Major General Charles H. Gerhardt, asked Howie if he could move his battalion to the edge of town all by itself. Howie replied "Will do." Moments later he was killed by a shellburst.

Both battalions were now cut off, mainly by German shellfire. Efforts to break through to them with food, ammunition and medical supplies failed. A column of half-tracks and tank destroyers tried to negotiate sunken roads that were clogged with wrecked vehicles and dead German transport horses, but progress under the German barrage was impossible.

On the night of July 17, riflemen of the 116th Infantry Regiment finally broke through to the two isolated battalions. The following morning the final assault on Saint-Lô was launched. A task force under the command of Brigadier General Norman D. Cota, the assistant division commander, picked its way through antitank artillery and mortar fire to a square close to the town's cemetery. Using the square as a base of operations, infantry, tanks and tank destroyers then moved forward to seize key points in the town. By 5 p.m., after a series of skirmishes, Saint-Lô was in American hands. As the troops pushed into the center of town, the body of Major Howie was draped with an American flag, taken aboard a jeep and transported to the center of Saint-Lô. There it was gently laid on a pile of rubble before the old Romanesque church of Sainte Croix to serve as a symbol of the casualties suffered at Saint-Lô. All around it lay the ruins of the devastated town.

The Germans attempted a counterattack that night, but their forces were so badly weakened that it failed.

Saint-Lô, like Caen, had finally fallen, and the Allies were at last emerging from the sodden hedgerow country onto firm, dry ground. But all of this had come at a tremendous cost. The British, Americans and Canadians had suffered 122,000 casualties since the Normandy landings. The Allies had inflicted tremendous losses on the enemy—over 115,000 men were killed, wounded or missing—but they still had not been able to smash through the German defenses and get on with the liberation of the rest of France. Before that could be accomplished, another massive attack would be required.

SHAMBLES AT CHERBOURG

From atop newly won Fort du Roule, U.S. VII Corps commander Major General J. Lawton Collins views smoking Cherbourg harbor facilities set afire by Germans.

CLEARING A PASSAGE INTO A VITAL HARBOR

When, after more than a week of battle, the U.S. VII Corps won the badly needed port of Cherbourg at the end of June 1944, it seemed to Allied engineers that the harbor could be cleared in three weeks. Reconstruction plans that had been drawn up more than a year in advance had taken into account German sabotage, and special teams of divers had undergone extensive training in the muddy waters of England's Thames River, learning how to search out and defuse mines.

But when the damage was surveyed, it proved much more extensive than anyone had foreseen. The Germans had left basins and docks blocked by more than 55 scuttled ships, barges and smaller craft, and by overturned cranes and dynamited bridges. They had also wrecked docking and unloading facilities, including piers, wharves, storehouses, railways and utilities, in addition to 95 per cent of the crucial deepwater quay area that was needed by the Allies for their supply ships.

Hundreds of mines hampered clearing operations. Not satisfied with wrecking a railway bridge, the Germans had mined the sections of it that remained above water. And to confuse the Allies, they had marked minefields where there were none—and then booby-trapped the signs. The problem was worse in the water. No one could tell where or when a mine might go off—or what might trigger it. Some mines were so sensitive to changes in the magnetic field that the mere presence of a ship 125 feet above was enough to detonate them. During the course of the work, more than 200 mines went off, sinking three minesweepers and seven other craft and damaging three more.

In spite of the dangers, the clearing operations proceeded at fever pitch. By the 16th of July—three weeks after the capture of Cherbourg—four Liberty ships unloaded the first supplies in the harbor. But many more weeks would be required before the port could begin to meet the quota of 8,000 tons of cargo per day set for it by the planners—10 times the peacetime amount.

The first U.S. Naval Salvage unit rolls up to a statue of Napoleon at Cherbourg harbor on July 6, 1944. The statue overlooked the Avant Port du Commerce, a valuable anchorage that had been so thoroughly blocked and mined by the Germans that it took five weeks to clear it.

The remains of a bridge and a scuttled barge awash in a sea of debris block an entrance to the deepwater Avant Port du Commerce, which was needed by Liberty ships at Cherbourg. Seven more vessels—one of them heavily mined—and a 100-ton floating crane clogged the basin itself.

Readying Cherbourg to receive ships, the U.S.S. Pinon reels in torn German torpedo nets and their buoys to replace them with new nets and buoys spanning the harbor mouth.

BOOBY TRAPS AND BLOCKED BOAT BASINS

Clearing Cherbourg harbor of all of the wreckage and mines left behind by the Germans required great resourcefulness.

While engineers built docks and blasted holes in the sea wall to facilitate immediate unloading onto the shore, salvage units labored in the murky water. Sunken vessels were patched at low tide and pumped free of water so they could be floated away at high tide; vessels too badly damaged to patch were raised by pontoons strapped to them when the tide ran out. A sunken submarine-lifting vessel had to be blasted into manageable pieces by explosives, and toppled cranes were cut into sections by divers using acetylene torches.

Removing mines proved a nightmarish task. Minesweepers had to contend with not only three types of mines commonly used by the Germans—those detonated by magnetic, acoustic or direct contact with a ship—but also a fourth kind the Allies dubbed "Katies." These concrete-encased contraptions rested on the floor of the harbor two to three fathoms down, well out of the reach of ordinary minesweepers, and exploded as ships passed overhead. Some Katies had been set to go off only after several ships had sailed over them. Other mines had delayed-action fuses that detonated up to 85 days after being set.

To locate mines and obstacles, divers, hooked up by telephone to launches that followed on the surface, spent six weeks scouring the entire harbor floor. The divers walked along lines sunk to guide them through the darkness. When they found a mine, they identified it by touch and then dismantled it if they could, or had it raised to the surface where sharpshooters waited to explode it.

Clearing mines seemed a never-ending task—a single barge sunk by the Germans concealed more than 65 mines of differing varieties, which took divers three weeks to remove. Two weeks of intensive minesweeping were required to open a narrow passage for ships, and three and a half months were needed before the harbor could be considered safe.

A geyser erupts outside the breakwaters of Cherbourg harbor as two British minesweepers detonate an underwater mine in July 1944. Sixteen sweeps were made every morning to set off delayed-action mines.

The tension of his task evident in his face, a member of the U.S. Navy Salvage team uses a hacksaw to cut a bundle of electrical cables laid by the Germans to trigger the mines they had hidden in Cherbourg.

A member of a bomb disposal squad saws through the detonating cap of a delayed-action mine discovered in a Cherbourg cellar. Attached to a pipe, the mine had been set to spray noxious chemicals into the street.

British sailors help members of a specially trained team put on diving suits used when scouring Cherbourg harbor for mines.

A U.S. Navy Salvage ship moors alongside an overturned 550-foot-long whaler that was later used to extend a rebuilt pier.

A floating crane swings over the wreckage of a 1,700-ton submarine-lifting vessel blocking a harbor basin. The vessel's bridge had already been removed.

Smoke billows up from a sea wall at Cherbourg harbor as U.S. Army engineers use dynamite to open one of three breaches that allowed unloading on the beach.

U.S. troops begin breaking up concrete rubble with jackhammers to clear a dock in Cherbourg harbor.

Derricks used for unloading cargo line a 4,200-foot wooden pier being built up and out from a sea wall.

With no deep-draft berths yet available, the first Liberty ship to enter Cherbourg harbor had to have its cargo unloaded and ferried to the shore by an LCT.

THE TRICKY TASK OF UNLOADING SUPPLIES

The Allies needed supplies so badly that they could not afford to wait while Cherbourg harbor was cleared of all mines, obstacles and rubble. As soon as a channel was opened through the harbor in mid-July, ships began unloading cargo. LCTs and DUK-Ws ferried supplies from the vessels to the beach front.

But even when overloaded by 100 per cent, as was frequently the case, the amphibian lighters could manage only a few thousand tons of supplies a day, far short of Allied needs. Creating deepwater berths for ships for direct unloading was vital.

Working both night and day, engineers cleared and repaired a severely damaged breakwater, the Digue du Homet, in four days. Then they built five wooden piers along the breakwater and filled the gaps to form a continuous quay 2,700 feet long. Next they laid railroad tracks to provide access to train ferries. On August 9 the first Liberty ship docked alongside the quay.

By November, Cherbourg was handling more than 14,000 tons of supplies a day—6,000 tons more than the goal set for it. Against all odds, the harbor had become the most important port in the continental supply network, responsible for half the supplies brought in by American forces.

The harbor's first Liberty ship lowers a net containing Signal Corps wire spools to a waiting DUK-W.

Laden with cargo, a DUK-W plows through swells on its way to the beach-front unloading area.

A British train ferry and two Liberty ships unload their cargo at the rebuilt Digue du Homet breakwater in August 1944. By the end of the month, Cherbourg harbor had handled almost 300,000 tons of essential supplies.

Traffic backs up at the beach front as newly arrived two-and-a-half-ton trucks wait for incoming freight. DUK-Ws lined up in the second and third rows were to pick up supplies from ships anchored in the outer harbor.

A scant month after salvage operations got under way, a locomotive is hoisted ashore from the seatrain Texas by the booms of a crane ship moored alongside. Lighter railroad cars were rolled directly onto tracks.

2

While American troops were still struggling through the hedgerows north of Saint-Lô, General Bradley, commander of the U.S. First Army, gave his aide, Major Chester B. Hansen, a top-priority order. Hansen was to locate a large mess tent and have it set up adjacent to the general's command-post truck. The tent must have a wooden floor, and Hansen was to install in it the largest map of the Normandy beachhead that he could find.

By now Bradley was fed up with the agonizing and extremely costly progress of the hedgerow fighting. He had been ordered by General Montgomery to find a way to break out of the beachhead, and he intended to study the map until he came up with a solution. For that purpose he needed a map that would show in detail every road and terrain feature of the beachhead area. He also needed a floor, because heavy rains had recently turned the Normandy countryside into a sea of mud and he expected to do a lot of pacing before the map.

When Hansen took his problem to the headquarters commandant—the officer in charge of housekeeping around the command post—he met with some resistance at first. "Now you're pampering the old man," the headquarters commandant said. "Who ever heard of a wooden floor in a tent in the field?"

But with the authority of a three-star general behind him, Hansen got what he wanted. A floor was constructed of planks, the tent was set up, and an enormous eight-foot map of the Normandy beachhead was installed.

Bradley spent the next two nights in the tent studying the map, sketching in division and corps boundaries with colored pencils and marking roads and rivers. As he paced back and forth, he devised a plan. First Army troops would attack the enemy along a narrow front—but not until after Allied heavy bombers had pounded the Germans so hard that they would be unable to fight back when the ground assault got under way.

Ground and air efforts would have to be coordinated with great precision. To gain the maximum advantage from the bombing, the infantry would have to be as close as possible to the target area, ready to move as soon as the planes completed their runs. As Bradley studied the map, his attention fastened on the old road running east-west from Saint-Lô to Périers. Built by the Romans, the road was ruler-

BREAKOUT

straight; it could serve as a marker that would clearly set off the Americans from the Germans on the other side of it, a marker that would be readily recognizable from the air. First Army troops were now approaching this road, and with some luck they would soon be in position to push across it for an attack to the south.

Using a colored pencil, Bradley drew a rectangle on the map, covering an area three and a half miles wide and a mile and a half deep, south of the Périers–Saint-Lô road. This would be the critical area of battle; the bombers would fly in parallel to the road and carpet-bomb the rectangle. Then, upon completion of the bombing, two infantry divisions would assault enemy positions, tear open a large gap and hold back the sides for a motorized infantry division to come through. The motorized division would dash all the way to Coutances, 15 miles to the southwest. Two armored divisions would then follow. While one provided protection against German attacks on the flank to the east, the other would go barreling down to Avranches—a distance of 30 miles—and turn the corner into Brittany.

This was the plan for what came to be known as the Normandy breakout. Given the code name *Cobra,* the operation would later be fairly described by Bradley as "the most decisive battle of our war in western Europe."

On July 10, two days after Bradley first hatched his plan, General Montgomery called a conference at his headquarters at Creuilly with Bradley and General Dempsey of the British Second Army, his two top subordinates. In the course of the meeting, Bradley informed Montgomery of his plan for the breakout. He explained that the attack could not get started until his dwindling supplies of ammunition had been replenished and First Army troops were within hailing distance of the Périers–Saint-Lô road.

Understanding Bradley's need for time, Montgomery decided to do whatever he could to enlarge the scope of the offensive and ensure its success. He ordered Dempsey to make a "massive stroke" in the Caen-Falaise area. Three armored divisions of the British VIII Corps—the 7th, the 11th and the Guards—would be set aside for the attack. The armored divisions would be supported by the Canadian II Corps and the British XII Corps. Thus, instead of being struck by *Cobra* alone, the Germans now would receive a double blow. The new operation was code-named *Goodwood,* and planning for it began.

On July 13, three days after meeting with Bradley and Dempsey, Montgomery sent a message to General Eisenhower that said, "Am going to launch a very big attack next week." He explained that the British Second Army would push forward in the area south of Caen and the U.S. First Army would follow up with an assault west of Saint-Lô. Montgomery took pains to point out that the success of the operation would depend to a large extent upon having "the whole weight" of Allied air power behind it. If all went well, he said, *Goodwood* might have "far-reaching results."

Eisenhower took this to mean that Montgomery intended a breakout in the Caen area—an assumption that was to lead to misunderstandings later. "With respect to the plan," he wrote, "I am confident that it will reap a harvest from all the sowing that you have been doing during the past weeks. . . . I am not discounting the difficulties, nor the initial losses, but in this case I am viewing the prospects with the most tremendous optimism and enthusiasm. I would not be at all surprised to see you gaining a victory that will make some of the old classics look like a skirmish between patrols." Ike assured Montgomery that he could count on Bradley "to keep his troops fighting like the very devil, twenty-four hours a day, to provide the opportunity your armored corps will need, and to make the victory complete."

On July 14 one of Montgomery's aides, Lieut. Colonel Christopher Dawnay, arrived in London to brief the War Office on *Goodwood.* He stated that its "real object is to muck up and write off the enemy troops" and indicated that Montgomery "has no intention of rushing madly eastward and getting Second Army so extended that the flank might cease to be secure." He did add, however, that Montgomery stood "ready to take advantage of any situation which gives reason to think that the enemy is disintegrating." Despite Dawnay's assurances to the contrary, Allied air commanders were sure from the magnitude of the air support requested that Montgomery intended to achieve a breakout. An aerial bombardment of such scope surely would not be needed just to tie down German troops.

Goodwood was set for July 17, *Cobra* for the 18th. Air Chief Marshal Sir Arthur Tedder gave Montgomery his assurance that he would arrange for the heavy air support required by "the far-reaching and decisive plan." What Tedder arranged, in fact, was a stupendous show—the largest number of planes yet brought together in support of a ground attack. All told, some 1,600 British and American heavy bombers, plus another 400 medium bombers and fighter-bombers, were called for. These were to drop a total of 7,800 tons of bombs on German defenses; 2,500 tons were earmarked for the industrial suburbs of Caen, where the Germans were holed up, another 650 tons for the fortified village of Cagny just south of Caen and still more for other enemy positions in the target area.

Special care was taken to coordinate the air and ground attacks and to avoid a costly interval that would give the Germans time to recover. The bombers must not be allowed to crater the roads that the armored units would use in their drive forward. The planes were to use 260-pound fragmentation bombs to avoid this. As soon as the saturation bombing was completed, the armored divisions of O'Connor's VIII Corps, supported by 720 artillery pieces, would dash across two railroad embankments and seize the Bourguébus ridge, a commanding feature of the Falaise plain. The plain offered splendid tank country, and the main road beyond the ridge ran straight to Falaise, 15 miles to the south.

Thanks to the commander of Army Group B, Field Marshal Rommel, the Germans were prepared for the *Goodwood* offensive. Rommel had deployed his forces in depth to prevent a breakthrough. Facing the British along a 70-mile front was General Eberbach's Panzer Group West, consisting of four corps made up of eight divisions in the line and five divisions in reserve. Eberbach's battle positions were organized into five defensive zones: first the deeply entrenched infantry, then the tanks, next a band of fortified villages, then 88mm guns, artillery and rocket launchers emplaced on the Bourguébus ridge, and finally, reserve divisions positioned approximately five miles to the rear.

To make sure everything was in readiness, Rommel made a final inspection of these defenses on the afternoon of July 17. On his way back to his headquarters, his car was spotted by British planes. Rommel called out to his driver to take cover, but the fighters swooped in so quickly that

the driver was killed at the wheel. The automobile swerved into a tree, and Rommel was thrown to the road. Suffering from concussion, he was carried unconscious to a village that by one of the War's strange ironies was called Sainte-Foy-de-Montgommery. He survived the accident and was sent home to Germany to recuperate, but his illustrious military career was at an end.

The German dispositions that Rommel had so carefully nurtured were suddenly weakened on the eve of *Goodwood*, when Hitler became convinced that an Allied landing near the mouth of the Seine was imminent. The Führer ordered Field Marshal von Kluge, who had replaced Rommel as commander of Army Group B, to send a panzer division from the Caen area to Lisieux, not far from the river's mouth. Kluge protested to OKW, the German High Command, citing the dangers on the Caen front. "We aren't strong enough there," he said. He preferred to take his chances on another landing and to keep the panzer division where it was.

"I'll transmit your opinion to the Führer," the staff officer at OKW said.

"Never mind," Kluge said quickly. "You don't have to tell him anything more. I just wanted to talk it over with you."

The *Goodwood* air bombardment got under way at 5:30 on the morning of July 18. RAF Pathfinders dropped flares, and then 1,000 Lancasters and Halifaxes let loose a torrent of bombs. An infantryman, who watched while waiting for his outfit to move out, later wrote down his impressions: "The bombers flew in majestically and with a dreadful, unalterable dignity, unloaded and made for home; the sun, just coming over the horizon, caught their wings as they wheeled. Now hundreds of little black clouds were puffing round the bombers as they droned inexorably to their targets and occasionally one of them would heel over and plunge smoothly into the huge pall of smoke and dust that was steadily growing in the south. Everyone was out of their vehicles now, staring in awed wonder till the last wave dropped its bombs and turned away."

The RAF bombing lasted 45 minutes. When it was over, the unnerved German survivors climbed from their shelters to find villages and farmhouses around them obliterated. In minutes they had to dash for cover again as 571 American Eighth Air Force heavy bombers came over and pounded the area. Though the bombardiers found it difficult to sight bombs accurately through the smoke and dust raised by the earlier bombing, they nevertheless managed to eliminate many of the assault guns and panzer grenadiers at Démouville. Despite the intensity of the British and American bombing, the backbone of General Eberbach's defense system, the 88mm guns on the Bourguébus ridge, escaped serious damage.

Following the bombing, Canadian troops attacked the industrial suburbs of Caen across the Orne River from the city. In spite of the careful advance planning for the raid, bomb craters in the roads slowed the Canadians and gave the Germans time to recover from the bombing and stiffen their defenses. It took the Canadians the rest of the day and well into the night to clear the industrial area. At the same time, the British tanks moved out on schedule, 32 in a wave. The tanks lost formation as they entered the dust and smoke

raised by the bombs, but they encountered little opposition where the bombs had fallen. Dazed German infantrymen staggered toward them to surrender; others were too stunned even to rise from their foxholes.

Bomb craters in the paths of the tanks forced some of them to detour and slowed their progress. And in areas where bombs had not fallen, the Germans fought back hard, and many of the tanks were hit. "I watched through the periscope, fascinated, as though it was a film I was seeing," Lance Corporal Ron Cox later remembered. "Then suddenly there was a tremendous crash and shudder. We had been hit. It was a glancing blow but the track was broken. The next shot would follow as soon as the enemy gun could be reloaded. Wally Herd shouted, 'Bail out!' As we bailed out and ran, crouched down away from the tank, it was hit a second time and smoke began to pour from it."

For all the difficulties, the VIII Corps advanced more than

Taking cover behind cow carcasses, two American infantrymen advance under heavy fire along the Carentan-Périers road on July 22, 1944. "We must have seen a thousand dead cows in Normandy, perhaps two thousand," wrote one Allied observer. "One could never get used to that appalling sweet sickly stench." Most of the livestock was killed by Allied saturation bombing and the artillery shelling of both sides.

three miles in little over an hour. By noon the British appeared to be on the verge of a complete penetration of the German defenses. Then they came within range of the antitank guns on the Bourguébus ridge. Under the impact of heavy 88mm fire, they wavered and fell back. So effective were the guns that the Germans referred to the exploding British tanks as "Tommy cookers" and "Ronson lighters" because "they light up the first time."

That night, planes of the supposedly depleted Luftwaffe struck the 7th Armored Division while it was attempting to cross a railway bridge near Cagny. "It was worse than the *bocage*," Private Robert Boulton recalled. "All I remember of *Goodwood* is sitting one night in a traffic jam waiting to cross a bridge and the non-existent Luftwaffe being very existent. When we did get across, tanks and trucks were on fire all over the place."

The Second Army's casualties from the day's fighting were fearsomely high. Canadian troops who took the industrial suburbs of Caen—giving the Allies control of the entire city at last—suffered a total of 1,500 casualties and lost 200 tanks. The British VIII Corps attacking southeast of Caen and at Cagny lost an additional 1,500 men and 270 tanks. One regiment had 57 of its 61 tanks knocked out. It was replaced by another regiment, which quickly lost 49 more tanks.

At the termination of the first day of fighting, General Montgomery issued a communiqué saying that "early this morning British and Canadian troops of Second Army attacked and broke through into the area east of the Orne and southeast of Caen." That same night, he sent an optimistic message to the chief of the Imperial General Staff in London: "Operations this morning a complete success. The effect of the air bombing was decisive and the spectacle terrific." He added that there were three armored divisions in the open country south of Caen and concluded by saying, "Situation very promising and it is difficult to see what the enemy can do at present."

The British attack was renewed the next morning, bringing more heavy losses. Elements of the 11th Armored Division, attempting to climb the Bourguébus ridge, were repeatedly turned back, and the 7th, 11th and Guards Divisions were reduced to battered remnants on the road to Falaise. Before the day ended, the losses had climbed to 1,100 men and 131 tanks. In one unit only nine of 63 tanks remained serviceable.

Another thwarted push on the following day, July 20, brought 1,000 more casualties and the loss of 68 additional

Heavily armed youths of the 12th SS Panzer (Hitler Jugend) Division ready themselves for battle. The division, which consisted mainly of teenage volunteers, was created in June of 1943 and had its baptism of fire in Normandy a year later. "The young S.S. troops were detestable young beasts," a British officer recalled, "but, like good infantry, they stood up and fought it out when overrun." In the fighting that raged around Caen, nearly 90 per cent of them were killed, wounded or captured.

tanks. A heavy thunderstorm in the late afternoon turned the ground beyond Caen into a swamp, and *Goodwood* came to a halt.

Montgomery let it be known that he was satisfied with the offensive. His men had advanced nearly six miles, taken 2,000 prisoners, secured all of the Caen area, seized 34 square miles of territory and exhausted Eberbach's reserves. But all this had been accomplished at immense cost. The VIII Corps had lost more than 3,500 men. The Canadian II Corps had suffered 1,956 casualties. Tank losses amounted to 36 per cent of all British tanks on the Continent.

Above all, the offensive had not produced the breakout that members of Eisenhower's staff had led themselves to expect. A furor resulted. At the headquarters of Air Chief Marshal Sir Trafford Leigh-Mallory, staff members spoke of Montgomery's "failure." "Seven thousand tons of bombs for seven miles," said one air marshal. Eisenhower himself was furious, and there were rumors that Montgomery was going to be sacked.

When word reached Montgomery of the uproar at headquarters he responded quickly. "A number of misunderstandings" had arisen concerning the attack, he said. He had never thought of breaking through the enemy defenses; he

had hoped merely to mount a threat to Falaise to keep the Germans occupied.

Eisenhower did not fire his ground commander. Instead, he decided to swallow his wrath and write to Montgomery to make sure that the two saw "eye to eye on the big problems." Ike said he had been "extremely hopeful and optimistic" that *Goodwood* would achieve a breakthrough, but "that did not come about." As a consequence, he was "pinning our immediate hopes on Bradley's attack." Eisenhower urged Montgomery to have Dempsey strike again when *Cobra* was launched.

Montgomery replied that he had already told Dempsey to resume his attack and to give the impression of a major advance toward Falaise and Argentan. Satisfied with this explanation, Ike replied, "We are apparently in complete agreement that vigorous and persistent offensive effort should be sustained by both First and Second Armies."

Although *Goodwood* failed to achieve a breakout, the operation had forced the Germans to commit the bulk of their strength in the Caen area and had chewed up four German divisions. That was as much as Montgomery's representative, Colonel Dawnay, had claimed for the offensive when he explained to the War Office that it was designed to

A wounded Canadian soldier, his arm crudely bandaged by the photographer who took this picture, dashes off to rejoin his comrades in the assault on Colombelles, an industrial suburb of Caen. In the first day of this hard-fought battle, the Canadian II Corps lost approximately 1,500 men and 200 tanks.

"muck up and write off enemy troops." But by using the words "broke through" in his communiqué at the close of the first day's action, Montgomery had created the impression that *Goodwood* had produced the long-awaited breakout. As a result of his unfortunate choice of words, an operation that had in fact achieved its purpose was regarded as a failure by many Allied strategists.

On July 21, the day after the attack petered out, Field Marshal von Kluge wrote to Hitler that "in the face of the total enemy air superiority, we can adopt no tactics to compensate . . . except to retire from the battlefield. I came here with the firm resolve to enforce your command to stand and hold at all cost. The price of that policy is the steady and certain destruction of our troops. . . . The flow of matériel and personnel replacement is insufficient and artillery and antitank weapons and ammunition are far from adequate. . . . Despite all our efforts, the moment is fast approaching when our hard-pressed defenses will crack."

General Alfred Jodl, Chief of the German Armed Forces Operations Staff, read the letter and suggested to the Führer that the Germans should start thinking about a withdrawal from France. Surprisingly, Hitler agreed. But before the idea could be implemented, fighting erupted again. It was the start of *Cobra*, the second part of the Allied offensive, which had been delayed for four days by rain.

Cobra had to be quick and decisive. If the Germans were allowed to get set again, Bradley had warned his staff, "we go right back to this hedge fighting and you can't make any speed. This thing must be bold."

To ensure its boldness, Bradley had traveled to England on July 19, the day after the *Goodwood* air strike, for a conference at Air Chief Marshal Leigh-Mallory's headquarters near London. What he wanted, he said, was a "blast effect," to be achieved by a massive concentrated bombing of his rectangular target area. But to avoid slow-ups caused by the cratering of roads and the destruction of villages, he asked that nothing heavier than 100-pound fragmentation bombs be used. And he recommended that the planes make lateral bomb runs—approaching parallel to the Périers–Saint-Lô road instead of coming in over the heads of American troops. He urged that the sun be used for concealment: if the attack turned out to be scheduled for the morning, the

bombers could fly from east to west; if the jump-off was to take place in the afternoon, they could fly in the opposite direction—with the sun at their tails.

Bradley was anxious to minimize the interval between the bombing and the start of the ground attack. He suggested a safety zone of no more than 1,000 yards between the ground forces and the area that would be hit by high-flying heavy bombers so that the troops could move out immediately against the stunned Germans. The air commanders wanted a 3,000-yard safety margin, but agreed to a compromise. The troops would withdraw 1,200 yards. The heavy bombers would strike no closer than 1,450 yards. Fighter-bombers, which attacked at lower altitudes and more accurately, would cover the 250-yard interval. But as the plans jelled, the rains came.

During the four-day delay, the First Army rested, and the men got hot meals, showers, clothing changes and some surprisingly good food. "It was amazing," one regimental report later said, "how many cows and chickens wandered

into minefields . . . and ended up as sizzling platters."

In England the weather began clearing on Sunday, July 23. Leigh-Mallory set the *Cobra* bombardment for 1 p.m., July 24, and flew to Normandy that morning to witness the operation. One hour before the bombardment was scheduled to begin, American troops in the battle area pulled back the agreed 1,200 yards. In the wake of their withdrawal, German troops moved across the Périers–Saint-Lô road and set up outposts in the vacated territory. The sky was overcast and Leigh-Mallory decided to postpone the bombing because of poor visibility. His message reached England only a few minutes before the first of 1,600 bombers started arriving over the target area.

Unaware that they were supposed to turn back, three groups of fighter-bombers flew over the heads of American troops and then out over the German positions. Large numbers of heavy bombers also failed to get word of the change in plans, but visibility was so limited that the first 500 of these planes did not release their bombs and only

Covered with branches and camouflage netting to blend with the surrounding trees, a 66-foot observation platform affords British artillerymen a commanding view of German-held territory near the Normandy town of Cheux. Located on the edge of the thickly wooded hedgerow country, where ground visibility was often limited, artillery spotters manning the platform could pinpoint the muzzle flashes of enemy guns and direct artillery onto the targets.

Supreme Allied Commander Dwight D. Eisenhower (left) meets on July 5 in Normandy with the men who planned and executed the Allied breakout: Lieut. General Omar N. Bradley (center), the commander of the American ground forces, and Major General J. Lawton Collins, the commander of the VII Corps.

35 aircraft in the second formation dropped theirs—after making three runs to identify the target. But more than 300 bombers in the third formation dropped 550 tons of high explosives and 135 tons of fragmentation bombs before turning back.

Some of the bombs fell on American ground positions and killed 25 men, wounded another 131 and left some units in such shock that the men were unable to stir.

Bradley was horrified. He had expected the bombers to make a lateral approach, along the road, but the planes had come in over the heads of his troops. He protested to Leigh-Mallory, saying that he had left the July 19 meeting with "a clear understanding they would fly parallel to that road." Leigh-Mallory replied that he had been forced to leave the conference before that part of the discussion, but he promised to check into the matter and call Bradley back.

The size of the bombs used also disturbed Bradley. He had expected 100-pound fragmentation bombs—but the ones dropped had all been bigger and more powerful.

The abortive bombing had sown confusion up and down the line. Word that Leigh-Mallory had called off the bombardment had reached General Collins, the commander of the attacking American VII Corps, shortly before the bombs began landing. Collins did not know whether *Cobra* had been delayed or was proceeding according to plan after all.

As he ordered his troops to the jump-off point, he was surprised to discover that the enemy had moved into the area earlier vacated by the Americans. Two infantry divisions now had to struggle to take back the ground that had been given up for their own safety. One battalion gained a single hedgerow; two other battalions fought eight hours to reduce a strong point. Enemy artillery fire was heavy, and all advancing units took heavy casualties.

Across the Périers–Saint-Lô road, the German Panzer Lehr Division waited. The division commander, Major General Fritz Bayerlein, was sure that the bombing signaled the beginning of a major attack. Yet his communications were so badly mangled that he found it extremely difficult to coordinate a defensive effort. When the Americans failed to push across the road, he congratulated his troops for turning back a major attack. His losses were relatively light, his front line was intact, and he had committed no reserves. Then he made a fateful decision: he moved more troops

into the rectangular target area, unaware that the saturation bombing had been rescheduled for 11 o'clock the following morning, July 25.

The raid had been carefully worked out by the ground and air commanders. More than 1,500 B-17s and B-24s would fly over the target area and drop 3,300 tons of bombs; 400 medium bombers would release another 650 tons, and 550 fighter-bombers would drop more than 200 tons of high explosives and napalm. The bombardment was to be intensified by 125,000 rounds fired by artillery. To prevent a recurrence of the tragedy of the day before, the bombardiers were ordered not to release bombs above the Périers–Saint-Lô road. A special weather plane was to check visibility in the early morning. If the weather was good, the heavy bombers would fly in as low as possible and the bombardiers would sight the targets visually instead of using instruments.

Before the attack got under way, Bradley received the promised telephone call from Leigh-Mallory, who said that he had checked with the Air Force and found the overhead approach to the target area had not been a mistake. The air planners were opposed to a lateral run because it would mean approaching and entering the rectangular target area through its narrow side. The planes not only would have to fly dangerously close together but also would be exposed for a longer period of time to German antiaircraft guns, deployed across the entire length of the rectangle. If Bradley wanted the air bombardment resumed, Leigh-Mallory made it clear that the First Army commander would have to agree to let the planes come in over the heads of the troops. Bradley was angry at what he considered a breach of faith by the Air Force, but he acquiesced because he could see no alternative.

Americans on the ground were elated when they caught sight of the majestic armada. Correspondent Ernie Pyle, who had joined the men of the 4th Division for the *Cobra* operation, stood out in the open with them, transfixed by the sight of the oncoming planes.

"We spread our feet and leaned far back trying to look straight up, until our steel helmets fell off," he wrote. "And then the bombs came. They began like the crackle of popcorn and almost instantly swelled into a monstrous fury of noise that seemed surely to destroy all the world ahead of us." A wall of dust and smoke rose into the sky and "sifted around us and into our noses. The bright day grew slowly dark from it." And all the while the noise grew, becoming "an indescribable caldron of sounds."

As Pyle and the GIs watched, "there crept into our consciousness a realization that the windrows of exploding bombs were easing back toward us, flight by flight, instead of gradually forward, as the plan called for. Then we were horrified by the suspicion that those machines, high in the sky and completely detached from us, were aiming their bombs at the smoke line on the ground—and a gentle breeze was drifting the smoke line back over us! An inde-

scribable kind of panic came over us. We stood tensed in muscle and frozen in intellect, watching each flight approach and pass over, feeling trapped and completely helpless. And then all of an instant the universe became filled with a gigantic rattling as of huge ripe seeds in a mammoth dry gourd. I doubt that any of us had ever heard that sound before, but instinct told us what it was. It was bombs by the hundred, hurtling down through the air above us.

"Many times I've heard bombs whistle or swish or rustle, but never before had I heard bombs rattle. I still don't know the explanation of it. But it is an awful sound. We dived. Some got into a dugout. Others made foxholes and ditches and some got behind a garden wall. I was too late for the

Closely guarded by a Canadian soldier, a despondent German officer sits with his head in his hands after being captured south of Caen during the Goodwood operation. Between D-Day and the 25th of July, the Canadian and British troops took approximately 11,500 Germans prisoner.

dugout. The nearest place was a wagon shed. The rattle was right down upon us. I remember hitting the ground flat, all spread out like the cartoons of people flattened by steam rollers, and then squirming like an eel to get under one of the heavy wagons in the shed.

"An officer whom I didn't know was wriggling beside me. The bombs were already crashing around us. We lay with our heads slightly up—like two snakes—staring at each other . . . in a futile appeal, our faces about a foot apart, until it was over."

For the second time in two days bombs had fallen on Americans. Bomb loads from 35 heavy bombers and 42 medium bombers exploded inside the American lines. One hundred eleven men were killed and 490 wounded. Among the victims was Lieut. General Lesley J. McNair, a senior member of the U.S. Army staff in Washington, who had joined a frontline battalion as an observer. Infantry command posts, an artillery-fire-direction center and vehicles were wrecked, communications were disrupted, and troops were buried in their foxholes.

Many men who were unharmed physically suffered concussion and shock. "A lot of the men were sitting around after the bombing in a complete daze," wrote a company commander. "I called battalion and told them I was in no condition to move, that everything was completely disorganized and it would take me some time to get my men back together, and asked for a delay. But battalion said no, push off. Jump off immediately."

As word of the casualties reached higher headquarters, resentment mounted. Eisenhower was so upset that he decided he would never again use heavy bombers in support of a ground attack.

In spite of the tragic losses, the bombing had achieved its intended effect. Across the Périers–Saint-Lô road, 1,000 men of the Panzer Lehr Division had perished, and the survivors were stunned. The division commander, General Bayerlein, later reported, "my front lines looked like the face of the moon, and at least 70 per cent of my troops were out of action—dead, wounded, crazed or numbed. All my forward tanks were knocked out, and the roads were practically impassable."

Some of the survivors would be deaf for 24 hours. Three battalion command posts simply vanished, along with a whole parachute regiment. Only a dozen tanks remained operable. As Bayerlein frantically tried to restore a semblance of order by calling up units from the rear, American

56

P-38s, P-47s and P-51s and British Typhoons continued to blast his troops and tanks.

Now the ground attack got under way. Three American infantry divisions moved forward. General Collins intended them to take the towns of Marigny and Saint-Gilles by the end of the day so that he could send his motorized infantry and armor roaring down through the gap. But progress was slowed by the hedgerows, and by nightfall neither Marigny nor Saint-Gilles had fallen. The next day, Collins nevertheless sent his armor rolling through the infantry. One column was ordered to seize Marigny and turn southwest for Coutances, while the second column was to enter Saint-Gilles and block any effort the Germans might make to interfere with the drive to Coutances.

Saint-Gilles fell to the 2nd Armored Division in the afternoon, but infantrymen of the motorized 1st Division—who had been charged with freeing the road—could not clear the Germans from the high ground around Marigny that day. The town finally fell the third morning, and the way was open for the thrust to Coutances.

The situation was fluid now, but still fraught with danger. German troops, tanks and antitank guns lay concealed behind the hedgerows; they frequently closed in behind American mobile units and cut them off from the rear.

Bomb craters, wrecked vehicles and traffic congestion hindered the advance. But by evening Bradley knew that *Cobra* was achieving its purpose. "Things on our front really look good," he told Eisenhower. Instead of halting to consolidate his gains, he decided to go all out to smash the Germans, who by now were so demoralized that they were incapable of organizing a coordinated defense.

Seeing the enemy in flight in "bits and pieces," Bradley figured that the Germans' only hope was to regroup behind the Sée River at Avranches. Even there they could hardly make a stand unless fresh troops were brought up—and no such troops were available.

Meanwhile, Lieut. General George S. Patton Jr. had been waiting impatiently in an apple orchard on the Cotentin Peninsula for his Third Army to swing into action. But since the Third Army was not due to become operational until August 1, Bradley ordered Patton to see to it that the VIII Corps got to Avranches in a hurry.

Patton put two armored divisions at the head of the VIII Corps' advance, and late on July 28, Coutances fell to his armored thrust. The units hardly had time to savor their

U.S. troops dig out comrades who were buried when Allied bombs fell short of target during the July 25 air strike that preceded the Cobra breakout operation in Normandy. The bombings produced some 600 American casualties.

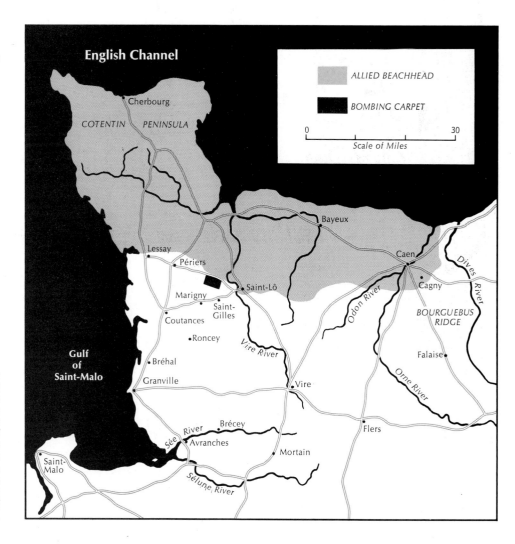

By the third week in July 1944, the Allies controlled a large part of Normandy, including all of the Cotentin Peninsula, and were ready to break out of their beachhead. For the offensive, Lieut. General Omar N. Bradley devised a plan whereby Allied planes would "carpet bomb" a rectangle measuring three and a half by one and a half miles (shown in red) south of the Périers–Saint-Lô road. The bombing was designed to tear a hole in the German lines through which the U.S. First Army could plunge south toward Coutances and Avranches and achieve the crucial breakout.

victory; by now they had their eyes set on Avranches, 30 miles farther down the road.

The Germans were in full retreat. Vehicular columns fled pell-mell to the south. Burning vehicles and tanks lined almost every road; unused mines lay scattered alongside the highways and in the haste of withdrawal, the German troops neglected to set off bridge demolitions.

Near Roncey, a huge German force had become bottled up trying to escape down the Cotentin Peninsula, and Allied aircraft discovered the traffic jam—at least 500 enemy vehi-cles stalled bumper to bumper around the town. On the afternoon of July 29, squadrons of fighter-bombers attacked for six hours, and American artillery, tanks and tank destroyers joined in. At the end of the attack more than 100 tanks and 250 vehicles lay wrecked or abandoned.

The speed of the Americans' advance actually spread confusion through their own ranks, for, while racing around the countryside, units were getting out of touch and running into one another. In order to keep the momentum going, generals directed traffic at the critical intersections.

Pockmarked with hundreds of craters, the countryside near Saint-Lô bears the scars of saturation bombing for Operation Cobra, the breakout from the Normandy beachhead. On July 25, 1944, some 2,500 Allied planes dropped 4,000 tons of high explosives and bombs on a rectangular area of five and a quarter square miles where the German forces were massed.

Along the West coast of the Cotentin Peninsula, the advance was even more hectic. The two armored divisions leading the VIII Corps were roaring down the road to Avranches. So many enemy soldiers were surrendering that frontline units could not handle them all. "Send them to the rear disarmed without guards" became the order of the day.

Outside Bréhal, 16 miles north of Avranches, the Germans had blocked the road with heavy logs. Four P-47s were called in and tried to blast an opening in the roadblock, but not until the lead tank charged into the barrier and broke through could the American armored column resume its drive to Avranches. As the column closed in on the German Seventh Army command post, three and a half miles north of the town, General Hausser and his staff officers managed to make a hairbreadth escape through a gap between the onrushing vehicles.

Just before nightfall on July 30, troops of the 4th Armored Division crossed the undefended highway bridges over the Sée River and entered Avranches. Behind them a large German vehicular column came rolling down the coastal road from Granville. The vehicles bore red crosses, and the Americans assumed that they carried German wounded. The first few trucks were allowed to cross the bridge into town. Then the German soldiers inside the trucks opened fire. An American tank knocked out the lead vehicles, bringing the column to a halt. The Germans piled out and came toward the bridge with their hands raised in surrender. When the vehicles were inspected, they were found to be loaded with ammunition.

Now a second and larger German column came down the road to Avranches and lobbed a shell into the Americans at the bridge, striking an ammunition truck and setting it on fire. The Americans withdrew, abandoning the bridge and several hundred prisoners. The German column then crossed the bridge; some of the vehicles turned eastward to escape toward Mortain, others bumped into Americans and confused fighting took place.

For the Germans the situation had become, as Kluge called it, a "*Riesensauerei*"—roughly, one hell of a mess. "It's a madhouse here," he reported over the telephone on the morning of July 31 as he tried to describe what was happening. "You can't imagine what it's like. Commanders are completely out of contact."

Kluge was told that higher headquarters wanted to know whether he was setting up defenses somewhere in the rear. He laughed. "Don't they read our dispatches? Haven't they been oriented? They must be living on the moon."

To Kluge it was all too clear that the German left flank along the Cotentin west coast had collapsed. "Someone has got to tell the Führer," he said to his chief of staff, General Günther Blumentritt, without suggesting who was to perform that unpleasant task, "that if the Americans get through at Avranches they will be out of the woods and they'll be able to do what they want."

Kluge pulled in troops from Brittany, ordering them to race to Pontaubault, four miles below Avranches, and to make sure the Americans did not seize the bridge there across the Sélune River. But when the first German elements arrived on the afternoon of July 31, they found the bridge already in American hands. Now there was nothing to stop the Americans from entering Brittany or from turning left and eastward toward the Seine River and Paris.

American armored divisions swept up more than 4,000 prisoners on the 31st; the infantry divisions behind them took an additional 3,000. Of the 28,000 enemy soldiers captured by the First Army in July, 20,000 were bagged during the last six days of the month. One German corps was smashed, another soundly defeated. Hausser's Seventh Army had been wrecked.

Cobra marked a change from slow and costly advances through the hedgerows to electrifying thrusts against defeated, disorganized and demoralized enemy forces. Allied casualties were light and morale soared. The sight of German prisoners "so happy to be captured that all they could do was giggle" dimmed the bitter memories of the costly earlier fighting.

To the Allied soldiers—racing past abandoned and destroyed equipment, past the stench and decay of dead soldiers, horses, cows and pigs—a quick end to the war appeared to be in sight.

CAUGHT IN THE CROSS FIRE

Seeking shelter during an air raid, frightened French women crouch against a wall near Caen, where thousands of civilians perished in the July 1944 fighting.

61

LIBERATION'S HIGH COST

During the summer of 1944, as the war raged through the northwestern corner of France, hundreds of thousands of men, women and children found themselves caught between the opposing forces. While Allied planes and artillery relentlessly bombarded towns and villages where the enemy was hiding, retreating Germans mined, burned, shelled and booby-trapped buildings, roads and bridges. Dazed civilians saw their homes and shops go up in flames, their livestock killed, their wheat fields ground to dust, and their loved ones buried alive beneath mountains of rubble. In Normandy alone nearly 187,000 buildings were damaged, 133,500 were completely demolished and 356,000 people were left homeless.

Thousands of French civilians picked up the few possessions they could carry and set off down the road to get away from the fighting. Those who were lucky rode bicycles, mules and in horse-drawn carts. But most people traveled on foot, pushing wheelbarrows or lugging their belongings on their backs. Often they did not know where they were going or even where they would find their next meal. Some holed up in trenches, tunnels, caves and quarries or slept within the solid walls of châteaux and medieval cathedrals. A few refugees even sought protection inside cemetery vaults and the padded cells of asylums. Others fled to nearby towns, villages or farms, only to be forced to flee again when the bombing and shelling caught up with them or when retreating Germans, searching for quarters, took over their shelters.

So great was the suffering that many Frenchmen were too numb to celebrate when Allied troops finally arrived to liberate them. "Some of the refugees in front of us remained impassive or stupefied in the midst of the gesticulations and cries of other inhabitants of the town," one Norman recalled. "The end of their anguish left them immobile, smiling stupidly, or lifting their arms without conviction. . . . Later, of course, we cried out with joy; but this first minute brought too much emotion. We only wanted to weep in a corner."

Straddling the pavement and the street, a disabled German tank blocks the entranceway of a shop—to the dismay of a French townswoman.

As shells fly overhead, a boy clutches his dog before shattered windows in the Brittany town of Dinard. The town was liberated by Americans in August 1944.

Rendered homeless by bombing and shelling, a little girl in Normandy pulls a cart bearing her doll and other possessions past an enormous pile of rubble.

Displaced civilians, fleeing Pont-l'Abbé on the coast of Brittany, hasten down a battle-scarred street.

Nuns evacuated from Caen receive a helping hand from men of the RAF, who drove them to Bayeux.

THE AGONIES
OF THE DISPOSSESSED

No matter where they went, the refugees could not escape the dangers and privations of war. When they were on the road, they risked stepping on German mines. And Allied planes—firing at almost every moving target—were a constant terror.

Even when the fleeing civilians managed to find a place to stay, they lived in fear and squalor. In Caen one building for 600 was invaded by 6,000; its wine cellar was so crammed that some people slept inside a wine press. Hospitals were jam-packed as well, and they were often without gas, electricity or water.

Food was so scarce that refugees had to scramble to find enough to live on. They butchered the animals killed by shells, salvaged food from wrecked stores and stole German supplies. Sometimes the fighting raged so fiercely they could not even forage for food and had to spend days without any nourishment.

With nowhere to go, a woman and her dog make a home for themselves under a roadside cart. Her farm was turned into a charred ruin by the fighting.

Elderly refugees hobble along a country road. So suddenly did the war come to their village, they barely had time to grab a few possessions before fleeing.

A bewildered girl shows the strain of fleeing from a farm near Argentan. Children were so overwhelmed by events that they often feared their liberators.

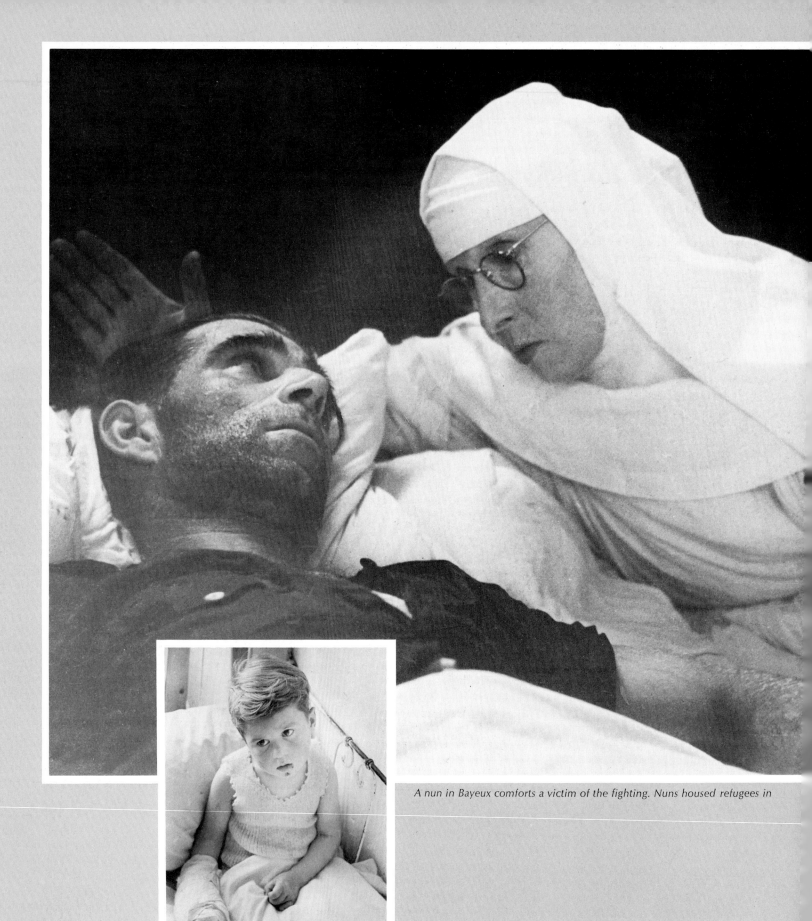

A nun in Bayeux comforts a victim of the fighting. Nuns housed refugees in

An injured boy stares listlessly from a hospital bed.

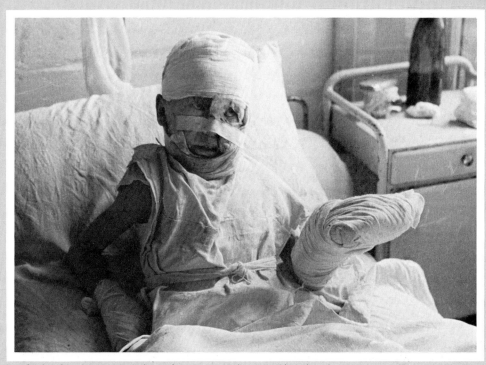

Swathed in bandages, a little boy who was severely injured by a bomb recovers in a hospital at Bayeux.

their churches and took care of the wounded.

Wounded during the battle for Argentan, a priest describes the battle he witnessed from his cathedral.

In a cave once used for brewing beer and
more recently for hiding valuables from
the Germans, a woman cooks for her husband.

Townspeople in a 19th Century fort at Tours
share a meal while American and German
forces battle over the city in August of 1944.

Exhausted civilians catch up on sleep in the
solidly built cloister of the cathedral of Caen,
while the battle rages outside in the streets.

A nun in the hospital ward of the quarry
of Fleury-sur-Orne near Caen watches over a
cauldron of soup while men chop wood.

In a crowded soup kitchen in Dreux, refugees
—most of them from the Paris area—are
served food from captured German stores.

Women taking shelter in a château chat with
a visiting RAF medical officer. The refugees slept
on thick piles of straw covering the floor.

A grieving woman is led away by a neighbor after coming back to her home in Saint-Marcouf and finding the body of her husband, who had been killed by a shell.

A handful of the 20,000 inhabitants of Laval who had fled to nearby farms return with their furniture.

A refugee points out his village on a map to a U.S. officer who was arranging his journey home.

A DESOLATION IN COMING HOME

For the dispossessed there was no greater disappointment after the joy of liberation than to return to their towns and cities and find ruins where their houses had once stood. Bulldozers, shoving the wreckage into mountainous heaps, sometimes made it impossible for previous residents to salvage anything at all of their former lives.

Many rushed to their towns and villages only to discover that the mines had not been cleared away from the streets and that they would have to wait for engineers to remove them. The citizens of Saint-Lô were barred from entering their city for eight weeks. And what they saw when at last they reentered was a complete wasteland. Saint-Lô was not the only town so ravaged. Of Normandy's 3,400 other towns and villages, 586 had to be completely rebuilt following liberation.

In the liberated city of Troyes, French girls tear down a German sign.

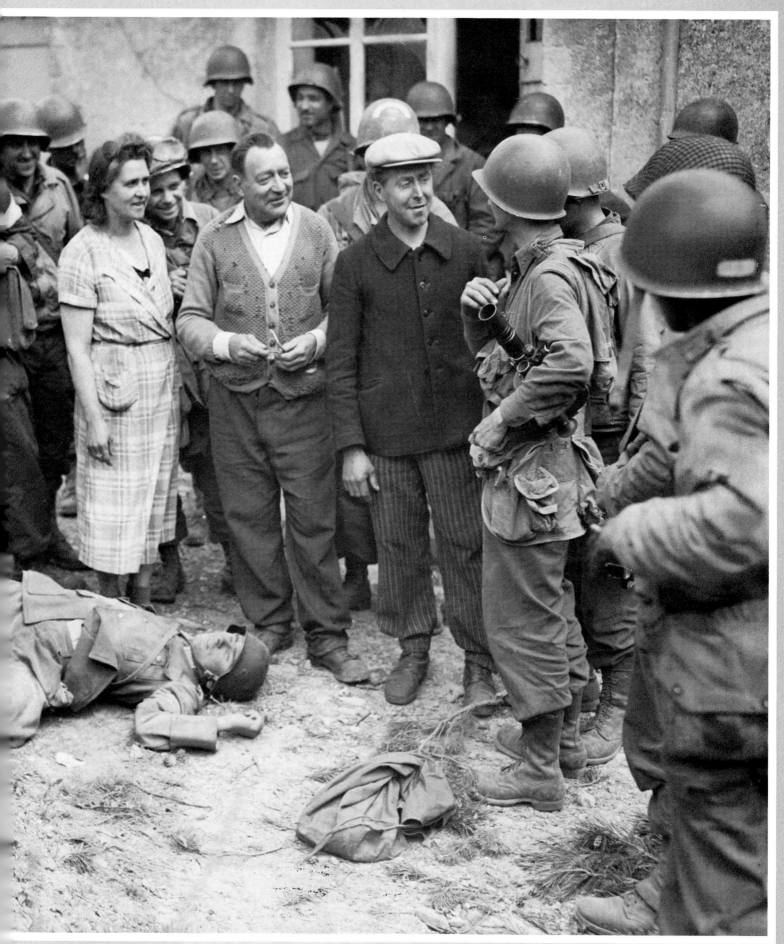

A Normandy villager (in cap) tells Americans why he killed the German on the ground—the German had treated him poorly, forcing him to work for a pittance.

3

Bradley's *Cobra* operation tore a funnel-shaped hole in the German defenses that was 10 miles wide at Avranches and narrowed to a single road and a bridge at Pontaubault. Through this opening poured more and more U.S. troops. The breakout was accompanied by a shift in the high command. Bradley took over the newly formed U.S. Twelfth Army Group, which included the First Army, under the soft-spoken infantry expert Lieut. General Courtney H. Hodges, and the Third Army, under the fiery and aggressive General Patton. Montgomery's command, the Twenty-first Army Group, now consisted solely of British and Canadian troops.

The Third Army swung into action on August 1. The new force included the VIII Corps—already in action under Patton's direction—and the XV Corps. In 48 hours, Patton squeezed two armored divisions through the bottleneck formed by the one road and bridge at Pontaubault. On their heels came other units, wriggling along the highways clogged with debris and dead animals, past wrecked vehicles and stacks of hastily abandoned mines, and through shattered villages and towns.

There was nothing to stop Patton's surge. The only weapon the Germans could bring to bear initially was the badly weakened Luftwaffe. By a superhuman effort, German pilots made the attempt, repeatedly strafing and bombing the tightly packed units moving down the corridor from Avranches. But the German aerial attack failed to halt the massive flow of men and machines from the Cotentin to the verdant, wide-open countryside to the south.

As the American tanks and motorized units burst out of the narrow end of the funnel and charged into Brittany *(map, page 90)*, the whole character of the fighting abruptly changed. "Suddenly the war became fun," war correspondent James Wellard later wrote. "It became exciting, carnivalesque, tremendous. It became victorious and even safe."

Patton and his armored-division commanders were old cavalrymen, brought up in the hell-for-leather tradition by which horsemen rode off in a cloud of dust and chased the enemy over the landscape while higher headquarters wondered where they were. The armored divisions traveled so fast that they frequently ran out of the range of radios, and supply outfits had to struggle to catch up with tanks and motorized infantry and service them on the run. "Within a couple of days we were passing out rations like Santa Claus

THE GERMANS ON THE RUN

on his sleigh, with both giver and receiver on the move," said one armored-division officer. "The trucks were like a band of stagecoaches making a run through Indian country. We got used to keeping the wheels going, disregarding the snipers and hoping we wouldn't get lost or hit."

Patton's orders from Bradley were to overrun the Brittany peninsula and capture some ports to ease the critical supply situation. Two crack armored divisions were assigned this mission. The 6th Armored Division was to dash out to the end of the peninsula and try to grab Brest, Brittany's biggest port; meanwhile, the 4th Armored Division would slice down to the southwest to seal off the peninsula and occupy Lorient and Vannes in the Quiberon Bay area, where the Allies planned to construct a huge supply complex.

The dash across Brittany was a brilliant but bitterly frustrating operation. The 4th Armored raced 40 miles from Pontaubault on the afternoon of August 1 and bumped into a hastily formed German defensive unit outside Rennes. Refusing to be slowed down, the division swept around the western edge of the city in two parallel columns, and the 8th Division's 13th Infantry Regiment came down from Avranches to clear out the Germans. The defenders made a show of force, but seeing the hopelessness of their situation, they prepared to leave, burning everything they could not take with them. As American troops moved into the city and accepted the kisses and wine of the liberated and overjoyed inhabitants, the Germans, in trucks and on foot, moved out the other side. By confining their movements to small back-country roads, they avoided the Americans and escaped to Saint-Nazaire, 65 miles to the south.

Below Rennes, the 4th Armored Division's commander, Major General John S. Wood, halted the division and pondered his next move. Wood's orders from Patton called for him to turn southwest and go streaking down to Lorient. But Wood was tempted to turn east and head for central France, where the main battle with the Germans was sure to occur.

While Wood was considering this alternative, his immediate superior, General Middleton, the capable, meticulous VIII Corps commander, suddenly appeared at Wood's command post. "What's the matter?" Middleton asked facetiously. "Have you lost your division?"

"No," Wood replied. "They"—meaning the Allied high command—"are winning the war the wrong way." The right way, as far as he was concerned, was to turn to the east and outflank the Germans.

Middleton decided on a compromise. He told Wood to go as far as the Vilaine River, southwest of Rennes, and await further orders. But when Patton's chief of staff, Major General Hugh J. Gaffey, learned of this development, he immediately ordered Wood to follow the original plan and proceed to Lorient as fast as possible. The delay cost Wood a whole day and enabled the German garrison at Lorient to get ready to meet and turn back his assault.

The 6th Armored Division also lost a crucial day through a similar mix-up. The division commander, Major General Robert W. Grow, was at a crossroad in Pontaubault on August 1, directing his tanks and troops through the bottleneck at the bridge, when Patton arrived on the scene. Patton said he had bet Montgomery £5 that American troops would be in Brest, 200 miles away, by Saturday night, only four days off, and he ordered Grow to hit the road at once.

Grow asked Patton whether he should worry about anything except Brest and was told no. "Take Brest," Patton said simply. Grow quickly sent his troops racing westward toward the vital port.

Unaware of Patton's order to Grow, Middleton began to fume. He wondered why Grow had bypassed Saint-Malo, a small but valuable port just around the corner from Pontaubault, with scarcely a sidelong glance. Middleton sent Grow a note by messenger ordering him to divert the 6th Armored from the drive toward Brest and to take Saint-Malo.

Bitterly disappointed over being diverted from their exciting dash toward Brest, Grow and his chief of staff were sitting in the sun drinking coffee in a wheat field, discussing plans for an attack toward Saint-Malo, when once again Patton appeared. It was evident at a glance that Grow was not driving toward Brest, and Patton was angry. "What in hell are you doing sitting here?" he shouted in his high-pitched voice. "I thought I told you to go to Brest."

Grow said his advance had been halted.

"On what authority?" Patton demanded.

"Corps order, sir." Grow's chief of staff handed Middleton's message to Patton. "I'll see Middleton," said Patton. "You go ahead where I told you to go."

The halt had cost the 6th Armored 24 hours. With the

help of Frenchmen who pointed out where small groups of Germans were hiding, the troops bypassed potential opposition and reached the outskirts of Brest by Sunday, August 6—too late for Patton to win his bet.

Grow ordered Combat Command B of his division to attack toward Brest. The unit ran into heavy opposition, and Grow decided to see whether he could persuade the Germans to surrender before a major battle developed. He sent an officer and a sergeant in a white-draped jeep to deliver a surrender ultimatum to the German commander, Colonel Hans von der Mosel, at Brest.

Mosel refused to surrender, and the 6th Armored prepared to attack the city. The next day, the Brest defenders were reinforced by the German 2nd Parachute Division under Lieut. General Herman B. Ramcke, who replaced Mosel as fortress commander. Meanwhile, another German reinforcement unit blundered into the rear of the 6th Armored. This outfit turned out to be the better part of an infantry division sent from Morlaix, near Brittany's north coast. A confused and furious battle erupted, and all but a few of the infantrymen were prevented from reaching Brest.

The 6th Armored now turned again to attack the city. The Germans, under orders from Hitler to deny the port to the Allies at all cost, resisted fiercely. Elements of the 8th Infantry Division were brought up to help out. It would be six weeks before Brest fell, and the 6th Armored would be relieved and two divisions called in to join the 8th Division before the Germans finally yielded. As for the port, the Germans left it completely wrecked.

Meanwhile, at the base of the Brittany peninsula, infantrymen of the 83rd Division had launched an attack on Saint-Malo, and a bitter fight had developed. The commander of the heavily fortified town, Colonel Andreas von Aulock, promised Kluge, the Army Group B commander, to make it "another Stalingrad."

Asked by the French inhabitants to spare the historic port town—home of the 16th Century explorer Jacques Cartier—Aulock referred the request to Hitler. Hitler replied that in warfare there was no such thing as a historic city. "You will fight to the last man," he said. Aulock ordered all civilians to evacuate the town. A long and pathetic parade of men, women and children carrying suitcases and pushing carts and baby carriages came over into the American lines.

The Germans occupied strong defensive positions in a fortified complex covering Saint-Malo and the surrounding area. The defenses were dominated by a heavily reinforced 18th Century fort known as the Citadel, which was dug into a rocky promontory near the harbor. German coastal batteries on the nearby island of Cézembre opened fire on the Americans on the outskirts of town, and a shell knocked the spire off the Saint-Malo cathedral. Fires broke out; Saint-Malo burned for more than a week, and demolitions set by the Germans destroyed the port, quays, locks, breakwaters and harbor machinery.

As troops of the 83rd Division moved in, they faced belts of double-apron barbed wire, large minefields, rows of steel gates, antitank obstacles, underground pillboxes, iron rail fences and concrete bunkers. Bullets and shell fragments were so heavy in the town's streets that engineers dynamited passageways for the infantry to advance from house to house. Ten artillery battalions, including 8-inch guns and 240mm howitzers, joined with tank destroyers and tanks to pound German strong points. Medium bombers attacked Aulock's Citadel headquarters but had little effect on the underground installations.

The Americans captured a German chaplain and prevailed upon him to try to persuade Aulock to give up. The chaplain was permitted by the Germans to visit their commander, but he made no headway. "A German soldier does not surrender," Aulock said.

With the failure of the chaplain's peacemaking efforts, the mayor of the neighboring village of Saint-Servan-sur-Mer came forward with the information that he knew a French woman who had been on intimate terms with Aulock. The woman was now in Allied territory, and the mayor suggested that she make a telephone call to the German colonel. A telephone line from Saint-Servan to the Citadel was still in service, and a call was duly placed. But Aulock, unmoved by romantic considerations, sent word that he was too busy to come to the phone.

Deep inside the Citadel, Aulock told his troops: "Anyone deserting or surrendering is a common dog." For more than a week, the bombardments and attacks went on. On August 11, medium bombers dropped 1,000-pound bombs on the Citadel. Then troops of the 83rd attacked with Bangalore torpedoes and flamethrowers; demolition charges, mortar

Along the bomb-ravaged road between Caen and Falaise, a Canadian casualty is tended by a medic while a German tank burns only a few yards away. In August 1944, fighting raged along the 21-mile-long road from Caen to Falaise for nine days as the Canadian First Army battered its way through the tough German defenses. The Canadian advance—which produced more than 2,000 casualties—was, in General Eisenhower's eyes, a remarkable achievement. "Ten feet gained on the Caen sector," the Supreme Commander said, "was equivalent to a mile elsewhere."

and artillery fire were used, all to no avail. On the 13th, tank destroyers, artillery and medium bombers struck; two days later, following another medium-bomber attack, infantry assault teams were driven off by machine-gun fire. Finally, on August 17, just before planes were to attack with napalm, a white flag was raised over the Citadel.

The Brittany campaign had liberated thousands of square miles and thousands of joyous Frenchmen, but it failed to secure the supply ports that were its main objective. With troops and supplies piling up in England for delivery to Allied forces on the Continent, the failure to capture even a single port intact was a major frustration. For the time being, however, this concern was obscured by momentous developments to the east.

On August 5 the Third Army's XV Corps, under Major General Wade H. Haislip, had emerged from the bottleneck at Pontaubault and headed southeast for Mayenne and Laval. The XV Corps' drive was part of a plan devised by

General Montgomery as U.S. troops were breaking out of Normandy. The operation's success confronted the Germans with two poor alternatives. They could pull troops from the Caen sector to plug the gap at Avranches or they could go on making an all-out defense in the Caen area. If they chose to weaken the Caen defenses, they would give the British and Canadians a chance to break through in that sector, and if they decided to keep their troops there, they would face being cut off by the XV Corps' swing eastward.

In less than half a day, the XV Corps covered 30 miles, with the Germans nowhere in sight. Haislip's tanks pushed 45 miles more to Le Mans within the next three and a half days. The American troops were now 85 miles southeast of Avranches and threatening the two German armies west of the Seine with encirclement.

Hitler still clung to the notion that the situation could be stabilized. He believed that Kluge could counterattack, regain Avranches and restore the old Normandy front. Then the static warfare that had hemmed in the Allies and kept

them confined to a relatively small area through June and most of July could be renewed, and the Americans who had already passed through the bottleneck at Pontaubault would be cut off and could be dealt with in good time.

Hitler ordered Kluge to attack to the west through Mortain to reach the coast at Avranches, thereby separating the U.S. First and Third Armies, and then to turn north and throw the Allies into the sea. The Führer even decided to release some of his carefully hoarded divisions from the Pas-de-Calais and bring additional units up from southern France for the attack.

By August 6, four panzer divisions had been assembled and were ready to strike toward Avranches. "The decision in the Battle of France depends on the success of the attack," the Führer announced in an order of the day. The Germans, he said, had "a unique opportunity, which will never return, to drive into an extremely exposed enemy area and thereby change the situation completely."

Standing directly in the path of the Germans was the American 30th Infantry Division, a veteran outfit. Its men had spent a grueling 49 days fighting in the hedgerows and had been sent to a rest area at Tessy-sur-Vire after *Cobra*. Now they had moved into the Mortain area to relieve the 1st Division, which had been ordered southward to protect the flank of Haislip's rapidly advancing XV Corps. The 30th Division had barely taken over its new sector when a warning message, based on intercepts of German radio traffic deciphered by the British code-breaking system, *Ultra*, arrived from VII Corps headquarters. "Enemy counterattack

expected vicinity Mortain . . . within twelve hours." Twenty minutes later, around midnight, the Germans struck.

The first intimation the 30th Division troops had that the attack was under way came from the rumble of tanks moving north of the town. The motors did not sound like those of American tanks. Artillery battalions quickly began to fire at the noises in the darkness at a range of 5,000 yards, which was soon reduced to 1,000.

One of the chief German objectives was Hill 317, just east of Mortain, which was the key to the entire area because of the excellent observation it afforded. The hill was held by the 2nd Battalion of the 120th Infantry Regiment.

When daylight broke on August 7, the troops on the hill discovered that the Germans had surrounded them. By 11 o'clock the Americans were in need of food, medical supplies and ammunition. Yet they were cut off and would have to wait several days before being rescued. They came to be known as the "Lost Battalion."

North of Mortain the panzers penetrated seven miles, but fearful of Allied air power, they halted at daybreak, pulled off the road and took cover under camouflage nets. At Saint-Barthélemy, 50 tanks accompanied by infantry overran two companies of the 30th Division's 117th Regiment. To the south of Mortain, in the Romagny area, panzers came within 250 yards of a regimental command post.

On the road to Avranches, the Germans penetrated four miles before being stopped by P-47s and rocket-firing Typhoons. The attackers were perilously close to breaking through the 30th Division—so close that General Hobbs, the division commander, could later say, "with a heavy onion breath the Germans would have achieved their objective." General Bradley immediately ordered six divisions brought into the area to reinforce the 30th and alerted still another division for possible commitment.

The Germans had been told by their weather forecasters to expect a heavy fog on the morning of August 7, and they were counting on it to conceal their movements. But the day dawned bright and clear, and they were forced by overwhelming Allied air power to hide in the forests under camouflage nets. Roaring overhead by the hundreds, the Allied fighter-bombers bombed and strafed concentrations of vehicles. "The activities of the fighter-bombers are

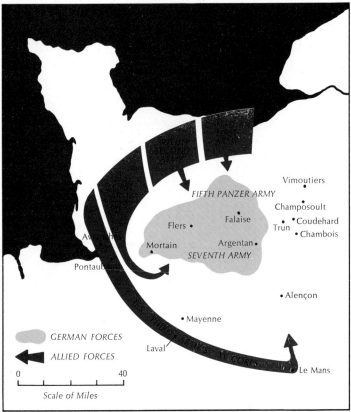

GERMAN FORCES

ALLIED FORCES

0   40

Scale of Miles

Following the breakout from the Normandy hedgerow country at the beginning of August 1944, troops of the U.S. Third Army dashed 85 miles to the southeast from Avranches. Meanwhile, the Canadian First Army, the British Second Army and the American First Army pressed in on the Germans from the north and west. The combined actions of these three armies threatened the German Fifth Panzer and Seventh Armies with encirclement, but Hitler, who was determined to drive a wedge between the American forces, ordered his Seventh Army to counterattack to the west through Mortain toward Avranches. The attack succeeded only in making the Germans more vulnerable to the threatened encirclement.

almost unbearable," Lieut. General Hans von Funck, the 47th Panzer Corps' commander, reported to Kluge at Army Group B. "We could do nothing against them, we could make no further progress," said Major General Heinrich von Lüttwitz, the 2nd Panzer Division's commander.

Clearly, the counterattack had failed. On August 8 the Canadians launched an attack down the Caen-Falaise road spearheaded by 600 tanks. The assault penetrated the German defenses for three miles and raised the specter of a linkup with Haislip's forces in the south that would completely cut off the Germans. Kluge thought it madness to go on sticking his head deeper into the noose at Mortain. He must pull out now or face the possibility that all of Army Group B would be destroyed.

The fighting continued inconclusively around Mortain throughout August 8. The positions remained largely unchanged, and on August 9 Hitler ordered a stronger attack toward Avranches. His officers in the field were appalled. The Seventh Army chief of staff, Brigadier General Rudolph-Christoph Gersdorff, later called the order "the apex of conduct of a command ignorant of front line conditions, taking upon itself the right to judge the situation from East Prussia." The Seventh Army commander, General Hausser, said bitterly: "This will be the death blow not only to the Seventh Army but to the entire Wehrmacht in the West."

Meanwhile, the embattled Lost Battalion was still holding out under intense pressure. The Germans had tried to dislodge the Americans by assault, but the slopes were too steep and the defensive fire too strong. Twice the Germans sent parties up the hill with white flags to demand surrender, and twice the Americans refused.

Two light planes tried to drop supplies to the men by parachute, but German antiaircraft fire chased them away. Several C-47 cargo planes then dropped food and ammunition. Using shells normally employed to scatter propaganda leaflets to the enemy, artillery units fired bandages, adhesive tape and morphine to the beleaguered troops. French civilians living in the single farmhouse on the hill helped out by sharing their few chickens, potatoes and cabbages.

Not until August 11—with the threat to their rear growing by the hour—did the Germans decide to break off the Mortain attack and withdraw from around the hill. The Americans had suffered 300 casualties, but 370 survivors walked down the hill. The men had held off the Germans for five days, and their observations of enemy movements had made it possible for Allied planes and guns to exact a heavy toll of enemy troops and weapons, including almost 100 tanks.

Meanwhile, Bradley had ordered Haislip to turn north after capturing Le Mans (map, opposite), and his tanks were now streaking toward Alençon. On August 12 they went roaring past the town, and the next day they came within sight of Argentan. The corps commander was sure he could go all the way to Falaise and link up with the Canadians pushing toward Falaise from the north; together they could prevent the escape of the two German armies in Normandy.

But then, in one of the most controversial orders of the War, General Bradley told Haislip to halt where he was. All sorts of explanations were later advanced for the failure to close the gap. Bradley said he wanted to avoid a head-on collision between Americans and Canadians and a "calamitous battle between friends." He pointed out that Allied planes had dropped time bombs in the gap—land mines that were set to explode where Haislip's men would pass. Ultra intercepts indicated that the Germans might attack Haislip from the rear; Bradley was therefore concerned lest the XV Corps get separated too widely from the First Army to the west, thus allowing space for the Germans to get through. He also feared that Haislip's corps might cross the boundary separating Montgomery's Twenty-first Army Group from Bradley's Twelfth Army Group. It was necessary, Bradley felt, to await Montgomery's invitation to penetrate farther into the zone reserved for British-Canadian operations. No such invitation was forthcoming.

Bradley went on to make the point that the German divisions inside the unclosed pocket were about to stampede through the Argentan-Falaise gap and might trample any thin line of American troops that could be established there. He preferred, he said, "a solid shoulder at Argentan to a broken neck at Falaise."

Montgomery's failure to invite Bradley into his zone may have stemmed from the fact that the Canadians were already preparing to resume their attack from the north toward Falaise. The attack was launched on August 14. The way was opened by a massive air bombardment at night.

The Canadians then moved forward in three waves—160 tanks in the first wave, 90 in the second and motorized infantry in the third.

Neil Stewart, a shell loader in a Sherman tank under the command of a man named Forsyth, later recalled the attack in all of its terrible detail. "We charged down a hill in the center of the mass of tanks. There was a small stream at the foot of the hill which had apparently escaped notice on the maps. Tanks circled around frantically searching for a crossing place. After some short delay the tanks and other vehicles were able to cross, but our formations had been seriously disrupted. . . .

"Our squadron had spread out widely. Close control had been lost at the crossing of the creek, and tanks simply roared toward the sun. I could see several hit and burning, and a number of wrecked German antitank guns. But we could not yet see any German tanks. Sandy Forsyth took us, along with a number of other tanks, along the left side of the attack line and into a large wheat field. We shot up some German infantry and a frantic '88' crew trying to get their gun into action in our direction. We could hear heavy artillery shells exploding to our left front, as the Canadian and British guns hammered the German positions.

"About one hour after the charge started, our luck changed. I saw two or three tanks burning very close to us. Crews still alive were scrambling out and flopping down into the wheat to hide from fire from woods to our left. Then a gush of blood from the open hatches of our turret marked the end of Sandy Forsyth. An armour-piercing shot had hit him squarely in the face. His large body, decapitated as if by a great cleaver, slumped to the turret floor amid the spent shell casings."

Almost at once the tank shuddered and stopped. "Smoke poured in from the engine and a tongue of flame leaped along the drive shaft below us. We had taken a shell in the engine compartment. I can still remember our gunner, Bill Brown, leaning back into the turret to help me get out. I had to crawl under the master gun, over Sandy's remains, and out the hatch." Stewart and the other tankers lay in the wheat field until after dark and then made it safely back to their own lines.

The attack brought the Canadians within three miles of Falaise. The Germans were now confined to a pocket 40 miles long and 13 miles wide shaped like a giant horseshoe, with a 25-mile opening in the east. The Canadians held the northern prong. Beyond them to the west, the British were strung out to the town of Flers, and still farther on, the U.S. First Army was deployed around the curving part in the west. Haislip's XV Corps held the southern prong. The gap between the Canadians near Falaise and the Americans south of Argentan was beginning to narrow. Most of the ground inside the pocket lay within the range of Allied artillery, and all of it was vulnerable to air attacks.

The Germans could scarcely move without being fired on; Eisenhower later described the pocket as "one of the greatest killing grounds of any of the war areas." The official U.S. Army report later noted that "the carnage wrought during the final days as artillery of the two Allied Armies and the massed air forces pounded the ever-shrinking pocket was perhaps the greatest of the war. The roads and fields were littered with thousands of enemy dead and wounded, wrecked and burning vehicles, smashed artillery pieces, carts laden with the loot of France overturned and smoldering, dead horses and cattle swelling in the summer's heat."

On August 15, Kluge entered the pocket to size up the situation and determine a course of action for the Germans. After visiting the headquarters of General Josef "Sepp" Dietrich's Fifth Panzer Army, the field marshal and his small party suddenly disappeared. A frantic search was organized.

When Hitler learned of Kluge's disappearance, he was sure the field marshal was trying to make contact with the Allies to arrange the surrender of the German forces in the West. That evening, however, Kluge returned to Dietrich's headquarters and explained that a plane had strafed his vehicle and knocked out his radio. Allied aircraft had forced him and his small party to remain in a ditch all day long.

Hitler now wanted Kluge to attack, to broaden the gap between the Canadians and the Americans. On August 16, however, Kluge recommended to Hitler that the troops be immediately withdrawn from the pocket. "No matter how many orders are issued," Kluge said, "the troops cannot, are not able to, are not strong enough to defeat the enemy. It would be a fateful error to succumb to a hope that cannot be fulfilled."

That afternoon, although Hitler's permission had not ar-

Dead horses and shattered carts of a German transport column litter a ravine after the Allies trapped some 60,000 Germans in the Argentan-Falaise pocket in August of 1944. So great was the devastation that one Allied officer said, "it was as if an avenging angel had swept the area bent on destroying all things German." More than 220 tanks, 860 artillery pieces, 130 antiaircraft guns and 7,130 vehicles were destroyed or damaged, and nearly 2,000 horses and 10,000 Germans were killed. The anguish of the soldiers who lived through the ordeal is reflected in the dazed expression on the face of the paratrooper shown at far right.

rived, Kluge ordered the troops to start withdrawing to the east by night. Several nights would be needed to get all of the troops out—if the sides of the pocket could be prevented from closing in and the exit held open. The shoulders of the gap were crucial. If the Germans were to escape, Kluge had to prevent the Americans at Argentan and the Canadians at Falaise from advancing.

The Canadians entered Falaise on August 16, and the gap was now only 20 miles wide. Montgomery proposed to Bradley that the Canadians and Americans close the pocket near the villages of Trun and Chambois, to the northeast of Argentan. If this could be done, four panzer corps, a parachute corps and two regular corps—at least 100,000 men—would be trapped.

Bradley was not sure that the Americans could advance to Chambois. He had already sent two of Haislip's four divisions eastward toward the Seine with the intention of cutting the Germans off farther to the east. No sooner had the two divisions departed Argentan than the Germans launched heavy attacks to keep their escape route open.

On the night of August 16, the Germans started their movement out of the pocket. Though in dire danger, they did not panic. Instead, they marched out in good order and in accordance with the rigid timetable Kluge had ordered established for them.

On August 17 the Canadians churned forward to within two miles of Trun. The Germans holding the northern shoulder were fighting hard, but their escape route was becoming more and more constricted. And at the southern shoulder, they were struggling to drive the Americans off

the Bourg–Saint-Léonard ridge. The battle seesawed, with the Germans first gaining the high ground, then losing it.

By this point, Hitler had decided to relieve Kluge. On July 20 there had been an attempt on Hitler's life; the Führer had barely escaped being killed by a bomb that exploded at his headquarters in East Prussia. A number of Army officers had been involved in the attempt, and there were allegations that Kluge had been one of them. In addition, Hitler remained convinced that Kluge had tried to surrender to the Allies when he disappeared in the pocket. Even more to the point, Hitler felt Kluge was to blame for the disaster now confronting the Germans in France.

In little more than two weeks, the Western Front had disintegrated. Where once there had been carefully delineated sectors and orderly troop dispositions, chaos now prevailed. Two German armies were on the brink of total destruction.

On the afternoon of August 17, Field Marshal Walter Model arrived from the Eastern Front to take over Kluge's command. Model was known as the Führer's fireman because of his demonstrated ability to overcome crises. But what he faced in Normandy was perhaps beyond saving. Before officially assuming command, he familiarized himself with the situation and observed the German troop movement eastward. Despite road congestion and Allied artillery fire, the withdrawal was still orderly. But gasoline was running so low that some tanks and self-propelled guns had to be destroyed or abandoned. By now some divisions were reduced to battalion size.

On the afternoon of the 18th, Model reported to Hitler

that the troops in the pocket were so exhausted they could no longer be expected to fight. The best that could be hoped for was to try to get them out of the pocket. With that in mind, Model formed the remnants of 10 divisions into four task forces.

The Canadians took Trun that day, and the Americans almost reached Chambois. The gap was now narrowed to less than 10 miles, and the Germans were fighting bitterly to keep it open.

Model officially assumed command of Army Group B at midnight, August 18, and Kluge left for Germany by car. Before departing, he wrote a letter to Hitler. Then, on the road to Metz, he took his life by swallowing potassium cyanide. Hitler would later claim that Kluge's letter included an admission of guilt for the defeat in the West, but what Kluge really wrote was a plea to the Führer to end the War.

"When you receive these lines," he said, "I shall be no more. I cannot bear the accusation that I sealed the fate of the West by taking wrong measures. I have been relieved of command. The evident reason is the failure of the armored units in their push to Avranches and the consequent impossibility of closing the gap to the sea. That order had been *completely* out of the question. It presupposed a state of affairs that did not exist. Both Rommel and I, and probably all the leaders here in the West, who have experienced the struggle with the English and Americans and their wealth in matériel, foresaw the development that has now appeared. Our views were *not* dictated by pessimism but by sober recognition of the facts.

"Should the new weapons in which you place so much hope . . . not bring success—then, my Führer, make up your mind to end the war. The German people have suffered so unspeakably that it is time to bring the horror to a close.

"I have steadfastly stood in awe of your greatness, your bearing in this gigantic struggle, and your iron will. If fate is stronger than your will and your genius, that is destiny. You have made an honorable and tremendous fight. History will testify this for you. Show now that greatness that will be necessary if it comes to the point of ending a struggle which has become hopeless."

That night the pocket was only six miles deep and seven miles wide. Under savage artillery fire, remnants of the German divisions, improvised task forces, stragglers and service units moved wearily along roads and fields clogged with the wreckage of vehicles, dead soldiers and horses. When the morning mist rose on August 19, the gap remained barely open. The Germans still coming through it were pounded mercilessly by Allied aircraft.

Just east of Trun and Chambois, 1,500 Polish troops, aided by 80 tanks, held a ridge called Mont Ormel. From this position, the Poles fired their artillery at a German column moving bumper to bumper along the Chambois-Vimoutiers highway. Dense smoke from burning vehicles blackened the sky. The air was filled with the stench of death and burned flesh. And everywhere dead Germans and destroyed equipment littered the ground.

The German 3rd Parachute Division was one of the last units to leave the pocket during the night of August 19. The exodus was led by Lieut. General Eugen Meindl, commander of the 2nd Parachute Corps. Meindl made his plans and briefed unit commanders and noncommissioned officers. The men slept a few hours and ate what little food they had. Their weariness seemed to have vanished. They believed they had a good chance of getting out. They were buoyed by rumors that Model had brought two divisions across the Seine and was planning to attack toward the mouth of the pocket on the following morning.

At 10:30 p.m., the paratroopers moved out in two columns. Forty-five minutes later they were fired on by a tank near the Trun-Argentan highway. Not long afterward they ran into some Allied strong points, and the columns were scattered. Meindl reached the Dives River around midnight with a small command group and about 20 paratroopers. After searching for a crossing site, he found a ford where the water was only five feet deep, but the riverbank on the opposite side was covered with dense underbrush, and above the bank Meindl could make out the silhouettes of three Allied tanks.

Covered by the sound of small-arms and artillery fire, Meindl and his task force crossed the river and circled around the hill crowned by the tanks. Almost immediately they ran into machine-gun fire from a concealed tank 30 yards away. The paratroopers crawled past the tanks. Flares suddenly illuminated the area, forcing them to freeze to the ground. Reduced to about 15 men, the little group slowly worked its way out of the field by creeping along a furrow and then headed eastward.

On the morning of August 20, the whole plain was covered with German columns and small groups moving along the roads and over the countryside. The Poles on Mont Ormel now had a choice of moving targets to fire at. Suddenly remnants of two German divisions appeared out of the east and engaged the Poles, keeping them from disrupting further the German troop movements.

Late that afternoon, Meindl organized a column of vehicles, loaded each vehicle with wounded soldiers and marked the sides with Red Cross flags. He halted all traffic for a quarter of an hour, then ordered the vehicles to move out in close formation. Allied troops in the area held their fire. "Not a shot was fired on the column," Meindl later said, "and I can openly acknowledge the feeling of gratitude to the chivalrous enemy." Half an hour after the vehicles had disappeared, Allied artillery fire started pounding the Germans once again.

In the early hours of August 21, while rain kept the Allied planes grounded, Meindl assembled his troops on a road near Coudehard and sent them eastward. Within two hours, they were inside the lines of the 2nd SS Panzer Division near Champosoult.

The Germans who still remained in the pocket were caught in what was described by General Lüttwitz as a "hurricane" of Allied fire. In the midst of this storm, Volkswagens, carts, trucks, tanks, vehicles and weapons went flying through the air, disintegrating in flashes of fire and puffs of smoke. Flames leaped skyward from burning gasoline tanks. Ammunition exploded. Horses ran about crazed with terror. Congestion at a bridge at the Dives produced a nightmarish scene, later described by Lüttwitz: the bodies of dead men, horses, vehicles and other equipment had been "hurled from the bridge into the river to form there a gruesome tangled mass."

A Canadian soldier named Duncan Kyle, who served at Argentan-Falaise, later recalled: "Germans charred coalblack, looking like blackened tree trunks, lay beside smoking vehicles. One didn't realize that the obscene mess was human until it was poked at. I remember wishing that the Germans didn't have to use so many horses. Seeing all those dead animals on their backs, their legs pointing at God's sky like accusing fingers, their bellies bloated, some ripped open. . . . That really bothered me."

The defeat was the worst suffered by the Germans since an entire army of 275,000 Axis soldiers surrendered to Allied forces at the conclusion of the Tunisian campaign in May 1943. In the Argentan-Falaise pocket, an estimated 10,000 men were killed and 50,000 captured, and approximately 220 tanks were destroyed.

No one knew exactly how many men had escaped. Model reported that 40 to 50 per cent of the trapped forces made it, but his estimate was surely high. The six or seven panzer divisions that managed to make their way out of the pocket were shattered remnants totaling no more than 2,000 men, 62 tanks and 26 artillery pieces. The best estimate of the number of troops who escaped was 40,000. Of vital importance to the Germans was the fact that the total included an army commander, four corps commanders (Meindl was one of them), 12 division commanders. These critically needed combat leaders and their staffs would later fight again.

Even for those who got out of the pocket the ordeal was not over. They were threatened by another encircling arm, formed by the two divisions of the XV Corps that had left Argentan on August 15 on Bradley's orders to drive to the Seine. On August 19 the divisions had reached the river near Mantes-Gassicourt, barely 30 miles downstream from Paris. The 5th Armored Division continued down the left bank, pushing the Germans toward the mouth of the river where the current is strong, the banks far apart and the water difficult to cross.

On the night of August 19, as a torrential rain was falling, soldiers of the U.S. 79th Division walked single file across a narrow dam in the Seine, each man touching the one ahead to keep from falling into the river. At daybreak others paddled across. A treadway bridge was installed, and by nightfall of August 20 a substantial American force was across the Seine and ready to drive toward Germany.

As British, Canadian and American units surged triumphantly eastward, they left a large part of northwestern France liberated behind them. The German forces in the Normandy beachhead had been eliminated.

AN AMERICAN BLITZKRIEG

Pausing at Orleans, France, on August 17, 1944, American officers watch through field glasses as an M10 tank destroyer fires across the Loire at a German tank.

GENERAL PATTON'S SPECTACULAR DRIVE

When Lieut. General George S. Patton Jr. hurled his newly activated Third Army southward from Normandy through the gap at Avranches on the first day of August, 1944, he unleashed an American blitzkrieg that would take its place among the War's most spectacular campaigns. While the VIII Corps raced westward 200 miles to reach the coveted port of Brest in six days, tanks of the XV Corps wheeled to the southeast, then turned north to help block the escape of more than 60,000 Germans in the Argentan-Falaise pocket. Meanwhile, the XX Corps and the XII Corps swung farther south for parallel sweeps along the Loire River. "The whole Western Front has been ripped open," German Field Marshal Günther von Kluge frantically radioed Hitler as his shattered Seventh Army reeled back across the Seine.

Patton was possessed with what General Dwight D. Eisenhower termed "an extraordinary and ruthless driving power." The flamboyant general believed that destiny had chosen him to be a great warrior. He customarily wore a lacquered helmet liner and ivory-handled pistols and practiced making ferocious faces in the mirror. He sought to emulate Napoleon's military successes in his campaigns and studied the military feats of Alexander the Great, Julius Caesar and William Tecumseh Sherman. He lived by three maxims: "An ounce of sweat is worth a gallon of blood," "Attack! Attack! Attack!" and Stonewall Jackson's "Never take counsel of your fears."

The maxims paid off. Patton pushed his armored spearheads up to 70 miles a day, bypassed centers of resistance and ordered his men to "continue until gasoline is exhausted, then proceed on foot." By the end of August the Third Army had swept eastward 400 miles to Verdun and had reached the Meuse River, liberating almost 50,000 square miles of territory in the process.

Patton had hoped to reach the Rhine by the first week of September, before enemy forces had time to regroup. From there, he could bring the blitzkrieg home to Berlin. But then something happened over which he had no control: he ran out of gas.

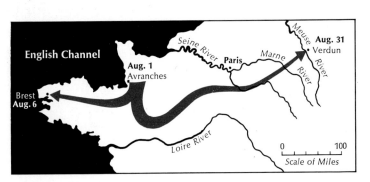

An MP waves on a convoy laden with supplies. By August 31 the Third Army drive (below) had reached Brest in the west and Verdun in the east.

With his top subordinates and his English bull terrier Willie, Third Army commander George S. Patton Jr. waits for Eisenhower to show up for a meeting.

Townspeople of Saint-Brieuc in Brittany welcome the crew of a *Third Army* tank, still bearing steel blades for slicing through Normandy hedgerows.

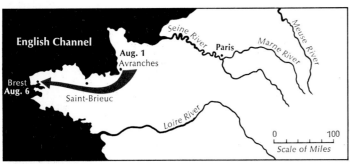

With orders from Patton to take Brest—200 miles away—the VIII Corps drove south from Avranches and west across Brittany in less than a week.

A U.S. infantryman takes aim at a sniper during street fighting in Saint-Malo on August 8. The infantry followed up the tanks and cleared out cities and towns.

Third Army troops move into Angers on the 10th of August after a successful attack that netted 2,000 prisoners. From Angers the Third Army swept east along

A low wall lends cover as troops of the 79th Division ferret out snipers left in Laval by the Germans, who also set up roadblocks and wrecked bridges.

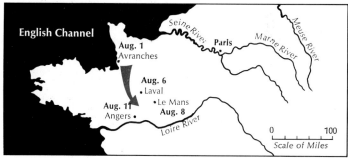

Patton ordered eastward his three corps not committed in Brittany; in eight days the Third Army had taken Le Mans, almost halfway to Paris.

the north bank of the Loire River—a flank that eventually extended 485 miles.

The smoke of battle hangs low over a highway as a Third Army tank on its way into Dreux, just west of Paris, rolls past wrecked German armor.

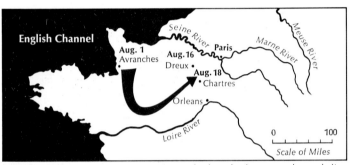

By the middle of August, Patton's forces had pushed to a north-south line cutting through Chartres, bringing them within 20 miles of the Seine River.

Citizens of Chartres celebrate liberation as Major General Lindsay M. Silvester,

commander of the XX Corps' 7th Armored Division, waves from his armored car on August 16. The Germans held out in parts of the town for two more days.

Accompanied by infantry, a XX Corps tank rolls across the French countryside near Montereau on August 25, 1944. Of Patton's nine divisions, six were infantry.

With German machine-gun fire spraying the water around them, U.S. Army engineers ferry a vehicle on a pontoon across the Seine at Montereau.

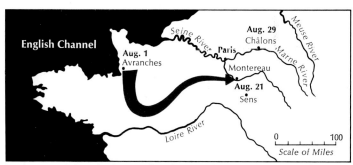

By August 25 the Third Army had bypassed Paris and crossed the Seine River. The objective was now the German border, only 200 miles away.

RUNNING OUT OF GAS WITH VICTORY IN THE AIR

The Third Army's lightning advance consumed between 500,000 and 600,000 gallons of gasoline every 50 miles. As the army raced eastward, supply lines became stretched to the breaking point.

Special convoys were organized, but the transport trucks used more than 300,000 gallons of gas a day. Patton arranged for Air Transport Command C-47s to shuttle supplies—more than 500 tons on a single day. Enemy supplies helped—100,000 gallons of gas found at Châlons-sur-Marne and 37 carloads of gas and oil at Sens. And Patton pretended not to notice when his men raided other Allied units for fuel.

As August drew to a close, however, most of Patton's gasoline was diverted to the First Army in the north. On August 31 gas delivery ended, and the Third Army ground to a halt. In the first week of September it would start again—but, as Patton angrily pointed out, only after the enemy had been given time to gather its forces.

While an amused Frenchman looks on, the crew of a Third Army half-track consumes Army rations and some French bread in the streets of Verdun.

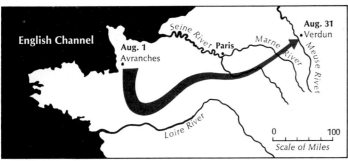

Undaunted by dwindling supplies of gasoline, the Third Army rolled on to Verdun and the Meuse before being halted abruptly by empty gas tanks.

Out of gasoline, dejected Third Army soldiers rest beside their half-track at the foot of a gigantic Verdun memorial to soldiers who died during World War I.

During the weeks following D-Day in Normandy, before the Allied armies broke out of their embattled beachhead, their commanders often looked wistfully south to Italy and North Africa, where U.S., Free French and British forces were hastily making preparations to invade France's Mediterranean coast. This operation, code-named *Anvil,* was to be a mighty assault on the scale of the Normandy and Sicily landings: an armada of 880 ships, preceded and protected by 2,000 bombers and fighter planes, would on the first day put ashore some 94,000 troops (and 367,000 within one month), whose mission was to drive due north up the Rhone River Valley with all possible speed. At the very least, the bold thrust would relieve German pressure on the Normandy beachhead. If all went as planned, the forces from Normandy and from southern France would complete the liberation of France by autumn.

But *Anvil*'s background did not inspire confidence in its future. Dogged by supply shortages, and by plain bad luck, the operation had repeatedly been delayed and altered. Worse, there had been bitter staff-level arguments over the strategic merits of the invasion—arguments that put terrible strains on relations between *Anvil*'s American backers and its British opponents. Worst of all, the opposition was led by a man so powerful, so eloquent and so stubborn that the invasion might well be scrubbed before the troops boarded their ships for southern France. That man was Prime Minister Winston Churchill.

The idea of invading southern France was first suggested officially in August 1943, four months after planning for the Normandy invasion had begun. The Combined Chiefs of Staff proposed the operation as a small-scale diversion to help the Normandy assault: a modest force would land in the south at the same time Normandy was invaded, thereby pinning down German units that might otherwise reinforce the defenders up north. However, when the Big Three met in November at Teheran, Stalin urged that *Anvil* be increased to a large-scale diversion, and President Roosevelt supported him. Churchill, outvoted, agreed to the change. But soon he began working against the operation through the British Chiefs of Staff, for it was obvious that *Anvil*'s added strength would have to be drawn from the Allied armies campaigning in Italy, stripping them of the surplus

4

SOUTHERN FRANCE'S D-DAY

manpower needed to mount one of his own pet strategies.

Basically, Churchill wanted to use those troops to open an entirely new major theater in Europe—one that would further Britain's interests in the eastern Mediterranean. He argued for a strong Allied drive north from Italy into Yugoslavia through the Alpine pass known as the Ljubljana Gap—"that gap," said Eisenhower, "whose name I can't even pronounce." These forces, perhaps with aid from amphibious landings at the head of the Adriatic, would then drive north to Vienna, blocking the westward advance of the Soviet armies and Soviet Communism. Whatever the merits of this plan, the Americans rejected it because of the mountainous terrain, and because they saw the Balkan route as a politically motivated detour that would do nothing to shorten the War. They considered a large-scale version of *Anvil* essential to the success of the Normandy invasion and not, as Churchill insisted, an unnecessary duplication of effort.

In spite of Churchill's misgivings, plans for *Anvil* went forward. The U.S. Seventh Army, most of whose troops had been parceled out among other forces after the Sicily victory, was revitalized, and it was decided that for the invasion Lieut. General Mark W. Clark, who was then commanding the Fifth Army in Italy, would succeed General Patton as Seventh Army commander. In December 1943 Clark called in the commander of his 3rd Infantry Division, Major General Lucian K. Truscott Jr., and appointed him to *Anvil*'s most important field command—leading the assault. Jutjawed, squint-eyed and perpetually scowling, Truscott was a tough, outspoken, aggressive soldier almost universally admired by his men and his superiors.

Truscott, who had been a cavalry lieutenant colonel at the start of the War, was a perfect choice to lead the invasion spearhead. His credentials included a wealth of experience in amphibious operations. In 1942 he had studied the methods of the British Commandos, accompanied them on the ill-fated Dieppe raid and helped organize the commando-like U.S. Rangers. He later distinguished himself as a task force commander in the invasion of North Africa and as a division commander in Sicily and Italy; during those campaigns he forged his 3rd Infantry Division into one of the great combat outfits of the War.

While Truscott and Clark continued fighting their way up the Italian boot, the Seventh Army opened a secret headquarters in a sprawling Moorish-style school on the outskirts of Algiers. The *Anvil* planning staff established liaison with the Navy, the Services of Supply and the Army Air Forces. They also arranged for close contact with the Free French forces, most of whom would follow Truscott's spearhead ashore as an integral force in order to avoid language problems in combat. To select a landing area, the planners systematically sifted through masses of photographs, records and intelligence reports on France's southern coastline and its defenses.

There were two logical target areas, but both had disadvantages. The first was a 45-mile stretch of coast midway between Marseilles and the Spanish border that had the finest landing beaches in southern France. But there was no major port in the area. Moreover, this part of the French coast was out of the range of Allied tactical aircraft based in Italy, Corsica and Sardinia. The second choice would have been the beaches just west of Marseilles, a port with a handling capacity of 20,000 tons a day and the hub of a road and rail network that led to the Rhone Valley. However, the marshy Rhone delta that enveloped Marseilles would cause many landing problems.

The planners therefore looked farther east to a 45-mile stretch of the famed Riviera coast between the Bay of Cavalaire and the anchorage at Agay *(map, page 102)*. Here, too, there were disadvantages—the beaches were narrow and cramped and at intervals cliffs fronted on the sea—but on balance this was the best area that was available, and it was chosen.

In planning tactics for the invasion, the staff faced a bewildering array of imponderables. *Anvil* ranked third in priority behind the invasion of Normandy and the Italian campaign; with every essential item in short supply, especially landing craft, the staff had to base its plans on troops, matériel and shipping whose quantity and delivery date were at best uncertain. And since the scale of *Anvil* was constantly in doubt, the planners had to prepare several different versions of the invasion and ensuing operations—and continually update them as newer surveys were completed on German troop deployment. It was frustrating work, but the magnitude of *Anvil* was eventually settled at 10 divisions, which gave the Seventh Army a solid basic plan for the main assault and a number of preliminary attacks.

For all practical purposes, the mounting of *Anvil* could not begin until the fall of Rome freed the seasoned combat divisions that Truscott would lead in the landings. But the road to Rome was blocked—interminably, it seemed—by resolute German defenses at Monte Cassino, north of Naples. In an attempt to break the bottleneck, Churchill created another one: he persuaded the Combined Chiefs to outflank Monte Cassino with an ill-starred amphibious landing 70 miles north at Anzio. Launched on January 22, 1944, the operation went so poorly that a month later Truscott, whose 3rd Division had led the first wave ashore, was promoted to commander of the VI Corps in the hope that he would break out of the besieged beachhead. It was also decided that General Clark was too valuable in Italy to be spared for the invasion of southern France; he was replaced as commander of the Seventh Army by Major General Alexander M. Patch, a veteran of the fighting on Guadalcanal. And since the Anzio operation had tied up landing craft that might have been used for *Anvil*, the Combined Chiefs were forced to postpone the landings in southern France.

The impasses at Anzio and Monte Cassino were finally broken in May, and then events moved swiftly. On June 4 the Allies took Rome; two days later Normandy was invaded, and on June 11 Truscott was ordered to start preparing for *Anvil* with three divisions of his choice.

Truscott chose two of the most experienced divisions in Italy. One was his old 3rd Division, now under the command of Major General John W. O'Daniel, a hard-bitten soldier aptly nicknamed Iron Mike, who keyed up his troops to fight the Germans by shouting, "Hate 'em! Hate 'em!" The other outfit was the 45th Division under Major General William W. Eagles, whose mild, professorial appearance belied his uncompromising toughness. Truscott considered both these selections obvious, but his third choice—the 36th Division—was not. The 36th had twice been badly mauled in the Italian campaign and was led by a new commander, Major General John E. Dahlquist, who had no combat experience at the head of a division. But the 36th had redeemed itself at Anzio, and Truscott chose it "because of its outstanding performance during the action following the breakout from the beachhead." These divisions, the nucleus of Truscott's revamped VI Corps, were

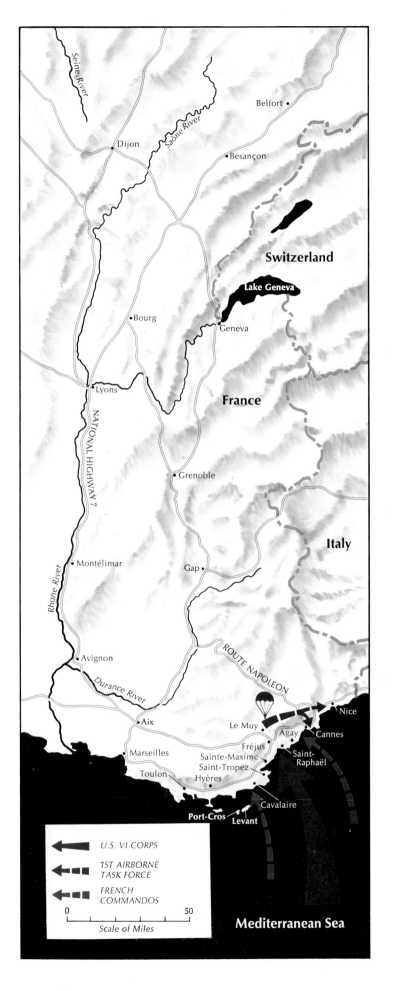

The Allied invasion of southern France got under way on August 15, 1944, when French commandos landed at Cap Nègre and west of Cannes shortly before 2:00 a.m. with the vital mission of blocking roads leading to the beachhead area from the west and east. At 4:30 a.m., troops of the 1st Airborne Task Force were dropped 12 miles inland to seize the highway junction at Le Muy. The main assault began at 8:00 a.m., when three divisions of the American VI Corps landed in the area between Cavalaire and Agay. Troops of these units managed to push inland 10 miles the first day. On D-plus-1, they were followed by the French II Corps, which came ashore near Saint-Tropez, over beaches already secured by the U.S. 3rd Division, then swung west to march on Toulon and Marseilles.

withdrawn from the line one by one and sent to the Naples area for invasion training.

On June 15 Truscott was called to Algiers to meet General Patch, the new head of the Seventh Army. Patch was a talented administrator who complemented Truscott's dynamic leadership in battle with organizing skill, patience for detail and the tact of a diplomat. "I was fully aware of his fine reputation," Truscott later wrote; on reporting to Patch, Truscott found him to be "thin and wiry, simple in dress and forthright in manner—obviously keenly intelligent with a dry Scottish sense of humor."

Patch made a different impression on his other top subordinate, General Jean de Lattre de Tassigny, whom Charles de Gaulle had appointed commander of *Anvil*'s Free French forces. De Lattre found Patch to be "deeply religious, of mystic turn of mind." Patch had shown his reverence on a hot day in Algiers when he was disconsolate because the invasion was apparently being argued to death. "With emotion," de Lattre later recalled, "he took from the drawer of his desk a box of sweets that had come from home that morning and offered them to me as if our mutual disappointment had opened his family circle to me, and said, 'Ah General, there's not much more we can do.' Then, after a silence: 'We must pray.'"

De Lattre himself was a formidable and courageous soldier. Imprisoned by the Germans as a dangerous French patriot, he had three times escaped and been recaptured. On his fourth attempt he was successful; he joined the Free French forces in North Africa and served with gallantry, most recently leading the hard-fought amphibious landing that resulted in the reconquest of Elba. He was proud, opinionated and something of a martinet—"a terrible man to serve," said one of his officers, who then added, "but I wouldn't care to serve under anyone else."

Predictably, Truscott and de Lattre rubbed each other the wrong way. Their first meeting was arranged by de Lattre, who invited Truscott to what turned out to be a long, stiff meal. "Conversation lagged during the luncheon," Truscott reported. "Everyone attended to the business of eating, the sounds of mastication dominating the scene. It finally came to a close and we learned the reason for the cool reception. De Lattre was in a towering rage." It seemed that Truscott had violated military protocol by inspecting some of de

Lattre's troops without his personal permission and in his absence. "It was a slight to him," Truscott remarked, "and to the honor of France." De Lattre burst into an angry tirade over the matter, but Truscott cut him short, saying that "if that was all he had to discuss, we were wasting our time." Afterward, the two came to regard each other with wary respect, but it took all of Patch's diplomacy to smooth over their occasional clashes.

By early July de Lattre's forces were growing. Four Free French divisions, which had been instrumental in breaking the German line near Monte Cassino, were withdrawn from the line in Italy and put into training south of Naples.

Meanwhile, Truscott's VI Corps had been beefed up by the addition of some 10,000 American and British paratroopers, who would land behind the beaches on D-day; these troops, later designated the 1st Airborne Task Force, went into training outside Rome and were formed into an effective fighting unit in less than one month. Some of Patch's French-speaking soldiers remained in training in North Africa and would sail for France from there. Like the French units in Italy, their ranks were filled with thousands of veteran fighting men who had fled from the homeland and an enormous hodgepodge of volunteers from France's far-flung empire: Somalis, New Caledonians, Tahitians, Antilleans, Indochinese, Pondicherrians, Syrians, Lebanese, Algerians, Moroccans, Tunisians, men from French Equatorial Africa and West Africa, plus Foreign Legionnaires from a score of nations. The colonial soldiers had little in common, but all of them could be counted on to fight.

Even as preparations gained momentum, so did Churchill's efforts to abort the invasion, reduce its size or change its direction. He still insisted that the operation was "sheer folly," and that it would serve "no earthly purpose," especially since Normandy had already been invaded successfully. However, a new reason for the operation had arisen shortly after D-Day in Normandy. The U.S. Army Chief of Staff, General George C. Marshall, had flown to England on June 8 to help Eisenhower explain that more than 40 new American divisions had recently completed their training in the United States; they were ready and needed for the assault on Germany but could not be sent into action because the Normandy forces might not be able to capture and clear enough ports in northern France to handle the influx. The solution, Marshall said forcefully, was to capture Marseilles and use its fine facilities as a port of entry for divisions shipped directly from the United States. Eisenhower said he had to have Marseilles.

Churchill remained adamant. In a nonstop barrage of letters and cables, he hectored Roosevelt to abandon *Anvil*. On June 29 the President replied in a message that fairly sighed with weariness: "My dear friend, I beg you let us go ahead with our plan." Churchill replied that he was "deeply grieved," but the Combined Chiefs of Staff scheduled the operation for August 15.

Churchill continued his attack, shifting to a target more conveniently located in London—Eisenhower. Through July and into August, the Prime Minister subjected the Supreme Commander to what Ike described as one of the most severe trials of his life. Churchill wept: he charged the U.S. with "bullying" Britain by not adopting his grand strategy. He threatened: at one point he told Eisenhower that he might go to the King and "lay down the mantle of my high office," which indeed would have thrown the Allied war effort into turmoil. And that was just the beginning.

By August 1 the American armies were pouring out of the Normandy beachhead, increasing *Anvil*'s potential dramatically. If Patch's northbound Seventh Army and Patton's eastbound Third Army could link up, they would trap the enemy forces west of the Rhone and south of the Loire, forcing the Germans in France to surrender and liberating that whole immense bypassed territory in one great rush.

Churchill persevered. On August 5 he assailed Eisenhower with his most determined anti-*Anvil* argument. Arriving at Ike's advance headquarters near Portsmouth for a hastily arranged lunch, he disarmingly fed milk to the general's black kitten, Shaef, and then went on the offensive. Arguing for closer tactical connection between the two invading forces, he urged that the units assigned to the Riviera assault be sent instead to capture the ports of Brittany—Brest, Lorient and Saint-Nazaire—where he assumed "they could walk in like tourists." Such landings, he asserted, would not only open those ports for Allied use but also put troops ashore in position to strengthen the Allies' southern flank in the sweep east across France.

Eisenhower replied that the proposal was impossible. As he later told the story, he informed Churchill that he expected the Brittany ports to be "stubbornly defended" and "effectively destroyed once we had captured them"; but "we did not expect this destruction to be so marked at Marseilles" because "capture should be so swift as to allow little time for demolition." Even Churchill's steadfast supporter, General Sir Henry Maitland Wilson, the Supreme Allied Commander in the Mediterranean theater, had said that *Anvil* could not be postponed again. But Churchill persisted mercilessly. According to Eisenhower's Naval aide, Commander Harry Butcher, "Ike said no, continued saying no all afternoon, and ended up saying no in every form of the English language at his command. . . . He was practically limp when the PM departed."

Three days later, Churchill apparently bowed to the inevitable. He cabled Roosevelt and agreed to the assault: "I pray God that you may be right." Then he went right on with his obstructive campaign. His final concession of defeat did not come until August 10, when the British Chiefs of Staff ordered General Wilson to execute the invasion as scheduled on August 15.

Those last five days capped a hectic final period of preparation for the invasion forces in dozens of encampments and staging areas up and down the Italian coast. By August 12 all of the 94,000 soldiers who would land on the Riviera beaches were crammed aboard their ships, with the largest flotilla riding at anchor in the Bay of Naples. General Patch (recently promoted to lieutenant general) and General Truscott boarded the command ship *Catoctin* with Vice Admiral Henry Kent Hewitt, whose huge Western Task Force was to deliver the Seventh Army into combat. The ships began leaving on a staggered schedule.

Late on the brilliant afternoon of August 13, the few officers in the Naples fleet who knew of Churchill's dogged opposition were amazed to see his familiar figure moving among the ships aboard a British motor launch, his pudgy fingers outthrust in his famous V-for-Victory sign. The Prime Minister, making a grand Churchillian gesture, had come to wish *bon voyage* to his least-favorite operation. The troops aboard the transports greeted him with cheers, and the men of the 3rd Division serenaded him with their marching song, "The Dog Face Soldier." Churchill beamed. There was a story that he even permitted himself a rueful joke about his long and bitter resistance to the invasion. *Anvil* had been renamed *Dragoon* on August 1 to maintain security, and the new name, Churchill said, was entirely fitting: he had, after all, been dragooned into accepting the operation.

From their scattered ports, the flotillas of the Seventh Army invasion fleet converged on their rendezvous off the coast of Corsica. Behind the ships carrying the VI Corps came the vessels bearing de Lattre's French Army B, which would start landing on the day after D-day, D-plus-1. On board, the troops received their last briefings, and unit commanders studied the latest updated intelligence reports on German troop deployments.

The Germans' static coastal defenses, known as the Mediterranean Wall, were not as formidable as those the Allies had encountered in Normandy, and German air and naval forces were negligible. But 200 guns of medium and heavy caliber had been massed in the Toulon area, with nearly as many at Marseilles, and 45 more batteries were strewn along the coast between the Rhone and Agay, some of them camouflaged as Riviera cabanas and refreshment stands. In addition, some 600 concrete pillboxes and other strongholds faced the sea between Marseilles and Nice, and the beaches were seeded with mines and anti-invasion obstacles, many of them with 75mm shells rigged to explode on contact. Inland, the flowering meadows of Provence bristled with needle-pointed pine poles designed to destroy gliders and to impale paratroopers. However, conscripted French laborers had deliberately dug only shallow postholes, so that many of the poles would topple at a touch.

These defenses and the personnel manning them were controlled by German Army Group G, headquartered near Toulouse, some 260 miles from the threatened coast. The commanding officer was General Johannes Blaskowitz, a competent, correct product of the German general staff system, whose only black mark was that he had run afoul of Adolf Hitler at the outset of the War. As commander of the army besieging Warsaw, Blaskowitz had received notice that the Führer intended to drop by for a field-kitchen meal and wanted no frills laid on. Blaskowitz, failing to realize that Hitler wanted a genuinely spartan meal, had the tables elaborately set with paper cloths and decorated with flow-

ers. The Führer arrived, took one look at the tables and stalked away indignantly without eating. "From that moment on," reported Field Marshal Albert Kesselring, "Hitler regarded Blaskowitz with suspicion."

One of the two armies in Blaskowitz' group, the Nineteenth, under Lieut. General Friedrich Wiese, held the Riviera coast; he commanded or had within calling range no less than 10 divisions. But that strength was somewhat deceptive. One of Wiese's divisions was totally occupied in the French Alps fighting strong Resistance units, some of them members of de Gaulle's formally organized FFI (Forces Françaises de l'Intérieur), others belonging to the Maquis guerrilla bands who took their name from the word for the scrubby underbrush of the French hill country. Several other divisions were of poor quality; their troops were young and inexperienced or they were heavily diluted by ragtag collections of Poles, Armenians, Georgians, Ukrainians, Azerbaijanis—soldiers who had been captured on the Eastern Front and who had opted to serve under German officers rather than waste away in prison camps or labor battalions. The abilities and the loyalties of the foreign troops were dubious at best.

However, Wiese's army was no paper tiger. Four of his divisions were highly rated formations, and Truscott took them seriously. And then there was the powerful 11th Panzer Division, with 14,000 top-quality troops and 200 tanks. At last report, the 11th Panzer had been stationed near Bordeaux, approximately 400 miles west of the attack zone, and like all of the German panzer divisions, it could not be sent into action without direct permission from Hitler himself. But the division could move quickly and hit hard whenever the order came.

Unbeknownst to the invasion forces, the Germans knew all about the attack—only the exact landing area was in doubt. German intelligence had reported large and small indications of an imminent strike by the Allies. Various French units had very suddenly been pulled out of the fighting in Italy, and the Germans were well aware of de Gaulle's pledge that the next destination of his forces would be France itself. A German agent in Naples had reported the appearance on the north Italian coast of the U.S.S. *Augusta,* a heavy cruiser with too much firepower to be sent there unless a new invasion was in the offing. And in July an

American Red Cross worker in Rome had been overheard saying, "I've got to get to Naples by August 1, because I'm going to be in on the invasion of southern France a few weeks after that."

Blaskowitz and Wiese were just as worried as Truscott about the location of the 11th Panzer Division. Blaskowitz had begged OKW, the German High Command at the Wolf's Lair in East Prussia, for permission to move the armored division to the Riviera coast, and a draft order to that effect had been prepared. But General Jodl, Hitler's operations chief, had delayed presenting the order to the Führer until the 13th of August, when he was convinced that an invasion was looming.

Hitler read the order and brightened on reaching a passage that called for "resistance by all available means" along the coast of southern France. That meant moving the 11th Panzer, and he signed the appropriate order.

Word crackled down through Hitler's elaborate chain of command to Army Group G headquarters near Toulouse. Chief of Staff Major General Heinz von Gyldenfeldt rushed into Blaskowitz' office shouting, "Here's the order! It just came through!" Moments later Gyldenfeldt was on the phone to the Nineteenth Army, informing Wiese that the 11th Panzer had been released to his command. The division was loaded on 33 trains and headed eastward on August 14, but the unit was soon forced by Allied air attacks to abandon the trains and take to the roads.

As darkness fell on the soft, fragrant Languedoc countryside, armored cars emblazoned with skulls and crossbones led the tanks of the 11th Panzer Division east toward Avignon on the Rhone. To avoid further air attacks, the division had been instructed to use back roads and to travel only at night. But Major General Wend von Wietersheim, the division commander, was in a hurry, and he ignored the orders. According to his chief of staff, the 11th Panzer raced for the Rhone with its "vehicles bristling with foliage, speeding

along the main highways in broad daylight, leaving ample space between them, darting from one place of concealment to the next."

On the evening of August 14—when Wietersheim's advance units were within 15 miles of the Rhone and, far to the north, tanks of the U.S. Third Army were driving toward Chartres—the Allied invasion fleet made its Corsica rendezvous and steamed cautiously toward the coast of southern France. As darkness fell, advance elements of the Seventh Army debarked and set out on five preliminary operations designed to pave the way for the morning assault by Truscott's main force.

French Lieut. Colonel Georges-Régis Bouvet, commander of Operation *Romeo,* set off for the shore at Cap Nègre with 800 French commandos aboard 20 landing craft; their mission was to scale a cliff 350 feet high and destroy German artillery that would otherwise bombard the left flank of Truscott's VI Corps' landings.

Ahead of the main party of French commandos, bobbing along in a rubber boat, went nine men led by Sergeant Georges du Bellocq. They were to land near Cap Nègre on the beach at Rayol and knock out German blockhouses. Somehow the little party drifted to a landing west of Rayol. Now, in the darkness, du Bellocq was obsessed with the idea of "getting the hell out of this nameless beach." Crawling, climbing, bloodying their hands on barbed-wire obstacles, the commandos finally arrived at a network of trenches that du Bellocq thought was empty—until a voice to his left called, "Ludwig! Ludwig!" Du Bellocq sent a submachinegun burst in that direction, and the enemy soldier screamed once, then "gurgled and shut up"—the first German to die in the invasion of southern France. The sound of gunfire set off a lively fire fight—mostly among the Germans themselves. "From that moment on during the whole rest of the night," du Bellocq recalled, "the Jerries hardly left off shooting at one another."

In one of the 20 landing craft offshore, Bouvet heard the sound of the fracas and stared into the darkness, looking for a green signal that was to be flashed by one of his men ashore, marking his beach. There was no signal; either it— or his main force—was in the wrong place. The Canadian midshipman in charge of the LCI thereupon refused to take the commandos ashore. Bouvet, an experienced improviser, changed the Canadian's mind with a pistol jammed in the ribs. The landing craft touched shore a mile west of the assigned beach.

Then Bouvet and his French commandos went to work. They scaled the steep cliff, took the enemy by surprise, destroyed the gun emplacements, established a roadblock on the coastal highway, picked up du Bellocq's team and other advance units, seized Cap Nègre, killed some 300 Germans and took 700 prisoners—all this in about 12 hours while losing only 11 men killed and 50 wounded. They had established a bridgehead two miles deep and more than a mile wide, and there they stayed, awaiting troops of Truscott's VI Corps from the beachhead to the east.

A different kind of preliminary attack, code-named *Ferdinand,* was aimed at La Ciotat, between Marseilles and Toulon, where the Germans expected a major invasion to take place. Five transport planes dropped 300 life-size dummies dressed as American paratroopers and rigged with explosive charges and noisemaking equipment that simulated the sound of battle when jarred by contact with the ground. Germans of the 244th Infantry Division were fooled by the trick. Crying "Paratroopers! Paratroopers!" they encircled the invaders. When they received no answering fire, a few men prodded the dummies with fixed bayonets—only to detonate more charges. The diversionary effort was so successful that the next day it earned special mention in a broadcast by Radio Berlin; the German station denounced the fake paratrooper attack as something that "could have been contrived only by the lowest and most sinister type of Anglo-Saxon mind."

In the meantime, the American-Canadian 1st Special Service Force was staging Operation *Sitka,* 25 miles southeast of Toulon, on the picturesque, pine-clad islands of Port-Cros and Ile du Levant. Aerial photographs had shown strong artillery batteries on both islands, and some 2,000 men of the crack attack force were sent to wipe them out, even though a knowledgeable French informant insisted that the three 164mm guns on Levant had been destroyed in November 1942, when the Germans occupied the southern half of France and the French fleet was hastily scuttled in Toulon harbor. One large detachment, led in by scouts in kayaks and on electrically operated surfboards, scrambled

Hundreds of parachutes, streaming from U.S. transports on August 15, 1944—D-day in southern France—drop men and supplies to the 1st Airborne Task Force, whose American and British paratroopers had landed in the dark near Le Muy, 12 miles behind the invasion beaches. By the time of this drop, the soldiers had achieved their main objective: setting up roadblocks to keep German reinforcements from reaching the beachhead.

ashore on Levant and rushed inland without a shot being fired. They soon learned that the French informant was right; the Levant guns turned out to be dummies, skillfully fashioned from corrugated metal, wooden stakes and drainpipes. Just before dawn on August 15, the commander on Levant radioed General Patch: "Islands utterly useless. Suggest immediate evacuation. Killed: none. Wounded: two. Prisoners: 240. Enemy batteries dummies."

Soon afterward, while the troops on Levant were liquidating a last pocket of German resistance, radio contact broke off. Hours later, Patch decided to send an aide to find out what was going on. "In that case, general," said a visitor, "I wouldn't mind being in the party. It'll give me a chance to stretch my legs." The volunteer was U.S. Secretary of the Navy James Forrestal. (Dragoon was notable for the number of visiting dignitaries; a week later, at a critical point in the campaign, Truscott would have to take time out to entertain Eisenhower's political adviser, Ambassador Robert D. Murphy, and New York's Archbishop Francis J. Spellman.)

Meanwhile, at the opposite end of the assault area, a film star turned U.S. Navy lieutenant commander, Douglas Fairbanks Jr., presided over the mixed fortunes of Operation Rosie, designed to block the coastal roads from Cannes west to the invasion area. Fairbanks' forces consisted of two gunboats, a fighter-director ship with sound equipment to broadcast a recording of naval gunfire, and four fast PT boats carrying demolition teams of 67 French commandos. To distract the Germans from the commandos' mission, Fairbanks' little flotilla raced east toward Nice, making a fearful racket (and prompting Radio Berlin to announce later that Antibes and Nice had been bombarded by "four or five large battleships"). But when the commandos were put ashore well to the west of Cannes, they ran into atrocious luck. First, they stumbled into an unreported minefield, laid only a day or two before. Next, having failed to achieve their objectives, they tried to withdraw—only to be mistaken for Germans and shot up by a pair of prowling Allied fighter planes. Of the 67 Frenchmen, only 40 survived, and they were captured by the Germans.

The largest preliminary operation, code-named Rugby, was aimed at Le Muy, 12 miles inland from Fréjus in the eastern sector of the Allied assault area. Le Muy was an insignificant village except for the fact that two vital high-ways converged there. At Le Muy, the Route Napoleon (handsomely paved since Napoleon used it on his return from Elba) ran northward to Grenoble, and National Highway 7 branched west from the Route Napoleon to Avignon, thence north up the Rhone Valley. By seizing Le Muy and its environs, the Seventh Army could not only prevent German reinforcements from reaching the beachheads but also hold open the routes that the VI Corps needed to exploit its landings. Thus, in the predawn hours of August 15, little Le Muy became the main objective of the big Anglo-American 1st Airborne Task Force.

Commanding the division-sized group was the youngest major general in the American Army and an extraordinary soldier: Robert T. Frederick. Of willowy build and wearing a dandified little moustache, the 37-year-old Frederick resembled—in the words of a Canadian officer—"a bloody goddamned actor." But he was a fierce and brilliant fighter. He had been wounded nine times in the War, had won many decorations and had received a rare accolade from Winston Churchill: "If we had a dozen men like him, we would have smashed Hitler in 1942."

Frederick's first paratroop wave dropped at 4:30 on the morning of D-day. Most of the units landed on or near their targets, and by 6 p.m. the force had taken several villages and thrown blockades over the road network linking the invasion coast to the interior.

Le Muy itself held out, mostly because of what Frederick deemed a halfhearted attack by the British 2nd Independent Parachute Brigade. Frederick turned the job over to his American 550th Glider Infantry Battalion, which took Le Muy by noon on D-plus-1. The linkup with troops from the invasion beaches came about an hour later, when a tank named "The Anzio Express" clanked into town. By then the Seventh Army was in business along its invasion front.

The preinvasion bombardment and the landings of Truscott's VI Corps went like clockwork. At 5:50 that morning, an hour after first light, another actor-turned-officer, French liaison officer Jean-Pierre Aumont, looked up from a landing craft off the 3rd Division beaches and saw what appeared to be "glistening drops of radium caught in the rays of the rising sun." These were the first of some 1,300 American, British and French bombers, arriving unopposed

U.S. 45th Division infantrymen stream ashore and make their way inland through an opening in the sea wall near Sainte-Maxime in August 1944. Erected by the Germans, the concrete wall was 10 feet high and six feet thick—one of the most formidable obstacles on the Riviera. After repeated air and naval bombardments failed to open a breach, U.S. engineers had to go ashore and blast a passageway through it for troops and vehicles.

from Sardinia and Corsica to pound the Riviera for the next hour and 40 minutes. The long and wide-ranging bombing attacks drove the Germans under cover and destroyed, among other things, a bridge at Pont-Saint-Esprit. This was the last of six bridges across a 30-mile stretch of the lower Rhone, and its destruction left the 11th Panzer Division stranded on the wrong side of the river. The most formidable enemy unit had to mark time until it could improvise some means of crossing the river to reach the assault area.

At precisely 7:30 the bombing ceased and the big planes disappeared in the distance. One minute passed in what seemed to be a dead silence. Then another fury was unleashed, this time from the 400 guns of the Allied warships offshore. During the next 19 minutes they fired some 16,000 shells at German batteries and strong points. On schedule at 7:50 a.m., the naval guns fell quiet and the invasion craft headed into the ground fog cloaking the beaches.

The first elements landed right on time at 8 o'clock. On the VI Corps' left, Iron Mike O'Daniel's 3rd Division hit two beaches 13 miles apart and moved to pinch off the Saint-Tropez peninsula, a pastoral patch of vineyards and olive groves cut by narrow, winding roads. The assault troops met with hardly any German opposition. A French woman, witnessing the advance from her home overlooking Cavalaire-sur-Mer, was impressed by "the deep silence, so profound that not even a leaf seemed to be rustling." When the German soldiers finally did emerge from their pillboxes, where they had holed up during the preliminary bombardment, they seemed dazed.

General O'Daniel went ashore at 10:44 a.m. and set up his command post in a barnyard nearly a mile inland. Even as local farmers were trundling out welcoming kegs of wine, O'Daniel established radio communication with a friendly force. "Hello, Bouvet," said Iron Mike. "Well, we made it." Three and a half hours later, 3rd Division units joined up with Colonel Bouvet and his commandos, who, after seizing Cap Nègre, had stoutly defended their inland roadblock against German attack.

The 3rd Division's main D-day objective was the town of Saint-Tropez. But by the time infantry units arrived there to take the town, they found that the job had been all but done for them by some paratroopers of the 1st Airborne

Task Force who, having been dropped far off target, had joined local Resistance fighters in seizing the town. Thus, by nightfall on D-day the 3rd Division had achieved all its objectives and taken 1,600 prisoners while itself suffering only 264 casualties.

Meanwhile, in the VI Corps' center, General Eagles' 45th Division "Thunderbirds"—including many Cherokee and Apache Indians—had an equally easy time. By 8:30 a.m. the division was able to report the situation on its three beaches: "First three waves landed. . . . Enemy resistance light." Most of the German troops hastily withdrew from Sainte-Maxime, once a fashionable resort town with pastel-painted hotels, but Thunderbird units still had to root out a handful of enemy soldiers who made a last-ditch stand in a concrete bunker with a 3-inch gun. A tank was called in to end the fight. At point-blank range of 50 yards, the tank scored two direct hits, blowing the bunker to bits along with its seven defenders.

The 45th Division Thunderbirds accomplished all of their assigned D-day missions and took 205 prisoners while suffering 109 casualties.

On the VI Corps' right, in the 36th Division's sector, things went well at first. The division seized two of its three beaches with little trouble, and General Dahlquist followed the troops ashore at 10 a.m. But the third assault, scheduled for the afternoon, ran into a snag.

This attack was aimed at the little port of Fréjus, which commanded not only the highway to Le Muy and the interior but also an excellent coastal road to Toulon and Marseilles. Fréjus was badly needed and, on the theory that it would be resolutely defended and might require special treatment, the attack there was not scheduled to take place until 2 o'clock in the afternoon.

As the assault was about to get under way, Generals Truscott and Patch watched with Admiral Hewitt from their command ship, the *Catoctin*. The landing craft circled several thousand yards offshore, while drone boats—remote-controlled vessels filled with high explosives to be detonated over underwater obstacles—headed toward the Fréjus beach. But the boats soon began to behave crazily (German radio operators were later credited with jamming the remote controls). Truscott saw one of them that "went out of control, dashed wildly up and down the beach, turned out to sea to our consternation, then turned about again."

Intimidated by the berserk drone boats, the landing craft remained well offshore until 2:30, a half hour behind schedule. Then all the landing craft made an unplanned move. Recalled Truscott: "While we watched helplessly, to our profound astonishment the whole flotilla turned about and headed to sea again. Hewitt, Patch and I were furious."

The landing craft had been recalled by Rear Admiral Spencer Lewis, a veteran of the great Pacific sea battle at Midway. When the drones failed to breach the underwater obstacles off the Fréjus beach, Lewis tried to consult the 36th Division Commander, Dahlquist. But the general had gone ashore with the main force and was out of touch.

Admiral Lewis, unwilling to let the landing craft run the gauntlet of dangerous drones, decided to alter the Fréjus landing on his own responsibility. Instead, the men were immediately put ashore on an alternate beach nearby, and they moved to attack the port from the rear. When Dahlquist learned of the switch, he sent Lewis a message of thanks: "Appreciate your prompt action in changing plan. . . . Opposition irritating but not too tough so far." But Lewis' action, wrote Truscott, was "a grave error, which merited reprimand at least, and most certainly no congratulation. Except for the otherwise astounding success of the assault, it might have had even graver consequences."

An astounding success it had surely been, on the 36th Division's front as elsewhere; while suffering only 75 casualties, the 36th captured 236 prisoners on D-day and even took Fréjus without much trouble the next day. By then, the focal point of action had shifted to the west. For there, on D-plus-1, the French returned in force to their homeland.

"I kept my eyes closed so as not to be aware of too much happiness too soon." So said a French soldier of his homecoming. "And then I bent down and scooped up a handful of sand, with the feeling that what I was doing was a private act, separate from anybody else's." Many French soldiers had the same sense of exultation on touching the sand and soil of France. A witness to one French landing saw the troops "massed in the bows of the ship, fascinated by the beach; they jumped down with a single bound, bent down to pick up a handful of sand, then skipped like madmen to the nearest pine trees, where they regrouped, shaking each

Fighting in besieged Toulon, French soldiers turn a captured enemy field gun against the Germans. The eight-day struggle for the port, leading to the surrender of the Germans on August 28, 1944, was "really most extraordinary," said French Admiral André Lemonnier. "Some streets were deserted while others were crowded with civilian population who strolled by as if the battle were taking place kilometers away." Citizens often directed troops to strong points blocking the French advance.

other's hands, or embracing like brothers meeting again after a long absence."

As he had long since demonstrated, General de Lattre bowed to no man in his love for France. Yet of his own homecoming, the voluble commander reported only that at 11 p.m. in Saint-Tropez, "I reached the Hotel 'Latitude 43' where General Patch had set up his command." De Lattre had no time to indulge in patriotic reflections. The Allied plan called for his Army B—then consisting only of the II Corps and assorted smaller units, totaling about 16,000 men, but scheduled to be heavily reinforced by new landings day after day—to attack Toulon and Marseilles one after the other. Toulon was to be taken by September 4 and Marseilles 20 days later.

But de Lattre meant to do better than that, much better; on August 19 he asked Patch's permission to go after the two great ports simultaneously. "General Patch gave me a free hand," de Lattre wrote. "Then I suddenly saw the clear, grave eyes of the American commander soften. With hesitation that was full of shyness, he brought out his pocket-

book and from it he took a flower with two stems, which was beginning to fade: 'Look,' he said, breaking it in two and handing me one of the stems; 'a young girl gave me it on the slopes of Vesuvius on the day before we embarked. She said it would bring me luck. Let us each keep half.'"

De Lattre set in motion a neat plan to encircle Toulon and attack the port from all sides. Brigadier General Charles Diego Brosset marched his veteran Free French 1st Infantry Division due west along the coastal highway and cordoned off Toulon from the east. Major General Aimé de Goislard de Monsabert led his Algerian 3rd Infantry Division through the mountain fortifications north of Toulon, then moved south to invest the city from the north and the west. Meanwhile, Allied naval forces closed in on the forts defending Toulon's southern approaches. On the 19th of August the honor of opening the bombardment was fittingly awarded to a French battleship, the *Lorraine*. De Lattre started his land assault the next day.

The German commander of Toulon, Rear Admiral Heinrich Ruhfus, had at his disposal some 25,000 men, about 100

light guns and 60 heavy ones, 30 forts and scores of pill-boxes and minefields. He also had an order from Hitler requiring him to hold the city "to the last cartridge." Ruhfus did his best, but it was not nearly enough. By August 22 Toulon was isolated and doomed.

The assault continued for a week and took several odd turns. A German-speaking French colonel tapped the telephone lines leading to Cap Brun Fort and told its commander that new orders from the Führer required him to shout "Heil Hitler" three times, blow up his guns and surrender the fort. The German officer obeyed to the letter. While the Free French 1st Division marked time on Toulon's outskirts, General Brosset found an undefended road, jumped into his jeep and entered the city alone. He returned jubilant. "Get a move on," he shouted to his troops. "I've already kissed at least 200 girls." Through it all, French forces continually pressed inward, squeezing the defenders into an ever-shrinking perimeter.

At 8 a.m. on August 28, Admiral Ruhfus appeared before General de Lattre to surrender Toulon. De Lattre gave him three hours to turn over detailed plans of all minefields in the area: "I warned him unequivocally that, after that interval, he would be shot if in his sector a single one of my men trod upon a German mine. Three hours later I had the plans." He also had 17,000 prisoners. The French had lost some 2,700 men killed or wounded.

Even as the assault on Toulon began on August 20, Colonel Léon Jean Chappuis and his 7th Infantry Regiment of the Algerian 3rd Division peeled off from the attack force and followed a French tank column west toward Marseilles. Waiting there apprehensively were Major General Hans Schaefer and 16,000 German troops, many of whom had wandered into the city after their units were routed on the invasion beaches to the east. An outer defense ring had been established in the city's sprawling suburbs, with massive roadblocks on all four of the main highways leading into Marseilles. Within the city, the defenses were anchored on redoubts in the port area to the north and on the heights of Notre-Dame de la Garde to the south. The defense system seemed impressive, but it was riddled with gaps that the French were soon to exploit.

When Chappuis arrived outside Marseilles on August 21, he learned that the Resistance had started an uprising in the city and that his troops were needed to aid the fighters, who were under heavy German pressure. Chappuis was enthusiastic about the idea of breaking into the city at once, before more troops arrived, and so reported to headquarters. De Lattre and Monsabert arrived there from Toulon on August 22 to look over the situation. The doughty Monsabert favored an immediate attack, but de Lattre dismissed the proposal. The Resistance could at times be a bother, de Lattre explained to Monsabert, and he had no intention of allowing his troops to be "contaminated by the disorder of a city in a state of insurrection."

Monsabert furiously protested, banging his fist on a table—to no avail. But when he told Chappuis of de Lattre's negative decision, he added with a sly smile: "Those are the orders. But should you have the opportunity. . . ."

By 5 o'clock the next morning, two battalions of Chappuis' regiment were on the outskirts of Marseilles, enjoying a breakfast of wine and fruit provided by a delirious citizenry at the Madeleine crossroad. Monsabert arrived and marched into the city with the troops. They tried to arrange the surrender of the German garrison, but the effort failed. Fighting erupted—and there they were: some 800 French soldiers in the midst of 16,000 Germans. The rest of Monsabert's division was withdrawn from Toulon and arrived posthaste to join the battle for Marseilles.

It was an incongruous, untidy battle. "In a few yards," de Lattre wrote, "one passed from the enthusiasm of a liberated boulevard into the solitude of a machine-gunned avenue. In a few turns of the track, a tank covered with flowers was either taken by the assault of pretty, smiling girls or fired at by an 88mm shell." At one intersection, a warning was posted: "Beware, there is firing from the church."

That church, the historic Notre-Dame de la Garde, and its commanding heights were the objective of an all-out assault launched on August 25 by two companies of Algerian infantry and a French tank troop. At 11:30 a.m. two Sherman tanks, the "Jourdain" and the "Jeanne d'Arc," neared the church steps. The "Jeanne d'Arc" was destroyed by shellfire. The "Jourdain" was crippled by a mine, but its wounded commander, a Sergeant Lolliot, clambered out of the tank and attached the tricolor of France to the church's railing. At 4:30 p.m., Notre-Dame de la Garde finally fell.

Wrecked piers in Marseilles, dynamited by the Germans before they surrendered, greeted the victorious French when they took over the port on the 28th of August, 1944. However, reconstruction here proved a much easier job than it was in Cherbourg harbor, and within one month facilities were available for docking and unloading 26 vessels at a time.

While the battle was raging within Marseilles, a fierce and tireless contingent of warriors—6,000 in all—trotted barefoot beside their heavily laden mules through the hills rimming the city. They were Goumiers, Berber tribesmen from the Atlas Mountains of Morocco. The Goumiers had almost been left behind; in Italy they had refused to travel without their beloved mules, which required special transports. Moreover, there was official concern about their "violent instincts, which it would be regrettable to let them satisfy in France." But de Lattre saw to it that his Goumiers came along, and now they were sealing off the routes by which Schaefer's troops might escape from Marseilles.

Surrounded and cut off, with his bastions crumbling before assaults by the reinforced French, Schaefer decided to surrender the city, along with 7,000 surviving troops, on August 28—the same day that Toulon fell. General de Lattre sent a proud message to de Gaulle: "Today, D-plus-13, in Army B's sector there is no German not dead or captive."

De Lattre had captured Toulon a week ahead of the schedule, and Marseilles had fallen to his forces nearly a month before the target date. But not even that swift performance matched the speed that Truscott had in mind for his VI Corps' campaign. "Every military leader," the general wrote, "dreams of the battle in which he can trap the enemy without any avenues or means of escape and in which his destruction can be assured." In order to cut off and obliterate all of the German forces in southwestern France, Truscott had to move as quickly as Patton's Third Army in its race eastward.

Soon after his remarkable success on the invasion beaches, Truscott had sketched out flexible plans for exploiting whatever possibilities lay ahead. He had also established a provisional armored group, called Task Force Butler after its commander, Brigadier General Fred W. Butler, whom Truscott called "one of the most fearless men I ever met." On August 17—D-plus-2—Butler received his marching orders: he would drive northwest to the Durance River, holding his task force ready to head either north to Grenoble or west to

Montélimar on the Rhone. As Task Force Butler raced north, Truscott and Patch chose between those two objectives on August 20, and Truscott sent an urgent message to Butler: "You will move at first light 21 August with all possible speed to Montélimar. Block enemy routes of withdrawal up the Rhone valley in that vicinity."

Truscott was, as he described his tactics, trying "to set the stage for a classic—a 'Cannae'—in which we would encircle the enemy against an impassable barrier or obstacle and destroy him." In the fulfillment of that purpose, Montélimar, hitherto known best to bonbon fanciers as the nougat capital of France, was the key. Just north of the town, National Highway 7 ran through a narrow defile—the Cruas Gorge—between the Rhone and a commanding ridge several miles long and 1,000 feet high. Butler was to plug this bottleneck in the Germans' main retreat route. He would be followed to Montélimar by Dahlquist and elements of the 36th Division, looping northwest from the right flank of the VI Corps. By seizing and holding the dominant ridge in strength, the two forces would pin the German Nineteenth Army in a trap, to be dismembered at leisure.

To carry out his Cannae, Truscott set several other forces in motion. The 45th Division moved north, splitting Provence and herding German remnants westward toward the Rhone Valley and Highway 7. The 3rd Division formed what Truscott's war log tersely called the "bottom of nutcracker," driving the Germans north up the Rhone into the trap at Montélimar. Since that division had previously been assigned to a blocking position north of Toulon and Marseilles, protecting de Lattre's II Corps during its attacks on those cities, Truscott first had to persuade Patch to release the 3rd Division for his push north. That bit of persuasion took Truscott until August 24.

While these movements were taking place, General Frederick's 1st Airborne Task Force faced east, protecting the VI Corps' right flank. The paratroopers carried out their guard duty with casual efficiency—and, as it turned out, with considerable enjoyment as well. A *Yank* staff correspondent reported: "they called it the 'Champagne Campaign,' this war in the Maritime Alps, because of the way the champagne flowed in the celebrations of the liberated people at Antibes and Cannes and Nice. . . . But when they went back into the mountains, to their foxholes on the terraced hillsides under the shelter of the olive trees, they returned to a full-fledged war."

Truscott's vanguard forces plunged north. Butler's tanks roared through the countryside at top speed, pausing only to refuel or to crush the small German garrisons they encountered. At some times and places the infantrymen did not march; they rushed ahead at what they called the "Truscott trot," a pace just slightly short of double time. Reinforcements from the south also moved along at a brisk clip, but they were hopelessly outdistanced; many a GI made the whole advance without hearing a single shot. It was said by experienced newsmen who reported the drive that Truscott was out-Pattoning Patton.

Truscott had not overemphasized how important speed was in his drive toward the Montélimar gap. For on August 16, Hitler had signed an order authorizing General Blaskowitz to withdraw his armies from southern France. With the exception of the forces then penned up in Toulon, Marseilles and ports along the southwest coast of France, all German troops west of the Rhone and south of the Loire would retreat northward. By August 23 the 11th Panzer Division, which had finally managed to cross the Rhone on jerry-built barges, was racing north, clearing the way to Montélimar, preparing to make a gallant stand to hold open the vital pass beyond.

Yet Truscott's race-horse advance was not trouble-free. As early as August 21 his war journal carried an ominous entry: "36th fouled up."

The 36th Division had exhausted the gasoline supply provided for the beach assault, and to get its stalled vehicles moving again, General Truscott on August 22 had been forced to give the outfit 10,000 gallons of gasoline taken from the 45th Division. But even then the 36th did not move as smartly as Truscott wanted it to. For that, he blamed General Dahlquist.

On the 22nd of August Truscott flew north to see Dahlquist at his last reported stopover, Aspres, in central Provence. He found that the General was out in the field but learned, "to my profound dismay," that elements of Dahlquist's division and also of the corps' artillery, which the general should have sent on ahead to Montélimar, were still in bivouac. Angered, Truscott left a note of stiff reprimand at Dahlquist's headquarters.

He was to become angrier yet. On August 24, after returning to his headquarters 15 miles north of Saint-Tropez, Truscott flew north once again to meet with Dahlquist, whose entire division had now reached the vital ridge line north of Montélimar. Truscott was informed by Dahlquist that "he had launched an attack to capture the ridge that morning and his troops were now on the northern end." Reassured, Truscott again headed south, only to learn from aerial reconnaissance reports that German troops were still moving into Montélimar and through the gap. "In spite of assurances," Truscott stated, "our block, on Highway 7 was not effective."

On August 26, Truscott flew north yet again to confront Dahlquist, this time determined to make a radical move. "John," he said, "I have come here with the full intention of relieving you from your command. You have reported to me that you held the high ground north of Montélimar and that you had blocked Highway 7. You have not done so. You have failed to carry out my orders. You have just five minutes in which to convince me that you are not at fault."

Dahlquist said unhappily that his men had seized the wrong ridge—but the mistake had been rectified and the 36th Division was now in fact in position commanding Highway 7. Truscott was still dissatisfied, but he relented and left Dahlquist in command.

For the next two days, the VI Corps hammered the fleeing German Nineteenth Army, blasting tanks of the 11th Panzer Division, piling up destroyed trucks and guns. When de Lattre later passed through the area, he saw a terrible sight: "Over tens of kilometres there was nothing but an inextricable tangle of twisted steel frames and charred corpses—the apocalyptic cemetery of all the equipment of the Nineteenth Army, through which only bulldozers would be able to make a way."

But Dahlquist's delay had exacted a high cost. A large part of the Nineteenth Army had squeezed to safety through the gap held open by the 11th Panzer, which survived the battering to fight again and again on the road to Germany. Moreover, most of Blaskowitz' other army, the First, had evacuated the Bordeaux area and was escaping well to the north of the VI Corps' advance. But the closing of the Montélimar gap, although belated, did come in time to seal the fate of the last Germans in southwestern France. The rear guard of the First Army had little choice but to surrender or to die in pointless battle. In fact, nearly 20,000 Germans eventually surrendered in a single group.

Thus the invasion of southern France reached its strategic conclusion at Montélimar. Symbolically, the operation may be said to have ended on September 11, 1944, when American soldiers of Patton's Third Army linked up with some of de Lattre's men in the town of Saulieu, 40 miles west of Dijon. On September 15, the Seventh Army was absorbed into Eisenhower's command. For General Truscott, whose driving leadership and daring were major factors in the success of the operation, the campaign brought a promotion to lieutenant general—a rank that resulted in his transfer from the fighting VI Corps to the command of an army. He wound up the War back in Italy as the commander of the U.S. Fifth Army.

The controversy surrounding Operation *Anvil-Dragoon* did not end. Churchill still believed that the forces involved could have struck a more telling blow in a drive north from Italy. But even Churchill conceded that the invasion had "brought important assistance to General Eisenhower."

That was faint praise. The invasion summed up all the Allies had learned about amphibious operations. The landing was almost textbook perfect, and the subsequent drive north was extraordinary, with the Seventh Army covering nearly 500 miles in just one month despite logistic problems. Southwestern France, almost one third of the nation, was thereby liberated in concert with the rapid advances being made in northern France. The ports captured in the invasion would inject into the war against Germany a total of 905,000 American soldiers and 4,100,000 tons of matériel. Churchill may have had reservations about the operation, but U.S. Chief of Staff Marshall had none. *Anvil-Dragoon*, he said, was "one of the most successful things we did."

THE PARISIANS MASTER WAR

In chilly November, 1943, Parisians huddle on a grill to take advantage of warm air rising from the subway. Fuel for home heating was rationed by the Germans.

"DESPERATE STRUGGLE FOR EXISTENCE"

Passing a pork store named "To the Royal Ham," a frustrated shopper grimaces after noticing an all-too-familiar sign: "Today, Nothing."

In June 1940, as the triumphant German Army neared Paris, more than two million citizens fled the city, leaving behind only 700,000. But the fugitives could not escape the conquerors, and as they drifted back in the following months, they found Paris transformed almost beyond recognition.

Motor vehicles had virtually disappeared from the city streets—except for autos and trucks used by the Germans. Paris was unheated and unlighted most of the time—except for districts with public buildings and German quarters. In the capital of haute cuisine, Parisians considered themselves lucky to dine on dishes they would have scorned in peacetime: heifer's udder, sheep's lungs, fricassee of alley cat. In the capital of haute couture, once-fashionable women improvised gloves from turkey skin and hats from wood shavings. Practically everything was in short supply—except the Germans' repressive measures.

"Everyday life," a Parisian wrote, "became a desperate struggle for existence," and conditions grew steadily worse. The Germans rationed and price-fixed essential items and issued coupons that theoretically permitted Parisians to buy enough to survive. The meat and bread rations were about half the normal consumption. The wine ration was set at about two quarts a week, which the average Parisian was used to consuming in four meals. The coal ration was as low as 50 kilos (110 pounds) per month per family—enough to heat a one-room apartment for five days. But by spring, 1941, most necessities were rarely available in adequate supply. Occupation troops had first call on all foodstuffs.

The Parisians suffered helplessly under the regimen of shortages; their protests were ignored, and they could not rebel against armed men. They made do without everyday necessities. "We have forgotten," noted one local writer, "what such things as rice, butter, soap, coffee, and eggs are like." The most galling aspect of the Occupation was that many of these items were not really scarce. Some shopkeepers had plenty of coffee, but they were obliged to post signs reading, "The coffee that we roast and grind is not for sale, it is for the exclusive use of the German troops."

Aspiring to makeshift elegance in footwear, a Parisienne puts the finishing touches on a pair of homemade shoes fashioned of raffia with cardboard soles.

Legs pumping, two men on a tandem bicycle run a ventilating system ordinarily powered by electricity.

DARKNESS FALLS ON THE "CITY OF LIGHT"

The Parisians, proud of the capital's fame as the "City of Light," resented Occupation policies that consigned them to darkness much of the time. The Germans confiscated most of the French coal supply for their own use, with the result that electricity for Paris was drastically reduced. Most sections of the city were put on a schedule of rotating blackouts.

While the power was cut off, businesses carried on as best they could. Some shopkeepers moved goods onto the sidewalks to trade in daylight. Several movie theaters kept their projectors running on current from generators powered by sturdy bicyclists. The Gaumont Palace, one of Paris' biggest theaters, calculated that four men, pedaling at the rate of 13 miles an hour for six hours, could produce enough electricity for two full-length features.

Faced with blackouts and the curfew, many families chose to spend the evenings in their living rooms under a single, flickering light bulb. They played cards, Monopoly, dominoes and mah-jongg, and at 9:15 every night they pressed their ears against radios to listen to the forbidden broadcasts of the BBC. Yet even these modest pleasures faded as the Germans' fuel supplies dwindled. Slowly but steadily the Occupation authorities extended the blackouts in Paris. By 1944 the current flowed through the city only one hour a day: between 11 p.m. and midnight.

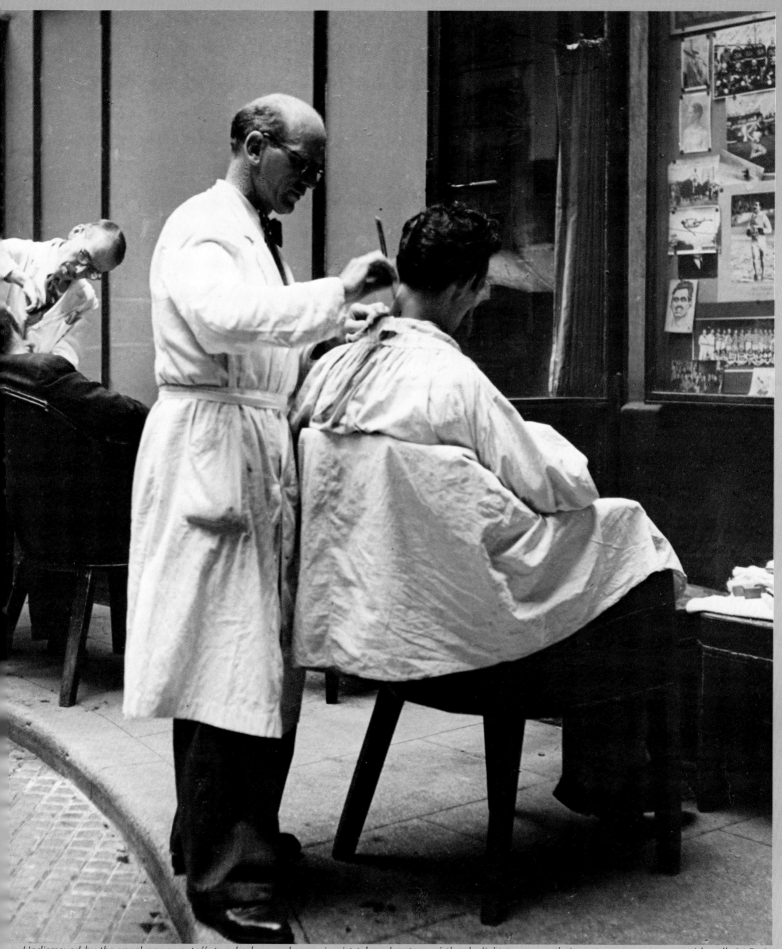

Undismayed by the usual power cutoff, two barbers and a manicurist take advantage of the daylight to groom their customers on a sunny sidewalk in Paris.

LEARNING TO SURVIVE THE FUEL SHORTAGE

A Paris housewife stuffs paper into a makeshift stove that could boil a liter of water in 12 minutes.

Thomas Kernan, an American who worked in occupied Paris before the United States entered the War, believed that "the hardships of the food shortage did not compare with the really terrible suffering caused by the fuel famine." Fuel for cooking was so scarce, he noted, that "a housewife could warm a dish on odd occasions only." Many women did heat small quantities of food with an ingenious device called *le réchaud papier*—the paper stove—that was fueled with scraps of paper *(left)* sprinkled with water for slow burning. There was a catch, though: paper was in short supply, too.

In the winter Parisians had to wear heavy outdoor clothing in their frigid apartments, and many, tired of shivering there, sought relief in the heated confines of post offices and subways. The museums and churches of Paris became as popular as the prewar cafés; there, said a newspaper article, the people "discovered a passion for archaeology, and a tireless devotion to some obscure saint, whose effigy was fanned by gentle blasts of warm air."

But the relief they were able to find was only temporary. "A hideous sight became gruesomely familiar in city streets," a Paris observer wrote. "Men and women, but especially children, blew fiercely at their hands in an effort to warm them. Their fingers were red and swollen. Unnatural bulges on them gaped with cracks or oozed pus from running sores."

"There comes a point," wrote Kernan, "where the human spirit can no longer withstand it." He cited the case of a housewife—"as patriotic as any"—who became so desperate that she asked the authorities to billet German officers in her home in a Paris suburb. "That was the only way she could get coal to heat the house, for no longer could she endure hearing her children crying from the cold."

Risking stiff fines to heat their frigid rooms, coal-less residents of Paris slip through the streets dragging branches that they cut illegally from the city's trees.

123

A bicycle-driven taxi slogs through the snow toward the Opera House in central Paris. This nearly empty square was often the scene of prewar traffic jams.

GETTING THERE
IN SLOW MOTION

Day after day, the Parisians faced a stern battle just to get from their homes to jobs and stores across town. Frenchmen had to apply to the German authorities for permission to keep their cars, and those who received permits and gas rations generally found that gasoline pumps were dry.

Those who managed to keep their cars on the road ran them on a fuel produced by burning wood or charcoal in bolted-on devices called gasogenes.

Public transportation took up some of the slack. A record number of Parisians rode the subway, packed in shoulder to shoulder in second-class cars, while German troops traveled free in first class. Citizens who had relied on taxis paid high prices for rides in horse-drawn carriages

and *vélo-taxis*—two-wheeled carts driven by men pedaling bicycles. Parisians in a hurry might even catch an express *vélo-taxi* propelled by four veterans of the world's greatest bicycle race, the Tour de France.

But most Parisians—two out of three by 1944—depended on their own bicycles. "The entire city is pedaling 'round," wrote a newsman, "from nuns, going out to buy food or to make house-to-house collections, to respectable magistrates."

Using a *specially rigged bicycle, a clever Parisian moves a bed across town.*

A driver stokes his fuel converter; it powered his car by burning charcoal.

On their wedding day, a bride and groom start their honeymoon in a flower-bedecked coach fashioned from an automobile and towed by an old nag.

At a restaurant, hungry Parisians watch a chef as he serves the day's special, described on a chalkboard: croquette of horsemeat in mushroom and wine sauce, potatoes and vegetables. The bottom line of the sign reminds the customers that the serving is "ONE DISH . . . THAT'S ALL!"

Searching for edibles, two French women rummage through a pile of garbage in front of Les Halles, Paris' central market. On one occasion there was a minor riot at Les Halles. Women, queued up to purchase potatoes, clashed with German soldiers who requisitioned the supply.

CHRONIC HUNGER IN THE CULINARY CAPITAL

Throughout the Occupation, the average Parisian lived on less than a third of his peacetime diet—and lost from five to 20 pounds. Moreover, he used up a good deal of his energy and time waiting in long lines for his meager fare.

It took the persistence and skills of a detective to find the makings of a square meal. People camped overnight outside of butcher stores rumored to have a meat delivery scheduled for the next morning. They bicycled far into the countryside to forage for fresh vegetables, eggs, meat and cheese. They also took to raising rabbits in bathtubs, poultry in rooftop coops and vegetables on the grounds of the Tuileries and the Luxembourg Gardens. Many sought out black marketeers who sold provisions at up to 20 times the price set by the Germans. A half pound of coffee, for example, was officially priced at 17 cents but sold for $2.75 on the black market.

Parisians bore up under their deprivations with bitter humor. According to one of their food-shortage jokes, their meat ration was so tiny that it could be wrapped in a subway ticket—if the stub had not been punched by the conductor. If the ticket had been punched, said the joke, the meat would fall through the hole.

5

As the Allies' massive seaborne invasion force was nearing the coast of southern France on August 14, 1944, events in northern France were about to take a dramatic turn of their own. There, as Allied ground troops tightened the noose around the German forces trapped in the Argentan-Falaise pocket, General Patton decided to pay a call on the U.S. XV Corps commander, General Haislip. At his headquarters south of Argentan, Haislip knew that the orders Patton was bringing with him would shape the future of the war in Europe and would determine the fate of Paris and its four million inhabitants.

The corps commander had reason to hope that these orders would conform to his wish for a swift, straight drive to liberate the French capital. Haislip spoke fluent French and had studied as a young officer at the Ecole de Guerre in Paris. He had under his command the only French division in Europe, the French 2nd Armored, and he felt keenly that Frenchmen must strike the ultimate symbolic blow for France by liberating Paris.

But Patton and the top Allied planners had more important objectives in mind. For the time being, Patton told Haislip, there would be no Allied effort to liberate the city. Two divisions of Haislip's XV Corps were to forge ahead only as far as Dreux, 45 miles from Paris, while the rest of the corps stayed at Argentan.

Haislip, bitterly disappointed, begged Patton to let the French 2nd Armored march on Paris. "George, you are wrong, you know," he said. "It will mean more to the French than anything else to think the only division they have in Europe is the first one to get into Paris and it will really jolly them up. It will thrill the whole country."

"Oh, to hell with that," replied Patton, unmoved. "We are fighting a war now."

In conveying the orders to Haislip, Patton was putting into effect the thinking of his superior, General Eisenhower. Ike was well aware of the immense spiritual uplift to the French—and to the whole Allied world—that would accompany the liberation of Paris. Yet his primary military objective clearly lay elsewhere: if his armies could thrust to the Rhine, now only 250 miles away, before the reeling Germans had time to regroup, the War might be ended in short order. But Eisenhower had another reason for not wanting to free the city. He knew that it would be a costly

A DIABOLICAL PLAN THWARTED

venture. Street fighting within a heavily defended Paris, a 24-page planning document from Allied Supreme Headquarters had warned, could result "in the destruction of the French capital." In addition, once taken, Paris would require "a civil affairs commitment equal to maintaining eight divisions in operation. . . . Paris food and medical requirements alone are 75,000 tons for the first two months, and an additional 1,500 tons of coal daily are likely to be needed for public utilities."

With the arrival of supplies still limited to the harbor at Cherbourg and the invasion beaches, Eisenhower already was operating on a logistical shoestring; even now, he was stripping incoming divisions of jeeps and trucks intended for battlefield use and assigning them to supply convoys. The round trip between Cherbourg and Paris was more than 400 miles, and each supply convoy would consume hundreds of gallons of gasoline at a time when, as Eisenhower would later recall, "I hurt every time I had to give up a gallon." His American field commander, General Bradley, put it another way: "If Paris could pull in its belt and live with the Germans a little longer, each 4,000 tons we saved would mean gasoline enough for a three days' motor march toward the German border."

The Allied plan was to go all out toward Germany. In the process, two arms—Montgomery's Twenty-first Army Group to the north and Bradley's Twelfth Army Group to the south—would be thrown around Paris, embracing the great city without storming it. The timetable called for the liberation of the city no earlier than the middle of September. But the plans for Paris were destined to be overwhelmed by events. Conspiring to upset the timetable were the urgent and inexorable will of the French to rule again in their capital, a contest between Communists and Gaullists for power in the city, the determination of Adolf Hitler to leave the French capital in ruins and, not least, the reluctance of a German general to become known to history as the man who destroyed Paris.

While the Allied leaders were debating what to do about Paris, the citizens of the great city were suffering from a variety of shortages and inconveniences. They were in dire need of food, electricity, municipal transport—and perhaps most of all, a renewal of their self-respect. In addition to the brutality of the German Occupation, the Parisians had endured hundreds of grating indignities. Each day, 250 elite German troops behind a brass band blaring "Preussens Glorie" ("Prussia's Glory") paraded down the Champs-Elysées from the Arc de Triomphe to the Place de la Concorde. The swastika flapped from the top of the city's most visible landmark, the Eiffel Tower, while the banned French tricolor could be viewed publicly in only one spot, a glass case in the Army Museum of Les Invalides.

The most potent and persistent force for a quick liberation of Paris was Charles de Gaulle. From his headquarters in Algeria, de Gaulle headed the French Committee of National Liberation, the central organization guiding the Free French war effort and coordinating the coalition of Communist, Gaullist and other anti-German guerrillas in France known as the Resistance. However, de Gaulle was far from being established as the unquestioned leader of France. He had formidable rivals in the Resistance—primarily Communists—who had the advantage of jockeying for position from within the country. In addition, many Allied officials considered him a pest, and even to his beleaguered countrymen he was little more than a voice from beyond, known to them by his BBC broadcasts.

De Gaulle realized that in order to become the acknowledged leader of liberated France, he would have to be recognized as the liberator of Paris. He understood, too, that if the city's civilian population, spurred by strident Communist factions in the Resistance, were to rise up and expel the Germans before he got to Paris, "on my arrival they would bind my brows with laurel, invite me to assume the place they would assign me, and thenceforth pull all the strings themselves."

Against that gloomy prospect, de Gaulle had been preparing for the assumption of power with painstaking care and consummate skill. His chances improved greatly on December 30, 1943, when Eisenhower visited Algiers and met with him for the first time. Near the end of the session, Ike said, "You were originally described to me in an unfavorable sense. Today, I realize that that judgment was wrong." "Splendid!" replied de Gaulle. "You are a man! For you know how to say, 'I was wrong!'" De Gaulle then went on to say to Ike: "It must be French troops that take possession of the capital." He meant forces under his own control as head of the French Committee of National Liberation. Eisenhower agreed.

In July of 1944, de Gaulle had taken another step toward becoming the undisputed leader of France. He traveled to Washington, D.C., to confer with President Roosevelt, who formally recognized him as the leader of a de facto French government sanctioned by the Allies to rule in liberated territory.

Now, in August 1944, as the Allied troops swept eastward across France, teams of Gaullist administrators, police, supply officers and even a traveling court-martial board followed close behind them, taking control of local governments in the name of the French Committee of National Liberation and Charles de Gaulle. These auxiliaries were under stern and specific orders to prevent Communist-dominated Resistance committees from gaining control of the newly liberated French cities and towns.

To de Gaulle the French Communists at this transitional stage of the war represented at least as fearsome a menace as the Germans. They were particularly powerful in the Paris Resistance, where they had an estimated 25,000 fighters under arms. To prevent a take-over by Communist factions in the city, de Gaulle methodically infiltrated his own representatives into the Paris Resistance. Among these was the 29-year-old General Jacques Chaban-Delmas, de Gaulle's top military man in Paris.

Chaban-Delmas had not the slightest doubt about the nature of the Leftist threat. "Whatever the cost," he later said, "the Communists would launch their insurrection, even if the result was the destruction of the most beautiful city in the world." He was right. The Communists, determined to challenge the Gaullists for power in Paris every step of the way, were convinced that their political advantage lay in fomenting rebellion in the city. If the uprising succeeded—and they believed it would—they could ride the wave of popular acclaim in France and deny de Gaulle the power he coveted.

Roger Villon, the Communist chief of staff of the Paris Resistance, was resolute in his belief that de Gaulle should not "march into Paris at the head of a conquering army and find the city gratefully prostrated at his feet." Villon was egged on by the commander of Communist military forces in Paris—Colonel Rol. Born Henri Tanguy, he had served in the Spanish Civil War (and taken his *nom de guerre* from a comrade killed in that conflict). Rol was a dedicated party member whose courage and devotion to the cause were acknowledged even by his enemies. Like his Gaullist opposite number, Chaban-Delmas, Rol realized the importance of the prize now involved. "Paris," he said, "is worth 200,000 dead."

In his headquarters in East Prussia, Hitler was determined to reduce Paris to such a shambles that neither the Gaullists nor the Communists would stand to gain from its liberation. To carry out his plans, Hitler summoned to Rastenburg in the early part of August an officer from the Western Front who, in the words of an OKW superior, had "never questioned an order, no matter how harsh it was." Physically, Major General Dietrich von Choltitz hardly fit the autocratic Prussian stereotype. He was a pudgy little man, and although his face, as described by a colleague, was "as expressionless as the fat Buddha's," he possessed a certain burgomaster jollity.

But Choltitz' reputation as a wrecker of cities was fearsome. In May 1940, as a lieutenant colonel, he had ordered the heart of Rotterdam bombed to rubble, leaving 718 Dutch dead and 78,000 wounded or homeless. The siege of Sebastopol in the Crimea, where he won general's rank, left him with an arm wound and only 347 able-bodied men out

Portly Major General Dietrich von Choltitz, the German commander of Paris, vowed to "personally shoot down in my own office the next man who comes to me suggesting we abandon Paris without a fight." But the defense he set up outside the city was soon overcome by the advancing French 2nd Armored Division.

of the original 4,800 in his regiment; but he took the city, and demolished it. And during the retreat from Russia, Choltitz covered the German rear, leaving behind only scorched earth. Such was his notoriety that he was widely blamed for the August 1944 destruction of Warsaw, where more than 100,000 died; in fact, he had been on the Western Front at the time. Choltitz was keenly—and ruefully—aware of his infamy. "It is always my lot," he said, "to defend the rear of the German army. And each time it happens I am ordered to destroy each city as I leave it."

In recent days, Choltitz had been greatly distressed by Germany's continuing defeats and had felt much in need of a boost to his flagging faith and spirit. As he arrived at Hitler's headquarters, he felt sure the Führer could provide the uplift he needed. What he encountered instead was one of the most bizarre and unsettling experiences of his life.

Hitler, still shaken by the July 20 assassination attempt, launched into a tirade shortly after greeting Choltitz. "Since the 20th of July, Herr General," he cried, "dozens of generals—yes, dozens—have bounced at the end of a rope because they wanted to prevent me, Adolf Hitler, from continuing my work."

Choltitz was aghast. "He was in a state of feverish excitement," he later said. "Saliva was literally running from his mouth. He was trembling all over and the desk on which he was leaning shook with him. He was bathed in perspiration and became more agitated."

Hitler came to the point. "Now," he said to Choltitz, "you're going to Paris." The city "must be utterly destroyed. On the departure of the Wehrmacht, nothing must be left standing, no church, no artistic monument." Even the water supply would be cut off, so that—in the Führer's words—"the ruined city may be a prey to epidemics."

Choltitz later recalled Hitler's harangue with dismay. "I was convinced there and then," he said, that "the man opposite me was mad!" His confidence in Hitler shattered, Choltitz left the meeting more despondent than ever—and, perhaps for the first time in his military career, questioning his own resolve to carry out an order.

Soon afterward, he paid a visit to Field Marshal von Kluge, commander of Army Group B, just six days before Kluge committed suicide. "I'm afraid, my dear Choltitz," said Kluge at the end of the meeting, "Paris may become a rather disagreeable assignment for you. It has the air of a burial place about it." Choltitz' reply was full of grim sarcasm. "At least," he said, "it will be a first class burial."

In Paris, Choltitz set up his headquarters in the elegant Hôtel Meurice, near the Place de la Concorde. From his bedroom window he could look down on the lush treetops of the Tuileries. There, in the days that followed, the stout German spent long hours in lonely contemplation of his dilemma. He was haunted by the thought that the man to whom he had sworn blind obedience was mad and that his country's cause was lost. As a patriotic German soldier, he was prepared to defend Paris against the advancing Allies; but, sensitive to the city's beauty and traditions, he was loath to destroy it. To disobey Hitler's orders would endanger his own life and the lives of his wife and children in Germany. Yet he knew that if he carried out the Führer's directives, history would damn him as the man who destroyed one of the world's most glorious cities.

As he pondered his problem, Choltitz was confronted with a situation that was to directly affect his decision: unrest in the city's police force. The gendarmes had long been caught in a cruel dilemma of their own, despised by the Parisians for carrying out the harsh Occupation orders of the Germans, yet distrusted by the Occupation authorities. As one of his first acts as commander of Paris, Choltitz set about disarming the police. In retaliation, the police made it clear that the Germans had good reasons for concern. A Resistance group within the police department called a strike for August 15, grimly warning: "Police who do not obey this order to strike will be considered traitors and collaborators." The strike was highly effective: only a handful of the gendarmes manned their posts. Events were now moving at such a pace as to force Choltitz' hand.

On the gray, damp Saturday morning of August 19, Amedée Bussière, the head prefect of the Paris police, awakened to the sound of a throng gathered outside the bedroom of his apartment at the Prefecture, the police headquarters on the Ile de la Cité opposite Notre-Dame. He hoped that his men were returning to duty, but he was mistaken. In the courtyard below, a slender blond man in a checked suit was addressing the crowd. As a trumpet sounded and voices lifted in the long-forbidden "Marseillaise," Yves Bayet, head of the Gaullist police faction in the Paris Police Committee of Liberation, proclaimed: "In the name of the Republic and Charles de Gaulle, I take possession of the Prefecture of Police."

On the previous day, the call for an uprising—including seizure of the Prefecture—had gone out from Communist Resistance leaders, who had hoped to keep the Gaullists ignorant of the plan until it was too late to do anything about it. But Alexandre Parodi, de Gaulle's top political representative in Paris, got word from an informer planted among the Communists—and Parodi, forewarned, struck first at the Prefecture. Ironically, this first major act of insurrection was led by the Gaullists—who, on orders from de Gaulle himself, had fiercely opposed open rebellion. But Gaullist leaders in Paris felt compelled to preempt the plans of their archrivals for power, the Communists. For their part, the Communists, hearing that they had been beaten to the punch at the Prefecture, immediately embarked on their plan to ambush German soldiers and vehicles all over Paris. Soon sharp gunfights could be heard across the city, as well-organized Resistance bands—Communist and Gaullist alike—began seizing police substations, post offices and government buildings. By nightfall, both sides had suffered heavy casualties; the Germans alone lost more than 50 killed and 100 wounded.

Late that night, Choltitz stood on the balcony of his hotel room, watching a girl in a red dress as she rode her bicycle through the Tuileries toward the Place de la Concorde. With Choltitz was Raoul Nordling, for 18 years the Swedish consul general in Paris and the managing director of the SKF factories, which made ball bearings that had helped keep the German war machine rolling. Choltitz, angered by the uprising in Paris, was nevertheless in a pensive mood. "I like those pretty Parisiennes," he said. "It would be a tragedy to have to kill them and destroy their city."

To Nordling, the destruction of Paris was unthinkable. He felt he owed much to the city in which he had spent his entire adult life—and that he deeply loved. He had already begun to pay that debt: during the week he had successfully negotiated with Choltitz for the release of more than 4,000 French political prisoners. With all his eloquence, Nordling now argued for the salvation of Paris.

"I am a soldier," Choltitz said. "I get orders. I execute them." From the area around the Resistance-held Prefecture came a spatter of gunfire. "I'll get them out of their Prefecture," Choltitz vowed. "I'll bomb them out of it."

"Do you realize," Nordling asked, "your near misses will fall on Notre-Dame and the Sainte-Chapelle?"

That could not be helped, Choltitz replied to Nordling. "You know the situation. Put yourself in my place. What alternative do I have?"

Nordling answered the plaintive question immediately. He proposed a cease-fire "to pick up the dead and wounded" of the spreading insurrection; if the cease-fire was successful, it might be turned into a full-fledged truce. The idea appealed to Choltitz: a truce would release troops, now tied down in the attempt to quell the uprising, to man the defense line Choltitz was setting up around Paris.

Two hours after his meeting with Nordling, as he considered the proposed truce, Choltitz received an order from Hitler instructing him to prepare the Seine bridges for destruction. "Paris," the Führer declared, "must not fall into the hands of the enemy except as a field of ruins."

Choltitz, a hard-bitten soldier for 29 of his 49 years, now faced his most agonizing decision. As an experienced tactician, he knew that Hitler's order could not halt the Allied advance. The Americans were already across the river north and south of the city. "What military value could the destruction of the bridges possibly have in this situation?" Choltitz later wrote. "Even if only three of the 60 bridges were to remain intact, the entire action would prove militarily worthless. . . . Additionally, I myself needed the bridges for troop movements within the city."

Beyond the military considerations, Choltitz found himself being influenced by more basic human emotions. "In what state of mind could I, without necessity, destroy this city, which had endured, calmly and wisely, though grudgingly, for four years under German occupation?" he asked himself. "It had been my firm commitment from the very beginning as a decent soldier to protect the civilian population and their magnificent city to the greatest extent possible." Weighing all of the factors that had pressed so heavily on him since his arrival in Paris, Choltitz made up his mind: he would accept a cease-fire.

Acting as an intermediary, Nordling outlined the terms of

his proposed cease-fire to Gaullist contacts he had cultivated in the Paris Resistance during the Occupation. Then, at a hastily convened early-morning meeting, Chaban-Delmas and his Gaullist associates presented the truce to Resistance leaders. Unfortunately for the Communists, who wanted to continue the fight, the deck was stacked against them. With communications difficult in the city and with events surging ahead at a tremendous clip, only one of their leaders—Roger Villon—was informed of the meeting; in fact, only six of the 16 Resistance chiefs eligible to vote were present.

Villon spoke out against the cease-fire. "The people of Paris have risen and are ready to liberate the capital themselves," he said. "To make them lay down their arms would be to curb their spirit and balk them of their victory." But the prevailing sentiment in the meeting was against Villon. The Germans were still too strong to be defeated, said the Gaullists, and Choltitz might destroy the city. The cease-fire proposal passed five to one.

Under the terms of the truce, Choltitz agreed to recognize members of the FFI, the coalition of Gaullist, Communist and other underground Resistance fighters, as regular troops and to treat them as prisoners of war if captured, instead of executing them as terrorist guerrillas. The Germans also accepted the FFI occupation of public buildings already seized (these by now included the Hôtel de Ville, which housed the municipal government and had been taken over by the Communist factions in the Resistance in response to the Gaullist occupation of the Prefecture). The FFI, for its part, agreed not to attack German-held strongholds and to allow German troop movements along several major arteries.

Little by little, as word of the cease-fire spread across the city, the firing stopped. A curtain of silence descended on the buildings whose courtyards, hallways and staircases had echoed during the day with gunfire. The FFI set up mobile kitchens, where exhausted Resistance fighters were given a snack, some hot coffee and two packs of cigarettes each.

But the truce quickly began to crumble. Colonel Rol, the Communist military leader, furious at the agreement that had been concluded without his consent a few hours before, feverishly began to undermine it, hoping ultimately to gain control in Paris. "The order is insurrection," Rol told his followers. "As long as there is a single German left in the streets of Paris, we shall fight."

Slowly but steadily throughout the day, along sweeping boulevards and in dark alleys, the uprising regained its lost momentum; four truckloads of German soldiers were ambushed and doused with Molotov cocktails, which sent the burned occupants screaming through the narrow streets. Fearful of German retribution, Gaullists sought desperately to stop the shooting. "Rol and the men around him are leading Paris to a massacre!" cried Chaban-Delmas. But Rol held fast, and the rebellion spread.

At the Hôtel Meurice, Choltitz' glum contemplation of the truce breakdown was interrupted by a telephone call. At the other end of the line was General Jodl, Hitler's operations chief, wanting to know how much progress Choltitz had made in executing Hitler's order to destroy the city. In fact, Choltitz had done little. He tried to excuse the delay by claiming that his troops had been totally occupied with quelling the insurrection. This was the first indication Jodl (or through him, Hitler) had of the extent of the Paris uprising. For a few moments he seemed dumbstruck. Then, speaking deliberately but with a noticeable edge to his voice, Jodl concluded the conversation: "Whatever happens, the Führer expects you to carry out the widest destruction possible in the area assigned to your command."

The news from Paris, which jolted Hitler and Jodl, disturbed Eisenhower as well. When he first heard that the Resistance was fighting in the city, Ike was—he later said—

Wearing American combat gear, members of the French 2nd Armored Division fire rifles and a bazooka at German forces fighting a delaying action at Châteaufort, eight miles southwest of Paris, on August 24, 1944. To enable the Free French to put a modern army in the field, the United States provided about 3.25 million tons of equipment, including more than 1,400 tanks and almost 50.2 million small arms.

"damned mad." It was "just the kind of situation I didn't want, a situation that wasn't under our control, that might force us to change our plans before we were ready for it." Because of the fighting, he faced the dismal prospect of a meeting with de Gaulle, whom he quite rightly suspected of intending to try "to get us to change our plans to accommodate his political needs."

After a precarious flight from Algiers (his plane got lost in fog over the English Channel while trying to link up with a British fighter escort), de Gaulle landed at Cherbourg; his plane had fuel for only two more minutes of flying. Promptly informed of the uprising in Paris, he sprang into action. He flew off in his refueled plane to present his case to Eisenhower at Ike's forward headquarters not far away.

When the two men met, Eisenhower explained to de Gaulle how he planned to pinch off Paris and let it hang there for later plucking. According to Eisenhower, de Gaulle "immediately asked us to reconsider on Paris. He made no bones about it; he said there was a serious menace from the Communists in the city." To Eisenhower, this was a political argument, running counter to strategy—and he found it unacceptable.

Ike suspected that the Germans were reinforcing Paris, and "we might get ourselves in a helluva fight there." But de Gaulle insisted that the prompt liberation of Paris was of paramount importance, and he backed his plea with a threat. He was ready if necessary, he said, to remove Major General Jacques Leclerc's French 2nd Armored Division, now temporarily attached to the American V Corps under Major General Leonard Gerow, from the Allied command and send it to Paris on his own authority. Eisenhower merely smiled—serene in his belief that the 2nd Armored was so dependent on American equipment and supplies that it "couldn't have moved a mile if I didn't want it to."

De Gaulle had been rebuffed, but he was far from defeated. Departing, he turned to an aide and asked: "Where is General Leclerc?"

At that moment, and throughout the next nerve-fraying day of Monday, August 21, General Leclerc was at Argentan, more than 100 miles from Paris. There, as de Gaulle later wrote, the 2nd Armored Division was being kept under "close supervision of General Gerow . . . as if someone

feared it might make off toward the Eiffel Tower." In fact, Leclerc was straining to do just that. He was an impetuous man, who had been waiting for four years for such an opportunity. His real name was not Leclerc but Jacques-Philippe de Hauteclocque. He had taken the pseudonym to protect the family he had left behind in Occupied France. In July 1940, some three weeks after France's surrender, he had bicycled across the Pyrenees and into Spain; from there he had traveled to London to join de Gaulle. His first command, in French Equatorial Africa, had consisted of three officers, two missionaries, seven farmers and five civil servants, equipped with a single dugout canoe. Now, on August 21, 1944, he commanded 16,000 men with 2,000 vehicles—and he was eagerly awaiting the signal to lead his countrymen back into Paris.

As it happened, Eisenhower had miscalculated in assuming that Leclerc's division was unable to move without American help. In recent days, the French regiments had deliberately failed to report their vehicle losses so that their gasoline ration would not be cut. They also continued to requisition fuel and ammunition for vehicles and weapons that had been lost in the fighting around the Argentan-Falaise pocket. In nighttime forays, moreover, men of the French 2nd Armored had taken additional supplies from Allied dumps. By this unorthodox means, Leclerc had squirreled away enough gasoline and ammunition to get his division to Paris.

Yet, as a professional soldier, Leclerc still respected what he called the "rules of military subordination," and at least for the moment, he was willing to settle for a token advance on Paris. In strict secrecy, Leclerc ordered Lieut. Colonel Jacques de Guillebon, at the head of a force of about 150 men in tanks, armored cars and personnel carriers, to reconnoiter the routes toward—and, if the opportunity arose, into—Paris. As General Bradley later related it, Gerow himself first spotted the wayward column after it had passed through Chartres. "And just where in hell do you think you're going?" Gerow asked a French captain. The reply, accompanied by a smile and a shrug: "To Paris—yes?" The V Corps commander was outraged at such blatant insubordination. He halted the armored column in its tracks and sent it back to Argentan.

While Leclerc had been scouting the possibilities for a

march into Paris, radical Resistance forces inside the city were urging the populace to greater action. Three new Resistance newspapers—*Le Parisien Libéré, Défense de la France* and *Libération*—appeared in the capital on August 21. Each of the papers, sired by the Communist forces of Colonel Rol, carried the huge headline, *Aux Barricades!*—the stirring battle cry that had echoed throughout Paris' revolution-filled past.

Despite danger to themselves and to their beloved city, Parisians within the next two days would answer that call by building more than 400 barricades. People of all ages tore up paving stones, felled trees, ripped up railings, turned over cars and trucks, then piled the debris in boulevards and alleyways to hamper German movement. In Saint Germain des Prés, on the corner of the Rue St. Jacques, battered pictures of Hitler and other Nazi leaders were hung on the barricades in exposed positions where attacking Germans would have to fire on them. "Hour by hour, methodically, the barricades close in round the Germans like a trap," wrote an observer. "Patiently, cunningly, with all the vast fury of insurgent Paris, the spider's web is woven."

As the street fighting flared, the Resistance made steady gains. Dozens of key buildings—newspaper offices, government headquarters and Elysée Palace, home of French heads of state—fell into FFI hands. At the Bank of France, the tricolor hung from the façade, while Resistance fighters divvied up a treasure stored inside that was more prized than money in luxury-starved Paris—400,000 bottles of cognac, three million cigars and 235 tons of sugar.

Meanwhile, at a violent conclave of factional leaders, top Resistance chiefs debated whether to try to restore the shattered cease-fire. An angry voice denounced the truce with Choltitz: "You don't make gentlemen's agreements with murderers!" Chaban-Delmas, the Gaullist general, furiously retorted: "You want to massacre 150,000 people for nothing!" Declared Roger Villon, the Communist political leader: "I've never seen such a gutless French general." And then, playing his trump card, Villon vowed that if the truce were restored, the Communists would "plaster every wall in Paris with a poster accusing the Gaullists of stabbing the people of Paris in the back." Alexandre Parodi, the Gaullist political chief, gave in. "My God," he said. "They're going to destroy Paris now. Our beautiful Notre-Dame will be

bombed to ruins." But Villon was unmoved. "So what if Paris is destroyed?" he said. "We will be destroyed along with it. Better Paris be destroyed like Warsaw than that she live another 1940."

Fortunately for Paris, however, the fate of the city rested in the hands of Choltitz. He had chosen to ignore—as long as he could—Hitler's order to immolate the city. Anticipating reprisal from the Führer, he said to an aide: "I will sit on the last bridge and blow myself up along with it because it will be the only thing left for me."

As the violence spread, Choltitz made a desperate gesture to calm the rampaging French patriots. Food supplies were dwindling, and he offered to turn some meat over to the Resistance. When the Frenchmen proudly refused to take it from German hands, a face-saving compromise was arranged and the meat was sent to Nordling, who then gave it to the Resistance. But the offering had little effect: the fighting had taken on an irresistible momentum.

Choltitz decided to meet with Nordling and try another tack. As the two men faced each other across a decanter of whiskey in the German commander's headquarters at the Hôtel Meurice, Choltitz said wryly: "Your truce, Herr Consul General, doesn't seem to be working very well." Nordling agreed and commented that perhaps the only man who could calm Paris, Charles de Gaulle, was elsewhere. In matter-of-fact tones, Choltitz asked a wholly unanticipated question: "Why doesn't someone go to see him?"

In his many years as a diplomat, Nordling had rarely been so astonished. Hesitating, groping for the explicit meaning of the question, he asked if Choltitz would authorize someone to pass through the German lines to seek out the Allied command.

"Why not?" asked Choltitz.

Taking a sheet of paper from his jacket, Choltitz explained that it contained the formal orders for Paris' demolition. So far, he said, he had managed to resist the orders, but time was running out. Only the presence in Paris of Allied troops could prevent the debacle. "You must realize," he said, "that my behavior in telling you this could be interpreted as treason." He paused, then added: "Because what I am really doing is asking the Allies to help me."

When Nordling, as a neutral diplomat, volunteered to

approach the Allies, Choltitz quickly wrote a pass to enable him to get out of the city and make contact with the Allied command and, ultimately, with de Gaulle: "The Commanding General of Greater Paris authorizes the Consul General of Sweden R. Nordling to leave Paris and its line of defense." Then, ushering Nordling out of his office, Choltitz offered a farewell admonition. "Go fast," he said. "Twenty-four, forty-eight hours are all you have."

As Nordling was leaving the German headquarters, he was struck by a troubling thought: perhaps de Gaulle and the Allied commanders would view him less as the well-meaning Swedish consul general than as the purveyor of SKF ball bearings to Germany. To clear the way for his mission, he decided to take with him two men with strong Gaullist connections: Alexandre de Saint-Phalle, treasurer of the Resistance in Paris, and Jean Laurent, who in 1940 had served with de Gaulle in the Ministry of Defense.

Added to the party on Choltitz' advice was Emil "Bobby" Bender, ostensibly the representative of a Swiss paper-pulp company but actually an agent of Abwehr, the German intelligence arm, whose status could be counted on to shepherd the party past security checkpoints. Since 1940, Bender had been a familiar figure in Paris nightclubs; now, to protect himself or from real affection for Paris, he agreed to help save the city (he had already helped Nordling arrange for the release of French political prisoners).

A fifth member joined the group; he called himself "Arnoux" and claimed to be a Red Cross representative. He was, in fact, Colonel Claude Ollivier, head of the British intelligence service in France. Finally, self-invited, was an Austrian nobleman, Baron Erich Posch-Pastor von Camperfeld, who had opposed the Nazis, been interned at Dachau, later escaped to France and joined the Resistance.

That afternoon came a near-fatal hitch in the plan. As he was getting ready to leave, 62-year-old Raoul Nordling slumped to the floor of the Swedish consulate with a heart attack, which, though it proved to be mild, nonetheless precluded any possibility of his leading the mission. Hastily picked to replace him was the one other man in the city whose initials and last name matched those on the Choltitz pass: Raoul Nordling's brother Rolf.

And so the oddly assorted group finally set out—five men in Nordling's car and Bobby Bender in his speedy little Citroën—only to be stopped near the village of Trappes by a German soldier, clad for comfort in the August heat in a polka-dot bathing suit but wearing his helmet and brandishing a submachine gun. At that point, Bender made up for any past sins he may have committed: shouting angrily, he showed his Abwehr papers, along with the Choltitz pass, to an SS captain who had come to investigate. The captain rejected them. "I don't give a damn what general signed it," he said of the pass. "Since the 20th of July, we don't obey Wehrmacht generals." Furious, Bender demanded that the officer call Choltitz' headquarters for orders. Minutes later, Rolf Nordling and his group were on their way.

But they were unable to make contact with the Allied command until the next morning. By that time, Leclerc's tanks were already rolling toward Paris, spurred by an entirely separate two-man mission that had set forth from the beleaguered capital to seek arms from the Allies and had changed its purpose en route.

Major Roger Gallois was Colonel Rol's chief of staff. Two days earlier, Rol, whose insurrection required more weapons to fill willing but empty hands, had jumped at an offer from Dr. Robert Monod, who led a double life as the official health inspector for the Paris area and medical chief for the Resistance. Monod agreed to guide a Rol emissary through the German lines to "establish a liaison with the Allies and ask for arms." Rol chose Gallois for the job.

Gallois and Monod traveled only 18 miles that first day and night before stopping to rest in the village of Saint-Nom-la-Breteche. The two were longtime friends, and as they talked by candlelight, Monod, an anti-Communist especially resentful of Communists planted in his own office, urged Gallois not to help Rol grasp control of Paris by insurrection. Instead, the doctor said, Gallois should try to get the Allies to go to Paris as quickly as possible, so the city would be saved from destruction by the Germans. Gallois listened carefully. "Robert," he said finally, "I think you're right." With those words, Gallois changed goals: instead of seeking arms for Colonel Rol, he would try to convince Allied commanders that they, and not the insurrectionists, must accomplish the liberation of Paris.

The next day, Gallois came upon an American soldier, eating canned rations by the side of the road. "I come from

Paris," Gallois dramatically declared, "with a message for General Eisenhower!"

"Yeah?" said the American. "So what?"

Despite that massive display of disinterest, Gallois was placed in a jeep and taken to the headquarters of General Patton, whose Third Army had crossed the Seine that same day. When he had first heard of the Paris uprising, Patton had been less than sympathetic: "They started their goddamned insurrection. Now let them finish it." Aroused from sleep, he was hardly in better humor. "Okay," he told the disheveled French Resistance officer. "I'm listening. What's your story?" And when Gallois finished talking, Patton flatly turned down his plea: the Resistance would have to "accept the consequences" of its own insurrection, he said.

Still, Gallois must have impressed Patton; at any rate, he was soon on his way by jeep to General Bradley's headquarters at Laval, where he arrived on the morning of August 22.

There, Brigadier General Edwin L. Sibert, Bradley's intelligence officer, who had been alerted by Patton's headquarters, was waiting impatiently to meet with Gallois and to get a firsthand account of the situation in Paris. Sibert had delayed a flight with Bradley to Eisenhower's new headquarters at Grandchamp, just outside Falaise, where he was to attend a conference with the Supreme Commander. Gallois, his failure to convince Patton still rankling, passionately poured out his fears for the preservation of Paris and the survival of its populace. "The people of Paris want to liberate their capital themselves and present it to the Allies," he said. "But they cannot finish what they have started. You must come to our help or there is going to be a terrible slaughter."

Sibert was silent. But as he gathered his papers before leaving, he confided some information to Gallois that gave cause for hope. "Your impatient lion, Leclerc, is coming today," he said, knowing that the French general was later to meet with Bradley. "We may have some news for him tonight." Sibert had one other piece of news that he did not share with Gallois: Eisenhower was wavering about Paris.

It had become increasingly evident to Ike that the French capital was in real peril. Just as Choltitz dreaded being known to history as the man who destroyed Paris, Eisenhower had no wish to be responsible for contributing to the city's ruin by doing nothing to save it. Beyond that, Ike was having second thoughts about the military considerations, thoughts he expressed that morning in a cable to his superior in Washington, U.S. Army Chief of Staff Marshall. He acknowledged the fact that Paris' supply needs made it desirable to delay its liberation, but, he added, "I do not believe this is possible. If the enemy tries to hold Paris with any real strength, he would be a constant menace to our flank. If he largely concedes the place, it falls into our hands whether we like it or not."

Finally, there was the matter of de Gaulle, about whom Ike's feelings were ambivalent. Eisenhower was often annoyed by the towering Frenchman's "hypersensitiveness and extraordinary stubbornness." But at the same time, he knew that, to many, de Gaulle was the embodiment of French nationalism—as well as the leader who had been given Roosevelt's blessing.

Moreover, Eisenhower now had before him a letter, written by de Gaulle after their last disagreeable meeting and personally delivered by French General Alphonse Juin. It implicitly placed the consequences for failure to seize Paris—a move now necessary "even if it should produce fighting and damage in the interior of the city"—upon Eisenhower. It also renewed the threat to send Leclerc and the French 2nd Armored Division to Paris on their own. Ike had

Masters turned slaves, Germans who once used the Hôtel Majestic as headquarters are forced to clean the streets in front of it after the liberation of Paris. Fences were built to keep Parisians from attacking the Germans.

a feeling that—fuel or no fuel—de Gaulle meant to try exactly that. For the attention of his chief of staff, Lieut. General Walter Bedell Smith, Eisenhower wrote on the letter's margin: "It looks as though we shall be compelled to go into Paris." Whatever doubt remained was dispelled when Bradley and his staff arrived to report Gallois' description of the situation in Paris. "Well, what the hell, Brad," said Ike. "I guess we'll have to go in."

Explaining his reasons for sending troops to Paris, Eisenhower later wrote: "My hand was forced by the actions of the Free French forces inside the city. . . . Information indicated that no great battle would take place and it was believed that the entry of one or two Allied divisions would accomplish the liberation of the city. For the honor of first entry General Bradley selected General Leclerc's French 2nd Division."

Leclerc and Gallois were waiting fretfully on the airstrip at Bradley's headquarters when they first got the word from Sibert. "You win," shouted the intelligence officer as his light plane taxied to a stop. "They've decided to send you straight to Paris." Then, Bradley's plane landed. "The decision has been made to enter Paris," he said quietly, "and the three of us share in the responsibility for it: I, because I have given the order; you, General Leclerc, because you are going to execute it; and you, Major Gallois, because it was largely on the basis of the information you brought us that the decision was made." To Leclerc, Bradley added, "I want you to remember one thing above all. I don't want any fighting in Paris. It's the only order I have for you."

Around dusk, Major General Jacques Leclerc leaped from his plane on the field at Argentan and cried: *"Mouvement immediat sur Paris!"*

Leclerc's drive for Paris started shortly before dawn on Wednesday, August 23, as the French 2nd Armored Division roared out of its bivouac near Ecouché and headed for Paris—slipping and sliding through a lashing rainstorm along winding country roads. The weather could not dampen the ardor of the men, volunteers all, gathered from every corner of the French Empire. There were soldiers from Indochina, Chad, Senegal, Tunisia, Morocco, French Equatorial and Central Africa. Although they were French citizens, most had never been to France until recently, and

Paris was still but a hazy vision. Yet this was the moment they had been waiting for. "A French officer came along and told us we were first for Paris and everybody was tremendously excited," said a soldier. "When we moved off it seemed more like 50 mph than our usual 20."

For his part, Bradley was determined that Leclerc's movement into Paris should not be turned into a triumphant lark. He was aware of the French troops' reputation for being undisciplined—what one American First Army Officer had described as their "casual manner of doing almost exactly what they please, regardless of orders." Therefore, Bradley placed general supervision of the operation under the First Army commander, General Hodges, and gave direct control to the V Corps commander, General Gerow, whose understanding was that he should permit entry into Paris only "in case the degree of fighting was such as could be overcome by light forces."

As the French 2nd Armored set forth, the urgency of its mission was heightened by the delayed appearance at Bradley's headquarters of Rolf Nordling and his strange little delegation from Paris. Nordling's report made it grimly clear that Choltitz could not delay much longer before beginning the demolition of the city. "Tell Hodges to have the French division hurry the hell in there," Bradley ordered one of his staff officers. Then he added, "Tell him to have the 4th Division ready to get in there too. We can't take any chances on that general changing his mind and knocking hell out of the city."

As it happened, a small segment of the U.S. 4th Infantry Division was already on the way to Paris, following the French 2nd Armored, which it had been ordered to assist by seizing the Seine River crossing sites south of the city. Now the rest of the division's troops, veterans of Utah Beach, Cherbourg and the hedgerow fighting in Normandy, began pulling up stakes for the 132-mile trip from Carrouges to Paris.

Although the last thing Leclerc wanted was American (or any other non-French) help, there could be no blinking the fact that his force was making little headway—owing less to enemy opposition than to the weather and to what Bradley later described as a "Gallic wall" of joyously cheering and crowding humanity. Leclerc's orders were to barge straight through Rambouillet and Versailles to Paris. But at Ram-

Carrying badly needed food supplies, Allied planes prepare to land at a Parisian airfield as part of a hastily organized airlift to the French capital. When the Allies liberated Paris on August 25, they discovered that there was only one day's supply of food remaining in the city. On General Eisenhower's orders, planes began shuttling 3,000 tons of food, soap and medical items from Great Britain to Paris at the rate of 500 tons a day.

bouillet, still 30 miles from the capital, he got word that the Germans had moved 60 tanks into the area. On his own authority, he therefore decided to cut 17 miles east to Arpajon and Longjumeau. In doing so, he neglected to inform his American superiors, an omission that, when they heard of it, seemed to confirm their fears about the wayward French.

Meanwhile, de Gaulle had arrived from his temporary command post at Le Mans and had ensconced himself in the magnificent Château de Rambouillet, on the doorstep of Paris, where the leaders of France from Louis XVI to Napoleon had stayed. That night, while the wet, weary men of the 2nd Armored bedded down in nearby woods, Leclerc arrived to confer with his leader. The two discussed Leclerc's battle plan, already being put into effect, and de Gaulle belatedly approved it, virtually without comment. But as Leclerc left, de Gaulle voiced a fear that during these last days had pressed so heavily upon him. "Go fast," he said. "We cannot have another Commune"—a grim refer-

ence to the bloodshed during the Franco-Prussian War in 1871, when Frenchmen, bitterly divided by economic inequalities, had fought one another in the streets of Paris.

Leclerc moved out again at dawn, Thursday, August 24, 1944, aiming three columns toward the southwestern corner of Paris. One column swung west and headed past Versailles, along the route originally assigned to the entire division; its purpose was to draw the enemy away from the main points of attack. A second column thrust through the Chevreuse valley toward Toussus-le-Noble; it would enter Paris through the Porte de Vanves. The third would make the major effort, pushing through the towns of Longjumeau, Antony and Fresnes to strike the capital from the south, at the Porte d'Orléans.

As the three columns slogged forward through a steady drizzle, celebrating throngs continued to slow their progress. Even General Leclerc was caught up in the excitement of the hour. On the way, he stopped in a small town to

CITY IN REBELLION

Sidewalk superintendents offer words of advice to a Resistance machine gunner in an Henri Cartier-Bresson picture taken during Paris' preliberation revolt.

HISTORIAN WITH A CAMERA AND A CAUSE

"The photographer cannot be a passive spectator," said Henri Cartier-Bresson, the distinguished French photographer, and he was true to his injunction during the six turbulent days of rebellion leading to the liberation of Paris on August 25, 1944. After years of forced absence, Cartier-Bresson had returned to his beloved city not just as a historian with a camera but also as a working member of the Resistance. Caught up in the revolt, he recorded it with intimacy and candor in the pictures shown on these pages.

Cartier-Bresson's road back to Paris had been long and hard. Sent to Germany as a prisoner of war in 1940, he spent 36 months in grim prison camps and labor battalions. "Captivity became my nationality," he said. He held 30 different jobs while in prison camps but preferred working on farms, "as it was easier to escape from there, and we were well fed." Twice he escaped and was recaptured. On the third try he made his way back to France.

Eventually, armed with false papers identifying him as one Barbet, Cartier-Bresson went home to Paris and joined the FFI (Forces Françaises de l'Intérieur) as it furtively fomented the uprising against the Germans. "Our work was awkward," he said, "as we tried to know as little as possible about each other." He also joined a handful of FFI photographers who shared his determination to record the revolt. They were well organized when the fighting erupted. "We had friends who telephoned and told us where the action was, and I made sure a photographer was on the spot, or I would go myself."

Amid gunfire and exploding Molotov cocktails, Cartier-Bresson worked to capture the faces of the people—"Human faces are such a world!"—and to record their reactions. His pictures show vividly the Parisians' business-like calm and solidarity in the face of battle; it was as if the years of captivity and hardship and humiliation were a festering sore that they had coolly resolved to lance. "At the liberation," said Cartier-Bresson, "we felt that the abscess had burst, that the pus was going to come out, and it would be more a relief than a glory."

Ingenious Resistance fighters, preparing for a motorized attack on the Germans, mount and load a machine gun on the back of a flat-bed truck.

Women and children on the Rue des Martyrs pass along cobblestones —"the man-in-the-street's weapon," Cartier-Bresson called them—to be used in building a barricade. By erecting and defending more than 400 barricades, the Parisians bottled up the Germans in the center of the city.

Young Parisians, manning a barricade made out of an overturned truck, watch Cartier-Bresson take their picture from another defense point just down the street from them. The numerous barricades in this area were constructed primarily to guard the central headquarters of the Paris police, seen in the background to the left of the cathedral of Notre-Dame.

A Resistance sharpshooter, under cover in an arcade on the Rue de Rivoli, takes aim at a German making a last-ditch stand on the rooftop of a building across the street. Other FFI fighters wear arm bands bearing the Resistance symbol, the cross of Lorraine, which identified them to fellow patriots but could be discarded quickly if Germans closed in.

Braving heavy German fire, Resistance stretcher-bearers evacuate two wounded women to a first-aid station in nearby Place du Théâtre Français. Parisian casualties during the liberation totaled some 2,300 rebels and 2,600 civilians. The Germans paid a higher price: 7,700 dead or wounded.

White sheets (left), signifying the surrender of Germans inside the Hôtel Continental, are hung out over the Rue de Castiglione, while

Parisians gather to watch the mopping-up operations. The German defenders forced the French to clear out the hotel room by room.

Armed with shotguns, gendarmes herd captured German enlisted men past the Louvre to a detention area, where prisoners were registered and sent to POW camps. The first gendarme wears civilian trousers under his uniform jacket, suggesting that he had been fighting for the Resistance and had dressed hastily for his official role after order was restored.

High-ranking German officers wait for the next order from their FFI captors. "Much has been said about how scared the Germans were to be taken prisoner by the FFI," commented Cartier-Bresson, "but really this was exaggerated, as there was no particular violence on the part of the FFI toward the Germans. It came, rather, from the Parisian crowds."

Resistance fighters help themselves to weapons taken from a captured bank that the Germans had used as an arms depot during the Occupation. "The people came for arms as they knew there was a depot," said Cartier-Bresson years later. "I still have an attractive revolver from there."

THE TIME OF DELIVERANCE

Exuberant Parisians wave to the soldiers of the French 2nd Armored Division who have come to liberate the French capital on the 25th of August, 1944.

"THE DAY THE WAR SHOULD HAVE ENDED"

When French and American troops rolled into Paris on August 25, 1944, the city suddenly exploded with joy. To an American captain who was there on that glorious day, it seemed that "a physical wave of human emotion picked us up and carried us into the heart of Paris. It was like groping through a dream." Thousands of Parisians surged into the streets, chanting "Merci! Merci!," singing the "Marseillaise" and waving homemade American and French flags.

So many people swarmed around the Allied vehicles that a French soldier compared his tank to "a magnet passing through a pile of steel filings." A British journalist reported that "the pent-up delirious crowds just wanted to touch us, to feel if we were real." Soldiers were kissed until their faces turned red and hugged until they thought their ribs would crack. Girls clambered over tanks and trucks, shoving paper forward for autographs. Smiling civilians thrust long-hoarded bottles of fine wine, flowers and fruit at the soldiers—anything that might convey the gratitude they felt. One U.S. major counted a total of 67 bottles of champagne in his jeep by the time he reached the Seine. It was, said American private—and author—Irwin Shaw, "the day the war should have ended."

But there were still more than 20,000 Germans in the Paris area, and a lot of fighting took place even while the celebrating was going on. In streets where Allied soldiers battled with the enemy, Parisians leaned out of their windows, completely disregarding the shooting, and cheered the men on. Some residents even lowered bottles of wine on strings down into the open turrets of Allied tanks. Drunk with excitement, or from the wine that was lavished upon them, some soldiers, engaged in house-to-house fighting, took such foolhardy chances that they lost their lives. Nevertheless, that day the Allied forces conquered Paris, losing only 628 men, while more than 3,000 Germans were killed and 10,000 prisoners taken.

Paris was free at last, and the Free French leader, General Charles de Gaulle, arrived on the scene to assert his authority over the nation.

General Jacques Leclerc (far left), commander of the French 2nd Armored Division, rides with French soldiers past the cathedral of Notre-Dame.

Men of Leclerc's division attack the Chamber of Deputies. Defended by 500 German soldiers until August 25, it was one of the last strongholds to fall.

A triumphant Leclerc and his defeated enemy, General Dietrich von Choltitz (seated), leave police headquarters amid excited crowds after agreeing on surrender

Free at last to vent their hatred, Parisians vandalize a portrait of Hitler.

terms. That evening Choltitz was taken from the city to an Allied prison camp.

FREEDOM FOR PARISIANS, CAPTIVITY FOR GERMANS

When Paris was liberated, the German occupiers suddenly became prisoners, and the Parisians had a chance to take revenge on their enemies. They mutilated portraits of Nazi leaders, ripped down swastikas and threw clothes and papers out of buildings where Germans had lived. When the military commander of Paris, General Dietrich von Choltitz, was taken to police headquarters, people spat on him and clawed at his uniform. They did not know that Choltitz had saved their city by disobeying Hitler's orders to burn Paris to the ground.

The Germans were not the only ones who suffered. Their French mistresses were also rounded up. Their heads were shaved and their bared breasts were painted with swastikas. They were decked with signs that said, "I whored with the Boches," and were paraded through the streets.

While prisoners were filing through Paris, de Gaulle was planning a parade of another sort. The general was determined to establish himself as the leader of France. Arriving in the city on the 25th of August, he broadcast that he would parade with French troops the next day at 3:00 p.m. "We must have this parade," he told his American liaison officer. "This parade is going to give France political unity."

On August 26, just before the start of the victory parade, General de Gaulle (saluting) inspects troops of the French 2nd Armored Division with General Leclerc.

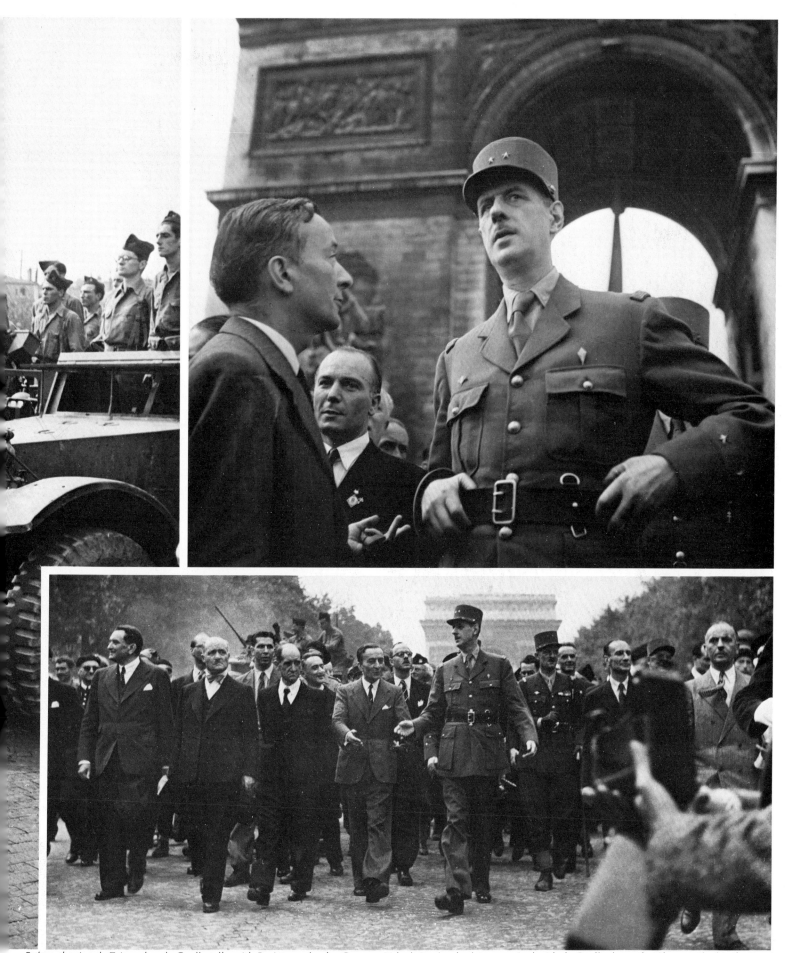

Before the Arc de Triomphe, de Gaulle talks with Resistance leader Georges Bidault (top), who later marched with de Gaulle down the Champs-Elysées (bottom).

Part of the enthusiastic throng that gathered to welcome de Gaulle waits in vain in the Place de l'Opéra for the general, who took another route.

CHEERING A NEW LEADER

Thousands of Frenchmen watched as de Gaulle marched down the Champs-Elysées on August 26. Cheering civilians lined both sides of the avenue, packed rooftops and windows, climbed up lampposts, flagpoles and trees. One septuagenarian stood atop a ladder 12 feet above the sidewalk.

Few men have known a more supremely satisfying moment of triumph than the one de Gaulle enjoyed now. But the moment was about to be rudely interrupted.

Ecstatic civilians, mingling tears with cheers, greet de Gaulle along the parade

route. As early as 7 o'clock in the morning people had started streaming in from the Paris suburbs on bicycles or on foot to view the 3 o'clock victory parade.

163

Hundreds of panic-stricken spectators dash for cover as shooting begins in the Hôtel de Ville area, where the de Gaulle party made a stop during the parade.

164

Close to the cathedral of Notre-Dame, some parents huddle with their frightened children alongside a jeep as a wave of gunfire sweeps through the square.

PANDEMONIUM ON THE AVENUES

As de Gaulle's victory parade headed out of the Champs-Elysées into the Place de la Concorde, a shot suddenly rang out. Thousands of spectators fell to the pavement or scurried to take cover behind the tanks of Leclerc's division. De Gaulle, however, walked indifferently to an open car, which took him to the Hôtel de Ville—Paris' city hall—where he made a brief stop. Then just as he was leaving the Place de l'Hôtel de Ville, machine guns and rifles began rattling from the buildings on the square.

No one knew who started the shooting, but in the street almost every man who had a gun—and hundreds did—started wildly shooting at the windows. Unmoved, de Gaulle rode on to the final stop on his itinerary, the cathedral of Notre-Dame. As he alighted from his automobile, there was more firing. Calmly, the general strode on with the same unhurried, unwavering step into the cathedral.

While shots crackle inside Notre-Dame, de Gaulle sings the "Magnificat."

A FINAL DESPERATE ROUND OF GUNFIRE

When de Gaulle entered the partially darkened cathedral of Notre-Dame, shooting broke out inside the church. The frightened congregation cowered on the floor, prompting André Le Troquer (above, left), one of de Gaulle's ministers, to remark: "I can see more rear ends than faces."

Unruffled, the general moved 190 feet down the aisle to his seat of honor. "He walked straight ahead in what appeared to me to be a hail of fire," a BBC correspondent reported in amazement, "without hesitation, his shoulders flung back. It was the most extraordinary example of courage that I've ever seen."

The shooting persisted, and de Gaulle cut the church service off after the "Magnificat" and quietly left the cathedral. His conduct under fire greatly impressed the people of France. "After that," concluded an American newsman who had watched the general in the cathedral, "de Gaulle had France in the palm of his hand."

A Resistance fighter aims at rooftops near Notre-Dame, hoping to hit unseen

snipers, while a French soldier rushes to take up another firing position. The jittery young gunmen frightened the pedestrians almost as much as the snipers did.

With calm finally settled over the city of Paris, Parisians and newly arrived American soldiers sip wine at a café in Montmartre and attempt to carry on a conversation with the aid of English-French dictionaries.

cathedral of Notre-Dame. The liberation accomplished, the majority of the Allied troops moved on to free other parts of France from German domination.

6

As Paris was being liberated, Allied spearheads elsewhere along the 200-mile front in northern France were crossing the Seine River. The original invasion plans called for a lengthy pause on the Seine's banks to allow time for a build-up of the supplies and service troops needed to feed and fuel the Allied war machine in its final thrust to Germany. But that stopover had been predicated on a much slower and more methodical Allied advance against continued stiff German resistance. Eisenhower and his planners had not foreseen the sudden collapse of the German armies in Normandy; now, with the dispirited enemy formations fleeing across northern France toward the sanctuary of their homeland, an Allied pause was out of the question. The obvious course was to keep the Germans on the run and, by maintaining constant pressure, give them no chance to sort out their battered formations and establish a defensive line anywhere in northeastern France.

The Supreme Allied Commander knew that this strategy was risky. Already the supply system was straining to keep up with the accelerated advance of the combat troops. Although Cherbourg was now open, that port alone could not begin to meet the demands of the armies. None of the captured Brittany ports had been put into operation; the major Mediterranean ports had yet to fall to the forces that had invaded southern France. Most supplies were still coming over the Normandy beaches. Moreover, there were not enough trucks to carry the supplies from the beaches to the front lines; those available were being driven around the clock, without maintenance, and they were beginning to show signs of wear. Stocks of gasoline were rapidly diminishing, and the farther the troops advanced, the more acute the fuel shortage became.

Despite nagging doubts about supply, no one in the Allied camp argued for stopping at the Seine. If the British, Canadian and American armies could maintain their pace and drive across the German border, the war might well be over before winter. But on the question of how best to pursue the enemy beyond the Seine, a bitter controversy arose, pitting the British against the Americans.

Eisenhower's plans for the advance beyond the Seine required the division of the Allied armies into two great columns. One, the Twenty-first Army Group under Montgomery, would surge northeastward through Belgium and

NIGHTMARE IN HOLLAND

into the Ruhr, Germany's industrial heart, whose factories and coal mines were essential to the German war effort. The other column, Bradley's American Twelfth Army Group, would drive eastward through France and lunge into the Saar, another major German industrial area. The two prongs of the Allied thrust would be separated by the Ardennes, a region of dense forests and difficult terrain in lower Belgium and Luxembourg.

Montgomery vehemently disagreed with this plan of attack. On August 23, as the Allied vanguards were forging bridgeheads across the Seine, he met with Eisenhower to argue for a single, massive thrust north of the Ardennes through Belgium, with the Twelfth and the Twenty-first Army Groups marching side by side, 40 divisions strong. The power and momentum of such a consolidated force, Montgomery asserted, would overwhelm the Germans before they had an opportunity to regroup and thereby bring a quick end to the war in Europe. If the Allies attacked with two thrusts, as originally planned, Montgomery told Eisenhower, the steadily diminishing supplies would be spread too thin, the front would be weak everywhere and inevitably the advance would peter out. Winter would set in and the war would drag on.

Eisenhower refused to accept Montgomery's argument. To confine both army groups to one sector, he felt, would invite a German counterattack in another. At the same time, the Supreme Commander realized that along the route the British were to take through Belgium lay objectives worthy of a special effort. A thrust into Belgium could overrun V-1 launching sites, whose rockets were still falling on England. It could cut off escape for the German Fifteenth Army, the force that had waited in the French Pas-de-Calais for an Allied invasion that never came. Most important, it could secure the great port of Antwerp and relieve the Allied logistic crisis.

With this in mind, Eisenhower decided on a compromise solution. He would split the American Twelfth Army Group and send General Hodges' First Army into Belgium alongside Montgomery's forces. That would leave Patton's Third Army by itself in the drive into the Saar, but help would soon be forthcoming from the Allied forces that had invaded southern France and were driving north. Accordingly, Eisenhower gave first priority on supplies to the major thrust into Belgium. Patton, for the meantime, would get less.

Eisenhower's concession to Montgomery was not designed to please the American field generals. General Bradley, commander of the Twelfth Army Group, insisted that Montgomery did not need an entire American army on his flank—one corps should be enough. The volatile Patton asserted with characteristic bravado that his army could cross the German border in 10 days if he were given enough supplies. But Eisenhower stuck by his decision, and Patton termed it "the most momentous error of the war."

As the Allied armies plunged across the Seine toward Belgium and Germany, the pursuit of the disintegrating enemy forces turned into a headlong rush. Soldiers rode on tanks and in trucks, trailers, jeeps and captured German automobiles. They followed sun-scorched roads all day, their eyes bloodshot and watering from the sun, wind, dust and weariness. At night the drivers squinted to keep sight of the taillights on the racing vehicles ahead.

The countryside became a blur, and progress was seldom interrupted for long. At times German rear guards set up roadblocks, usually a few trees felled across the highway, forcing Allied reconnaissance units into short but nasty engagements. Allied vanguards sometimes found their way blocked by piles of debris: burned-out tanks and trucks, and the carcasses of dead horses, from which hungry French civilians had cut chunks of flesh to eat. But bulldozers were called forward, the wreckage was quickly cleared, and the advance resumed.

As Allied forces approached, fleeing Germans destroyed supply installations, blew up fuel depots, abandoned ammunition dumps and raided ration stocks. They dismantled their antiaircraft guns, burned their barracks and headed for home. Many discarded their uniforms, donned civilian clothes and took off on their own.

"There was a quality of madness about the whole debacle of Germany's forces in the West," the First Army's operations officer later wrote. "Isolated garrisons fought as viciously as before, but the central planning and coordination were missing. It looked very much as though Adolf Hitler might be forced into surrender long before the American and British units reached the Rhine. That was the avowed opinion of Allied soldiers on the western front, and

German prisoners were of the same mind, often stating that it couldn't last for another week."

Patton, taking a page from the German book, maintained the blitzkrieg that his Third Army had begun in Normandy. From the right bank of the Seine his forces raced 100 miles, crossing the Marne River and capturing the town of Châlons-sur-Marne. The Germans were unable to organize serious resistance.

On the morning of August 31, in a heavy rain, elements of the Third Army approached the Meuse River at Commercy, 150 miles east of Paris. A light-tank company overran German outposts, knocked out artillery emplacements, seized a bridge and crossed the river. Another column took a bridgehead 10 miles north of Commercy at Saint-Mihiel. Meanwhile, six of Patton's armored columns drove eastward to Epernay, passed Reims, rolled through the Argonne Forest and by noon on August 31 were across the Meuse.

At this juncture, Patton's army was less than 60 miles from the border of Germany. But his supply lines had finally stretched to the breaking point. On the last day of August he had no gasoline at all.

Bitter with frustration, Patton and his staff railed at Eisenhower's decision to give priority on supply to the British Second Army and the U.S. First Army in their drive into Belgium. With no opposition in sight, Patton was forced to park his armor because the gas tanks were dry. To his staff he confided that he faced two enemies—the Germans and his own high command. "I can take care of the Germans," he stormed, "but I'm not sure I can win against Montgomery and Eisenhower.'" His appeals for more gasoline came to no avail. "My men can eat their belts," he bellowed, "but my tanks have gotta have gas."

In the meantime, in the center of the Allies' advance General Hodges' First Army had also made impressive gains. Pushing off from the Seine near Paris and heading northeast, First Army troops rolled back the Germans and liberated the town of Soissons.

At the village of Braine, not far from Soissons, a French railroad stationmaster stopped some American tankers traveling at a fast clip through his town. He told them that a German train was due in 15 minutes. No one listened except Sergeant Hollis Butler of the 3rd Armored Division. His antiaircraft gun section had not fired for several days, and he thought it was time to shoot some live ammunition at a real target, even though it was on the ground.

Pulling his guns out of the column, Butler set them up to cover the railroad. When the train arrived, the crews fired and disabled the locomotive, then turned machine guns on the cars. Advancing in squad formation, Hollis' men captured the 36-car train. French Resistance members appeared to march the German survivors away, and the Americans resumed their advance. From their efforts came a bonus. The stranded train blocked the tracks, and when a second train carrying more Germans pulled into the railroad station a little while later, it was easily captured by an American artillery outfit.

Farther along the way, other elements of the First Army liberated the city of Laon and forged ahead, crossing the Belgian border near Mons and cutting off a mass of Germans, part of the Fifth Panzer Army, fleeing from coastal regions toward their homeland. The German force was strafed by Allied fighter planes and encircled finally by First Army troops. In three days of action some 25,000 Germans were captured. General Hodges, heady with optimism, remarked that with 10 more days of good weather, the war might well be over.

The words were hardly out of Hodges' mouth, however, when he was compelled to curtail his operations. The same hateful problem that had afflicted Patton, the lack of gasoline, forced him to stop one entire corps for three days. His other two corps kept moving, but as they thrust through Luxembourg and Belgium and approached the German border, the advance sputtered fitfully and trucks ran out of gas. Despite its priority on supply, the First Army, like the Third, was coming to the end of its tether.

To the left of the Americans, the British and the Canadian armies had been making great strides in their thrust northward along the French coast. On August 30 elements of the Canadian First Army liberated Rouen, the capital of Normandy. During the first week of September, the Canadians invested the English Channel ports of Le Havre, Boulogne, Calais and Dunkirk, and seized the V-1 launching sites in the Pas-de-Calais.

On the Canadians' right, the British Second Army liberated the city of Amiens on August 31 and captured General

A U.S. tank destroyer fires its 90mm cannon at point-blank range to silence a German pillbox blocking the Allies' path through a Brest street.

BESIEGING BREST'S LAST-DITCH DEFENDERS

The phenomenal speed with which the Allied forces crossed Brittany—200 miles in six days—led them to expect the quick capitulation of their chief target, the port city and German submarine base of Brest. But they did not reckon on the stubbornness of Lieut. General Herman B. Ramcke, commander of some 30,000 crack troops who had been ordered by Hitler to hold out to the last man.

The Germans had turned the city into a huge fortress by constructing elaborate minefields, antitank ditches and concrete dugouts. The Allied troops measured their progress in yards as they took on General Ramcke's 75 strong points, including several old forts, one after another.

On September 18, six weeks after it had begun, the siege ended when the last of the Germans gave themselves up—except for Ramcke, who had escaped. But with nowhere left to go, he surrendered the following day.

Downcast German General Ramcke and his dog are held captive at Allied headquarters.

Eberbach, formerly head of Panzer Group West, now the Seventh Army commander. British armored columns flowed through northern France, rushed across the Belgian frontier and took the capital city of Brussels on September 3. On the next day they took the port of Antwerp, and then, a few days later, the British advance also began to run out of gas. Various units of the Second Army had been dropping out of the pursuit as their vehicles ran dry. Finally, after covering 250 miles in six days, the British advance stopped along the Belgian-Dutch border northeast of Brussels.

In their drive the British had won a major prize, the port of Antwerp. They had seized its wharves and docks before the Germans had had a chance to demolish them. The port's vast capacity was being counted on to ease the Allied logistic crisis, and its nearness to the German border meant that the Allies should not have any problem funneling supplies to their front line.

But Antwerp was to be of no immediate help to the Allies. Its outlet to the sea, the 60-mile Schelde Estuary, was guarded by powerful German forces. So long as the Germans held the banks of this waterway, no Allied ship could run the gauntlet to Antwerp. Yet the British commanders sent no forces to clear the Schelde's banks.

The failure to clear the seaward approaches to Antwerp was attributed later to the sheer exhaustion of the British troops after their long and magnificent drive into Belgium. Another compelling reason, perhaps, was the fact that the attention of the Allied commanders was focused not on Antwerp but on Germany itself. Lieut. General Brian G.

Horrocks, commander of the Second Army's XXX Corps, summed up their attitude in his memoirs: "My eyes were entirely fixed on the Rhine and everything else seemed of subsidiary importance."

The first week of September was a time of infectious optimism in the Allied camp. "We have now reached a stage," Montgomery wired Eisenhower on September 4, "where one really powerful and full-blooded thrust toward Berlin is likely to get there and thus end the German war." The Allied Intelligence Committee in London echoed Montgomery's assertion in a report on September 8 that "organized resistance under the control of the German High Command is unlikely to continue beyond December 1, 1944, and it may end even sooner." At that time, the British War Office estimated: "If we go at the same pace as of late, we should be in Berlin by the 28th of September."

There were few dissenters from this rosy view. One who felt otherwise was Colonel Oscar W. Koch, Third Army intelligence chief. Koch warned that the enemy was still capable of a last-ditch struggle. "Barring internal upheaval in the homeland and the remote possibility of insurrection within the Wehrmacht," he wrote, "the German armies will continue to fight until destroyed or captured."

But Koch's minority opinion went unnoticed as optimism swept through all levels of the Allied ranks. The spectacular dash across France, with its brilliant successes against a demoralized enemy, had veiled the commanders' eyes to the reality of the Allied situation. The troops were exhausted. Moreover, their equipment was in need of maintenance,

An American soldier supervises a German prisoner of war as he dismantles a booby trap in a Chartres doorway. Retreating Germans not only booby-trapped objects as small as electric irons but also often employed nonmetal mines that defied detection by conventional methods.

Standing proudly in his jeep, General Patton, commander of the U.S. Third Army, triumphantly crosses a pontoon bridge over the Seine River on August 26, 1944. Later that day, Patton sent a wry message to General Eisenhower to mark the occasion: "Dear Ike: Today I spat in the Seine."

and ceaseless driving had crippled many of their vehicles. Worse, only a trickle of supplies was arriving at the front. The French railway system had been wrecked by air attacks and French Resistance saboteurs.

An Allied innovation called the Red Ball Express, an endless belt of trucks on two parallel one-way routes between Normandy and the forward divisions, proved inadequate to meet the enormous supply demand. The U.S. First and Third Armies required more than 800,000 gallons of gasoline a day. The trucks of the Red Ball Express, operated round the clock, mainly by black service troops, carried great quantities of fuel but burned up an additional 300,000 gallons a day just getting it there.

By the second week of September, after the Allied advance had sputtered, faltered and was crawling to a halt, Allied soldiers began to notice a definite change in the weather. The summer warmth was receding, replaced by frequent rain, fog, mist and cold. Fall was approaching, and winter would not be far behind. Even more alarming were the unmistakable indications of firmer German resistance—a shade more artillery and mortar fire.

The strengthened German defense was no accident. Hit-

ler, shocked into action by the fall of Antwerp, had been taking drastic measures. The foundation of his plan of defense was the West Wall—known to the Allies as the Siegfried Line—a belt of fortifications completed in 1940 that ran along the German border from Switzerland to the Netherlands. Hitler decreed that his forces would fight as long as possible in front of the West Wall, and then pull back and make a stand within the Wall itself, which boasted a formidable array of pillboxes, troop shelters, command posts and tank obstacles.

Early in September Hitler dispatched General Kurt Student to the Belgian-Dutch border to set up defensive positions along the numerous canals that traversed that area.

In what he called "an improvisation on the grandest scale," General Student managed to throw together a makeshift defense, borrowing and confiscating staff, troops and matériel. He was particularly helped by the audacious Major General Kurt Chill, who, retreating with remnants of his own division and two others, had perceived the critical situation along the border, where the British advance threatened. Chill postponed his withdrawal and established straggler collecting points, so that by nightfall of September

4, he had assembled a "crazy-quilt mob" of men from almost every conceivable source. He used them to form a firm line of defense.

To provide a figure around whom his demoralized troops might rally, Hitler recalled from retirement Field Marshal von Rundstedt and appointed the wise old soldier commander in chief in the West. Rundstedt moved quickly and brilliantly to resurrect a protective line along the western approaches to Germany. In one of his first moves, he devised a plan to save the Fifteenth Army, which was trapped in Belgium with its back to the sea.

Following Rundstedt's design, three divisions were left behind to hold the seaward approaches to Antwerp, while 86,000 men of the Fifteenth Army shoved off at night in boats and ferries and crossed the Schelde Estuary to the Beveland peninsula in the German-occupied Netherlands. From there they moved quietly inland down a single road, deep into the Netherlands. Had the British pushed just 15 more miles north after capturing Antwerp, they could have cut the neck of the peninsula and prevented the German escape. But again, because of either exhaustion or shortsightedness, they decided not to press on.

After saving part of the Fifteenth Army, Rundstedt skillfully deployed what units he could pull together in the Netherlands, as well as reserve formations from Germany, against the sputtering advances of the U.S. First and Third Armies. The German units formed a continuous if not altogether solid line from the North Sea to the Swiss frontier.

As the Germans were building up their forces, Montgomery met with Eisenhower in Brussels on September 10 to appeal, once again, for a single massive Allied thrust into Germany. In view of the critical Allied supply situation, Montgomery argued, there simply were not enough resources to keep all the armies pushing forward on a broad front. It would be far more logical, he insisted, to halt Patton's Third Army and the Canadian First Army, giving them just enough supplies to maintain a defensive posture, and to throw full support behind the British Second Army and the American First Army. Those two armies would attack together through the Netherlands and seize the Ruhr. As a preliminary to this main attack, Montgomery laid before Eisenhower a bold and daring scheme, known as Operation *Market-Garden*.

Montgomery proposed dropping three divisions of the Allied First Airborne Army, the Allies' strategic reserve, along a highway connecting the three Dutch cities of Eindhoven, Nijmegen and Arnhem. The airborne troops would seize a series of bridges that spanned canals and three large rivers, clearing the road and holding it open. This phase of the operation was called *Market*. Then, in a coordinated venture called *Garden,* British armored units would dash up the passageway over the bridges and through the cities to link up with the airborne troops. The British tanks would drive 99 miles, all the way to the Zuider Zee, then wheel to the east, outflanking the German West Wall, and go on to seize the Ruhr.

The boldness of this concept startled Montgomery's fellow commanders, who knew him as prudent and meticulous. "Had the pious, teetotaling Montgomery wobbled into SHAEF [Supreme Headquarters, Allied Expeditionary Force] with a hangover, I could not have been more astonished than I was by the daring adventure he proposed," General Bradley later recalled.

Eisenhower was intrigued. Ever since mid-July he had been itching to use his airborne reserve, most of which had dropped into Normandy during the invasion and had thereafter returned to England. Three and a half divisions of paratroopers and glider infantry—the U.S. 82nd and 101st Airborne, the British 1st Airborne and a Polish brigade—were rested, retrained and ready for more action. Eisenhower had asked his planners frequently to find something for the airborne units to do, something, as he put it, "with imagination and daring." Late in August and early in September, the planners had proposed no fewer than 18 different airborne operations. None of them ever got under way, usually because the ground troops, in their hectic dash across France, had overrun the airborne targets before the operations could commence. *Market-Garden* seemed just what he was waiting for.

Furthermore, Eisenhower saw *Market-Garden* as providing the impetus to get the Allies across the Rhine before the supply situation forced another halt and enabled enemy troops to recoup behind the river. Ike again turned thumbs down on Montgomery's demand that he halt the Canadians and the U.S. Third Army in favor of a single thrust by the British and the U.S. First Army, but he gave his approval to

Market-Garden and promised Montgomery sufficient supplies to carry it off.

Having received Eisenhower's approval of the operation on September 10, Montgomery was eager to get started immediately, before the deteriorating weather and a resurgence of German power lessened its chances of success. He picked September 17 as the jump-off date, a deadline that allowed the planners only seven days, hardly enough time to map out such a complex enterprise with thoroughness.

It was obvious to the planners that *Market-Garden* had great potential for failure. Any nagging doubts, however, were soon swept away by the urgency and excitement of planning the largest airborne assault of the war. The Allied commanders were firm in their conviction that the element of surprise would win the bridges and thus ensure a swift passage by the armored column. Behind their optimism lay the assumption that the Germans were incapable of organized resistance. The enemy troops were few, they be-

As everyone pitches in to help out, cans of gasoline bound for Patton's gas-hungry Third Army are unloaded from a C-47 by Air Evacuation Nurse Irene Steffens. Airlifts brought in up to 12,000 gallons a day, a mere trickle in comparison to the 450,000 gallons that Patton required.

lieved, and ill-trained, capable of mustering only a feeble defense. Those Germans could easily be brushed aside.

This belief persisted in the face of disturbing reports to the contrary. Dutch Resistance disclosed that two panzer divisions, the 9th and the 10th SS, battered from their Normandy experience, had stopped in the vicinity of Arnhem to rest and refit. The report was ignored. When the Allies' own intelligence confirmed the Dutch information, Eisenhower's chief of staff, General Smith, deeply concerned about *Market-Garden's* prospects, carried the disquieting report to Montgomery and argued for a revision of the plan. "Montgomery simply waved my objections airily aside," Smith wrote later.

Other evidence of strong German units in the *Market-Garden* area was similarly discounted. The intelligence chief of the British I Airborne Corps, 25-year-old Major Brian Urquhart, laid aerial reconnaissance photos of the Arnhem area on the desk of his superior, Lieut. General Frederick A. M. Browning. Unmistakably, the photos showed German tanks. Browning studied them for a time and told Urquhart not to worry, the tanks were probably in need of repair. After this blithe dismissal of his indisputable evidence, Urquhart's anxiety about *Market-Garden* became so intensified that he was ordered to go on leave. "I had become such a pain around headquarters that on the very eve of the attack I was being removed from the scene," he recalled later. "I was told to go home."

While the Allied armies waited anxiously for ammunition, food and gasoline to come forward, most of the front remained static. On the right flank, elements of General Patch's Seventh Army, which had surged up from the Mediterranean beachhead, made contact with units of Patton's army on September 11, forty miles west of Dijon. With more gasoline at last available, Patton managed to move eastward from the Meuse to grab bridgeheads across the Moselle River, 30 miles from the German border. After foiling a German counterattack, his troops bogged down in the face of increased resistance.

Farther north, on September 11, a First Army patrol in Luxembourg waded across the Our River and set foot on German soil. The soldiers climbed a hill, looked around and returned. Less than a week later, a corps of the First Army crossed into Germany near the border city of Aachen and

penetrated the West Wall, but then, overextended and ill-supplied, the unit came to a halt in the face of a fresh German infantry division that had been rushed to the front from East Prussia.

On the coastal flank, the Canadians were inching doggedly toward the Schelde Estuary, Antwerp's yet unopened gateway to the sea, where they would find powerful defenders: three divisions of the Fifteenth Army held there as guardians when the bulk of that army escaped under the noses of the Allies.

All along the extended Allied front, from the North Sea to Switzerland, the American, British, Canadian and French armies were at a virtual standstill. Frustrated by the lack of progress, the Allied high commanders glued their eyes to a single target—the Netherlands—and awaited the onset of Operation *Market-Garden*.

September 17, a Sunday, D-day for *Market-Garden*, dawned hazy but cleared into a beautiful, calm, late summer day with perfect flying conditions. From 24 airfields in Britain, 1,545 C-47s and 478 gliders, protected by 1,131 fighter planes, took to the air and soon were streaming toward their targets: the British 1st Airborne Division to the city of Arnhem, the U.S. 82nd Airborne Division to Nijmegen, the U.S. 101st Airborne Division to the vicinity of Eindhoven.

As the airborne armada neared its drop and landing zones along the 65-mile corridor in the Netherlands, it ran into lighter German opposition than expected. Within a few minutes, 16,500 parachutists and 3,500 glider troops were floating down to earth. Dutch civilians were strolling home from church and sitting down to Sunday dinner when the parachutes, white for soldiers and colored for equipment, blossomed overhead shortly after 1 p.m. "What is it?" a little boy asked his grandfather. "I don't know," the old man said. "But it looks like the end of the war."

The men of the British 1st Airborne Division—the "Red Devils" under Major General Robert E. Urquhart (no relation to Major Brian Urquhart)—came to earth on the north bank of the Lower Rhine, eight miles west of Arnhem and their key objective, the huge highway span over the river in the city. Assembling quickly, they began their march to the bridge, meeting at first almost no opposition.

However, they had gone only a short distance when the

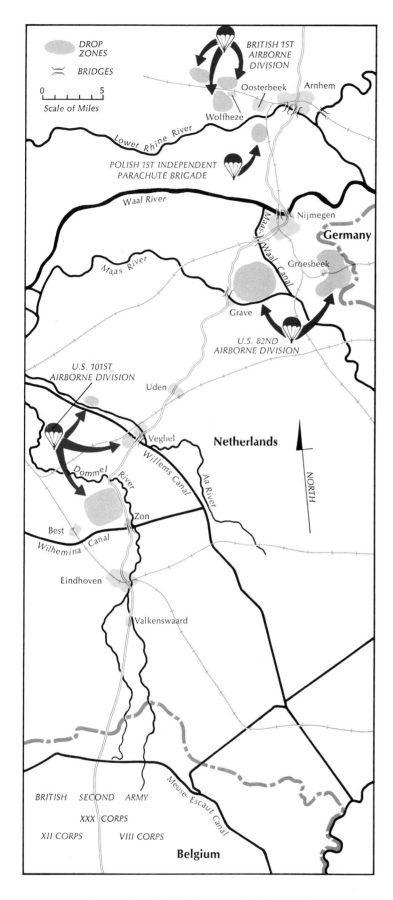

DROP ZONES

BRIDGES

0 — 5
Scale of Miles

BRITISH 1ST AIRBORNE DIVISION

Arnhem
Oosterbeek
Wolfheze

Lower Rhine River

POLISH 1ST INDEPENDENT PARACHUTE BRIGADE

Waal River

Maas River

Maas-Waal Canal

Nijmegen
Germany

Groesbeek

Grave

U.S. 82ND AIRBORNE DIVISION

U.S. 101ST AIRBORNE DIVISION

Uden

Veghel

Netherlands

NORTH

Dommel River

Willems Canal

Aa River

Zon

Best

Wilhemina Canal

Eindhoven

Valkenswaard

Meuse-Escaut Canal

BRITISH SECOND ARMY

XXX CORPS

XII CORPS   VIII CORPS

Belgium

Operation Market-Garden, the Allied invasion of the Netherlands, began on September 17, 1944, when Anglo-American airborne troops landed near Arnhem, Nijmegen and Eindhoven. They were to seize seven vital bridges and hold open a corridor for tanks of the British Second Army to drive into Germany and bring about an early end to the War.

situation suddenly changed. "One moment we were marching steadily toward Arnhem," recalled Sergeant Major Harry Callaghan, "the next, we were scattered in the ditches. Snipers had opened fire, and three dead airborne soldiers lay across the road."

The sniper fire presaged a more disturbing development. Although they were unaware of it, the British had dropped near a German hornet's nest that was beginning to buzz angrily. As it happened, their drop zones were barely two miles from the headquarters of German Army Group B; its commander, Field Marshal Model, at first thought that the British had launched a daring raid to kidnap him and his staff. Ordering the evacuation of his headquarters, a resort hotel, he leaped into a staff car and raced 18 miles east to the headquarters of Lieut. General Wilhelm Bittrich, commander of the 2nd SS Panzer Corps. He found that Bittrich had already reacted to the invasion—with great foresight, as it turned out.

Bittrich had a hunch that the Allies were bent on forging a bridgehead across the Rhine en route to the Ruhr, and for this they would need the bridges at Arnhem and Nijmegen. He quickly committed his two SS panzer divisions, the 9th and 10th—the very forces whose presence in the *Market-Garden* area the Allied commanders had discounted. Bittrich sent the 9th SS Panzer Division to Arnhem to hold the span across the Lower Rhine. He ordered the 10th Panzer to race to Nijmegen to defend the bridges there.

A couple of hours later, the Germans found a copy of the entire *Market-Garden* plan of operation in a wrecked American glider. The plan included the schedule and locations of reinforcement and supply drops to take place over the next two days. Thanks to that carelessness, the Germans would be ready.

Meanwhile, German troops, bolstered by growing numbers of tanks from the 9th SS Panzer Division, had swiftly cut the main roads over which the British were marching to Arnhem. Consequently, only one unit—the 500 men of Lieut. Colonel John D. Frost's 2nd Battalion, 1st Parachute Brigade—made it to the north end of the bridge.

Frost's men launched an attack across the bridge during the night but were thrown back. The Germans, in force, tried unsuccessfully to bull their way across the bridge from the southern end. Then they brought in troops and laid siege to the British-held houses. Although casualties were increasing and ammunition, food rations and medical supplies were running out, the British refused to give up. They fought savagely from houses and in the streets, waiting for the rest of the 1st Airborne to relieve them.

The rest of the 1st Airborne, however, could not get through to Frost. The Germans had blocked the roads into town, forcing the other two battalions of the 1st Parachute Brigade to make a stand in Oosterbeek, a western suburb of Arnhem. To make matters worse, the division's radio sets, for no apparent reason, were not working.

General Urquhart, desperate for word from Frost, set off for the front with a few members of his staff. They quickly became caught up in the fighting and found themselves surrounded behind German lines. For the next 36 hours, the commander of the 1st Airborne was a fugitive trying to evade capture. He leaped fences in Dutch backyards, lost his way once and hid out in an attic before he finally escaped and made his way to British positions.

While the British situation was deteriorating, the U.S. 82nd Airborne Division, landing in the middle of the *Market-Garden* sector, was moving swiftly to capture a series of bridges in and near the city of Nijmegen. By fortuitous accident, the span at the village of Grave quickly fell into American hands. Above the jump zone near the Maas River bridge south of Nijmegen, the green light in one trans-port—the signal to leap—flicked on belatedly. When the 16 paratroopers from that plane landed, they found themselves only 600 yards from the bridge. Although the rest of the company was nowhere around, the men, led by Lieutenant John S. Thompson, charged the bridge, spraying it with machine-gun fire. Thompson's men knocked out a flak tower that protected the bridge and quickly overwhelmed the handful of German defenders.

About six miles to the northeast, other paratroopers of the 82nd Airborne grabbed two more bridges, and by the end of the day, only one crucial objective remained in German hands—the highway bridge over the Waal River in the city of Nijmegen. The assault there had been delayed by another mission. Before leading his troops to Nijmegen, the 82nd's commander, Brigadier General James M. Gavin, ordered them to seize and hold a ridge east of the city, the only high ground in the otherwise flat countryside; the rise of land commanded the highway and bridges over which the British ground forces would advance. If the Germans held this position, they could close the highway and choke off the ground assault coming up from the south.

Capturing the height took all afternoon, and it was not until nightfall that Gavin was able to free a battalion to move toward Nijmegen and the division's most important objective, the 1,960-foot bridge over the Waal.

If the 82nd had been able to attack the bridge at the outset, the troops would have found scant opposition. But

The youthful commander of the U.S. 82nd Airborne Division, Brigadier General James M. Gavin, checks his weapons and combat gear before taking off from England for Operation Market-Garden in the Netherlands. The division had been through some of the War's toughest actions in Sicily, Italy and Normandy, but Gavin called the assignment to take the bridge spanning the river at Nijmegen the 82nd's most difficult battle.

An American paratrooper lands upside down in Holland, narrowly missing a haystack that would have softened the blow. During Operation Market-Garden, the largest airborne operation of the War, 35,000 men dropped from planes and gliders. Of these, more than 11,000 were killed, wounded or captured. Many were dead before they hit the ground.

as the light started to fade and the leading company rushed through the streets of Nijmegen heading for the bridge, the first contingents of the 10th SS Panzer Division rolled across the span from the other bank and fanned out against the southern end of the bridge.

An American assault on the bridge that night ended in failure. The next morning, September 18, the men of the 82nd tried again. A company of paratroopers advanced through the back streets, cheered by crowds of Dutch who tossed them fruit and flowers. As the soldiers neared the bridge, the crowds quieted and thinned ominously. Dug in around a traffic circle in a grassy park at the foot of the bridge, the Germans lay in wait. They allowed the Americans to advance to within two blocks of the bridge and then opened up with a machine gun and antiaircraft guns. The paratroopers, ducking from street to street, inched their way to within one block of the bridge and then were stopped.

The Germans clung tenaciously to the bridge, denying the Allies the vital link between the ground forces and the beleaguered paratroopers in Arnhem, 11 miles to the north. American troops at Nijmegen could only await reinforcement from the ground troops advancing up the corridor.

Meanwhile, in the southernmost sector of *Market-Garden,* the U.S. 101st Airborne Division had landed north of Eindhoven and, with great speed and relative ease, seized the village of Veghel and its four rail and highway crossings over the Aa River and the Willems Canal. Then they turned their attention to the south and the vital highway bridge over the Wilhelmina Canal at the village of Zon.

The airborne troops advancing toward Zon met little opposition until they reached the outskirts of town. There, their vanguard came under fire from a German 88mm gun. A bazooka team crept undetected to within 50 yards of the gun and blew it up with one shot. The Americans then ducked and dodged their way forward through the village streets, shooting as they moved along. When they were within a stone's throw of the canal and their objective, a tremendous roar went up and debris rained down on them. The Germans had blown the bridge.

Without hesitation, several paratroopers dived into the canal and swam across, under fire from a house on the far bank. Other American soldiers found a tiny boat, rowed across and quickly subdued the German opposition.

Working feverishly, engineers used lumber brought by Dutch civilians to erect a footbridge across the destroyed span, and a regiment of the 101st walked across in single file. Repairing the bridge for vehicular traffic, however, required heavy equipment that the paratroopers lacked. That would have to wait until the arrival of the ground forces coming up from the Belgian-Dutch border.

Four miles south of Zon, the next morning, September 18, men of the 101st Airborne marched virtually unopposed into Eindhoven to the cheers of the populace. "The recep-

tion was terrific," one soldier noted. "The air seemed to reek with hate for the Germans." Amid the celebration, however, the men of the 101st could not help but notice the conspicuous absence of another contingent in Eindhoven. The British armored column, the thread that was supposed to stitch together the isolated holdings of the three airborne divisions, was nowhere in sight. Expected the previous evening, the ground forces had yet to arrive at Eindhoven.

On the afternoon of September 17, as the paratroopers were landing along the corridor, the British Second Army's XXX Corps moved out of its bridgehead on the Meuse-Escaut Canal and began clanking north up the highway. Its commander, General Horrocks, hoped to adhere to a rigorous timetable: Eindhoven, 13 miles away, by nightfall; Nijmegen, 41 miles farther, by midnight on September 19; and Arnhem, 11 miles farther, by September 21. He realized that his troops faced tremendous hazards. The narrow roadway could accommodate only two tanks abreast. Furthermore, for much of the route, the highway was elevated as it ran across the Dutch flatlands and was thus exposed to enemy observation and gunfire.

Horrocks' worst fears were quickly realized. The Guards Armored Division, the vanguard of the XXX Corps, had scarcely gotten across the Belgian-Dutch border when it ran into a German ambush. German antitank guns that were concealed in the pine woods close to the highway knocked out nine of the Guards' lead tanks, and the advance jarred to a halt. While the British officers fumed at the delay, the British infantry flanking the highway moved forward and cleared out the enemy guns, armored bulldozers pushed the wreckage out of the way, and the column got rolling again. But this first encounter established a pattern that would plague the XXX Corps for another day: a maddening, jerky, stop-and-go progression that would put the advance far behind schedule.

By nightfall of September 17, the ground column was still six miles south of Eindhoven, and not until late in the afternoon of the next day did the British tanks make their way into town—24 hours behind schedule. With crowds of jubilant Dutch civilians their only encumbrance, they moved through Eindhoven to the destroyed bridge at Zon. Working feverishly, British engineers laid a pontoon bridge across the canal, and the tanks rumbled over it on the morning of September 19, D-plus-2.

From Zon the road north was clear and fast, and the tanks raced to Nijmegen in only a few hours. It began to look as though the operation might pick up sufficient speed to meet the schedule.

But the troops of the 10th SS Panzer Division holding the great highway bridge over the Waal at Nijmegen put an end to any British hopes of regaining the lost time. Firmly entrenched behind coils of barbed wire around the traffic circle at the foot of the bridge, the tough SS troops threw back an attack that afternoon by elements of the Guards Armored and the U.S. 82nd Airborne Divisions. The bridge, the last remaining obstacle in the path to Arnhem just 11 miles away, remained firmly in German hands.

Deeply concerned about the Red Devils at Arnhem, General Gavin proposed a desperate measure to unplug the corridor—an amphibious assault across the Waal in broad daylight. "There's only one way to take this bridge," he told his staff. "We've got to get it simultaneously from both ends." As Gavin conceived the assault, his paratroopers on the south bank would cross the river downstream from the bridge. Gaining the north bank, they would outflank the German position at the bridge and a lesser objective, a railroad bridge. The defenders of both bridges would be overwhelmed. At the same time, the armor from the British ground column would continue to hammer away at the Germans guarding the south end of the highway bridge.

Gavin realized that the river crossing was a gamble. His paratroopers had never tried an operation like it; some had never been in a small boat. But the head-on attacks at the main bridge had been blunted, with heavy casualties, and there seemed to be no practical alternative to a crossing. General Horrocks agreed, and he sent back an order for British boats for the paratroopers. The attack was set for the following day, September 20.

At this juncture of *Market-Garden*, German reinforcements were pouring into the area south of Nijmegen. Elements of the 1st Parachute and Fifteenth Armies, as well as a grab-bag assortment of other German units, stabbed viciously at the British column up and down the corridor, trying to cut the road leading north. The situation reminded Major General Maxwell Taylor of the Old West, "where small garrisons had to contend with sudden Indian attacks at any point along great stretches of vital railroad." His 101st Airborne troops coined a nickname for the 15-mile stretch of road they defended: Hell's Highway.

The Allied reinforcement and supply drops to the British on September 18 and 19 had been a failure. Forewarned of Allied intentions by the captured plans, German troops had overrun some of the drop zones, and bundles of ammunition and food had fallen into their hands.

Clearly, the situation was precarious. And to add to the Allies' anxiety, the commanders had received no word from the 1st Airborne troops at Arnhem. Because of the failure of their radio sets, the Red Devils could not get a message through. An 82nd Airborne intelligence unit did pass along an ominous message from the Dutch underground on September 18: "Dutch report Germans winning at Arnhem."

Allied planners had estimated that the troops at Arnhem could hold out for only four days without relief from the ground forces. On September 20, the fourth day, their fate rested on the outcome of General Gavin's amphibious charge across the Waal. Scheduled for 1 p.m., the assault was delayed because the British boats, held up by traffic jams along the road, had not arrived. They came finally at 2:40 p.m., 33 unwieldy contraptions of plywood and canvas that had to be put together by engineers.

Late in the afternoon, as Allied artillery and British tanks pounded the German defenders on both sides of the river, the first wave of paratroopers, 260 men, led by Major Julian Cook, launched their craft into the strong current of the Waal. Things went wrong from the outset. Some of the flimsy boats flipped over as the soldiers climbed in. Some of them were overloaded and sank. A scarcity of paddles reduced some paratroopers to stroking with their rifle butts. The boats, seized by the current, were swept in circles in the river, out of control.

As the men struggled to steer their craft, the Germans opened up with a hail of machine-gun and mortar fire. From a command post on the river's south side, Lieut. Colonel J. O. E. "Joe" Vandeleur of the Guards Armored watched in awe. "It was a horrible, horrible sight," he recalled. "Boats were literally blown out of the water. Huge geysers shot up as shells hit and small arms fire from the northern bank made the river look like a seething cauldron. I remember almost trying to will the Americans to go faster."

From this maelstrom of fire, about half of the boats emerged finally on the north bank of the river, deposited the survivors and returned for the next wave. Major Cook led the remnants of the assault force across a flat stretch and up an embankment, where they subdued the German defenders in savage hand-to-hand combat. Dashing along the top of the embankment, they gained the northern end of the railroad bridge, trapping a host of German soldiers on the span itself. As the Germans on the bridge tried to escape at the north end, they met concentrated American machine-gun fire. More than 260 were later found dead on the structure, and scores were taken prisoner.

Their numbers swelled by succeeding waves of paratroopers, the Americans then advanced on the highway bridge, their principal objective. At the same time, a British armored attack on the other side of the river finally cracked the German perimeter around the traffic circle at the foot of the span. Through an inferno of burning buildings and shellfire, four British tanks made a wild dash up the bridge approaches and rumbled onto the span. Dueling with German 88mm guns on the bank and machine-gunning the defenders on the span, three made it across the 1,960-foot structure. On the other side, at 7:15 p.m., they met the jubilant U.S. paratroopers who had survived the waterborne assault, an operation that General Horrocks later termed "the most gallant attack ever carried out" in the War.

Arnhem and the battered Red Devils were just 11 miles away. But to the consternation of the American airborne troops, the British armored force halted for the night. The men were weary, and the unit was running low on ammunition and gas. Moreover, the stretch of road to Arnhem offered the worst terrain yet—the road was high, arrow-straight and dangerously exposed. An armored attack down that road would require infantry on the flanks to overcome German resistance, and the British infantry had not yet caught up with the spearhead.

In the heat of the moment, the Americans could not understand why the British tankers did not rush at once to rescue their isolated comrades at Arnhem. "We had killed ourselves crossing the Waal to grab the north end of the bridge," said Colonel Reuben H. Tucker, whose 504th Regiment staged the amphibious operation. "We just stood there seething, as the British settled in for the night, failing to take advantage of the situation. We couldn't understand it. It simply wasn't the way we did things in the American army—especially if it had been our men hanging by their fingernails 11 miles away."

In the meantime, the Red Devils at Arnhem were enduring a hellish German siege. By the end of the second day, September 18, the city around the northern end of the great bridge across the Lower Rhine was littered with wreckage and covered by the stench of battle. Fires raged out of control, and heavy smoke smeared buildings with a greasy black film. Still, Colonel Frost and his dwindling band of paratroopers held out in the houses at the foot of the bridge. Even though they had been surrounded and under constant shellfire, they had not allowed a single German vehicle to cross the span.

Checking his perimeter around midnight on the 18th, Frost discovered that morale was still high among his exhausted and dirty troops. But the basements of the houses they occupied were filled with wounded. They were short of medical supplies and ammunition, and their rations were gone. The paratroopers ate fruit and whatever they could find in the houses.

The German tanks and artillery continued to pound the houses where the paratroopers were holed up through the next day. By the night of September 19, only half of Frost's original 500 men were capable of fighting. At the end of the following day, the number had dwindled to perhaps 150 or 200 men. In the cellars of the shell-pitted houses, the wounded, swathed in filthy bandages, were jammed to-gether so tightly that medics found it difficult to treat them. Frost himself now lay among them, seriously wounded by an artillery burst.

By the 20th the British had been driven from all but a few of the houses. Most men were down to the last of their ammunition, and Frost concluded that continued resistance was senseless. Shortly before dawn on September 21, he ordered the remnants of his gallant band to try to escape, two or three at a time. Only a few of the remaining 50 men who melted into the darkness got away. Most were captured, including Frost.

A little over two miles away, the rest of the 1st Airborne had been forced back into a U-shaped defensive position, with the open end facing the bend of the Lower Rhine. By September 21 the perimeter had been reduced to a pocket only a mile deep and a mile and a half wide. Into that pocket the Germans poured tons of explosives; so intense was their barrage that they were calling the contested area *Der Hexenkessel*—the witches' cauldron. Pounded mercilessly by the German guns, harassed by German snipers, the 1st Airborne troops nevertheless held out. With little food, water or medical supplies, they waited for the arrival of the ground column, and rescue.

The ground column departed Nijmegen on the morning of September 21, tanks rolling toward Arnhem along the elevated, exposed highway. Six miles short of the Arnhem bridge objective, a single German artillery piece knocked out the lead tanks and stopped the whole column. Once again the operation ground to a halt.

On the afternoon of the same day, the Allies made another effort to reinforce the 1st Airborne. The Polish 1st Independent Parachute Brigade, under the command of

Patients from St. Elisabeth's Hospital in Arnhem are led to safety by a Red Cross worker carrying a white flag. The patients were taken to a town 20 miles away after the hospital came under fire during fighting between German and British troops. The hospital was used by both sides to treat their wounded.

Major General Stanislaw Sosabowski, boarded transports in England for the flight to Arnhem. The Poles were supposed to have jumped into Holland two days earlier, but adverse weather conditions had kept their transports on the ground. In the interim, General Sosabowski, who had been skeptical of *Market-Garden's* chances to begin with, received sketchy reports that indicated a disaster at Arnhem. Now it seemed to him that his men were being committed to a suicidal effort to redeem a hopeless situation, not to reinforce success as originally intended.

His fears were justified. As the Poles jumped out of their C-47s into an area along the southern bank of the Lower Rhine across from the 1st Airborne perimeter, they floated down into murderous German fire from antiaircraft guns, artillery and small arms. Scores of the descending Polish paratroopers were slain or wounded. The dazed survivors assembled and dug in.

Sosabowski was still intent on reinforcing the Red Devils, however. According to the plan worked out for them, his men were to cross the Lower Rhine by means of a large ferry located on the south bank across from the British perimeter. Shortly after landing, Sosabowski discovered to his dismay that the ferry was nowhere to be found; it had been set adrift by the Germans. Although the Poles later tried to get across the river in a few small boats, German fire forced a halt. There was little Sosabowski could do but await the arrival of the British ground forces from the south.

All day on September 22, D-plus-6, fierce battles raged near Eindhoven and Nijmegen for possession of the *Market-Garden* corridor. That evening a handful of armored cars from the stalled XXX Corps, traveling on back roads, managed to slip through German lines and reach the Polish paratroopers. They were followed by a tank-infantry task force that reinforced Sosabowski's hard-pressed troops.

This was little comfort, however, to General Urquhart and the remaining Red Devils, who continued to fight courageously against superior German forces across the river. By September 24 there were so many British wounded that the makeshift aid stations and Dutch homes in the suburb of Oosterbeek were overflowing. With medical supplies exhausted and the wounded in pitiful condition, Urquhart arranged a truce and turned the injured paratroopers over to the Germans, who held the main hospital in Arnhem.

On the following day, Montgomery, despairing of further attempts to reinforce the Red Devils, finally ordered a withdrawal to save the ragged remains of the division. That night, in a driving rain that helped muffle the noise of movement, the exhausted and numbed survivors quietly left their foxholes. Following guidelines made from parachute tape, or holding hands in a line in the pitch-black darkness, they made their way to the riverbank. As their perimeter gradually thinned out, some of their comrades stayed behind to continue firing and mask the escape.

On the muddy north bank of the Lower Rhine, the Red Devils were met by boats sent up from the XXX Corps and paddled by courageous Canadian and British soldiers. During the night, under sporadic fire by German machine guns, some using tracers, scores of men were ferried to the south bank of the river. The light of dawn revealed to the Germans the extent of the British withdrawal. Still, hundreds of men remained at the river's edge. The Germans began firing, and many of the British plunged into the swift water. Some were swept away by the current or dragged down by the weight of their clothing. Others, as German tanks rumbled unimpeded toward the riverbank, stripped off their clothes and swam across. The remainder, too exhausted or too sick to try to swim, were captured.

The evacuation ended the ordeal of the Red Devils at Arnhem. Of some 10,000 British troops who landed and fought on the north bank of the Lower Rhine, fewer than 2,200 made it back across the river. The British 1st Airborne Division had ceased to exist.

And with the Germans still in possession of the Arnhem bridge, Operation *Market-Garden,* one of the most gallant but disastrous ventures of the War, came to a close. In their bid for a drive into Germany, the Allies had paid a stiff price—17,000 troops dead, wounded or captured.

In one sense *Market-Garden* achieved its objectives. The Allies won a corridor 60 miles long in the Netherlands, and they would continue to hold it. But they had failed to gain a bridgehead over the Rhine or to outflank the West Wall and thus place themselves in position to drive into the Ruhr and on to Berlin. They had been unable to extend their pursuit and bring Germany to collapse. With the failure of *Market-Garden,* the bright Allied vision of a quick end to the War evaporated. A long, hard winter loomed ahead.

THE EMBATTLED BRIDGE

The massive highway bridge at Arnhem, ultimate objective of Operation Market-Garden, lies strewn with debris after the British attempt to take the span failed.

A DARING PLAN TO CROSS THE RHINE

Major General Robert E. "Roy" Urquhart, the commander of the British 1st Airborne Division, stands in front of his headquarters at Arnhem.

On September 17, 1944, as 10,000 men of the British 1st Airborne Division were preparing to take off for German-occupied Holland, a paratrooper named Gordon Spicer remarked that their mission seemed likely to be "a fairly simple affair, with a few backstage Germans recoiling in horror at our approach."

The affair would prove to be anything but simple. The 1st Airborne's objective—the highway bridge over the Lower Rhine at Arnhem—was crucial to the success of the huge Allied operation called *Market-Garden,* the bold but hazardous scheme to get the Allies swiftly across the Rhine and into Germany. Success depended upon two things: the seizure of seven key bridges along a 65-mile corridor in southeastern Holland by Allied paratroopers and glidermen, and the eventual relief of this force by a British armored column driving up from the south.

What Gordon Spicer did not know was that everything had to work to perfection for the operation to succeed. If the narrow corridor designated for the armored column was blocked anywhere along the line, the tanks could be stopped, and the airborne forces beyond that point, cut off from support, would be threatened with annihilation. Pondering the hazards faced by the relieving force, one somewhat more knowledgeable officer observed: "It will be like threading seven needles with one piece of cotton and we only have to miss one to be in trouble."

All such misgivings went unheeded by the Allied planners. When Dutch Resistance sources reported that German panzer formations had moved into the area, their warning was ignored. When Lieut. General Frederick A. M. Browning got a look at the plans, he said to General Montgomery: "I think we might be going a bridge too far." Montgomery paid no attention to Browning.

The bridge that Browning was talking about was the one at Arnhem. Sergeant Walter Inglis of the British 1st Parachute Brigade, in keeping with the general euphoria, told friends the Arnhem bridge would be "a piece of cake." He and his cohorts would find it highly indigestible.

Hands raised in surrender, a British officer disguised as a Dutch civilian in a thwarted attempt to escape capture is questioned by Germans in Arnhem.

Under their billowing parachutes, men of the British 1st Airborne Division float to the ground west of Arnhem while paratroopers who have already landed

AN AIRDROP SURPRISING TO FRIEND AND FOE ALIKE

The paratroopers and the glidermen in the *Market-Garden* operation were to land in broad daylight, a risky maneuver that had been decided upon because night landings in Sicily and Normandy had resulted in disastrous foul-ups and confusion. The decision seemed to be the right one when the paratroopers floated down from the sky. There was no German machine-gun or small-arms fire. But to General Urquhart, commander of the 1st Airborne Division —known as the Red Devils—the silence seemed unreal.

The general had good reason to be ap-prehensive. His men still had a long way to go to reach their objective, the bridge at Arnhem. The landing sites—eight miles from the span—had been chosen to avoid the soft, boggy ground around the city. The distance between the airborne troops and their goal would give the Germans plenty of time to prepare a rude recep-tion for them.

The parachute of a British soldier hangs from a tree a few feet away from a camouflaged German tank.

rush to unload supplies from Horsa gliders.

In a field near Arnhem, gliders rest at the ends of the trails they scratched in the cultivated earth.

PICNICS ON THE WAY TO A BLOODY BATTLE

After the paratroopers had landed, Lieut. Colonel John D. Frost, colorful commander of the 2nd Battalion of the 1st Parachute Brigade, rallied his men with a hunting horn and led them onto a secondary road to Arnhem. They were charged with making a quick dash to the city to seize the bridge while the 1st and 3rd Battalions, following main roads, were to come in behind them and occupy the city and high ground to the north.

As the three battalions moved toward Arnhem, they encountered an unexpected hazard: the Dutch they were liberating. "Waving, cheering, and clapping their

ed, "they offered us apples, pears, something to drink. But they interfered with our progress and filled me with dread that they would give our positions away."

The Germans were quick to take advantage of the British soldiers' predicament. "One moment we were marching steadily toward Arnhem; the next, we were scattered in the ditches," recalled one officer. "Snipers had opened fire, and three dead airborne soldiers lay across the road."

As the enemy fire intensified, the 1st and 3rd Battalions bogged down. But Frost and his men, pushing along a lightly guarded secondary road, made it through to the city, and in the fading light of dusk they reached the northern end of the bridge. They moved quietly into buildings nearby and set up a base of operations for an

Checking the supplies in its jeep, a patrol led by a glider pilot—in the kilt he was wearing when he landed—prepares to move toward Arnhem. Jeep patrols set out first to scout the roads that the airborne troops would use.

Pausing for a moment on their push to Arnhem, two British soldiers enjoy an impromptu picnic provided by a grateful Dutch girl. British leaders found that the crowds of joyous civilians made it very difficult for their troops "to keep alive to the possibility of a German attack."

As Dutch civilians look on, British troops round up stray German soldiers near Arnhem. Earlier, when retreating Germans had poured through Arnhem on their way to Germany, the emboldened Dutch taunted them with scornful shouts of "Go home. The British and Americans will be here in a few hours."

German soldiers dash across a rubble-cluttered street in Arnhem (left), while British paratroopers cautiously advance through the ruins of a house (right).

Braced against a window sill, a British soldier takes aim at a target in the street (left). At right, German troops leap over a fence to take up new positions.

An aerial photograph shows the northern end of the 2,000-foot-long highway bridge (near top of picture) at Arnhem, scene of vicious fighting between the British and the Germans. The British 2nd Battalion held the northern end of the bridge from the cluster of buildings on either side of the approach ramp.

THE GERMANS SET THEIR TRAPS

When darkness came, Colonel Frost began his attack. "The sky lit up," he remembered later, "and there was the noise of machine-gun fire, a succession of explosions, the crackling of burning ammunition and the thump of a cannon." In that savage battle, Frost's men cleared the north end of the bridge, but fires and exploding ammunition on the span prevented their crossing it.

With the south end of the bridge still firmly in German hands and no relieving force in sight, Frost and his troops soon found themselves outnumbered and under siege. German tanks and artillery pounded the houses in which they were holed up. The basements were soon filled with wounded—some of whom glowed eerily from phosphorus shell fragments.

As casualties mounted and food, water and morphine ran low, the men waited desperately for help. Their hopes were as illusory as the vision seen by one of the shell-shocked wounded: "Look," he said peering from a window. "It's the Second Army ground column. On the far bank. Look. Do you see them?" His comrade sadly shook his head.

Enjoying some wine and a smoke, well-equipped Germans seem unconcerned by the British attack.

Alerted to the British invasion, Germans in a self-propelled gun patrol a tree-lined street in Arnhem.

German troops creep forward around a British drop

THE ERODING FOOTHOLD OF THE 2ND BATTALION

As Frost and his men tried valiantly to hang on until help arrived, the other troops of the British 1st Airborne Division were running into trouble advancing toward Arnhem. Germans suddenly seemed to be ev-

zone. In the action around Arnhem, fighting was at such close quarters that neither side could be sure who was on the other side of a hedge or in the next house

erywhere. As they swarmed over the area and enveloped entire units, they unknowingly trapped an important quarry—the 1st Airborne's commander, General Urquhart.

The general had joined the 3rd Battalion, but as opposition mounted, Urquhart and two other officers were cut off from the battalion and were forced to take refuge in a Dutch house. Trapped in an attic

while the fighting raged outside, Urquhart and his companions expected the Germans to burst in at any moment. When they failed to do so, "the idiocy of the situation forced itself upon me," and Urquhart suggested that the three make a break for it. "I don't know how you chaps feel," he said, "but we are less than useless cooped up here." However, only when British troops

began advancing down the street could the three make a run for it.

Urquhart had been missing for 36 hours and there were rumors circulating that he had been killed, wounded or captured. But when he returned to his headquarters he was greeted by his unruffled orderly with the words: "I'm glad you're back, sir. You tea and shaving water are ready."

A NEVER-ENDING WAIT FOR REINFORCEMENTS

While the Germans mercilessly pounded them, the tired, dogged men of the British 1st Airborne were sustained by one thought—airdrops would bring relief.

But the Germans closed in on the drop zones and greeted transports and gliders with hailstorms of mortar and antiaircraft fire. Some glider pilots, trying to escape the enemy barrage, released their planes too soon. The flimsy craft collided in mid-air and plowed into one another on the ground. Transports burst into flames and crashed; others—even though they were on fire—continued to hover over the drop zones. A doomed Dakota made repeated drops after its lower fuselage was engulfed in flames. An awestruck British officer who watched from the ground recalled later, "I couldn't take my eyes off the craft. Suddenly it wasn't a plane anymore, just a big orange ball of fire."

Most of the supplies fell behind German lines. In two days of drops, the enemy captured nearly 630 of the 690 tons of supplies that had been intended for the beleaguered airborne troops. "It was the cheapest battle we ever fought," said one German colonel. "We had free food, cigarettes and ammunition."

Even more disastrous for the British at Arnhem was the inability of the 1,500 men of the Polish 1st Independent Parachute Brigade to reach them. Grounded in England for two days by bad weather, the brigade finally took off on the afternoon of September 21. As the planes flew over Holland, the brigade commander, Major General Stanislaw Sosabowski, staring out of the window of his Dakota transport, saw huge traffic jams, burning vehicles and wreckage on the road north of Eindhoven. This could mean only one thing: the British relief column coming up from the south was under heavy German attack.

Sosabowski's sagging spirits received another jolt shortly afterward, when he spotted German tanks on the Arnhem bridge: obviously, the British paratroopers had not taken their main objective. Sosabowski bitterly concluded that his brigade was "being sacrificed in a complete British disaster." Moments later, as the Polish troops began to bail out over the drop zone, they were cut to pieces by German antiaircraft fire. Only half of them ever made it to Arnhem, and they arrived there too late to do much good.

British soldiers near Arnhem, exhausted by days of continuous fighting, anxiously await supply drops.

Polish paratroopers—who were to reinforce the British—wait in England to board planes for Arnhem

Urgently needed supplies for British troops float down to drop zones near Arnhem. Unknown to the plane crews, Germans had already overrun the zones.

Frantically waving table linen taken from a nearby hotel, British soldiers on the edge of a drop zone try to attract the attention of supply planes overhead.

hattered houses from which the British fought indicate the force of the German tank and artillery attack. The shellfire was so relentless that one German soldier

ZEROING IN ON
THE RED DEVILS

At the bridge, Frost's men had managed to hold on for almost 72 hours. But then Germ~~an tanks and artillery, working in relays~~

started systematically blasting the British positions. "It was the best, most effective fire I have ever seen," recalled a German private. "Starting from the rooftops, buildings collapsed like doll houses."

Frost ordered those who could to escape and then arranged a truce with the Ger-

mans to remove the injured. One of the wounded was Frost himself. As he was carried out on a stretcher, he said to the man lying next to him, "Well, we didn't get away with it this time, did we?" "No, sir," answered the man, "but we gave them a ~~damn good run for their money."~~

The bullet-riddled corpse of a German soldier lies where he fell from a car after a British attack

later admitted "I truly felt sorry for the British"

The crumpled bodies of two British soldiers rest next to a taunting milestone on a road to Arnhem

A British soldier wears a ragtag outfit assembled after he swam the Rhine.

TRAGIC COST OF A MISSION THAT FAILED

On the night of September 25, all hopes for reinforcement gone, the battered remnants of the British 1st Airborne Division began a quiet withdrawal under the noses of the Germans. Their feet wrapped up in cloth to muffle the sound of their boots, the survivors of the ill-fated operation filtered through the darkness to the north bank of the Lower Rhine and later were ferried or swam to safety. The division had lost 7,500 of its original 10,000 men.

But, said General Eisenhower afterward: 'No single performance by any unit . . . more highly excited my admiration.'

his contempt with a snarl and a gesture. One officer who recalled watching his men retreat remarked, "By God we had come out as we went in. Proud."

BIBLIOGRAPHY

Adelman, Robert H., and Colonel George Walton, *The Champagne Campaign*. Little, Brown and Co., 1969.

Amouroux, Henri, *La Vie des Français sous l'Occupation*, Vol. 1. Fayard, 1961.

Aron, Robert, *France Reborn: The History of the Liberation, June 1944–May 1945*. Charles Scribner's Sons, 1964.

Barber, Noel, *The Week France Fell: June 1940*. Macmillan London Ltd., 1976.

Baudot, Marcel, *Libération de la Normandie*. Librairie Hachette, 1974.

Bradley, Omar N., *A Soldier's Story*. Henry Holt and Co., 1951.

Buisson, Doctors Jules and Gilles, *Mortain et sa Bataille, 2 August–13 August 1944*. Imprimerie Maurice Simon, 1947.

Bullock, Alan, *Hitler: A Study in Tyranny*. Harper & Row, 1971.

Butcher, Captain Harry C., USNR, *My Three Years with Eisenhower*. Simon and Schuster, 1946.

Carell, Paul, *Invasion—They're Coming!* E. P. Dutton & Co., Inc., 1963.

Carr, William Guy, *Checkmate in the North: The Axis Planned to Invade America*. The Macmillan Company of Canada Ltd., 1944.

Carter, Ross S., *Those Devils in Baggy Pants*. Appleton-Century-Crofts, Inc., 1951.

Cartier-Bresson, Henri, *The World of Henri Cartier-Bresson*. The Viking Press, 1968.

Churchill, Winston S.:
The Second World War. Houghton Mifflin Co.
Vol. 5, *Closing the Ring*, 1951.
Vol. 6, *Triumph and Tragedy*, 1953.

Collins, Larry, and Dominique Lapierre, *Is Paris Burning?* Simon and Schuster, 1965.

Commission du Coût de l'Occupation, *Evaluation des Dommages Subis par la France: du fait de la Guerre et de l'Occupation Ennemie (1939-1945)*. Institut de Conjoncture, no date.

Cooke, David C., and Martin Caidin, *Jets, Rockets and Guided Missiles*. The McBride Co., 1951.

Craven, Wesley Frank, and James Lea Cate, eds., *The Army Air Forces in World War II*, Vol. 3, *Europe: Argument to V-E Day (January 1944 to May 1945)*. The University of Chicago Press, 1951.

Dank, Milton, *The French against the French: Collaboration and Resistance*. J. B. Lippincott Co., 1974.

Dawidowicz, Lucy S., *The War against the Jews 1933-1945*. Holt, Rinehart and Winston, 1975.

De Gaulle, Charles, *The Complete War Memoirs of Charles de Gaulle*. Simon and Schuster, 1972.

De La Ferte, Air Chief Marshal Sir Philip Joubert, *Rocket*. Philosophical Library, Inc., 1957.

Dornbusch, C. E.:
compiler, *Histories of American Army Units, World Wars I and II and Korean Conflict*. Special Services Division, Office of the Adjutant General, Department of the Army, 1956.
Histories: Personal Narratives, United States Army (A Checklist). Hope Farm Press, 1967.

Douglas, W. A. B., and Brereton Greenhous, *Out of the Shadows*. Oxford University Press, 1977.

Downing, David, *The Devil's Virtuosos: German Generals at War 1940-5*. St. Martin's Press, 1977.

DuJardin, Raoul, *Les Routes sans Oiseaux*. Flammarion, 1947.

Eisenhower, Dwight D., *Crusade in Europe*. Doubleday & Co., Inc., 1948.

Ellis, Major L. F., *Victory in the West*, Vol. 1, *The Battle of Normandy*. Her Majesty's Stationery Office, 1962.

Eparvier, Jean, *A Paris sous la Botte des Nazis*. Editions Raymond Schall, 1944.

Esposito, Brig. General Vincent J., USA (Ret.), chief ed., *The West Point Atlas of American Wars*, Vol. 2, *1900-1953*. Frederick A. Praeger, 1959.

Essame, H., *Patton: A Study in Command*. Charles Scribner's Sons, 1974.

Florentin, Eddy, *The Battle of the Falaise Gap*. Hawthorne Books, Inc., no date.

Flower, Desmond, and James Reeves, eds., *The Taste of Courage: The War, 1939-1945*. Harper & Brothers, 1960.

Gavin, Major General James M.:
Airborne Warfare. Infantry Journal Press, 1947.
On to Berlin: Battles of an Airborne Commander 1943-1946. The Viking Press, 1978.

Gosset, André, and Paul LeComte, *Caen: pendant la Bataille*. Ozanne et C., no date.

Grall, Jeanne, *1944: La Libération du Calvados en Images*. S.P.R.L. SODIM, 1977.

Greenfield, Kent Roberts, ed., *Command Decisions*. Office of the Chief of Military History, Department of the Army, 1960.

Haupt, Werner, *Rückzug im Westen 1944*. Motorbuch Verlag, 1978.

Howard, Michael, *Grand Strategy*, Vol. 4, *August 1942-September 1943*, History of the Second World War, United Kingdom Military Series, edited by J. R. M. Butler. Her Majesty's Stationery Office, 1972.

Huddleston, Sisley, *France: The Tragic Years 1939-1947*. The Devin-Adair Co., 1955.

Huston, James A., *Across the Face of France: Liberation and Recovery 1944-63*. Purdue University Studies, 1963.

Jane, Fred T., *Jane's All the World's Aircraft 1945/6*. David & Charles Ltd., 1970.

Johnson, Brian, *The Secret War*. British Broadcasting Corporation, 1978.

Jones, R. V., *Most Secret War*. Hamish Hamilton Ltd., 1978.

Kay, Anthony L., *Monogram Close-Up 4—Buzz Bomb*. Monogram Aviation Publications, 1977.

Kernan, Thomas D., *Report on France*. John Lane, 1942.

Kesselring, Albert, *Kesselring: A Soldier's Record*. William Morrow & Co., 1954.

Lang, Will, "Lucian King Truscott, Jr." LIFE, October 2, 1944.

Lantier, Maurice, *Saint-Lô au Bucher*. Imprimerie Jacqueline, no date.

Le Boterf, Hervé, *La Vie Parisienne sous l'Occupation: 1940-1944*, Vol. 1. Editions France-Empire, 1974.

LeFrançois, Auguste-Louis, *Quand Saint-Lô Voulait Revivre: Juillet à Noël 1944*. Imprimerie P. Bellée, no date.

MacDonald, Charles B., *Airborne*. Ballantine Books Inc., 1970.

McKee, Alexander, *Last Round against Rommel: Battle of the Normandy Bridgehead*. The New American Library, 1964.

Majdalany, Fred, *The Fall of Fortress Europe*. Hodder and Stoughton Ltd., 1968.

Manvell, Roger, *SS and Gestapo: Rule by Terror*. Ballantine Books Inc., 1969.

Matloff, Maurice, *United States Army in World War II, The War Department, Strategic Planning for Coalition Warfare: 1943-1944*. Office of the Chief of Military History, Department of the Army, 1959.

Maule, Henry:
Normandy Breakout. Quadrangle/The New York Times Book Co., 1977.
Out of the Sand: The Epic Story of General Leclerc and the Fighting Free French. Odhams Books Ltd., 1966.

Mellenthin, F. W. von, *German Generals of World War II: As I Saw Them*. University of Oklahoma Press, 1977.

Michael [pseud.], *France Still Lives*. Lindsay Drummond, 1942.

Montgomery of Alamein, Field-Marshal the Viscount, *The Memoirs of Field-Marshal the Viscount Montgomery of Alamein, K.G.* The World Publishing Co., 1958.

Monzein, A. and P., and Y. Chapron, *A la Charnière (Caen 1944)*. Flammarion, 1947.

Moorehead, Alan, *Eclipse*. Harper & Row, 1968.

Moran, Lord, *Churchill—Taken from the Diaries of Lord Moran—The Struggle for Survival 1940-1965*. Norman S. Berg, 1976.

Mordal, Jacques, *La Bataille de France 1944-1945*. B. Arthaud, 1964.

Morison, Samuel Eliot, *History of United States Naval Operations in World War II*, Vol. 11, *The Invasion of France and Germany 1944-1945*. Little, Brown and Co., 1975.

Piekalkiewicz, Janusz, *Arnhem 1944*. Charles Scribner's Sons, 1976.

Pogue, Forrest C., *George C. Marshall: Organizer of Victory—1943-1945*. The Viking Press, 1973.

Polnay, Peter de, *The Germans Came to Paris*. Duell, Sloan and Pearce, 1943.

Porter, Roy P., *Uncensored France*. The Dial Press, 1942.

Powley, A. E., *Broadcast from the Front (Canadian Radio Overseas in the Second World War)*. Hakkert, 1975.

Pyle, Ernie, *Brave Men*. Henry Holt and Co., 1944.

Renaudot, Françoise, *Les Français et l'Occupation*. Editions Robert Laffont, 1975.

Report of Operations: The Seventh United States Army in France and Germany 1944-1945, Vol. 1. Aloys Gräf, 1946.

Robichon, Jacques, *The Second D-Day*. Walker and Co., 1969.

Ryan, Cornelius, *A Bridge Too Far*. Popular Library, 1974.

St-Lô (7 July-19 July 1944), American Forces in Action Series. Historical Division, War Department, 1946.

Saunders, Hilary St. George, *Royal Air Force 1939-1945*, Vol. 3, *The Fight is Won*. Her Majesty's Stationery Office, 1975.

Sosabowski, Major-General Stanislaw, *Freely I Served*. William Kimber, 1960.

Stacey, Colonel C. P.:
The Canadian Army at War: Canada's Battle in Normandy. King's Printer, 1946.
The Canadian Army 1939-1945: An Official Historical Summary. King's Printer, 1948.
Not in Vain. University of Toronto Press, 1973.
Official History of the Canadian Army in the Second World War, Vol. 3, *The Victory Campaign (The Operations in North-West Europe 1944-1945)*. The Queen's Printer and Controller of Stationery, 1960.

Taggart, Donald G., *History of the Third Infantry Division in World War II*. Infantry Journal Press, 1947.

Tassigny, Marshal de Lattre de, *The History of the French First Army*. George Allen and Unwin Ltd., 1952.

Thompson, Robert Smith, *Pledge to Destiny—Charles de Gaulle and the Rise of the Free French*. McGraw-Hill Book Co., 1974.

Thornton, Willis, *The Liberation of Paris*. Harcourt, Brace & World, Inc., 1962.

Truscott, Lieut. General L. K., Jr., *Command Missions: A Personal Story*. E. P. Dutton and Co., Inc., 1954.

United States Army in World War II, The European Theater of Operations. Office of the Chief of Military History, Department of the Army:
Blumenson, Martin, *Breakout and Pursuit*, 1961.
Cole, Hugh M., *The Lorraine Campaign*, 1950.
MacDonald, Charles B., *The Siegfried Line Campaign*, 1963.
Pogue, Forrest C., *The Supreme Command*, 1954.
Ruppenthal, Roland G., *Logistical Support of the Armies*, 2 vols., 1959.

Urquhart, Major-General R. E., *Arnhem*. W. W. Norton & Co., Inc., 1958.

Vigneras, Marcel, *United States Army in World War II, Special Studies: Rearming the French*. Office of the Chief of Military History, Department of the Army, 1957.

Walter, Gérard, *Paris under the Occupation*. The Orion Press, 1960.

Warlimont, Walter, *Inside Hitler's Headquarters 1939-1945*. Frederick A. Praeger, 1964.

Werth, Alexander, *France 1940-1955*. Henry Holt and Co., 1956.

Whitcombe, Fred, ed., *The Pictorial History of Canada's Army Overseas 1939-1945*. Whitcombe, Gilmour & Co., 1947.

Wilmot, Chester, *The Struggle for Europe*. Harper & Brothers, 1952.

ACKNOWLEDGMENTS

The index for this book was prepared by Mel Ingber. For help given in the preparation of this book the editors wish to express their gratitude to Gérard Baschet, Editions de l'Illustration, Paris; Dana Bell, U.S. Air Force Still Photo Depository, Pentagon, Washington, D.C.; Leroy Bellamy, Prints and Photographs Division, Library of Congress, Washington, D.C.; Georges Bidault, Paris; Léon Bonin, Paris; Carole Boutté, Senior Researcher, U.S. Army Audio-Visual Activity, Pentagon, Washington, D.C.; Henri Cartier-Bresson, Paris; Huguette Chalufour, Editions Jules Taillandier, Paris; Yves Ciampi, Paris; Charles de Coligny, Curator, Musée de l'Ordre de la Libération, Paris; Cécile Coutin, Curator, Musée des Deux Guerres Mondiales, Paris; Cécile Dabosville, Les Moutiers-en-Cinglais, France; Mrs. Charles de Gaulle, Colombey-les-Deux-Eglises, France; Patrick Dempsey, Geography and Map Division, Library of Congress, Alexandria, Virginia; V. M. Destefano, Chief, Reference Library, U.S. Army Audio-Visual Activity, Pentagon, Washington, D.C.; Ken Dillon, Alexandria, Virginia; Robert Doisneau, Paris; Hans Dollinger, Wörthsee, Germany; Colonel Marcel Dugué-MacCarthy, Curator, Musée de l'Armée, Paris; Georges Févre, Paris; General James M. Gavin, Cambridge, Massachusetts; Dr. Paul German, Falaise, France; Government Institute for War Documentation, Amsterdam; Jeanne Grall, Curator, Archives Municipales, Caen, France; Nelly Guicheteau, Paris; Dr. Robert Guillermou, Evreux, France; Robert and Jeanne Halley, Caen, France; Al Hardin, The Army Library, Pentagon, Washington, D.C.; MacDonald Hastings, London; Dr. Matthias Haupt, Bundesarchiv, Koblenz, Germany; Werner Haupt, Bibliothek für Zeitgeschichte, Stuttgart, Germany; Thierry Hollier-Larousse, Le Mesnil-de-Louvigny, France; Roger Huguen, Saint-Brieuc, France; Jerry Kearns, Prints and Photographs Division, Library of Congress, Washington, D.C.; Lawrence Kennedy, Franconia, Virginia; Dr. Roland Klemig, Bildarchiv Preussischer Kulturbesitz, Berlin; Gene Kubal, The Army Library, Pentagon, Washington, D.C.; William H. Leary, National Archives and Records Service, Audio-Visual Division, Washington, D.C.; André Lebrun, Caen, France; Auguste Lefrancois, Saint-Lô, France; Donald S. Lopez, Assistant Director of Aeronautics, The National Air and Space Museum, The Smithsonian Institution, Washington, D.C.; Leonard McCombe, Long Island, New York; Major Mike Mandel, Chief of Photojournalism Branch, Office of the Chief of Public Affairs, Pentagon, Washington, D.C.; Colonel Jean Martel, Curator, Musée de l'Armée, Paris; Brün Meyer, Bundesarchiv, Freiburg, Germany; Henri Michel, President, Comité d'Histoire de la Deuxième Guerre Mondiale, Paris; Claude Monnerat, I.N.R.P., Paris; Municipal Museum, Nijmegen, The Netherlands; General Sir Richard O'Connor, D.S.O., M.C., London; Thomas Oglesby, National Archives and Records Service, Audio-Visual Division, Washington, D.C.; Emile Perez, Paris; Raoul Pérol, Institut Charles de Gaulle, Paris; Yves Perret-Gentil, Comité d'Histoire de la Deuxième Guerre Mondiale, Paris; Janusz Piekalkiewicz, Rösrath-Hoffnungsthal, Germany; Dr. Etienne Poilpré, Mathieu, Paris; Marianne Ranson, Comité d'Histoire de la Deuxième Guerre Mondiale, Paris; Michel Rauzier, Comité d'Histoire de la Deuxième Guerre Mondiale, Paris; John Riley, Special Projects Historian, Ships' Histories Branch, Naval Historical Center, Navy Yard, Washington, D.C.; Axel Schulz, Ullstein Bilderdienst, Berlin; Joseph Thomas, National Archives and Records Service, Audio-Visual Division, Washington, D.C.; Dominique Veillon, Comité d'Histoire de la Deuxième Guerre Mondiale, Paris; Dr. Jean Verdier, Sainte-Maxime, France; Chuck Vinch, Office of the Chief of Public Affairs, Pentagon, Washington, D.C.; Paul White, National Archives and Records Service, Audio-Visual Division, Washington, D.C.; Colonel Paul Willing, Curator, Musée de l'Armée, Paris; Marjorie Willis, Radio Times Hulton Picture Library, London; Marie Yates, U.S. Army Audio-Visual Activity, Pentagon, Washington, D.C. Particularly valuable sources for this book were: *Normandy Breakout* by Henry Maule, Quadrangle/The New York Times Book Company, 1977; and *Brave Men* by Ernie Pyle, Henry Holt and Company, 1944.

PICTURE CREDITS

Credits from left to right are separated by semicolons, from top to bottom by dashes.

COVER and page 1: Robert Capa from Magnum.

PARIS UNDER THE SWASTIKA—6, 7: Zucca/Tallandier from Magnum. 8: Zucca © Tallandier. 9, 10: Zucca/Tallandier from Magnum. 11: Zucca © Tallandier, Paris. 12, 13: Zucca/Tallandier from Magnum (2); Zucca © Tallandier, Paris. 14, 15: Bundesarchiv, Koblenz; Zucca/Tallandier from Magnum.

BATTLE OF THE HEDGEROWS—18, 19: Map by Elie Sabban. 21: Ministère de l'Equipement, Institut Géographique National, Paris—Wide World—UPI. 23: U.S. Army. 25: Radio Times Hulton Picture Library, London. 26: Ullstein Bilderdienst, Berlin—Bundesarchiv, Koblenz. 29: Frank Scherschel for LIFE.

SHAMBLES AT CHERBOURG—32, 33: U.S. Army. 34: National Archives. 35: U.S. Army. 36: National Archives. 37: U.S. Army, except bottom left, National Archives. 38, 39: U.S. Army (2); David E. Scherman for LIFE. 40, 41: U.S. Army. 42: National Archives. 43: U.S. Army. 44, 45: National Archives—U.S. Army; David E. Scherman for LIFE.

BREAKOUT—49: UPI. 50: Süddeutscher Verlag, Bilderdienst, Munich. 51: Wide World, courtesy Imperial War Museum, London. 52: Wide World. 53: U.S. Army. 55, 56: Wide World. 57: Map by Elie Sabban. 58: U.S. Air Force.

CAUGHT IN THE CROSS FIRE—60, 61: Ullstein Bilderdienst, Berlin. 62: Radio Times Hulton Picture Library, London. 63: U.S. Army. 64, 65: Top right, Wide World—Imperial War Museum, London. 66 through 69: Leonard McCombe from Radio Times Hulton Picture Library, London. 70, 71: Imperial War Museum, London; U.S. Army (2)—Imperial War Museum, London; George Rodger for LIFE; Imperial War Museum, London. 72, 73: Bob Landry for LIFE; National Archives—U.S. Army. 74, 75: UPI; U.S. Army.

THE GERMANS ON THE RUN—79: UPI. 80: Map by Elie Sabban. 83: Imperial War Museum, London; Ullstein Bilderdienst, Berlin.

AN AMERICAN BLITZKRIEG—86, 87: U.S. Army. 88: U.S. Army—Map by Elie Sabban. 89: U.S. Army. 90, 91: Photo Delaunay-Huguen, Saint-Brieuc—Map by Elie Sabban; U.S. Army. 92 through 97: U.S. Army, except maps by Elie Sabban. 98, 99: U.S. Army—Map by Elie Sabban; Ralph Morse for LIFE.

SOUTHERN FRANCE'S D-DAY—102: Map by Elie Sabban. 106: UPI. 109, 111: E. C. P. Armées, Paris. 113: U.S. Army.

THE PARISIANS MASTER WAR—116, 117: H. Roger-Viollet, Paris. 118, 119: © Almasy, Paris. 120, 121: H. Roger-Viollet, Paris; Photo Seeberger, Paris. 122: Collection Comité d'Histoire de la Deuxième Guerre Mondiale, Paris. 123, 124: Photo Robert Doisneau-Rapho, Paris. 125: Photo Seeberger, Paris (2)—Bibliothèque Nationale, Paris. 126, 127: H. Roger-Viollet, Paris; Roger Schall, Paris.

A DIABOLICAL PLAN THWARTED—130: Office of War Information photo by Weston Haynes, courtesy Imperial War Museum, London. 133 through 140: U.S. Army.

CITY IN REBELLION—142 through 153: Henri Cartier-Bresson.

THE TIME OF DELIVERANCE—154, 155: H. Roger-Viollet, Paris. 156: Photo Lapi, Musée de la Préfecture de Police, Paris. 157: Robert Capa for LIFE. 158, 159: Léon Bonin, Musée de la Préfecture de Police, Paris; U.S. Army. 160, 161: Frank Scherschel for LIFE; Rapho, Paris—UPI. 162, 163: Robert Capa from Magnum. 164, 165: Frank Scherschel for LIFE; Ralph Morse for LIFE. 166, 167: U.S. Army, courtesy Imperial War Museum, London; Ralph Morse for LIFE. 168, 169: Frank Scherschel for LIFE.

NIGHTMARE IN HOLLAND—173 through 177: U.S. Army. 179: Map by Elie Sabban. 180: U.S. Army, courtesy James M. Gavin. 181: U.S. Army. 184: Bundesarchiv, Koblenz.

THE EMBATTLED BRIDGE—186, 187, 188: Imperial War Museum, London. 189: Süddeutscher Verlag, Bilderdienst, Munich. 190, 191: Government Institute for War Documentation, Amsterdam, copied by Martin Vries; Imperial War Museum, London (2). 192: Imperial War Museum, London. 193: Imperial War Museum, London—Government Institute for War Documentation, Amsterdam. 194: Bundesarchiv, Koblenz; Imperial War Museum, London—Imperial War Museum, London; Bundesarchiv, Koblenz. 195: Imperial War Museum, London. 196, 197: Bundesarchiv, Koblenz (2); Imperial War Museum, London. 198: Imperial War Museum, London—Janusz Piekalkiewicz, Rösrath-Hoffnungsthal. 199: Government Institute for War Documentation, Amsterdam—Janusz Piekalkiewicz, Rösrath-Hoffnungsthal. 200, 201: Government Institute for War Documentation, Amsterdam; Imperial War Museum, London—Bundesarchiv, Koblenz. 202, 203: Imperial War Museum, London; Bundesarchiv, Koblenz.

INDEX

*Numerals in italics indicate an illustration
of the subject mentioned.*